Patricia Cornwell is one of the world's major international best-selling authors, translated into thirty-six languages across more than fifty countries. She is a founder of the Virginia Institute of Forensic Science and Medicine, a founding member of the National Forensic Academy, a member of the New York OCME Forensic Sciences Training Program's Advisory Board, and a member of the Harvard-affiliated McLean Hospital's National Council, where she is an advocate for psychiatric research.

In 2008 Cornwell won the Galaxy British Book Awards' Books Direct Crime Thriller of the Year – the first American ever to win this prestigious award. Her most recent bestsellers include *Scarpetta*, *Book of the Dead* and *The Front*. Her earlier works include *Postmortem* – the only novel to win five major crime awards in a single year – and *Cruel and Unusual*, which won the coveted Gold Dagger award in 1993. Dr. Kay Scarpetta herself won the 1999 Sherlock Award for the best detective created by an American writer.

Also by Patricia Cornwell

THE SCARPETTA NOVELS

Postmortem
Body of Evidence
All That Remains
Cruel and Unusual
The Body Farm
From Potter's Field
Cause of Death
Unnatural Exposure
Point of Origin
Black Notice
The Last Precinct
Blow Fly
Trace
Predator
Book of the Dead
Scarpetta
The Scarpetta Factor
Port Mortuary
Red Mist
The Bone Bed
Dust

ANDY BRAZIL SERIES

Isle of Dogs
Southern Cross
Hornet's Nest

WIN GARANO SERIES

The Front
At Risk

NONFICTION

Portrait of a Killer: Jack the Ripper – Case Closed

BIOGRAPHY

Ruth, A Portrait: The Story of Ruth Bell Graham

OTHER WORKS

Food to Die For: Secrets from Kay Scarpetta's Kitchen
Life's Little Fable
Scarpetta's Winter Table

Patricia Cornwell

Cause of Death

sphere

SPHERE

First published in the United States in 1996 by G. P. Putnam's Sons,
a division of Penguin Group (USA) Inc.
First published in Great Britain in 1996 by Little, Brown
Paperback edition published in 1997 by Time Warner Paperbacks
This paperback edition published in 2010 by Sphere

5 7 9 10 8 6

A CIP catalogue record for this book
is available from the British Library.

ISBN 978-0-7515-4468-8

Printed and bound in Great Britain by
Clays Ltd, St Ives plc

Papers used by Sphere are from well-managed forests
and other responsible sources.

MIX
Paper from
responsible sources
FSC® C104740

Sphere
An imprint of
Little, Brown Book Group
100 Victoria Embankment
London EC4Y 0DY

An Hachette UK Company
www.hachette.co.uk

www.littlebrown.co.uk

To Susanne Kirk

---

visionary editor and friend

And he said unto them the third time,
Why, what evil hath he done?
I have found no cause of death in him.

Luke 23:22

1

On the last morning of Virginia's bloodiest year since the Civil War, I built a fire and sat facing a window of darkness where at sunrise I knew I would find the sea. I was in my robe in lamplight, reviewing my office's annual statistics for car crashes, hangings, beatings, shootings, stabbings, when the telephone rudely rang at five-fifteen.

"Damn," I muttered, for I was beginning to feel less charitable about answering Dr. Philip Mant's phone. "All right, all right."

His weathered cottage was tucked behind a dune in a stark coastal Virginia subdivision called Sandbridge, between the U.S. Naval Amphibious Base and Back Bay National Wildlife Refuge. Mant was my deputy chief medical examiner for the Tidewater District, and, sadly, his mother had died last week on Christmas Eve. Under ordinary circumstances, his returning to London to get family affairs in order would not have constituted an emergency for the Virginia medical examiner system. But his assistant forensic pathologist was already out on maternity leave, and, recently, the morgue supervisor had quit.

"Mant residence," I answered as wind tore the dark shapes of pines beyond windowpanes.

"This is Officer Young with the Chesapeake Police," said someone who sounded like a white male born and bred in the South. "I'm trying to reach Dr. Mant."

"He is out of the country," I answered. "How may I help you?"

"Are you Mrs. Mant?"

"I'm Dr. Kay Scarpetta, the chief medical examiner. I'm covering for Dr. Mant."

The voice hesitated, then went on, "We got a tip about a death. An anonymous call."

"Do you know where this death supposedly took place?" I was making notes.

"Supposedly the Inactive Naval Ship Yard."

"Excuse me?" I looked up.

He repeated what he had said.

"What are we talking about, a Navy SEAL?" I was baffled, for it was my understanding that SEALs on maneuvers were the only divers permitted around old ships moored at the Inactive Yard.

"We don't know who it is but he might have been looking for Civil War relics."

"After dark?"

"Ma'am, the area's off-limits unless you have clearance. But that hasn't stopped people from being curious before. They sneak their boats in and always it's after dark."

"This scenario is what the anonymous caller suggested?"

"Pretty much."

"That's rather interesting."

"I thought so."

"And the body hasn't been located yet," I said as I continued to wonder why this officer had taken it upon himself to call a medical examiner at such an early hour when it was not known for a fact that there was a body or even someone missing.

"We're out looking now, and the Navy's sending in a few divers, so we'll get the situation handled if it pans out. But I just wanted you to have a heads up. And be sure you give Dr. Mant my condolences."

"Your condolences?" I puzzled, for if he had known about Mant's circumstances, why did he call here asking for him?

"I heard his mother passed on."

I rested the tip of the pen on the sheet of paper. "Would you tell me your full name and how you can be reached, please?"

"S. T. Young." He gave me a telephone number and we hung up.

I stared into the low fire, feeling uneasy and lonely as I got up to add more wood. I wished I were in Richmond in my own home with its candles in the windows and Fraser fir decorated with Christmases from my past. I wanted Mozart and Handel instead of wind shrilly rushing around the roof, and I wished I had not taken Mant up on his kind offer that I could stay in his home instead of a hotel. I resumed proofreading the statistical report, but my mind would not stop drifting. I imagined the sluggish water of the Elizabeth River, which this time of year would be less than sixty degrees, visibility, at best, maybe eighteen inches.

In the winter, it was one thing to dive for oysters in the Chesapeake Bay or go thirty miles offshore in the Atlantic Ocean to explore a sunken aircraft carrier or German submarine and other wonders worth a wet suit. But in the Elizabeth River, where the Navy parked its decommissioned ships, I could think of nothing enticing, no matter the weather. I could not imagine who would dive there alone in winter after dark to look for artifacts or anything, and believed the tip would prove to be a crank.

Leaving the recliner chair, I walked into the master bedroom where my belongings had metastasized throughout most of the small, chilly space. I undressed quickly and took a hurried shower, having discovered my first day here that the hot-water heater had its limitations. In fact, I did not like Dr. Mant's drafty house with its knotty pine paneling the color of amber and dark brown painted floors that showed every particle of dust. My British deputy chief seemed to live in the dark clutches of gusting wind, and every moment in his minimally furnished home was cold and unsettled by shifting sounds that sometimes caused me to sit up in my sleep and reach for my gun.

Swathed in a robe with a towel wrapped around my hair, I checked the guest bedroom and bath to make certain all was in order for the midday arrival of Lucy, my niece.

Then I surveyed the kitchen, which was pitiful compared to the one I had at home. I did not seem to have forgotten anything yesterday when I had driven to Virginia Beach to shop, although I would have to do without garlic press, pasta maker, food processor and microwave oven. I was seriously beginning to wonder if Mant ever ate in or even stayed here. At least I had thought to bring my own cutlery and cookware, and as long as I had good knives and pots there wasn't much I couldn't manage.

I read some more and fell asleep in the glow of a gooseneck lamp. The telephone startled me again and I grabbed the receiver as my eyes adjusted to sunlight in my face.

"This is Detective C. T. Roche with Chesapeake," said another male voice I did not know. "I understand you're covering for Dr. Mant, and we need an answer from you real quick. Looks like we got a diving fatality in the Inactive Naval Ship Yard, and we need to go ahead and recover the body."

"I'm assuming this is the case one of your officers called me about earlier?"

His long pause was followed by the rather defensive remark, "As far as I know, I'm the first one notifying you."

"An officer named Young called me at quarter past five this morning. Let me see." I checked the call sheet. "Initials S as in Sam, T as in Tom."

Another pause, then he said in the same tone, "Well, I got no idea who you're talking about since we don't have anybody by that name."

Adrenaline was pumping as I took notes. The time was

thirteen minutes past nine o'clock. I was baffled by what he had just said. If the first caller really wasn't police, then who was he, why had he called, and how did he know Mant?

"When was the body found?" I asked Roche.

"Around six a security guard for the shipyard noticed a johnboat anchored behind one of the ships. There was a long hose in the water, like maybe there was someone diving at the other end. And when it hadn't budged an hour later, we were called. One diver was sent down and like I said, there is a body."

"Do we have an identification?"

"We recovered a wallet from the boat. The driver's license is that of a white male named Theodore Andrew Eddings."

"The reporter?" I said in disbelief. "That Ted Eddings?"

"Thirty-two years old, brown hair, blue eyes, based on his picture. He has a Richmond address of West Grace Street."

The Ted Eddings I knew was an award-winning investigative reporter for the Associated Press. Scarcely a week went by when he didn't call me about something. For a moment, I almost couldn't think.

"We also recovered a nine-millimeter pistol from the boat," he said.

When I spoke again, it was very firmly. "His identification absolutely is not to be released to the press or anyone else until it has been confirmed."

"I already told everybody that. Not to worry."

"Good. And no one has any idea why this individual might have been diving in the Inactive Ship Yard?" I asked.

"He might have been looking for Civil War stuff."

"You speculate that based on what?"

"A lot of people like to look in the rivers around here for cannonballs and things," he said. "Okay. So we'll go on and pull him in so he's not down there any longer than necessary."

"I do not want him touched, and leaving him in the water a little longer isn't going to change anything."

"What is it you're gonna do?" He sounded defensive again.

"I won't know until I get there."

"Well, I don't think it's necessary for you to come here . . ."

"Detective Roche," I interrupted him. "The necessity of my coming to the scene and what I do when I'm there is not for you to decide."

"Well, there's all these people I've got on hold, and this afternoon it's supposed to snow. Nobody wants to be standing around out there on the piers."

"According to the Code of Virginia, the body is my jurisdiction, not yours or any other police, fire, rescue or funeral person's. Nobody touches the body until I say so." I spoke with just enough edge to let him know I could be sharp.

"Like I said, I'm going to have to tell all the rescue and shipyard people to just hang out, and they aren't going to be happy. The Navy's already leaning on me pretty hard to clear the area before the media shows up."

"This is not a Navy case."

"You tell them that. It's their ships."

"I'll be happy to tell them that. In the meantime, you just tell everyone that I'm on my way," I said to him before I hung up.

Realizing it could be many hours before I returned to the cottage, I left a note taped to the front door that cryptically instructed Lucy how to let herself in should I not be here. I hid a key only she could find, then loaded medical bag and dive equipment into the trunk of my black Mercedes. At quarter of ten the temperature had risen to thirty-eight degrees, and my attempts to reach Captain Pete Marino in Richmond were frustrating.

"Thank God," I muttered when my car phone finally rang.

I snatched it up. "Scarpetta."

"Yo."

"You've got your pager on. I'm shocked," I said to him.

"If you're so shocked, then why the hell'd you call it?" He sounded pleased to hear from me. "What's up?"

"You know that reporter you dislike so much?" I was careful not to divulge details because we were on the air and could be monitored by scanners.

"As in which one?"

"As in the one who works for AP and is always dropping by my office."

He thought a moment, then said, "So what's the deal? You have a run-in with him?"

"Unfortunately, I may be about to. I'm on my way to the Elizabeth River. Chesapeake just called."

"Wait a minute. Not that kind of run-in." His tone was ominous.

"I'm afraid so."

"Holy shit."

"We've got only a driver's license. So we can't be certain,

yet. I'm going to go in and take a look before we move him."

"Now wait a damn minute," he said. "Why the hell do you need to do something like that? Can't other people take care of it?"

"I need to see him before he's moved," I repeated.

Marino was very displeased because he was overly protective. He didn't have to say another word for me to know that.

"I just thought you might want to check out his residence in Richmond," I told him.

"Yeah. I sure as hell will."

"I don't know what we're going to find."

"Well, I just wish you'd let them find it first."

In Chesapeake, I took the Elizabeth River exit, then turned left on High Street, passing brick churches, used-car lots and mobile homes. Beyond the city jail and police headquarters, naval barracks dissolved into the expansive, depressing landscape of a salvage yard surrounded by a rusty fence topped with barbed wire. In the midst of acres littered with metal and overrun by weeds was a power plant that appeared to burn trash and coal to supply the shipyard with energy to run its dismal, inert business. Smoke-stacks and train tracks were quiet today, all dry-dock cranes out of work. It was, after all, New Year's Eve.

I drove on toward a headquarters built of boring tan cinder-block, beyond which were long paved piers. At the guard gate, a young man in civilian clothes and hard hat stepped out of his booth. I rolled my window down as clouds churned in the wind-swept sky.

"This is a restricted area." His face was completely devoid of expression.

"I'm Dr. Kay Scarpetta, the chief medical examiner," I said as I displayed the brass shield that symbolized my jurisdiction over every sudden, unattended, unexplained or violent death in the Commonwealth of Virginia.

Leaning closer, he studied my credentials. Several times he glanced up at my face and stared at my car.

"You're the chief medical examiner?" he asked. "So how come you're not driving a hearse?"

I had heard this before and was patient when I replied, "People who work in funeral homes drive hearses. I don't work in a funeral home. I am a medical examiner."

"I'm going to need some other form of identification."

I gave him my driver's license, and had no doubt that this sort of interference wasn't going to improve once he allowed me to drive through. He stepped back from my car, lifting a portable radio to his lips.

"Unit eleven to unit two." He turned away from me as if about to tell secrets.

"Two," floated back the reply.

"I got a Dr. Scaylatta here." He mispronounced my name worse than most people did.

"Ten-four. We're standing by."

"Ma'am," the security guard said to me, "just drive through and you'll find a parking lot on your right." He pointed. "You need to leave your car there and walk to Pier Two, where you'll find Captain Green. That's who you need to see."

"And where will I find Detective Roche?" I asked.

"Captain Green's who you need to see," he repeated.

I rolled my window up as he opened a gate posted with signs warning that I was about to enter an industrial area where spray painting was an imminent hazard, safety equipment was required and parking was at my own risk. In the distance, dull gray cargo and tank landing ships, and mine sweepers, frigates and hydrofoils intimidated the cold horizon. On the second pier, emergency vehicles, police cars and a small group of men had gathered.

Leaving my car as instructed, I briskly walked toward them as they stared. I had left my medical bag and dive gear in the car, so I was an empty-handed, middle-aged woman in hiking boots, wool slacks and pale army-green Schoffel coat. The instant I set foot on the pier, a distinguished, graying man in uniform intercepted me as if I were trespassing. Unsmiling, he stepped in my path.

"May I help you?" he asked in a tone that said halt as the wind lifted his hair and colored his cheeks.

I again explained who I was.

"Oh, good." He certainly did not sound as if he meant it. "I'm Captain Green with Navy Investigative Service. We really do need to get on with this. Listen," he turned away from me and spoke to someone else. "We gotta get those CPs off . . ."

"Excuse me. You're with NIS?" I cut in, for I was going to get this cleared up now. "It was my belief that this shipyard is not Navy property. If it is Navy property, I shouldn't be here. The case should be the Navy's and autopsied by Navy pathologists."

"Ma'am," he said as if I tried his patience, "this shipyard is a civilian contractor-operated facility, and therefore not Naval property. But we have an obvious interest because it appears someone was diving unauthorized around our vessels."

"Do you have a theory as to why someone might have done that?" I looked around.

"Some treasure hunters think they're going to find cannon-balls, old ship bells and whatnot in waters around here."

We were standing between the cargo ship *El Paso* and the submarine *Exploiter*, both of them lusterless and rigid in the river. The water looked like cappuccino, and I realized that visibility was going to be even worse than I had feared. Near the submarine, there was a dive platform. But I saw no sign of the victim or the rescuers and police supposedly working his death. I asked Green about this as wind blowing off the water numbed my face, and his reply was to give me his back again.

"Look, I can't be here all day waiting for Stu," he said to a man in coveralls and a filthy ski jacket.

"We could haul Bo's butt in here, Cap'n," was the reply.

"No way José," Green said, and he seemed quite familiar with these shipyard men. "No point in calling that boy."

"Hell," said another man with a long tangled beard. "We all know he ain't gonna be sober this late in the morning."

"Well, now if that isn't the pot calling the kettle black," Green said, and all of them laughed.

The bearded man had a complexion like raw hamburger. He slyly eyed me as he lit a cigarette, shielding it from the wind in rough bare hands.

"I hadn't had a drink since yesterday. Not even water," he swore as his mates laughed some more. "Damn, it's cold as a witch's titty." He hugged himself. "I should'a wore a better coat."

"I tell you what's cold is that one over yonder." Another worker spoke, dentures clicking as he talked about what I realized was the dead diver. "Now that boy's cold."

"He don't feel it now."

I controlled my mounting irritation as I said to Green, "I know you're eager to get started, and so am I. But I don't see any rescuers or police. I haven't seen the johnboat or the area of the river where the body is located."

I felt half a dozen pairs of eyes on me, and I scanned the eroded faces of what easily could have been a small band of pirates dressed for modern times. I was not invited into their secret club and was reminded of those early years when rudeness and isolation could still make me cry.

Green finally answered, "The police are inside using the phones. In the main building there, the one with the big anchor in front. The divers are probably in there too staying warm. The rescue squad is at a landing on the other side of the river where they've been waiting for you to get here. And you might be interested in knowing that this same landing is where the police just found a truck and trailer they believe belonged to the deceased. If you follow me." He began walking. "I'll show you the location you're interested in. I understand you plan on going in with the other divers."

"That's right." I walked with him along the pier.

"I sure as hell don't know what you expect to see."

"I learned long ago to have no expectations, Captain Green."

As we passed old, tired ships, I noticed many fine metal lines leading from them into the water. "What are those?" I asked.

"CPs—cathodic protectors," he answered. "They're electrically charged to reduce corrosion."

"I certainly hope someone has turned them off."

"An electrician's on the way. He'll turn off the whole pier."

"So the diver could have run into CPs. I doubt it would have been easy to see them."

"It wouldn't matter. The charge is very mild," he said as if anyone should know that. "It's like getting zapped with a nine-volt battery. CPs didn't kill him. You can already mark that one off your list."

We had stopped at the end of the pier where the rear of the partially submerged submarine was in plain view. Anchored no more than twenty feet from it was the dark green aluminum johnboat with its long black hose leading from the compressor, which was nestled in an inner tube on the passenger's side. The floor of the boat was scattered with tools, scuba equipment and other objects that I suspected had been rather carelessly gone through by someone. My chest tightened, for I was angrier than I would show.

"He probably just drowned," Green was saying. "Almost every diving death I've seen was a drowning. You die in water as shallow as this, that's what it's going to be."

"I certainly find his equipment unusual." I ignored his medical pontifications.

He stared at the johnboat barely stirred by the current. "A hookah. Yeah, it's unusual for around here."

"Was it running when the boat was found?"

"Out of gas."

"What can you tell me about it? Homemade?"

"Commercial," he said. "A five-horsepower gasoline-driven compressor that draws in surface air through a low-pressure hose connected to a second-stage regulator. He could have stayed down four, five hours. As long as his fuel lasted." He continued to stare off.

"Four or five hours? For what?" I looked at him. "I can understand that if you're collecting lobsters or abalone."

He was silent.

"What is down there?" I said. "And don't tell me Civil War artifacts because we both know you're not going to find those here."

"In truth, not a damn thing's down there."

"Well," I said, "he thought something was."

"Unfortunately for him, he thought wrong. Look at those clouds moving in. We're definitely going to get it." He flipped his coat collar up around his ears. "I assume you're a certified diver."

"For many years."

"I'm going to need to see your dive card."

I looked out at the johnboat and the submarine nearby as I wondered just how uncooperative these people intended to be.

"You've got to have that with you if you're going in," he said. "I thought you would have known that."

"And I thought the military did not run this shipyard."

"I know the rules here. It doesn't matter who runs it." He stared at me.

"I see." I stared back. "And I suppose I'm going to need a permit if I want to park my car on this pier so I don't have to carry my gear half a mile."

"You do need a permit to park on the pier."

"Well, I don't have one of those. I don't have my PADI advanced and rescue dive cards or my dive log. I don't have my licenses to practice medicine in Virginia, Maryland or Florida."

I spoke very smoothly and quietly, and because he could not rattle me, he became more determined. He blinked several times, and I could feel his hate.

"This is the last time I'm going to ask you to allow me to do my job," I went on. "We have an unnatural death here that is in my jurisdiction. If you would rather not cooperate, I will be happy to call the state police, the U.S. Marshal, FBI. Your choice. I can probably get somebody here in twenty minutes. I've got my portable phone right here in my pocket." I patted it.

"You want to dive"—he shrugged—"then go right ahead. But you'll have to sign a waiver relieving the shipyard of any responsibility, should something unfortunate happen. And I seriously doubt there are any forms like that here."

"I see. Now I need to sign something you don't have."

"That's correct."

"Fine," I said. "Then I'll just draft a waiver for you."

"A lawyer would have to do that, and it's a holiday."

"I am a lawyer and I work on holidays."

His jaw muscles knotted, and I knew he wasn't going to bother with any forms now that it was possible to have one. We started walking back, and my stomach tightened with dread. I did not want to make this dive and I did not like the people I had encountered this day. Certainly, I had gotten entangled in bureaucratic barbed wire before when cases involved government or big business. But this was different.

"Tell me something," Green spoke again in his scornful tone, "do chief medical examiners always personally go in after bodies?"

"Rarely."

"Explain why you think it is necessary this time."

"The scene of death will be gone the moment the body is moved. I think the circumstances are unusual enough to merit my taking a look while I can. And I'm temporarily covering my Tidewater District, so I happened to be here when the call came in."

He paused, then unnerved me by saying, "I certainly was sorry to hear about Dr. Mant's mother. When will he be back to work?"

I tried to remember this morning's phone call and the man called Young with his exaggerated southern accent. Green did not sound native to the South, but then neither did I, and that didn't mean either of us couldn't imitate a drawl.

"I'm not certain when he'll return," I warily replied. "But I'm wondering how you know him."

"Sometimes cases overlap, whether they should or not."

I was not sure what he was implying.

"Dr. Mant understands the importance of not interfering," Green went on. "People like that are good to work with."

"The importance of not interfering with what, Captain Green?"

"If a case is the Navy's, for example, or this jurisdiction or that. There are many different ways that people can interfere. All are a problem and can be harmful. That diver, for example. He went where he didn't belong and look what happened."

I had stopped walking and was staring at him in disbelief. "It must be my imagination," I said, "but I think you're threatening me."

"Go get your gear. You can park closer in, by the fence over there," he said, walking off.

2

Long after he had disappeared inside the building with the anchor in front, I was sitting on the pier, struggling to pull a thick wet suit over my dive skin. Not far from me, several rescuers prepared a flat-bottomed boat they had moored to a piling. Shipyard workers wandered about curiously, and on the dive platform, two men in royal blue neoprene tested buddy phones and seemed very thorough in their inspection of scuba gear, which included mine.

I watched the divers talk to each other, but I could not make out a word they said as they unscrewed hoses and fitted belts with weights. Occasionally, they glanced my way, and I was surprised when one of them decided to climb the ladder that led up to my pier. He walked over to where I was and sat beside me on my little patch of cold pavement.

"This seat taken?" He was a handsome young man, black and built like an Olympic athlete.

"There are a lot of people who want it, but I don't know where they are." I fought with the wet suit some more. "Damn. I hate these things."

"Just think of it as putting on an inner tube."

"Yes, that's an enormous help."

"I need to talk to you about underwater comm equipment. You ever used it before?" he said.

I glanced up at his serious face and asked, "Are you with a squad?"

"Nope. I'm just plain ole Navy. And I don't know about you, but this sure isn't the way I planned to spend my New Year's Eve. Don't know why anybody'd want to dive in this river unless they got some sort of fantasy about being a blind tadpole in a mud puddle. Or maybe if you got iron-poor blood and think all the rust in there will help."

"All the rust in there will do is give you tetanus." I looked around. "Who else here is Navy versus squad?"

"The two with the rescue boat are squad. Ki Soo down there on the dive platform is the only other Navy except our intrepid investigator with NIS. Ki's good. He's my buddy."

He gave an okay sign to Ki Soo, who gave it back, and I found all of this rather interesting and very different from what I had experienced so far.

"Now listen up." My new acquaintance spoke as if he had worked with me for years. "Comm equipment's tricky if you've never used it. It can be real dangerous." His face was earnest.

"I'm familiar with it," I assured him with more ease than I felt.

"Well, you gotta be more than familiar. You gotta be buddies with it, because like your dive buddy, it can save your life." He paused. "It can also kill you."

I had used underwater communication equipment on only one other dive, and was still nervous about having my regulator replaced by a tightly sealed mask fitted with a mouthpiece and no purge valve. I worried about the mask flooding, about having to tear it off as I frantically groped for my alternate air source, or octopus. But I was not going to mention this, not here.

"I'll be fine," I assured him again.

"Great. I heard you were a pro," he said. "By the way, my name's Jerod, and I already know who you are." Sitting Indian-style, he was tossing gravel into the water and seemed fascinated by the slowly spreading ripples. "I've heard a lot of nice things about you. In fact, when my wife finds out I met you, she's going to be jealous."

I was not certain why a diver in the Navy would have heard anything about me beyond what was in the news, which wasn't always nice. But his words were a welcome salve to my raw mood, and I was about to let him know this when he glanced at his watch, then stared down at the platform and met Ki Soo's eyes.

"Dr. Scarpetta," Jerod said as he got up. "I think we're ready to rock and roll. How about you?"

"I'm as ready as I'm going to be." I got up, too. "What's going to be the best approach?"

"The best way—in fact, the only way—is to follow his hose down."

We stepped closer to the edge of the pier and he pointed to the johnboat.

"I've already been down once, and if you don't follow the hose you'll never find him. You ever had to wade through a sewer with no lights on?"

"That one hasn't happened to me yet."

"Well, you can't see shit. And that's the same thing here."

"To your knowledge, no one has disturbed the body," I said.

"No one's been near it but me."

He watched as I picked up my buoyancy control vest, or BC, and tucked a flashlight in a pocket.

"I wouldn't even bother. In these conditions, all a flashlight's going to do is get in your way."

But I was going to bring it because I wanted any advantage I could possibly have. Jerod and I climbed down the ladder to the dive platform so we could finish preparations, and I ignored overt stares from shipyard men as I massaged cream rinse into my hair and pulled on the neoprene hood. I strapped a knife to my inner right calf, and then grabbed each end of a fifteen-pound weight belt and quickly hoisted it around my waist. I checked safety releases, and pulled on gloves.

"I'm ready," I said to Ki Soo.

He carried over communication equipment and my regulator.

"I will attach your air hose to the face mask." He spoke with no accent. "I understand you've used comm equipment like this before."

"That's correct," I said.

He squatted beside me and lowered his voice as if we were about to conspire. “You, Jerod and I will be in constant contact with each other over the buddy phones.”

They looked like bright red gas masks with a five-strap harness in back. Jerod moved behind me and helped me into my BC and air tank while his buddy talked on.

“As you know,” Ki Soo was saying, “you breathe normally and use the push-to-talk button on the mouthpiece when you want to communicate.” He demonstrated. “Now we need to get this nice and secure over your hood and tuck it in. There, you get the rest of your hair tucked in and let me make sure this is nice and tight in back.”

I hated buddy phones the most when I wasn’t in the water because it was difficult to breathe. I sucked in air as best I could as I peered out through plastic at these two divers I had just entrusted with my life.

“There will be two rescuers in a boat and they will be monitoring us with a transducer that will be lowered into the water. Whatever we say will be heard by whoever is listening on the surface. Do you understand?” Ki Soo looked at me and I knew I had just been given a warning.

I nodded, my breathing loud and labored in my ears.

“You want your fins on now?”

I shook my head and pointed at the water.

“Then you go first and I will toss them to you.”

Weighing at least eighty pounds more than when I had arrived, I cautiously made my way to the edge of the dive platform and checked again to make certain my mask was tucked into my hood. Cathodic protectors were like catfish whiskers trailing from the huge dormant ships, the water ruffled by wind. I steeled myself for the most unnerving giant stride I had ever made.

The cold at first was a shock, and my body took its time warming the water leaking into my rubber sheath as I pulled on my fins. Worse, I could not see my computer console or its compass. I could not see my hand in front of my face, and I now understood why it was useless to bring a flashlight. The suspended sediment absorbed light like a blotter, forcing me to surface at frequent intervals to get my bearings as I swam toward the spot where the hose led from the johnboat and disappeared beneath the surface of the river.

"Everybody ten-four?" Ki Soo's voice sounded in the receiver pressed against the bone of my skull.

"Ten-four," I spoke into the mouthpiece and tried to relax as I slowly kicked barely below the surface.

"You're on the hose?" It was Jerod who spoke this time.

"I've got my hands on it now." It seemed oddly taut, and I was careful to disturb it as little as possible.

"Keep following it down. Maybe thirty feet. He should be floating right above the bottom."

I began my descent, pausing at intervals to equalize the pressure in my ears as I tried not to panic. I could not see. My heart was pounding as I tried to will myself to relax and take deep breaths. For a moment I stopped and floated as I shut my eyes and slowly breathed. I resumed following the hose down and panic seized me again when a thick rusting cable suddenly materialized in front of me.

I tried to get under it, but I could not see where it was

coming from or going to, and I was really more buoyant than I wanted to be and could have used more weight in my belt or the pockets of my BC. The cable got me from the rear, clipping my K-valve hard. I felt my regulator tug as if someone were grabbing it from behind, and the loosened tank began to slide down my back, pulling me with it. Ripping open the Velcro straps of my BC, I quickly worked my way out of it as I tried to block out everything except the procedure I had been trained to do.

"Everything ten-four?" Ki Soo's voice sounded in my mask.

"Technical problem," I said.

I maneuvered the tank between my legs so I could float on it as if I were riding a rocket in cold, murky space. I re-adjusted straps and fought off fear.

"Need help?"

"Negative. Watch for cables," I said.

"You gotta watch for anything," his voice came back.

It entered my mind that there were many ways to die down here as I slipped my arms inside the BC. Rolling over on my back, I snugly strapped myself in.

"Everything ten-four?" Ki Soo's voice sounded again.

"Ten-four. You're breaking up."

"Too much interference. All these big tubs. We're coming down behind you. Do you want us closer?"

"Not yet," I said.

They were maintaining a prudent distance because they knew I wanted to see the body without distraction or interference. We did not need to get in each other's way. Slowly, I dropped deeper, and closer to the bottom, I realized the hose must be snagged, explaining why it was so taut. I was not sure which way to move, and tried going several feet to my left, where something brushed against me. I turned and met the dead man face to face, his body bumping and nudging as I involuntarily jerked away. Languidly, he twisted and drifted on the end of his tether, rubber-sheathed arms out like a sleepwalker's as my motion pulled him after me.

I let him drift close, and he nudged and bumped some more, but now I was not afraid because I was no longer surprised. It was as if he were trying to get my attention or wanted to dance with me through the hellish darkness of the river that had claimed him. I maintained neutral buoyancy, barely moving my fins for I did not want to stir up the bottom or cut myself on rusting shipyard debris.

"I've got him. Or maybe I should say he got me." I depressed the push-to-talk button. "Can you copy?"

"Barely. We're maybe ten feet above you. Holding."

"Hold a few minutes more. Then we'll get him out."

I tried my flashlight one last time, just in case, but it still proved useless, and I realized I would have to see this scene with my hands. Tucking the light back in my BC, I held my computer console almost against my mask. I could barely make out that my depth was almost thirty feet and I had more than half a tank of air. I began to hover in the dead man's face, and through the murkiness could make out only the vague shape of features and hair that had floated free of his hood.

Gripping his shoulders, I carefully felt around his chest, tracing the hose. It was threaded through his weight belt and

I began following it toward whatever it was caught on. In less than ten feet, a huge rusty screw blossomed before my eyes. I touched the barnacle-covered metal of a ship's side, steadying myself so I did not float any closer. I did not want to drift under a vessel the size of a playing field and have to blindly feel my way out before I ran out of air.

The hose was tangled and I felt along it to see if it might be folded or compressed in a way that might have cut off the flow of air, but I could find no evidence of that. In fact, when I tried to free it from the screw, I found this was not hard to do. I saw no reason why the diver could not have freed himself, and I was suspicious his hose had gotten snagged after death.

"His air hose was caught." I got on the radio again. "On one of the ships. I don't know which."

"Need some help?" It was Jerod who spoke.

"No. I've got him. You can start pulling."

I felt the hose move.

"Okay. I'm going to guide him up," I said. "You keep pulling. Very slowly."

I locked my arms under the body's from behind and began kicking with my ankles and knees instead of my hips because movement was restricted.

"Easy," I warned into the microphone, for my ascent could be no more than one foot a second. "Slowly. Slowly."

Periodically, I looked up but could not see where I was until we broke the surface. Then suddenly the sky was painted with slate-gray clouds, and the rescue boat was rocking nearby. Inflating the dead man's BC and mine, I turned him on his belly and released his weight belt, almost dropping it because it seemed so heavy. But I managed to hand it up to rescuers who were wearing wet suits and seemed to know what they were doing in their old flat-bottomed boat.

Jerod, Ki Soo and I had to leave our masks on because we still had to swim back to the platform. So we were talking by buddy phone and breathing from our tanks as we maneuvered the body inside a chicken-wire basket. We swam it flush against the boat, then helped the rescuers lift it in as water poured everywhere.

"We need to take his mask off," I said, and I motioned to the rescuers.

They seemed confused, and wherever the transducer was, it clearly wasn't with them. They couldn't hear a word we said.

"You need some help getting your mask off?" one of them asked as he reached toward me.

I waved him off and shook my head. Grabbing the side of the boat, I hoisted myself up enough to reach the basket. I pulled off the dead man's mask, emptied it of water, and laid it next to his hooded head with its straying long wet hair. It was then I knew him, despite the deep oval impression etched around his eyes. I knew the straight nose and dark mustache framing his full mouth. I recognized the reporter who had always been so fair with me.

"Okay?" One of the rescuers shrugged.

I gave them an okay, although I could tell they did not understand the importance of what I had just done. My reason was cosmetic, for the longer the mask caused pressure against skin fast losing elasticity, the slighter the chance that the indentation would fade. This was an unimportant concern to investigators and paramedics, but not to loved ones who would want to see Ted Eddings's face.

"Am I transmitting?" I then asked Ki Soo and Jerod as we bobbed in the water.

"You're fine. What do you want done with all this hose?" Jerod asked.

"Cut it about eight feet from the body and clamp off the end," I said. "Seal that and his regulator in a plastic bag."

"I got a salvage bag in my BC," Ki Soo volunteered.

"Sure. That will work."

After we had done what we could, we rested for a moment, floating and looking across muddy water to the johnboat and the hookah. As I surveyed where we had been, I realized that the screw Eddings's hose had snagged on belonged to the *Exploiter*. The submarine looked post-World War II, maybe around the time of the Korean War, and I wondered if it had been stripped of its finer parts and was on its way to being sold for scrap. I wondered if Eddings had been diving around it for a reason, or if, after death, he had drifted there.

The rescue boat was halfway to the landing on the other side of the river where an ambulance waited to take the body to the morgue. Jerod gave me the okay sign and I returned it, although everything did not feel okay at all. Air rushed as we deflated our BCs, and we dipped back under water the color of old pennies.

* * *

There was a ladder leading from the river to the dive platform, and then another to the pier. My legs trembled as I climbed, for I was not as strong as Jerod and Ki Soo, who moved in all their gear as if it weighed the same as skin. But I got out of my BC and tank myself and did not ask for help. A police cruiser rumbled near my car, and someone was towing Eddings's johnboat across the river to the landing. Identity would have to be verified, but I had no doubt.

"So what do you think?" a voice overhead suddenly asked.

I looked up to find Captain Green standing next to a tall, slender man on the pier. Green was apparently now feeling charitable, and reached down to help. "Here," he said. "Hand me your tank."

"I won't know a thing until I examine him," I said as I lifted it up, then the other gear. "Thanks. The johnboat with the hose and everything else should go straight to the morgue," I added.

"Really? What are you going to do with it?" he asked.

"The hookah gets an autopsy, too."

"You're going to want to rinse your stuff really good," the slender man said to me as if he knew more than Jacques Cousteau, and his voice was familiar. "There's a lot of oil and rust in there."

"There certainly is," I agreed, climbing up to the pier.

"I'm Detective Roche," he then said, and he was oddly dressed in jeans and an old letter jacket. "I heard you say his hose was caught on something?"

"I did, and I'm wondering when you heard me say that."

I was on the pier now and not at all looking forward to carrying my dirty, wet gear back to my car.

"Of course, we monitored the recovery of the body." It was Green who spoke. "Detective Roche and I were listening inside the building."

I remembered Ki Soo's warning to me and I glanced at the platform below where he and Jerod were working on their own gear.

"The hose was snagged," I answered. "But I can't tell you when that happened. Maybe before his death, maybe after."

Roche didn't seem all that interested as he continued to stare at me in a manner that made me self-aware. He was very young and almost pretty, with delicate features, generous lips and short curly dark hair. But I did not like his eyes, and thought they were invasive and smug. I pulled off my hood and ran my fingers through my slippery hair, and he watched as I unzipped my wet suit and pulled the top of it down to my hips. The last layer was my dive skin, and water trapped between it and my flesh was chilling quickly. Soon I would be unbearably cold. Already, my fingernails were blue.

"One of the rescuers tells me his face looks really red," the captain said as I tied the wet suit's sleeves around my waist. "I'm wondering if that means anything."

"Cold livor," I replied.

He looked expectantly at me.

"Bodies exposed to the cold get bright pink," I said as I began to shiver.

"I see. So it doesn't—"

"No," I cut him off, because I was too uncomfortable to listen to them. "It doesn't necessarily mean anything. Look, is there a ladies' room so I can get out of these wet things?" I cast about and saw nothing promising.

"Over there." Green pointed at a small trailer near the administration building. "Would you like Detective Roche to accompany you and show you where everything is?"

"That's not necessary."

"Hopefully, it's not locked," Green added.

That would be my luck, I thought. But it wasn't, and it was awful, with only toilet and sink, and nothing seemed to have been cleaned in recent history. A door leading to the men's room on the other side was secured by a two-by-four with padlock and chain, as if one gender or the other were very worried about privacy.

There was no heat. I stripped, only to find there was no hot water. Cleaning up as best I could, I hurried into a sweat suit, after-ski boots and cap. By now it was one-thirty and Lucy was probably at Mant's house. I hadn't even started the tomato sauce yet. Exhausted, I was desperate for a long hot shower or bath.

Because I could not get rid of him, Green walked me to my car and helped place my dive gear into the trunk. By now the johnboat had been loaded on a trailer and should have been en route to my office in Norfolk. I did not see Jerod or Ki Soo and was sorry I could not say good-bye to them.

"When will you do the autopsy?" Green asked me.

I looked at him, and he was so typical of weak people with

power or rank. He had done his best to scare me off, and when that had accomplished nothing he had decided we would be friends.

"I will do it now." I started the car and turned the heat up high.

He looked surprised. "Your office is open today?"

"I just opened it," I said.

I had not shut the door, and he propped his arms on top of the frame and stared down at me. He was so close, I could see broken blood vessels along his cheekbones and the wings of his nose, and changes in pigmentation from the sun.

"You will call me with your report?"

"When I determine cause and manner of death, certainly I will discuss them with you," I said.

"Manner?" He frowned. "You mean there's some question that he's an accidental death?"

"There can and will always be questions, Captain Green. It is my job to question."

"Well, if you find a knife or bullet in his back, I hope you'll call me first," he said with quiet irony as he gave me one of his cards.

I drove away looking up the number for Mant's morgue assistant and hoping I would find him home. I did.

"Danny, it's Dr. Scarpetta," I said.

"Oh, yes, ma'am," he said, surprised.

Christmas music sounded in the background and I heard the voices of people arguing. Danny Webster was in his early twenties and still lived with his family.

"I'm so sorry to bother you on New Year's Eve," I said,

"but we've got a case I need to autopsy without delay. I'm on my way to the office now."

"You need me?" He sounded quite open to the idea.

"If you could help me, I can't tell you how much I would appreciate it. There's a johnboat and a body headed to the office as we speak."

"No problem, Dr. Scarpetta," he cheerfully said. "I'll be right there."

I tried Mant's house, but Lucy did not pick up, so I entered a code to check the answering machine's messages. There were two, both left by friends of Mant, expressing their sympathy. Snow had begun drifting down from a leaden sky, the interstate busy with people driving faster than was safe. I wondered if my niece had gotten delayed and why she hadn't called. Lucy was twenty-three and barely graduated from the FBI Academy. I still worried about her as if she needed my protection.

My Tidewater District Office was located in a small, crowded annex on the grounds of Sentara Norfolk General Hospital. We shared the building with the Department of Health, which unfortunately included the office of Shell Fish Sanitation. So between the stench of decomposing bodies and decaying fish, the parking lot was not a good place to be, no matter the time of year or day. Danny's ancient Toyota was already there, and when I unlocked the bay I was pleased to find the johnboat waiting.

I lowered the door behind me and walked around, looking. The long low-pressure hose had been neatly coiled, and as I had requested one severed end and the regulator it was attached to were sealed inside plastic. The other end was still connected to the small compressor strapped to the inner tube. Nearby were a gallon of gasoline and the expected miscellaneous assortment of dive and boat equipment, including extra weights, a tank containing three thousand pounds per square inch of air, a paddle, life preserver, flashlight, blanket and flare gun.

Eddings also had attached an extra five-horsepower trolling engine that he clearly had used to enter the restricted area where he had died. The main thirty-five-horsepower engine was pulled back and locked, so its propeller would have been out of the water, and I remembered this was the position it was in when I saw the johnboat at the scene. But what interested me more than any of this was a hard plastic carrying case open on the floor. Nestled in its foam lining were various camera attachments and boxes of Kodak 100 ASA film. But I saw no camera or strobe, and I imagined they were forever lost on the bottom of the Elizabeth River.

I walked up a ramp and unlocked another door, and inside the white-tiled corridor, Ted Eddings was zipped inside a pouch on top of a gurney parked near the X-ray room. His stiff arms pushed against black vinyl as if he were trying to fight his way free, and water slowly dripped on the floor. I was about to look for Danny when he limped around a corner, carrying a stack of towels, his right knee in a bright red sports brace from a soccer injury that had necessitated a reconstruction of his anterior cruciate ligament.

"We really should get him in the autopsy suite," I said. "You know how I feel about leaving bodies unattended in the hall."

"I was afraid someone would slip," he said, mopping up water with the towels.

"Well, the only someones here today are you and me." I smiled at him. "But thank you for the thought, and I certainly don't want you to slip. How's the knee?"

"I don't think it's ever going to get better. It's already been almost three months and I still can barely go downstairs."

"Patience, keep up your physio, and yes, it will get better," I repeated what I had said before. "Have you rayed him yet?"

Danny had worked diving deaths before. He knew it was highly improbable that we were looking for projectiles or broken bones, but what an X-ray might reveal was pneumothorax or a mediastinal shift caused by air leaking from lungs due to barotrauma.

"Yes, ma'am. The film's in the developer." He paused, his expression turning unpleasant. "And Detective Roche with Chesapeake's on his way. He wants to be present for the post."

Although I encouraged detectives to watch their cases autopsied, Roche was not someone I particularly wanted in my morgue.

"Do you know him?" I asked.

"He's been down here before. I'll let you judge him for yourself."

He straightened up and gathered his dark hair into a ponytail again, because strands had escaped and were getting in his eyes. Lithe and graceful, he looked like a young Cherokee with a brilliant grin. I often wondered why he wanted to work here. I helped him roll the body into the autopsy suite, and while he weighed and measured it, I disappeared inside the locker room and took a shower. As I was dressing in scrubs, Marino called my pager.

"What's up?" I asked when I got him on the phone.

"It's who we thought, right?" he asked.

"Tentatively, yes."

"You posting him now?"

"I'm about to start," I said.

"Give me fifteen minutes. I'm almost there."

"You're coming here?" I said, perplexed.

"I'm on my car phone. We'll talk later. I'll be there soon."

As I wondered what this was about, I also knew that Marino must have found something in Richmond. Otherwise, his coming to Norfolk made no sense. Ted Eddings's death was not Marino's jurisdiction unless the FBI had already gotten involved, and that would not make sense, either.

Both Marino and I were consultants for the Bureau's Criminal Investigative Analysis program, more commonly known as the profiling unit which specialized in assisting police with unusually heinous and difficult deaths. We routinely got involved in cases outside of our domains, but by invitation only, and it was a little early for Chesapeake to be calling the FBI about anything.

Detective Roche arrived before Marino did, and he was carrying a paper bag and insisting that I give him gown, gloves, face shield, cap and shoe covers. While he was in the locker room fussing with his biological armor, Danny and I began taking photographs and looking at Eddings exactly as he had come to us, which was still in a full wet suit that continued to slowly drip on the floor.

"He's been dead a while," I said. "I have a feeling that whatever happened to him occurred shortly after he went into the river."

"Do we know when that was?" Danny asked as he fit scalpel handles with new blades.

"We're assuming it was sometime after dark."

"He doesn't look very old."

"Thirty-two."

He stared at Eddings's face and his own got sad. "It's like when kids end up in here or that basketball player who dropped dead in the gym the other week." He looked at me. "Does it ever get to you?"

"I can't let it get to me because they need me to do a good job for them," I said as I made notes.

"What about when you're done?" He glanced up.

"We're never done, Danny," I said. "Our hearts will stay broken for the rest of our lives, and we will never be done with the people who pass through here."

"Because we can't forget them." He lined a bucket with a viscera bag and put it near me on the floor. "At least I can't."

"If we forget them, then something is wrong with us," I said.

Roche emerged from the locker room looking like a disposable astronaut in his face shield and paper suit. He kept his distance from the gurney but got as close as he could to me.

I said to him, "I've looked inside the boat. What items have you removed?"

"His gun and wallet. I got both of them here with me," he replied. "Over there in the bag. How many pairs of gloves you got on?"

"What about a camera, film, anything like that?"

"What's in the boat is all there is. Looks like you got on more than one pair of gloves." He leaned close, his shoulder pressing against mine.

"I've double-gloved." I moved away from him.

"I guess I need another pair."

I unzipped Eddings's soggy dive boots and said, "They're in the cabinet over there."

With a scalpel I opened the wet suit and dive skin at the seams because they would be too difficult to pull off a fully rigorous body. As I freed him from neoprene, I could see that he was uniformly pink due to the cold. I removed his blue bikini bathing suit, and Danny and I lifted him onto the autopsy table, where we broke the rigidity of the arms and began taking more photographs.

Eddings had no injuries except several old scars, mostly on his knees. But biology had dealt him an earlier blow called hypospadias, which meant his urethra opened onto the underside of his penis instead of in the center. This moderate defect would have caused him a great deal of anxiety, especially as a boy. As a man he may have suffered sufficient shame that he was reluctant to have sex.

Certainly, he had never been shy or passive during professional encounters. In fact, I had always found him quite confident and charming, when someone like me was rarely charmed by anyone, least of all a journalist. But I also knew appearances meant nothing in terms of how people behaved when two of them were alone, and then I tried to stop right there.

I did not want to remember him alive as I made annotations

and measurements on diagrams fastened to my clipboard. But a part of my mind tackled my will, and I returned to the last occasion I had seen him. It was the week before Christmas and I was in my Richmond office with my back to the door, sorting through slides in a carousel. I did not hear him behind me until he spoke, and when I turned around, I found him in my doorway, holding a potted Christmas pepper thick with bright red fruit.

"You mind if I come in?" he asked. "Or do you want me to walk all the way back to my car with this."

I said good afternoon to him while I thought with frustration of the front office staff. They knew not to let reporters beyond the locked bulletproof partition in the lobby unless I was asked, but the female clerks, in particular, liked Eddings a little too much. He walked in and set the plant on the carpet by my desk, and when he smiled, his entire face did.

"I just thought there ought to be something alive and happy in this place." His blue eyes fixed on mine.

"I hope that isn't a comment about me." I could not help but laugh.

"Are you ready to turn him?"

The body diagram on my clipboard came into focus, and I realized Danny was speaking to me.

"I'm sorry," I muttered.

He was eyeing me with concern while Roche wandered around as if he had never been inside a morgue, peering through glass cabinets and glancing back in my direction.

"Everything all right?" Danny asked me in his sensitive way.

"We can turn him now," I said.

My spirit shook inside like a small hot flame. Eddings had worn khaki range pants and a black commando sweater that day, and I tried to remember the look in his eyes. I wondered if there had been anything behind them that might have presaged this.

Refrigerated by the river, his body was cold to my touch, and I began discovering other aspects of him that distorted the familiar, making me feel even more disturbed. The absence of first molars signaled orthodonture. He had extensive, very expensive porcelain crowns, and contact lenses tinted to enhance eyes already vivid. Remarkably, the right lens had not been washed away when his mask had flooded, and his dull gaze was weirdly asymmetrical, as if two dead people were staring out from sleepy lids.

I was almost finished with the external examination, but what was left was the most invasive, for in any unnatural death, it was necessary to investigate a patient's sexual practices. Rarely was I given a sign as obvious as a tattoo depicting one orientation or another, and as a rule, no one the individual was intimate with was going to step forth to volunteer information, either. But it really would not have mattered what I was told or by whom. I would still check for evidence of anal intercourse.

"What are you looking for?" Roche returned to the table and stood close behind me.

"Proctitis, anal tunneling, small fissures, thickening of the epithelium from trauma," I replied as I worked.

"Then you're assuming he's queer." He peered over my shoulder.

The color mounted to Danny's cheeks, and anger sparked in his eyes.

"Anal ring, epithelium are unremarkable," I said, scribbling notes. "In other words, he has no injury that would be consistent with an active homosexual lifestyle. And, Detective Roche, you're going to have to give me a little more room."

I could feel his breath on my neck.

"You know, he's been in this area a lot doing interviews."

"What sort of interviews?" I asked, and he was seriously getting on my nerves.

"That I don't know."

"Who was he interviewing?"

"Last fall he did a piece on the Inactive Ship Yard. Captain Green could probably tell you more."

"I was just with Captain Green, and he didn't tell me about that."

"The story ran in *The Virginian Pilot*, back in October, I think. It wasn't a big deal. Just your typical feature," he said. "My personal opinion is he decided to come back to snoop around for something bigger."

"Such as?"

"Don't ask me. I'm not a reporter." He glanced across the table at Danny. "I personally hate the media. They're always coming up with these wild theories and will do anything to prove them. Now this guy's kinda famous around here, being a big-shot reporter for the AP and all. Rumor has it when he gets with girls it's window dressing. You get beyond it and nothing's there, if you know what I mean." He had a cruel smile on his face, and I could not believe how much I did not like him when we had only met today.

"Where are you getting your information?" I asked.

"I hear things."

"Danny, let's get hair and fingernail samples," I said.

"You know, I take the time to talk to people on the street," Roche added as he brushed against my hip.

"You want his mustache plucked, too?" Danny fetched forceps and envelopes from a surgical cart.

"May as well."

"I guess you're going to test him for HIV." Roche brushed against me again.

"Yes," I replied.

"Then you're thinking he might be queer."

I stopped what I was doing because I'd had enough. "Detective Roche"—I turned around to face him, and my voice was hard—"if you are going to be in my morgue, then you will give me room to work. You will stop rubbing against me, and you will treat my patients with respect. This man did not ask to be here dead and naked on this table. And I don't like the word queer."

"Well, regardless of what you call it, his orientation might somehow be important." He was nonplussed, if not pleased by my irritation.

"I don't know for a fact that this man was or was not gay," I said. "But I do know for a fact that he did not die of AIDS."

I grabbed a scalpel off a surgical cart and his demeanor abruptly changed. He backed off, suddenly unnerved because

I was about to start cutting, so now I had that problem to cope with, too.

"Have you ever seen an autopsy?" I said to him.

"A few." He looked like he might throw up.

"Why don't you go sit down over there," I suggested none too kindly as I wondered why Chesapeake had assigned him to this case or any case. "Or go out in the bay."

"It's just hot in here."

"If you get sick, go for the nearest trash can." It was all Danny could do not to laugh.

"I'll just sit over here for a minute." Roche went to the desk near the door.

I swiftly made the Y incision, the blade running from shoulders to sternum to pelvis. As blood was exposed to air, I thought I detected an odor that made me stop what I was doing.

"You know, Lipshaw's got a really good sharpener out I wish we could get," Danny was saying. "It hone-grinds with water so you can just stick the knives in there and leave them."

What I was smelling was unmistakable, but I could not believe it.

"I was just looking at their new catalog," he went on. "Makes me crazy all the cool things we can't afford."

This could not be right.

"Danny, open the doors," I said with a quiet urgency that startled him.

"What is it?" he asked in alarm.

"Let's get plenty of air in here. Now," I said.

He moved fast with his bad knee and opened double doors that led into the hall.

"What's wrong?" Roche sat up straighter.

"This man has a peculiar odor." I was unwilling to voice my suspicions right then, especially to him.

"I don't smell anything." He got up and looked around, as if this mysterious odor might be something he could see.

Eddings's blood reeked of a bitter almond smell, and it did not surprise me that neither Roche nor Danny could detect it. The ability to smell cyanide is a sex-linked recessive trait that is inherited by less than thirty percent of the population. I was among the fortunate few.

"Trust me." I was reflecting back skin from ribs, careful not to puncture the intercostal muscles. "He smells very strange."

"And what does that mean?" Roche wanted to know.

"I won't be able to answer that until tests are conducted," I said. "In the meantime, we'll thoroughly check out all of his equipment to make sure everything was functioning and that he didn't, for example, get exhaust fumes down his hose."

"You know much about hookahs?" Danny asked me, and he had returned to the table to help.

"I've never used one."

I undermined the midline chest incision laterally. Reflecting back tissue, I formed a pocket in a side of skin, which Danny filled with water. Then I immersed my hand and inserted the scalpel blade between two ribs. I checked for a release of bubbles that might indicate a diving injury had caused air to leak into the chest cavity. But there were none.

"Let's get the hookah and the hose out of the boat and bring them in," I decided. "It would be good if we could get hold of a dive consultant for a second opinion. Do you know anyone around here we might be able to reach on a holiday?"

"There's a dive shop in Hampton Roads that Dr. Mant sometimes uses."

He got the numbers and called, but the shop was closed this snowy New Year's Eve, and the owner did not seem to be at home. Then Danny went out to the bay, and when he returned a brief time later, I could hear a familiar voice talking loudly with him as heavy footsteps sounded along the hallway.

"They wouldn't let you if you were a cop," Pete Marino's voice projected into the autopsy suite.

"I know, but I don't understand it," Danny said.

"Well, I'll give you one damn good reason. Hair as long as yours gives the assholes out there one more thing to grab. Me? I'd cut it off. Besides, the girls would like you better."

He had arrived in time to help carry in the hookah and coils of hose, and was giving Danny a fatherly lecture. It had never been hard for me to understand why Marino had terrible problems with his own grown son.

"You know anything about hookahs?" I asked Marino as he walked in. He looked blankly at the body. "What? He's got some weirdo disease?"

"The thing you're carrying is called a hookah," I explained.

He and Danny set the equipment on top of an empty steel table next to mine.

"Looks like dive shops are closed for the next few days," I added. "But the compressor seems pretty simple—a pump driven by a five-horsepower engine which pulls air through a filtered intake valve, then through the low-pressure hose connected to the diver's second-stage regulator. Filter looks all right. Fuel line is intact. That's all I can tell you."

"The tank's empty," Marino observed.

"I think he ran out of gas after death."

"Why?" Roche had walked over to where we were, and he stared intensely at me and the front of my scrubs as if he and I were the only two people in the room. "How do you know he didn't lose track of time down there and run out of gas?"

"Because even if his air supply quit, he still had plenty of time to get to the surface. He was only thirty feet down," I said.

"That's a long way if maybe your hose has gotten hung up on something."

"It would be. But in that scenario, he could have dropped his weight belt."

"Has the smell gone away?" he asked.

"No, but it's not as overpowering."

"What smell?" Marino wanted to know.

"His blood has a weird odor."

"You mean like booze?"

"No, not like that."

He sniffed several times and shrugged as Roche moved past me, averting his gaze from what was on the table. I could not believe it when he brushed against me again though he had plenty of room and I had given him a warning. Marino was big and balding in a fleece-lined coat, and his eyes followed him.

"So, who's this?" he asked me.

"Yes, I guess the two of you haven't met," I said. "Detective Roche of Chesapeake, this is Captain Marino with Richmond."

Roche was looking closely at the hookah, and the sound of Danny cutting through ribs with shears on the next table was getting to him. His complexion was the shade of milk glass again, his mouth bowed down.

Marino lit a cigarette and I could tell by the expression on his face that he had made his decision about Roche, and Roche was about to know it.

"I don't know about you," he said to the detective, "but one thing I discovered early on, is once you come to this joint, you never feel the same about liver. You watch." He tucked the lighter back inside his shirt pocket. "Me, I used to love it smothered in onions." He blew out smoke. "Now, on the pain of death you couldn't make me touch it."

Roche leaned closer to the hookah, almost burying his face in it, as if the smell of rubber and gasoline was the antidote he needed. I resumed work.

"Hey, Danny," Marino went on, "you ever eat shit like kidneys and gizzards since you started working here?"

"I've never ate any of that my entire life," he said as we removed the breastplate. "But I know what you mean. When I see people order big slabs of liver in restaurants, I almost have to dive for the door. Especially if it's even the slightest bit pink."

The odor intensified as organs were exposed, and I leaned back.

"You smelling it?" Danny asked.

"Oh, yeah," I said.

Roche retreated to his distant corner, and now that Marino had had his fun, he walked over and stood next to me.

"So you think he drowned?" Marino quickly asked.

"At the moment I'm not thinking that. But certainly, I'm going to look for it," I said.

"What can you do to figure out he didn't drown?"

Marino was not very familiar with drownings, since people rarely committed murder that way, so he was intensely curious. He wanted to understand everything I was doing.

"Actually, there are a lot of things I'm doing," I said as I worked. "I've already made a skin pocket on the side of the chest, filled it with water and inserted a blade in the thorax to check for bubbles. I'm going to fill the pericardial sac with water and insert a needle into the heart, again to see if any bubbles form. And I'll check the brain for petechial hemorrhages, and look at the soft tissue of the mediastinum for extraalveolar air."

"What will all that show?" he asked.

"Possibly pneumothorax or air embolism, which can occur in less than fifteen feet of water if the diver is breathing inadequately. The problem is that excessive pressure in the lungs can result in small tears of the alveolar walls, causing hemorrhages and air leaks into one or both pleural cavities."

"And I'm assuming that could kill you," he said.

"Yes," I said. "That most certainly could."

"What about when you come up and go down too fast?" He had moved to the other side of the table so he could watch.

"Pressure changes, or barotrauma, associated with descent or ascent aren't very likely in the depth he was diving. And as you can see, his tissues aren't spongy as I would expect them to be were he a death by barotrauma. Would you like some protective clothing?"

"So I can look like I work for Terminex?" Marino looked in Roche's direction.

"Just hope you don't get AIDS," Roche wanly said from far away.

Marino put on apron and gloves as I began explaining the pertinent negatives I needed to look for in order to also rule out a death by decompression or the bends, or drowning. It was when I inserted an eighteen-gauge needle into the trachea to obtain a sample of air for cyanide testing that Roche decided to leave. He rapidly walked across the room, paper rattling as he collected his evidence bag from a counter.

"So we won't know anything until you do tests," he said from the doorway.

"That's correct. For now his cause and manner of death are pending." I paused and looked up at him. "You'll get a copy of my report when it's complete. And I'd like to see his personal effects before you leave."

He would come no closer, and my hands were bloody.

I looked at Marino. "Would you mind?"

"It would be my pleasure."

He went to him, took the bag and gruffly said, "Come on. We'll go through it in the hall so you can get some air."

They walked just beyond the doorway, and as I continued

to work, paper rattled some more. I heard Marino drop the magazine from a pistol, open the slide and loudly complain that the gun had not been made safe.

"I can't believe you're carrying this thing around loaded," Marino's voice boomed. "Jesus Christ! You know, it's not like this is your friggin" lunch in a bag."

"It's not been processed for prints yet."

"Well, then you put on gloves and dump the ammo like I just did. And then you clear the chamber, the way I just did. Where'd you go? The Keystone Police Academy where they also must have taught you your gentlemanly manners?"

Marino went on, and it was now clear to me why he had taken Roche into the hall, and it wasn't for fresh air. Danny glanced across the table at me and grinned.

Moments later Marino returned to us shaking his head, and Roche was gone. I was relieved, and it showed.

"Good God," I said. "What is his story?"

"He thinks with the head God gave him," Marino said. "The one between his legs."

"Like I said," Danny replied, "he's been down here a couple of times before bothering Dr. Mant about things. But what I didn't tell you is he always talked to him upstairs. He never would come down to the morgue."

"I'm shocked," Marino drolly said.

"I heard that when he was in the police academy he called in sick the day they were supposed to come down here for the demo autopsy," Danny went on. "Plus, he just got transferred over from juvenile. So he's been a homicide detective for only about two months."

"Oh, now that's good," Marino said. "Just the kind of person we want working something like this."

I asked him, "Can you smell the cyanide?"

"Nope. Right now all I smell is my cigarette, which is exactly how I want it."

"Danny?"

"No, ma'am." He sounded disappointed.

"So far I'm seeing no evidence that this is a diving death. No bubbles in the heart or thorax. No subcutaneous emphysema. No water in the stomach or lungs. I can't tell if he's congested." I cut another section of heart. "Well, he does have congestion of the heart, but is it due to the left heart failing the right—just due to dying, in other words? And he does have some reddening of the stomach wall, which is consistent with cyanide."

"Doc," Marino said, "how well did you know him?"

"Personally, really not at all."

"Well, I'm going to tell you what was in the bag because Roche didn't know what he was looking at and I didn't want to tell him."

He at last slipped out of his coat and looked for a safe place to hang it, deciding on the back of a chair. He lit another cigarette.

"Damn, these floors kill my feet," he said as he went to the table where hookah and hose were piled, and leaned against the edge. "It must kill your knee," he said to Danny.

"Totally kills it."

"Eddings's got a Browning nine-millimeter pistol with a Birdsong desert brown finish," Marino said.

"What's Birdsong?" Danny placed the spleen in a hanging scale.

"The Rembrandt of pistol finishes. Mr. Birdsong's the guy you send your weapon to if you want it waterproofed and painted to blend with the environment," Marino answered. "What he does, basically, is strip it, sandblast it and then spray it with Teflon, which is baked on. All of HRT's pistols have a Birdsong finish."

HRT was the FBI's Hostage Rescue Team. I felt sure that given the number of stories Eddings had done on law enforcement, he would have been exposed to the FBI Academy at Quantico and its finest trained agents.

"Sounds like something Navy SEALs would have, too," Danny suggested.

"Them, SWAT teams, counterterrorists, guys like me." Marino was looking again at the hookah's fuel line and intake valves. "And most of us have Novak sights like he's got, too. But what we don't have is KTW metal-piercing ammo, also known as cop killers."

"He's got Teflon-coated ammo?" I glanced up.

"Seventeen rounds, one in the chamber. All with red lacquer around the primer for waterproofing."

"Well, he didn't get armor-piercing ammo here. At least not legally, because it's been outlawed in Virginia for years. And as for the finish on his pistol, are you certain it's Birdsong, the same company the Bureau uses?"

"Looks like Birdsong's magic touch to me," Marino replied. "'Course, there are other outfits that do similar work."

I opened the stomach as mine continued to close like a

fist. Eddings had seemed such a fan of law enforcement. I had heard he used to ride along with the police, and go to their picnics and their balls. He had never struck me as gung-ho about weapons, and I was stunned that he would have loaded a pistol with illegal ammunition notorious for being used to murder and maim the very people who were his sources and perhaps his friends.

"Gastric contents are just a small amount of brownish fluid," I continued. "He didn't eat near the time of death, not that I would have expected him to if he planned to dive."

"Any chance fuel exhaust could have gotten to him, say if the wind blew just right?" Marino continued studying the hookah. "Couldn't that also make him pink?"

"Certainly, we'll test for carbon monoxide. But that doesn't explain what I'm smelling."

"And you're sure?"

"I know what I'm smelling," I said.

"You think he's a homicide, don't you," Danny said to me.

"No one should be talking about this." I pulled a cord down from an overhead reel and plugged in the Stryker saw. "Not to the Chesapeake police. Not to anyone. Not until all tests are concluded and I make an official release. I don't know what's going on here. I don't know what was going on at the scene. So we must exercise even more caution than usual."

Marino was looking at Danny. "How long you been working in this joint?" he asked.

"Eight months."

"You heard what the doc just said, right?"

Danny looked up, surprised by Marino's change in tone.

"You know how to keep your mouth shut, right?" Marino went on. "That means no bragging to the boys, no trying to impress your family or your girlfriend. You got that?"

Danny held in his anger as he made an incision low around the back of the head, ear to ear.

"See, if anything leaks, me and the doc here are going to know where it came from," Marino continued an attack that seemed completely unprovoked.

Danny reflected back the scalp. He pulled it forward over the eyes to expose the skull, and Eddings's face collapsed, sad and slack, as if he knew what was happening and was grieving. I turned on the saw, and the room was filled with the high whine of blade cutting bone.

3

At three-thirty the sun had dipped low behind a veil of gray, and snow was several inches deep and hung like smoke in the air. Marino and I followed Danny's footsteps across the parking lot, for the young man had already gone, and I felt bad for him.

"Marino," I said, "you just can't talk to people like that. My staff knows about discretion. Danny did nothing to merit your treating him so rudely, and I don't appreciate it."

"He's a kid," he said. "You raise him right and he'll take good care of you. Thing is, you got to believe in discipline."

"It is not your job to discipline my staff. And I have never had a problem with him."

"Yeah? And maybe this is one time when you don't need a problem with him," he replied.

"I really would appreciate it if you wouldn't try to run my office."

I was tired and out of sorts, and Lucy still was not answering the phone at Mant's house. Marino had parked next to me, and I unlocked my driver's door.

"So, what's Lucy doing for the New Year?" he asked as if he knew my concerns.

"Hopefully, spending it with me. But I haven't heard from her." I got into the car.

"The snow started up north, so Quantico got hit first," he said. "Maybe she got caught. You know how 95 can be."

"She's got a car phone. Besides, she's driving from Charlottesville," I said.

"How come?"

"The Academy's decided to send her back to UVA for another graduate course."

"In what? Advanced Rocket Science?"

"Apparently, she's doing a special study in virtual reality."

"So maybe she got stuck somewhere between here and Charlottesville." He did not want me to leave.

"She could have left a message."

He stared around the parking lot. It was empty save for the dark blue morgue wagon, which was covered with snow. Flakes clung to his wispy hair and must have been cold on his balding head, but he did not seem to mind.

"Do you have New Year plans?" I started the engine, then the wipers to plow snow off the windshield.

"A couple of us guys are supposed to play poker and eat chili."

"That sounds like fun." I looked up at his big, flushed face as he continued staring off.

"Doc. I went through Eddings's apartment back in

Richmond and didn't want to get into it in front of Danny. I think you're going to want to go through it, too."

Marino wanted to talk. He did not want to be with the guys or alone. He wanted to be with me, but he would never admit that. In all the years I had known him, his feelings for me were a confession he could not make, no matter how obvious they might be.

"I can't compete with a poker game," I said to him as I fastened my shoulder harness, "but I was going to make lasagne tonight. And it doesn't look like Lucy's going to get in. So if—"

"It don't look like driving back after midnight would be a smart thing," he cut me off as snow swirled across the tarmac in small white storms.

"I've got a guest room," I went on.

He looked at his watch, and decided it was a good time to smoke.

"In fact, driving back now isn't even a good idea," I stated. "And it looks like we need to talk."

"Yeah, well, you're probably right," he said.

What neither of us counted on as he slowly followed me to Sandbridge was that when we arrived, smoke would be drifting up from the chimney. Lucy's vintage green Suburban was parked in the drive and blanketed with snow, so I knew she had been here for a while.

"I don't understand," I said to Marino as we slammed car doors shut. "I called three times."

"Maybe I'd better leave." He stood by his Ford, not sure what to do.

"That's ridiculous. Come on. We'll figure out something. There is a couch. Besides, Lucy will be thrilled to see you."

"You got your diving shit?" he said.

"In the trunk."

We got it out together and carried it up to Dr. Mant's house, which looked even smaller and more forlorn in the weather. At the back was a screened-in porch, and we went in that way and deposited my gear on the wooden floor. Lucy opened the door leading into the kitchen, and we were enveloped by the aroma of tomatoes and garlic. She looked baffled as she stared at Marino and the dive equipment.

"What the hell's going on?" she said.

I could tell she was upset. This had been our night to be alone, and we did not have special nights like this often in our complicated lives.

"It's a long story." I met her eyes.

We followed her inside, where a large pot was simmering on the stove. Nearby on the counter was a cutting board, and Lucy apparently had been slicing peppers and onions when we arrived. She was dressed in FBI sweats and ski socks and looked flawlessly healthy, but I could tell she had not been getting much sleep.

"There's a hose in the pantry, and just off the porch near a spigot is an empty plastic trash can," I said to Marino. "If you'd fill that, we can soak my gear."

"I'll help," Lucy said.

"You most certainly won't." I gave her a hug. "Not until we've visited for a minute."

We waited until Marino was outside, then I pulled her

over to the stove and lifted the lid from the pot. A delicious steam rose and I felt happy.

"I can't believe you," I said. "God bless you."

"When you weren't back by four I figured I'd better make the sauce or we weren't going to be eating lasagne tonight."

"It might need a little more red wine. And maybe more basil and a pinch of salt. I was going to use artichokes instead of meat, although Marino won't be happy about that, but he can just eat prosciutto. How does that sound?" I returned the lid to the pot.

"Aunt Kay, why is he here?" she asked.

"Did you get my note?"

"Sure. That's how I got in. But all it said was you had gone to a scene."

"I'm sorry. But I called several times."

"I wasn't going to answer a phone in somebody else's house," she said. "And you didn't leave a message."

"My point is that I didn't think you were here, so I invited Marino. I didn't want him to drive back to Richmond in the snow."

Disappointment glinted in her intense green eyes. "It's not a problem. As long as he and I don't have to sleep in the same room," she dryly remarked. "But I don't understand what he was even doing in Tidewater."

"Like I said, it's a long story," I answered. "The case in question has a Richmond connection."

We went out to the frigid porch and quickly swished fins, dive skin, wet suit and other gear in icy water. Then we carried all of it up to the attic, where nothing would freeze, and placed it on multiple layers of towels. I took as long a shower as the water heater would allow, and thought it unreal that Lucy, Marino and I were together in this tiny coastal cottage on a snowy New Year's Eve.

When I emerged from my bedroom, I found them in the kitchen drinking Italian beer and reading about making bread.

"All right," I said to them. "That's it. Now I take over."

"Watch out," Lucy said.

I shooed them out of the way and began measuring high gluten flour, yeast, a little sugar and olive oil into a large bowl. I turned the oven on low and opened a bottle of Côte Rôtie, which was for the cook to sip as she began her serious work. I would serve a Chianti with the meal.

"Did you go through Eddings's wallet?" I asked Marino as I chopped porcini mushrooms.

"Who's Eddings?" Lucy asked.

She was sitting on a countertop, sipping Peroni. Through the windows behind her snow streaked the gathering dark. I explained more about what had happened today, and she asked no further questions, but was silent as Marino talked.

"Nothing jumped out," he said. "One MasterCard, one Visa, AmEx, insurance info. Crap like that and a couple receipts. They look like restaurants, but we'll check. You mind if I get another one of these?" He dropped an empty bottle into the trash and opened the refrigerator door. "Let's see what else." Glass clattered. "He wasn't carrying much cash. Twenty-seven bucks."

"What about photographs?" I asked, kneading dough on a board dusted with flour.

"Nothing." He shut the refrigerator. "And as you know, he wasn't married."

"We don't know that he didn't have a significant relationship with someone," I said.

"That could be true because there sure isn't a hell of a lot we know." He looked at Lucy. "You know what Birdsong is?"

"My Sig's got a Birdsong finish." She looked over at me. "So does Aunt Kay's Browning."

"Well, this guy Eddings had a Browning nine-mil just like what your aunt's got and it has a desert brown Birdsong finish. Plus, his ammo's Teflon-coated and has red lacquer on the primer. I mean you could shoot the shit through twelve phone books in the friggin' pouring rain."

She was surprised. "What's a journalist doing with something like that?"

"Some people are just very enthusiastic about guns and ammo," I said. "Although I never knew Eddings was. He never mentioned it to me—not that he necessarily would have."

"I've never seen KTW in Richmond at all," Marino said, referring to the brand name of the Teflon-coated cartridges. "Legal or otherwise."

"Could he have gotten it at a gun show?" I asked.

"Maybe. One thing's for sure. This guy probably went to a lot of them. I ain't told you about his apartment yet."

I covered the dough with a damp towel and put the bowl in the oven on the lowest setting.

"I won't give you the whole tour," he went on. "Just the important parts, starting with the room where he's apparently been reloading his own ammo. Now where he's been shooting all these rounds, who knows. But he's got plenty of guns to choose from, including several other handguns, an AK-47, an MP5 and an M16. Not exactly what you use for varmint hunting. Plus, he subscribed to a number of survivalist magazines, including *Soldier of Fortune*, *U.S. Cavalry Magazine*, and *Brigade Quartermaster*. Finally" —Marino took another swallow of beer—"we found some videotapes on how to be a sniper. You know, special forces training and shit like that."

I folded eggs and Parmesan reggiano with ricotta. "Any hint as to what he may have been involved in?" I asked as the mystery of the dead man deepened and unsettled me more.

"No, but he sure as hell seemed to be after something."

"Or something was after him," I said.

"He was scared," Lucy spoke as if she knew. "You don't go diving after dark and carry along a waterproof nine-mil loaded with armor-piercing ammo unless you're scared. That's the behavior of someone who thinks there's a contract out on him."

It was then I told them about my strange early-morning phone call from an Officer Young who did not seem to exist. I mentioned Captain Green and described his behavior.

"Why would he call, if he's the one who did?" Marino frowned.

"Clearly, he didn't want me at the scene," I said. "And maybe if I were given ample information by the police, I would just wait for the body to come in, as I usually do."

"Well, it sounds to me like you were being bullied," Lucy said.

"I believe that was the overall plan," I agreed.

"Have you tried the phone number this nonexistent Officer Young gave you?" she asked.

"No," I said.

"Where is it?"

I got it for her and she dialed it.

"It's the number for the local weather report," she said, hanging up.

Marino pulled out a chair from the checker cloth-covered breakfast table and straddled it, his arms folded on top of the back. Nobody spoke for a while as we sifted through data that were getting only stranger by the minute.

"Listen, Doc." Marino cracked his knuckles. "I really gotta smoke. You going to let me or do I have to go outside?"

"Outside," Lucy said, jabbing her thumb toward the door and looking meaner than I knew she felt.

"And what if I fall into a snowdrift, you little runt?" he said.

"It's four inches deep out there. The only drift you're going to fall into is the one in your mind."

"Tomorrow we'll go out on the beach and shoot cans," he said. "Now and then you need someone to give you a little humility, Special Agent Lucy."

"You most certainly will not be shooting anything on this beach," I said to both of them.

"I guess we could let Pete open the window and blow smoke out," Lucy said. "But it just shows you how addicted you are."

"As long as you smoke fast," I said to him. "This house is cold enough as it is."

The window was stubborn, but no more so than Marino, who managed to get it open after a violent struggle. Moving his chair nearby, he lit up and blew smoke out the screen. Lucy and I placed silverware and napkins in the living room, deciding it would be cozier to eat in front of the fire than in Dr. Mant's kitchen or cramped, drafty dining room.

"You haven't even told me how you're doing," I said to my niece as she started working on the fire.

"I'm doing great."

Sparks swarmed up the chimney's sooty throat as she shoved more wood inside, and veins stood out in her hands, muscles flexing in her back. Her gifts were in computer science and, most recently, robotics, which she had studied at MIT. They were areas of expertise that had made her very attractive to the FBI's Hostage Rescue Team, but the expectation of her was cerebral, not physical. No woman had ever passed HRT's punishing requirements, and I worried that she was not going to accept her limits.

"How much are you working out?" I asked her.

She closed the screen and sat on the hearth, looking at me. "A lot."

"If your body fat gets much lower, you won't be healthy."

"I'm very healthy and actually have too much body fat."

"If you're getting anorexic, I'm not going to have my head in the sand about it, Lucy. I know that eating disorders kill. I've seen their victims."

"I don't have an eating disorder."

I came over and sat next to her, the fire warming our backs. "I guess I'll have to take your word on that."

"Good."

"Listen"—I patted her leg—"you've been assigned to HRT as their technical consultant. It has never been anyone's assumption that you will fast-rope out of helicopters and run four-minute miles with the men."

She looked over at me with flashing eyes. "You're one to talk about limitations. I don't see that you've ever let your gender hold you back."

"I absolutely know my limitations," I disagreed. "And I work around them with my mind. That is how I have survived."

"Look," she said with feeling, "I'm tired of programming computers and robots, and then every time something big goes down—like the bombing in Oklahoma City—the guys head off to Andrews Air Force Base and I get left. Or even if I go with them, they lock me in some little room somewhere like I'm nothing but a nerd. I'm not a goddamn nerd. I don't want to be a latchkey agent."

Her eyes were suddenly bright with tears and she averted them from me. "I can run any obstacle course they put me on. I can rappel, sniper-shoot and scuba-dive. More important, I can take it when they act like assholes. You know, not all of them are exactly happy to have me around."

I had no doubt of that. Lucy had always been an extremely polarizing human being, because she was brilliant and could be so difficult. She was also beautiful in a sharp-featured, strong way, and I frankly wondered how she survived at all on a special forces team of fifty men, not one of whom she would ever date.

"How is Janet?" I asked.

"They transferred her out to the Washington Field Office to do white-collar crime. So at least she's not far away."

"This must have been recent." I was puzzled.

"Real recent." Lucy rested her forearms on her knees.

"And where is she tonight?"

"Her family's got a condo in Aspen."

My silence asked the question, and her voice was irritated as she answered it. "No, I wasn't invited. And not just because Janet and I aren't getting along. It just wasn't a good idea."

"I see." I hesitated before adding, "Then her parents still don't know."

"Hell, who does know? You think we don't hide it at work? So we go to things together and each of us gets to watch the other being hit on by men. That's a special pleasure," she bitterly said.

"I know what it's like at work," I said. "It's no different than I told you it would be. What I'm more interested in is Janet's family."

Lucy stared at her hands. "It's mostly her mom. To tell you the truth, I don't think her dad would care. He's not going to assume it's because of something he did wrong, like my mother assumes. Only she assumes it's because of something you did wrong since you pretty much raised me and are my mother, according to her."

There was little point in my defending myself against the ignorant notions of my only sister, Dorothy, who unfortunately happened to be Lucy's parent.

"And Mother has another theory now, too. She says you're

the first woman I fell in love with, and somehow that explains everything," Lucy went on in an ironic tone. "Never mind that this would be called incest or that you're straight. Remember, she writes these insightful children's books, so she's an expert in psychology and apparently is a sex therapist, too."

"I'm sorry you have to go through all this on top of everything else," I said with feeling. I never knew quite what to do when we had these conversations. They were still new to me, and in some ways scary.

"Look"—she got up as Marino walked into the living room —"some things you just live with."

"Well, I got news for you," Marino announced, "the weather forecast is that this crap is going to melt. So come tomorrow morning, all of us should be able to get out of here."

"Tomorrow's New Year's Day," Lucy said. "For the sake of argument, why should we get out of here?"

"Because I need to take your aunt to Eddings's crib." He paused before adding, "And Benton needs to get his ass there, too."

I did not visibly react. Benton Wesley was the unit chief of the Bureau's Criminal Investigative Analysis program, and I had hoped I would not have to see him during the holidays.

"What are you telling me?" I quietly said.

He sat down on the sofa and regarded me thoughtfully for a pause. Then he answered my question with one of his own. "I'm curious about something, Doc. How would you poison someone underwater?"

"Maybe it didn't happen underwater," Lucy suggested. "Maybe he swallowed cyanide before he went diving."

"No. That's not what happened," I said. "Cyanide is very corrosive, and had he taken it orally, I would have seen extensive damage to his stomach. Probably to his esophagus and mouth, as well."

"So what could have happened?" Marino asked.

"I think he inhaled cyanide gas."

He looked baffled. "How? Through the compressor?"

"It draws air through an intake valve that's covered with a filter," I reminded him. "What someone could have done was simply mix a little hydrochloric acid with a cyanide tablet and hold the vial close enough to the intake valve for the gas to be drawn in."

"If Eddings inhaled cyanide gas while he was down there," Lucy said, "what would have happened?"

"A seizure, then death. In seconds."

I thought of the snagged air hose and wondered if Eddings had been close to the *Exploiter*'s screw when he suddenly inhaled cyanide gas through his regulator. That might explain the position he was in when I found him.

"Can you test the hookah for cyanide?" Lucy asked.

"Well, we can try," I said, "but I don't expect to find anything unless the cyanide tablet was placed directly on the valve's filter. Even so, things may have been tampered with by the time I got there. We might have better luck with the section of hose that was closest to the body. I'll start tox testing tomorrow, if I can get anybody to come into the lab on a holiday."

My niece walked over to a window to look out. "It's still coming down hard. It's amazing how it lights up the night. I can see the ocean. It's this black wall," she said in a pensive tone.

"What you're seeing is a wall," Marino said. "The brick wall at the back of the yard."

She did not speak for a while, and I thought of how much I missed her. Although I had seen little of her during her undergraduate years at UVA, now we saw each other less, for even when a case brought me to Quantico there was never a guarantee we would find time to visit. It saddened me that her childhood was gone, and a part of me wished she had chosen a life and a career less harsh than what hers must be.

Then she mused as she still gazed out the glass, "So we've got a reporter who's into survivalist weaponry. Somehow he's poisoned with cyanide gas while diving around decommissioned ships in a restricted area at night."

"That's just a possibility," I reminded her. "His case is pending. We should be careful not to forget that."

She turned around. "Where would you get cyanide if you wanted to poison someone? Would that be hard?"

"You could get it from a variety of industrial settings," I said.

"Such as?"

"Well, for example, it's used to extract gold from ore. It's also used in metal plating, and as a fumigant, and to manufacture phosphoric acid from bones," I said. "In other words, anyone from a jeweler to a worker in an industrial plant to an exterminator could have access to cyanide. Plus, you're going to find it and hydrochloric acid in any chemical lab."

"Well," it was Marino who spoke, "if someone poisoned Eddings, then they had to know he was going to be out in his boat. They had to know where and when."

"Someone had to know many things," I agreed. "For example, one would have had to know what type of breathing apparatus Eddings planned to use because had he gone down with scuba gear instead of a hookah, the MO would have had to be entirely different."

"I just wish we knew what the hell he was doing down there." Marino opened the screen to tend to the fire.

"Whatever it was," I said, "it seems to have involved photography. And based on the camera equipment it appears he had with him, he was serious."

"But no underwater camera was found," Lucy said.

"No," I said. "The current could have carried it anywhere, or it might be buried in silt. Unfortunately, the kind of equipment he apparently had doesn't float."

"I sure would like to get hold of the film." She was still looking out at the snowy night, and I wondered if she was thinking of Aspen.

"One thing's for damn sure, he wasn't taking pictures of fish." Marino jabbed a fat log that was a little too green. "So that pretty much leaves ships. And I think he was doing a story somebody didn't want him to do."

"He may have been doing a story," I agreed, "but that doesn't mean it's related to his death. Someone could have used his being out diving as an opportunity to kill him for another reason."

"Where do you keep the kindling?" He gave up on the fire.

"Outside under a tarp," I answered. "Dr. Mant won't allow it in the house. He's afraid of termites."

"Well, he ought to be more afraid of the fires and wind shear in this dump."

"In back, just off the porch," I said. "Thanks, Marino."

He put on gloves but no coat and went outside as the fire smoked stubbornly and the wind made eerie moaning sounds in the leaning brick chimney. I watched my niece, who was still at the window.

"We should work on dinner, don't you think?" I said to her.

"What's he doing?" she said with her back to me.

"Marino?"

"Yes. The big idiot's gotten lost. Look, he's all the way up by the wall. Wait a minute. I can't see him now. He turned his flashlight off. That's kind of weird."

Her words lifted the hair on my neck and instantly I was on my feet. I dashed into the bedroom and grabbed my pistol off the nightstand. Lucy was on my heels.

"What is it?" she exclaimed.

"He doesn't have a flashlight," I said as I ran.

4

In the kitchen, I flung open the door leading to the porch and ran into Marino. We almost knocked each other down.

"What the shit . . .?" he yelled behind a load of wood.

"There's a prowler," I spoke with quiet urgency.

Kindling thudded loudly to the floor and he ran back out into the yard, his pistol drawn. By now, Lucy had fetched her gun and was outside, too, and we were ready to handle a riot.

"Check the perimeter of the house," Marino ordered. "I'm going over here."

I went back in for flashlights, and for a while Lucy and I circled the cottage, straining eyes and ears, but the only sight and sound was our shoes crunching as we left impressions in the snow. I heard Marino decock his pistol as we reconvened in deep shadows near the porch.

"There are footprints by the wall," he said, and his breath

was white. "It's real strange. They lead down to the beach and then just disappear near the water." He looked around. "You got any neighbors who might have been out for a stroll?"

"I don't know Dr. Mant's neighbors," I replied. "But they should not have been in his yard. And who in his right mind would walk on the beach in weather like this?"

"Where on this property do the footprints go?" Lucy asked.

"Looks like he came over the wall and went about six feet inside the yard before backtracking," Marino answered.

I thought of Lucy standing before the window, backlit by the fire and lamps. Maybe the prowler had spotted her and had been scared off.

Then I thought of something else. "How do we know this person was a he?"

"If it ain't, I feel sorry for a woman with boats that big," Marino said. "The shoes are about the same size as mine."

"Shoes or boots?" I asked, heading toward the wall.

"I don't know. They got some sort of cross-hatch tread pattern." He followed me.

The footprints I saw gave me cause for more alarm. They were not from typical boots or athletic shoes.

"My God," I said. "I think this person was wearing dive boots or something with a moccasin shape like dive boots. Look."

I pointed out the pattern to Lucy and Marino. They had gotten down next to me, footprints obliquely illuminated by my flashlight.

"No arch," Lucy noted. "They sure look like dive boots or aqua shoes to me. Now that's bizarre."

I got up and stared out over the wall at dark, heaving water. It seemed inconceivable that someone could have come up from the sea.

"Can you get photos of these?" I asked Marino.

"Sure. But I got nothing to make casts."

Then we returned to the house. He gathered the wood and carried it into the living room while Lucy and I returned our attention to dinner, which I was no longer certain I could eat because I was so tense. I poured another glass of wine and tried to dismiss the prowler as a coincidence, a harmless peregrination on the part of someone who enjoyed the snow or perhaps diving at night.

But I knew better, and kept my gun nearby and frequently glanced out the window. My spirit was heavy as I slid the lasagne into the oven. I found the Parmesan reggiano in the refrigerator and began grating it, then I arranged figs and melon on plates, adding plenty of prosciutto for Marino's share. Lucy made salad, and for a while we worked in silence.

When she finally spoke, she was not happy. "You've really gotten into something, Aunt Kay. Why does this always happen to you?"

"Let's not allow our imaginations to run wild," I said.

"You're out here alone in the middle of nowhere with no burglar alarm and locks as flimsy as flip-top aluminum cans—"

"Have you chilled the champagne yet?" I interrupted. "It will be midnight soon. The lasagne will only take about ten minutes, maybe fifteen, unless Dr. Mant's oven works like everything else does around here. Then it could take until this time next year. I've never understood why people cook lasagne for hours. And then they wonder why everything is leathery."

Lucy was staring at me, resting a paring knife on a side of the salad bowl. She had cut enough celery and carrots for a marching band.

"One day I will really make lasagne coi carciofi for you. It has artichokes, only you use béchamel sauce instead of marinara—"

"Aunt Kay," she impatiently cut me off. "I hate it when you do this. And I'm not going to let you do this. I don't give a shit about lasagne right now. What matters is that this morning you got a weird phone call. Then there was a bizarre death and people treated you suspiciously at the scene. Now tonight you had a prowler who might have been in a damn wet suit."

"It's not likely the person will be back. Whoever it was. Not unless he wants to take on the three of us."

"Aunt Kay, you can't stay here," she said.

"I have to cover Dr. Mant's district, and I can't do that from Richmond," I told her as I again looked out the window over the sink. "Where's Marino? Is he still out taking pictures?"

"He came in a while ago." Her frustration was as palpable as a storm about to start.

I walked into the living room and found him asleep on the couch, the fire blazing. My eyes wandered to the window where Lucy had looked out, and I went to it. Beyond cold glass the snowy yard glowed faintly like a pale moon, and was pockmarked by elliptical shadows left by our feet. The brick wall was dark, and I could not see beyond it, where coarse sand tumbled into the sea.

"Lucy's right," Marino's sleepy voice said to my back.

I turned around. "I thought you were down for the count."

"I hear and see everything, even when I'm down for the count," he said. I could not help but smile.

"Get the hell out of here. That's my vote." He worked his way up to a sitting position. "No way I'd stay in this crate out in the middle of nowhere. Something happens, ain't no one going to hear you scream." His eyes fixed on me. "By the time anyone finds you, you'll be freeze-dried. If a hurricane don't blow you out to sea, first."

"Enough," I said.

He retrieved his gun from the coffee table, got up and tucked it in the back of his pants. "You could get one of your other doctors to come out here and cover Tidewater."

"I'm the only one without family. It's easier for me to move, especially this time of year."

"What a lot of bullshit. You don't have to apologize for being divorced and not having kids."

"I am not apologizing."

"And it's not like you're asking someone to relocate for six months. Besides, you're the friggin' chief. You should make other people relocate, family or not. You should be in your own house."

"I actually hadn't thought coming here would be all that

unpleasant," I said. "Some people pay a lot of money to stay in cottages on the ocean."

He stretched. "You got anything American to drink around here?"

"Milk."

"I was thinking more along the lines of Miller."

"I want to know why you're calling Benton. I personally think it's too soon for the Bureau to be involved."

"And I personally don't think you're in a position to be objective about him."

"Don't goad me," I warned. "It's too late and I'm too tired."

"I'm just being straight with you." He knocked a Marlboro out of the pack and tucked it between his lips. "And he will come to Richmond. I got no doubt about that. He and the wife didn't go nowhere for the holidays, so my guess is he's ready for a little field trip right about now. And this is going to be a good one."

I could not hold his gaze, and I resented that he knew why.

"Besides," he went on, "at the moment it ain't Chesapeake who's asking the FBI anything. It's me, and I have a right. In case you've forgot, I'm the commander of the precinct where Eddings's apartment is. As far as I'm concerned right now, this is a multi-jurisdictional investigation."

"The case is Chesapeake's, not Richmond's," I stated. "Chesapeake is where the body was found. You can't bulldoze your way into their jurisdiction, and you know it. You can't invite the FBI on their behalf."

"Look," he went on, "after going through Eddings's apartment and finding what I did—"

I interrupted him, "Finding what you did? You keep referring to whatever it is you found. You mean, his arsenal?"

"I mean more than that. I mean worse than that. We haven't gotten to that part yet." He looked at me and took the cigarette out of his mouth. "The bottom line is Richmond's got a reason to be interested in this case. So consider yourself invited."

"I'm afraid I was invited when Eddings died in Virginia."

"Don't sound to me like you felt all that invited this morning when you were at the shipyard."

I didn't say anything, because he was right.

"Maybe you had a guest on your property tonight so you would realize just how uninvited you are," he went on. "I want the FBI in this thing now because there's more to it than some guy in a johnboat you had to fish out of the river."

"What else did you find in Eddings's apartment?" I asked him.

I could see his reluctance as he stared off, and I did not understand it.

"I'll serve dinner first and then we'll sit down and talk," I said.

"If it could wait until tomorrow, it would be better." He glanced toward the kitchen as if worried that Lucy might overhear.

"Marino, since when have you ever worried about telling me something?"

"This is different." He rubbed his face in his hands. "I think Eddings got himself tangled up with the New Zionists," he finally said.

* * *

The lasagne was superb because I had drained fresh mozzarella in dishcloths so it did not weep too much during baking, and, of course, the pasta was fresh. I had served the dish tender instead of cooking it bubbly and brown, and a light sprinkling of Parmesan reggiano at the table had made it perfect.

Marino ate virtually all of the bread, which he slathered with butter, layered with prosciutto and sopped with tomato sauce, while Lucy mostly picked at the small portion on her plate. The snow had gotten heavier, and Marino told us about the New Zionist bible he had found as fireworks sounded in Sandbridge.

I pushed back my chair. "It's midnight. We should open the champagne."

I was more disturbed than I had supposed, for what Marino had to say was worse than I feared. Over the years, I had heard quite a lot about Joel Hand and his fascist followers who called themselves the New Zionists. They were going to cause a new order, create an ideal land. I had always feared they were quiet behind their Virginia compound walls because they were plotting a disaster.

"What we need to do is raid the asshole's farm," Marino said as he got up from the table. "That should have been done a long time ago."

"What probable cause would anybody have?" Lucy said.

"You ask me, with squirrels like him, you shouldn't need probable cause."

"Oh, good idea. You should suggest that one to Gradecki," she drolly said, referring to the U.S. attorney general.

"Look, I know some guys in Suffolk where Hand lives, and the neighbors say some really weird shit goes on there."

"Neighbors always think weird shit goes on with their neighbors," she said.

Marino got the champagne out of the refrigerator while I fetched glasses.

"What sort of weird shit?" I asked him.

"Barges pull up to the Nansemond River and unload crates so big they got to use cranes. Nobody knows what goes on there, except pilots have spotted bonfires at night, like maybe there's occult rituals. Local people swear they hear gunshots all the time and that there have been murders on his farm."

I walked into the living room because we would clean up later.

I said, "I know about the homicides in this state, and I've never heard the New Zionists mentioned in connection with any of them, or with any crime at all, for that matter. I've never heard they are involved in the occult, either. Only on-the-fringe politics and oddball extremism. They seem to hate America and would probably be happy if they could have their own little country somewhere where Hand could be king. Or God. Or whatever he is to them."

"You want me to pop this thing?" Marino held up the champagne.

"The new year's not getting any younger," I said. "Now let me get this straight." I settled on the couch. "Eddings had some link with the New Zionists?"

"Only because he had one of their bibles, like I already told you," Marino said. "I found it when we was going through his house."

"That's what you were worried about me seeing?" I looked quizzically at him.

"Tonight, yes," he said. "Because I'm more worried about her seeing it, if you want to know." He looked at Lucy.

"Pete," my niece spoke very reasonably, "you don't need to protect me anymore, even though I appreciate it."

He was silent.

"What sort of bible?" I asked him.

"Not any sort you've ever carried to Mass."

"Satanic?"

"No, I can't say it's like that. At least not like the ones I've seen, because it's not about worshiping Satan and doesn't have any of the sort of symbolism that you associate with that. But it sure as hell isn't something you'd want to read before going to bed." He glanced at Lucy again.

"Where is it?" I wanted to know.

He peeled foil off the top of the bottle and unwound wire. The cork popped loudly, and he poured champagne the way he poured beer, tilting the glasses sharply to prevent a head.

"Lucy, how about bringing my briefcase here. It's in the kitchen," he said, and he looked at me as she left the room and lowered his voice. "I wouldn't have brought it with me if I thought I was going to be seeing her."

"She's a grown woman. She's an FBI agent, for God's sake," I said.

"Yeah, and she gets whacked out sometimes, and you know that, too. She don't need to be looking at spooky stuff like this. I'm telling you, I read it because I had to, and I felt really creepy. I felt like I needed to go to Mass, and when have you ever heard me say that?" His face was intense.

I had never heard him say that, and I was uneasy. Lucy had been through hard times that had seriously frightened me. She had been self-destructive and unstable before.

"It is not my right to protect her," I said as she returned to the living room.

"I hope you're not talking about me," she said as she handed Marino his briefcase.

"Yeah, we were talking about you," he said, "because I don't think you should be looking at this."

Clasps sprang open.

"It's your case." Her eyes were calm as they turned to me. "I am interested in it and would like to help in even the smallest way, if I can. But I'll leave the room, if you want me to."

Oddly, the decision was one of the hardest ones I'd had to make, because my allowing her to look at evidence I wanted to protect her from was my concession to her professional accomplishment. As wind shook windows and rushed around the roof, sounding like spirits in distress, I moved over on the couch.

"You can sit next to me, Lucy," I said. "We'll look at it together."

The New Zionist bible was actually titled the *Book of Hand*, for its author had been inspired by God and had modestly named the manuscript after himself. Written in Renaissance script on India paper, it was bound in tooled black leather that was scuffed and stained and lettered with the name of someone I did not know. For more than an hour, Lucy leaned against me and we read while Marino prowled about, carrying in more wood and smoking, his restlessness as palpable as the fire's wavering light.

Like the Christian Bible, much of what the manuscript had to say was conveyed in parables, and prophesies and proverbs, thus making the text illustrative and human. This was one of many reasons why reading it was so hard. Pages were populated with people and images that penetrated to deeper layers of the brain. The Book, as we came to call it during the beginning of this new year, showed in exquisite detail how to kill and maim, frighten, brainwash and torture. The explicit section on the necessity of pogroms, including illustrations, made me quake.

I found the violence reminiscent of the Inquisition, and it was, in fact, explained that the New Zionists were here on earth to effect a new Inquisition, of sorts.

"We are in an age when the wrongful ones must be purged from our midst," Hand had written, "and in doing so we must be loud and obvious like cymbals. We must feel their weak blood cool on our bare skin as we wallow in their annihilation. We must follow the One into glory, and even unto death."

I read other ruminations and runes, and perused strange preoccupations with fusion and fuels that could be used to change the balance of the land. By the Book's end, a terrible darkness seemed to have enveloped me and the entire cottage. I felt sullied and sickened by the reminder that there were people in our midst who might think like this.

It was Lucy who finally spoke, for our silence had been unbroken for more than an hour. "It speaks of the One and their loyalty to him," she said. "Is this a person or a deity of some sort?"

"It's Hand, who probably thinks he's Jesus friggin' Christ," Marino said, pouring more champagne. "Remember that time we saw him in court?" He glanced up at me.

"That I'm not likely to forget any time soon," I said.

"He came in with this entourage, including a Washington attorney who has this big gold pocket watch and a silver-topped cane," he said to Lucy. "Hand is wearing some fancy designer suit, and he's got long blond hair in a ponytail, and women are waiting outside the courthouse to get a peek at him like he's Michael Bolton or something, if you can believe that."

"What was he in court for?" Lucy looked at me.

"He'd filed a petition for disclosure, which the attorney general had denied, so it went before a judge."

"What did he want?" she asked.

"Basically, he was trying to force me to turn over copies of Senator Len Cooper's death records."

"Why?"

"He was alleging that the late senator was poisoned by political enemies. In fact, Cooper died of an acute hemorrhage into a brain tumor. The judge granted Hand nothing."

"I guess Joel Hand doesn't like you too much," she said to me.

"I expect he doesn't." I looked at the Book on the coffee table, and asked Marino, "This name on the cover. Do you know who Dwain Shapiro is?"

"I was about to get to that," he said. "This is as much as we could pull up on the computer. He lived on the New Zionists' compound in Suffolk until last fall when he defected. About a month later he got killed in a carjacking in Maryland."

We were quiet for a moment, and I felt the cottage's dark windows as if they were big, square eyes.

Then I asked, "Any suspects or witnesses?"

"None anybody knows of."

"How did Eddings get hold of Shapiro's bible?" said Lucy.

"Obviously, that's the twenty-thousand-dollar question," Marino replied. "Maybe Eddings talked to him at some point, or maybe to his relatives. This thing ain't a photocopy, and it also says right in the beginning of it that you're not supposed to let your Book ever leave your hands. And if you're ever caught with someone else's Book, you can kiss your ass good-bye."

"That's pretty much what happened to Eddings," Lucy said.

I did not want the Book anywhere near us and wished I could throw it into the fire. "I don't like this," I said. "I don't like it at all."

Lucy looked curiously at me. "You're not getting superstitious on us, are you?"

"These people are consorting with evil," I said. "And I respect that there is evil in the world and it is not to be taken lightly. Where exactly in Eddings's house did you find this God-awful book?" I asked Marino.

"Under his bed," he said.

"Seriously."

"I'm very serious."

"And we're certain Eddings lived alone?" I asked.

"Appears that way."

"What about family?"

"Father's deceased, a brother's in Maine and the mother lives in Richmond. Real close to where you live, as a matter of fact."

"You've talked to her?" I asked.

"I stopped by and told her the bad news and asked if we could conduct a more thorough search of her son's house, which we'll do tomorrow." He glanced at his watch. "Or I guess I should say today."

Lucy got up and moved to the hearth. She propped an elbow on a knee and cupped her chin in her hand. Behind her, coals glowed in a deep bed of ashes.

"How do you know this bible originally came from the New Zionists?" she said. "Seems to me all you know is it came from Shapiro, and how can we be sure where he got it?"

Marino said, "Shapiro was a New Zionist until just three months ago. I've heard that Hand isn't real understanding when people want to leave him. Let me ask you something. How many ex-New Zionists do you know?"

Lucy could not say. Certainly, I couldn't either.

"He's had followers for at least ten years. And we never

hear anything about anyone leaving?" he went on. "How the hell do we know who he's got buried on his farm?"

"How come I've never heard of him?" she wanted to know.

Marino got up to top off our champagne.

He said, "Because they don't teach subjects like him at MIT and UVA."

5

At dawn, I lay in bed and looked out at Mant's backyard. The snow was very deep and piled high on the wall, and beyond the dune the sun was polishing the sea. For a while I shut my eyes and thought of Benton Wesley. I wondered what he would say about where I was living now, and what we would say to each other when we met later this day. We had not spoken since the second week of December, when we had agreed that our relationship must end.

I turned to one side and pulled the covers up to my ears as I heard quiet footsteps. Next I felt Lucy perch on the edge of my bed.

"Good morning, favorite niece in the world," I mumbled.

"I'm your only niece in the world." She said what she always did. "And how did you know it was me?"

"It had better be you. Someone else might get hurt."

"I brought you coffee," she said.

"You're an angel."

"'Yo,' to quote Marino. That's what everybody says about me."

"I was just trying to be nice." I yawned.

She bent over to hug me, and I smelled the English soap I had placed in her bathroom. I felt her strength and firmness, and I felt old.

"You make me feel like hell." I rolled on my back, placing my hands behind my head.

"Why do you say that?" She wore a pair of my loose cotton flannel pajamas and looked puzzled.

"Because I don't think I could even do the Yellow Brick Road anymore," I said, referring to the Academy's obstacle course.

"I've never heard anyone call it easy."

"It is for you."

She hesitated. "Well, it is now. But it's not like you have to hang out with HRT."

"For that I am thankful."

She paused, then added with a sigh, "You know, at first I was pissed when the Academy decided to send me back to UVA for a month. But it may end up being a relief. I can work in the lab, ride my bike and jog around the campus like a normal person."

Lucy was not a normal person, nor would she ever be. I had decided that in many sad ways, individuals with IQs as high as hers are as different from others as are the mentally impaired. She was gazing out the window and the snow was becoming bright. Her hair was rosegold in shy morning light, and I was amazed I could be related to anyone so beautiful.

"It may be a relief not being around Quantico right now, too." She paused, her face very serious when she turned back to me. "Aunt Kay, there's something I need to tell you. I'm not sure you're really going to want to hear this. Or maybe it would be easier if you didn't hear it. I would have told you yesterday if Marino hadn't been here."

"I'm listening." I was immediately tense.

She paused again. "Especially since you may be seeing Wesley today, I think you ought to know. There's a rumor in the Bureau that he and Connie have split."

I did not know what to say.

"Obviously, I can't verify that this is true," she went on. "But I've heard some of what's being said. And some of it concerns you."

"Why would any of it concern me?" I said too quickly.

"Come on." She met my eyes. "There have been suspicions ever since you started working so many cases with him. Some of the agents think that's the only reason you agreed to be a consultant. So you could be with him, travel with him, you know."

"That's patently untrue," I angrily said as I sat up. "I agreed to be the consulting forensic pathologist because the director asked Benton, who asked me, not the other way around. I assist in cases as a service to the FBI and—"

"Aunt Kay," she interrupted me. "You don't have to defend yourself."

But I would not be soothed. "That is an absolutely outrageous thing for anyone to say. I have never allowed a friendship with anyone to interfere with my professional integrity."

Lucy got quiet, then spoke again. "We're not talking about a mere friendship."

"Benton and I are very good friends."

"You are more than friends."

"At this moment, no, we are not. And it is none of your business."

She impatiently got up from my bed. "It's not right for you to get mad at me."

She stared at me but I could not speak, for I was very close to tears.

"All I'm doing is reporting to you what I've heard so you don't end up hearing it from someone else," she said.

Still, I said nothing, and she started to leave.

I reached for her hand. "I'm not angry with you. Please try to understand. It's inevitable I'm going to react when I hear something like this. I feel certain you would, too."

She pulled away from me. "What makes you think I didn't react when I heard it?"

I watched in frustration as she stalked out of my room, and I thought she was the most difficult person I knew. All our lives together we had fought. She never relented until I had suffered as long as she thought I should, when she knew how much I cared. It was so unfair, I told myself as I planted my feet on the floor.

I ran my fingers through my hair as I contemplated getting up and coping with the day. My spirit felt heavy, shadowed by dreams that were now unclear but I sensed had been strange. It seemed there had been water and people who were cruel, and I had been ineffective and afraid. In the bathroom I showered, then got a robe off a hook on the back of the door and found my slippers. Marino and my niece were dressed and in the kitchen when I finally appeared.

"Good morning," I announced as if Lucy and I had not seen each other this day.

"Yo. It's good all right." Marino looked as if he had been awake all night and was feeling hateful.

I pulled out a chair and joined them at the small breakfast table. By now the sun was up, the snow on fire.

"What's wrong?" I asked as my nerves tightened more.

"You remember those footprints out by the wall last night?" His face was boiled red.

"Of course."

"Well, now we've got more of them." He set down his coffee mug. "Only this time they're out by our cars and were left by regular boots with a Vibram tread. And guess what, Doc?" he asked as I already feared what he was about to say. "The three of us ain't going anywhere today until a tow truck gets here first."

I remained silent.

"Someone punctured our tires." Lucy's face was stone. "Every goddamn one of them. With some kind of wide blade, it looks to me. Maybe a big knife or machete."

"The moral of the story is that it sure as hell wasn't some misguided neighbor or night diver on your property," he went on. "I think we're talking about someone who had a mission.

And when he got scared off, he came back or somebody else did."

I got up for coffee. "How long will it take to get our cars fixed?"

"Today?" he said. "I don't think it's possible for you or Lucy to get your rides fixed today."

"It's got to be possible," I matter-of-factly stated. "We have to get out of here, Marino. We need to see Eddings's house. And right now it doesn't seem all too safe in this one."

"I'd say that's a fair assessment," Lucy said.

I moved close to the window over the sink and could plainly see our vehicles with tires that looked like black rubber puddles in the snow.

"They're punctured on the sides versus the tread, and can't be plugged," Marino said.

"Then what are we going to do?" I asked.

"Richmond's got reciprocal agreements with other police departments, and I've already talked to Virginia Beach. They're on their way."

His car needed police tires and rims, while Lucy's and mine needed Goodyears and Michelins because, unlike Marino, we were here in our personal vehicles. I pointed all this out to him.

"We got a flatbed truck on the way for you," he said as I sat back down. "Sometime during the next few hours they'll load up your Benz and Lucy's piece of shit and haul them into Bell Tire Service on Virginia Beach Boulevard."

"It's not a piece of shit," Lucy said.

"Why the hell did you buy anything the color of parrot shit? That your Miami roots coming out, or what?"

"No, it's my budget coming out. I got it for nine hundred dollars."

"What about in the meantime?" I asked. "You know they won't take care of this speedily. It's New Year's Day."

"You got that right," he said. "And it's pretty simple, Doc. If you're going to Richmond, you're riding with me."

"Fine." I wasn't going to argue. "Then let's get as much done now as we can so we can leave."

"Starting with your getting packed," he said to me. "In my opinion, you should boogie right on out of here for good."

"I have no choice but to stay here until Dr. Mant returns from London."

Yet I packed as if I might not be coming back to his cottage during this life. Then we conducted the best forensic investigation we could on our own, for slashing tires was a misdemeanor, and we knew the local police would not be especially enthused about our case. Ill-equipped to make tread-pattern casts, we simply took photographs to scale of the footprints around our cars, although I suspected the most we would ever be able to tell from them was that the suspect was large and wore a generic-type boot or shoe with a Vibram seal on the arch of the rugged tread.

When a youthful policeman named Sanders and a red tow truck arrived late morning, I took two ruined radials and locked them inside the trunk of Marino's car. For a while I watched men in jumpsuits and insulated jackets twirl hand-jacks with amazing speed as a winch held the Ford's front end rampant in the air, as if Marino's car were about to fly. Virginia Beach officer Sanders asked if my being the chief medical examiner might possibly be related to what had been done to our vehicles. I told him I did not think so.

"It's my deputy chief who lives at this address," I went on to explain. "Dr. Philip Mant. He's in London for a month or so. I'm simply covering for him."

"And no one knows you're staying here?" asked Sanders, who was no fool.

"Certainly, some people know. I've been taking his calls."

"So you don't see that this might be related to who you are and what you do, ma'am." He was taking notes.

"At this time I have no evidence that there is a relationship," I replied. "In fact, we really can't say that the culprit wasn't some kid blowing off steam on New Year's Eve."

Sanders kept looking at Lucy, who was talking to Marino by our cars. "Who is that?" he asked.

"My niece. She's with the FBI," I answered, and I spelled her name.

While he went to speak to her, I made one last trip inside the cottage, entering through the plain front door. The air was warmed by sunlight that blazed through glass, bleaching furniture of color, and I could still smell garlic from last night's meal. In my bedroom I looked around once more, opening drawers and riffling through clothes hanging in the closet while I was saddened by my disenchantment. In the beginning, I had thought I would like it here.

Down the hall I checked where Lucy had slept, then moved into the living room where we had sat until early morning reading the *Book of Hand*. The memory of that unsettled me like my dream, and my arms turned to gooseflesh. My blood was thrilled by fear, and suddenly I could not stay inside my colleague's simple home a moment longer. I dashed to the screened-in porch, and out the door into the backyard. In sunlight I felt reassured, and as I gazed out at the ocean, I got interested in the wall again.

Snow was to the top of my boots as I drew close to it, footprints from the night before gone. The intruder, whose flashlight Lucy had seen, had climbed over the wall and then quickly left. But he must have showed up later, or someone else must have, because the footprints around our cars clearly had been made after snow had quit falling, and they hadn't been made by dive boots or surf shoes. I looked over the wall and beyond the dune to the wide beach below. Snow was spun-sugar heaped in drifts with sea oats protruding like ragged feathers. The water was a ruffled dark blue and I saw no sign of anyone as my eyes followed the shore as far as they could.

I looked out for a long time, completely absorbed in speculations and worries. When I turned around to walk back, I was shocked to find Detective Roche standing so close he could have grabbed me.

"My God," I gasped. "Don't ever sneak up on me like that."

"I walked in your tracks. That's why you didn't hear me." He was chewing gum and had his hands in the pockets of a leather coat. "Being quiet's one thing I'm good at when I want to be."

I stared at him, my dislike of him finding new depths. He wore dark trousers and boots, and I could not see his eyes behind their aviator's glasses. But it did not matter. I knew what Detective Roche was about. I knew his type well.

"I heard about your vandalism and came to see if I could be of assistance," he said.

"I wasn't aware we called the Chesapeake police," I replied.

"Virginia Beach and Chesapeake have a mutual aid channel, so I heard about your problem on that," he said. "I have to confess that the first thing to go through my mind was there might be a connection."

"A connection to what?"

"To our case." He stepped closer. "Looks like someone really did a number on your cars. Sounds like a warning. You know, like just maybe you're poking your nose where someone doesn't think it belongs."

My eyes wandered to his feet, to his lace-up Gore-Tex boots made of leather the color of liver, and I saw the tread pattern they had left in the snow. Roche had big feet and hands, and was wearing Vibram soles. I looked back at a face that would have been handsome were the spirit behind it not so petty and mean. I did not say a word for a while, but when I did I was very direct.

"You sound a lot like Captain Green. So tell me. Are you threatening me, too?"

"I'm just passing along an observation."

He stepped even closer, and now I was backed against the wall. Melting snow heaped on top of it dripped down the collar of my coat while my blood ran hotter.

"By the way," he went on, edging ever nearer, "what's new with this case of ours?"

"Please step back," I said to him.

"I'm just not sure at all that you're telling me everything. I think you have a real good idea about what happened to Ted Eddings, and you're withholding information."

"We're not going to discuss that case or any other right now," I said.

"See? That puts me in a bad spot because I have people I answer to." I couldn't believe it when he placed his hand on my shoulder as he added, "I know you wouldn't want to cause me trouble."

"Don't touch me," I warned. "Don't push this any further."

"I think you and me need to get together so we can overcome our communication problem." He left his hand where it was. "Maybe we can catch dinner in some quiet little laid-back place. You like seafood? I know a real private place on the Sound."

I was silent as I wondered whether to jam my finger in his windpipe.

"Don't be shy. Trust me. It's all right. This isn't the Capital of the Confederacy with all these snobby old has-beens you got in Richmond. We believe in live and let live around here. You know what I mean?"

I tried to move past him and he grabbed my arm.

"I'm talking to you." He was beginning to sound angry. "You don't go walking off when I'm talking to you."

"Let go of me," I demanded.

I tried to wrench my arm away. But he was surprisingly strong.

"No matter how many fancy degrees you got, you're no match for me," he said under breath that smelled like spearmint.

I stared straight into his Ray-Bans.

"Get your hands off me now," I said in a loud, hard voice. "Now!" I exclaimed as if I would kill him instantly.

Roche suddenly let go, and I trudged with purpose through the snow as my heart flew off on its own. When I reached the front of the house, I stopped, out of breath and dazed.

"There are footprints in the backyard that should be photographed," I addressed everyone. "Detective Roche's footprints. He was just back there. And I want all of my belongings out of the house."

"What the hell do you mean he was just back there?" Marino said.

"We had a conversation."

"How the hell did he get back there without us seeing him?"

I scanned the street and did not see a car that might have been Roche's. "I don't know how he got back there," I said. "I guess he cut through someone else's backyard. Or maybe he came up from the beach."

Lucy did not know what to think as she looked at me. "You won't be coming back here?" she asked me. "Not at all?"

"No," I said. "I will not be coming back here ever again, if I have my way about it."

She helped me pack the remainder of my belongings, and

I did not relay what had happened in the backyard until we were in Marino's car driving fast on 64 West toward Richmond.

"Shit," he exclaimed. "The friggin' bastard hit on you. Goddamn it. Why didn't you yell?"

"I think his mission was to harass me on the behalf of someone else," I said.

"I don't care what his mission was. He still hit on you. You got to take out a warrant."

"Hitting on someone is not against the law," I said.

"He grabbed you."

"So I'm going to have him arrested for grabbing my arm?"

"He shouldn't have grabbed nothing." He was furious as he drove. "You told him to let go and he didn't. That's abduction. At the very least, it's simple assault. Damn, this thing's out of alignment."

"You've got to report him to Internal Affairs," Lucy said from the front seat, where she was fooling with the scanner because it was hard for her hands to be still. "Hey, Pete, the squelch isn't right," she added to him. "And you can't hear a thing on channel three. That's Third Precinct, right?"

"What do you expect when I'm way the hell near Williamsburg? You think I'm a state trooper?"

"No, but if you want to talk to one, I can probably figure that out."

"I'm sure you could tune in to the damn space shuttle," he irritably remarked.

"If you can," I said to her, "how about getting me on it."

6

We arrived in Richmond at half past two, and a guard raised a gate and allowed us into the secluded neighborhood where I very recently had moved. Typical for this area of Virginia, there had been no snow, and water dripped profusely from trees because rain had turned to ice during the night. Then the temperature had risen.

My stone house was set back from the street on a bluff that overlooked a rocky bend in the James River, the wooded lot surrounded by a wrought-iron fence neighboring children could not squeeze through. I knew no one on any side of me, and had no intention of changing that.

I had not anticipated problems when I had decided for the first time in my life that I would build, but whether it had been the slate roof, the brick pavers or the color of my front door, it seemed everyone had a criticism. When it had gotten to the point where my contractor's frustrated telephone calls were interrupting me in the morgue, I had threatened the neighborhood association that I would sue. Needless to say, invitations to parties in this subdivision, thus far, had been few.

"I'm sure your neighbors will be delighted to see you're home," my niece dryly said as we got out of the car.

"I don't think they pay that much attention to me anymore." I dug for my keys.

"Bullshit," Marino said. "You're the only one they got who spends her days at murder scenes and cutting up dead bodies. They probably look out their windows the entire time you're home. Hell, the guards probably call every one of them to let 'em know when you roll in."

"Thank you so much," I said, unlocking the front door. "And just when I was beginning to feel a little better about living here."

The burglar alarm loudly buzzed its warning that I had better quickly press the appropriate keys, and I looked around as I always did, because my home was still a stranger to me. I feared the roof would leak, plaster would fall or something else would fail, and when everything was fine, I took intense pleasure in my accomplishment. My house was two levels and very open, with windows placed to catch every photon of light. The living room was a wall of glass that captured miles of the James, and late in the day I could watch the sun set over trees on the river's banks.

Adjoining my bedroom was an office that finally was big enough for me to work in, and I checked it first for faxes and found I had four.

"Anything important?" asked Lucy, who had followed me while Marino was getting boxes and bags.

"As a matter of fact, they're all for you from your mother." I handed them to her.

She frowned. "Why would she fax me here?"

"I never told her I was temporarily relocating to Sandbridge. Did you?"

"No. But Grans would know where you are, right?" Lucy said.

"Of course. But my mother and yours don't always get things straight." I glanced at what she was reading. "Everything okay?"

"She's so weird. You know, I installed a modem and CD ROM in her computer and showed her how to use them. My mistake. Now she's always got questions. Each of these faxes is a computer question." She irritably shuffled through the pages.

I was put out with her mother, Dorothy, too. She was my sister, my only sibling, and she could not be bothered to so much as wish her only child a happy New Year.

"She sent these today," my niece went on. "It's a holiday and she's writing away on another one of her goofy children's books."

"To be fair," I said, "her books aren't goofy."

"Yeah, go figure. I don't know where she did her research, but it wasn't where I grew up."

"I wish you two weren't at odds." I made the same comment I had made throughout Lucy's life. "Someday you will have to come to terms with her. Especially when she dies."

"You always think about death."

"I do because I know about it, and it is the other side of life. You can't ignore it any more than you can ignore night. You will have to deal with Dorothy."

"No, I won't." She swiveled my leather desk chair around and sat in it, facing me. "There's no point. She doesn't understand the first thing about me and never has."

That was probably true.

"You're welcome to use my computer," I said.

"It will just take me a minute."

"Marino will pick us up about four," I said.

"I didn't know he left."

"Briefly."

Keys tapped as I went into my bedroom and began to unpack and plot. I needed a car and wondered if I should rent one, and I needed to change my clothes but did not know what to wear. It bothered me that the thought of Wesley would still make me conscious of what I put on, and as minutes crept forward I became truly afraid to see him.

Marino picked us up when he said he would, and somewhere he had found a carwash open and had filled the tank with gas. We drove east along Monument Avenue into the district known as the Fan, where gracious mansions lined historic avenues and college students crowded old homes. At the statue of Robert E. Lee, he cut over to Grace Street, where Ted Eddings had lived in a white Spanish duplex with a red Santa flag hanging over a wooden front porch with a swing. Bright yellow crime scene tape stretched from post to post in a morbid parody of Christmas wrapping, its bold black letters warning the curious not to come.

"Under the circumstances, I didn't want nobody inside, and I didn't know who else might have a key," Marino explained as he unlocked the front door. "What I don't need is some nosy landlord deciding he's going to check his friggin' inventory."

I did not see any sign of Wesley, and was deciding he wasn't going to show up when I heard the throaty roar of his gray BMW. It parked on the side of the street, and I watched the radio antenna retract as he cut the engine.

"Doc, I'll wait for him if you want to go on in," Marino said to me.

"I need to talk to him." Lucy headed back down the steps as I put on cotton gloves.

"I'll be inside," I said as if Wesley were not someone I knew.

I entered Eddings's foyer and his presence instantly overwhelmed me everywhere I looked. I felt his meticulous personality in minimalist furniture, Indian rugs and polished floors, and his warmth in sunny yellow walls hung with bold monotype prints. Dust had formed a fine layer that was disturbed anywhere police might recently have been to open cabinets or drawers. Begonias, ficus, creeping fig and cyclamen seemed to be mourning the loss of their master, and I looked around for a watering can. Finding one in the laundry room, I filled it and began tending plants because I saw no point in allowing them to die. I did not hear Benton Wesley walk in.

"Kay?" His voice was quiet behind me.

I turned and he caught sorrow not meant for him.

"What are you doing?" He stared as I poured water into a pot.

"Exactly what it looks like."

He got quiet, his eyes on mine.

"I knew him, knew Ted," I said. "Not terribly well. But he was popular with my staff. He interviewed me many times and I respected . . . Well . . ." My mind left the path.

Wesley was thin, which made his features seem even sharper, his hair by now completely white, although he wasn't much older than I. He did look tired, but everyone I knew looked tired, and what he did not look was separated. He did not look miserable to be away from his wife or from me.

"Pete told me about your cars," he said.

"Pretty unbelievable," I said as I poured.

"And the detective. What's his name? Roche? I've got to talk to his chief anyway. We're playing telephone tag, but when we hook up, I'll say something."

"I don't need you to do that."

"I certainly don't mind," he said.

"I'd rather you didn't."

"Fine." He raised his hands in a small surrender, and looked around the room. "He had money and was gone a lot," he said.

"Someone took care of his plants," I replied.

"How often?" He looked at them.

"Non-blooming plants, at least once a week, the rest, every other day, depending on how warm it gets in here."

"So these haven't been watered for a week?"

"Or longer," I said.

By now, Lucy and Marino had entered the duplex and gone down the hall.

"I want to check the kitchen," I added as I set down the can.

"Good idea."

It was small and looked like it had not been renovated since the sixties. Inside cupboards I found old cookware and dozens of canned goods like tuna fish and soup, and snack foods like pretzels. As for what Eddings had kept in his refrigerator, that was mostly beer. But I was interested in a single bottle of Louis Roederer Cristal Champagne tied in a big red bow.

"Find something?" Wesley was looking under the sink.

"Maybe." I was still peering inside the refrigerator. "This will set you back as much as a hundred and fifty dollars in a restaurant, maybe a hundred and twenty if you buy it off the shelf."

"Do we know how much this guy got paid?"

"I don't know. But I suspect it wasn't a whole lot."

"He's got a lot of shoe polish and cleansers down here, and that's about it," Wesley said as he stood.

I turned the bottle around and read a sticker on the label. "A hundred and thirty dollars, and it wasn't purchased locally. As far as I know, Richmond doesn't have a wine shop called The Wine Merchant."

"Maybe a gift. Explaining the bow."

"What about D.C.?"

"I don't know. I don't buy much wine in D.C. these days," he said.

I shut the refrigerator door, secretly pleased, for he and I had enjoyed wine. We once had liked to pick and choose and drink as we sat close to each other on the couch or in bed.

"He didn't shop much," I said. "I see no evidence that he ever ate in."

"It doesn't look to me like he was ever even here," he said.

I felt his closeness as he moved near me, and I almost could not bear it. His cologne was always subtle and evocative of cinnamon and wood, and whenever I smelled it anywhere, for an instant I was caught as I was now.

"Are you all right?" he asked in a voice meant for no one but me as he paused in the doorway.

"No," I said. "This is pretty awful." I shut a cabinet door a little too hard.

He stepped into the hallway. "Well, we need to take a hard look at his financial status, to see where he was getting money for eating out and expensive champagne."

Those papers were in the office, and the police had not gone through them yet because officially there had been no crime. Despite my suspicions about Eddings's cause of death and the strange events surrounding it, at this moment we legally had no homicide.

"Has anyone gone into this computer?" asked Lucy, who was looking at the 486 machine on the desk.

"Nope," said Marino as he sorted through files in a green metal cabinet. "One of the guys said we're locked out."

She touched the mouse and a password window appeared on the screen.

"Okay," she said. "He's got a password, which isn't unusual. But what is a little strange is he's got no disk in his backup drive. Hey, Pete? You guys find any disks in here?"

"Yeah, there's a whole box of them up there." He pointed at a bookcase, which was crowded with histories of the Civil War and an elaborate leather-bound set of encyclopedias.

Lucy took the box down and opened it.

"No. These are programming disks for WordPerfect." She looked at us. "All I'm saying is most people would have a backup of their work, assuming he was working on something here in his house."

No one knew if he had been. We knew only that Eddings was employed by the AP office downtown on Fourth Street. We had no reason to know what he did at home, until Lucy rebooted his computer, did her magic and somehow got into programming files. She disabled the screen saver, then started sorting through WordPerfect directories, all of which were empty. Eddings did not have a single file.

"Shit," she said. "Now that really is bizarre unless he never used his computer."

"I can't imagine that," I said. "Even if he did work downtown, he must have had an office at home for a reason."

She typed some more, while Marino and Wesley sifted through various financial records that Eddings had neatly stored in a basket inside a filing cabinet drawer.

"I just hope he didn't blow away his entire subdirectory," said Lucy, who was in the operating system now. "I can't store that without a backup, and he doesn't seem to have a backup."

I watched her type *undelete**.* and hit the enter key. Miraculously, a file named *killdrug.old* appeared, and after she was prompted to keep it, another name followed. By the time she was finished, she had recovered twenty-six files as we watched in amazement.

"That's what's cool about DOS 6," she simply said as she began printing.

"Can you tell when they were deleted?" Wesley asked.

"The time and date on the files is all the same," she replied. "Damn. December thirty-first, between one-oh-one and one-thirty-five A.M. You would have thought he'd already be dead by then."

"It depends on what time he went to Chesapeake," I said. "His boat wasn't spotted until six A.M."

"By the way, the clock's set right on the computer. So these times ought to be good," she added.

"Would it take more than half an hour to delete that many files?" I asked.

"No. You could do it in minutes."

"Then someone might have been reading them as he was deleting them," I said.

"That's what a lot of people do. We need more paper for the printer. Wait, I'll steal some from the fax machine."

"Speaking of that," I said, "can we get a journal report?"

"Sure."

She produced a list of meaningless fax diagnostics and telephone numbers that I had an idea about checking later. But at least we knew with certainty that around the time Eddings had died, someone had gone into his computer and had deleted every one of his files. Whoever was responsible wasn't terribly sophisticated, Lucy went on to explain, because a computer expert would have removed the files' subdirectory, too, rendering the undelete command useless.

"This isn't making sense," I said. "A writer is going to back up his work, and it is evident that he was anything but careless. What about his gun safe?" I asked Marino. "Did you find any disks in there?"

"Nope."

"That doesn't mean someone didn't get into it, and the house, for that matter," I said.

"If they did, they knew the combination of the safe and the code for the burglar alarm system."

"Are they the same?" I asked.

"Yeah. He uses his D.O.B. for everything."

"And how did you find that out?"

"His mother," he said.

"What about keys?" I said. "None came in with the body. He must have had some to drive his truck."

"Roche said there aren't any," Marino said, and I thought that odd, too.

Wesley was watching pages of undeleted files come off the printer. "These all look like newspaper stories," he said.

"Published?" I asked.

"Some may have been because they look pretty old. The plane that crashed into the White House, for example. And Vince Foster's suicide."

"Maybe Eddings was just cleaning house," Lucy proposed.

"Oh, now here we go." Marino was reviewing a bank statement. "On December tenth, three thousand dollars was wired to his account." He opened another envelope and looked some more. "Same thing for November."

It was also true for October and the rest of the year, and based on other information, Eddings definitely needed to supplement his income. His mortgage payment was a thousand dollars a month, his monthly charge card bills sometimes as much, yet his annual salary was barely forty-five thousand dollars.

"Shit. With all this extra cash coming in, he was sucking in almost eighty grand a year," Marino said. "Not bad."

Wesley left the printer and walked over to where I stood. He quietly placed a page in my hand.

"The obituary for Dwain Shapiro," he said. "*Washington Post*, October sixteenth of last year."

The article was brief and simply stated that Shapiro had been a mechanic at a Ford dealership in D.C., and was shot to death in a carjacking while on his way home from a bar late at night. He was survived by people who lived nowhere near Virginia, and the New Zionists were not mentioned.

"Eddings didn't write this," I said. "A reporter for the *Post* did."

"Then how did he get the Book?" Marino said. "And why the hell was it under his bed?"

"He might have been reading it," I answered simply. "And maybe he didn't want anyone else—a housekeeper, for example—to see it."

"These are notes now." Lucy was engrossed in the screen, opening one file after another and hitting the print command. "Okay, now we're getting to the good stuff. Damn." She was getting excited as text scrolled by and the LaserJet hummed and clicked. "How wild." She stopped what she was doing and turned around to Wesley. "He's got all this stuff about North Korea mixed in with info about Joel Hand and the New Zionists."

"What about North Korea?" He was reading pages while Marino went through another drawer.

"The problem our government had with theirs several years ago when they were trying to make weapons-grade plutonium at one of their nuclear power plants."

"Supposedly, Hand is very interested in fusion, energy, that sort of thing," I said. "There's an allusion to that in the Book."

"Okay," said Wesley, "then maybe this is just a big profile on him. Or better stated, the raw makings of a big piece on him."

"Why would Eddings delete the file of a big article he had not yet finished?" I wanted to know. "And is it a coincidence that he did this the night he died?"

"That could be consistent with someone planning to commit suicide," Wesley said. "And we really can't be certain he didn't do that."

"Right," Lucy said. "He wipes out all his work so that after he's gone, no one's going to see anything he doesn't want them to see. Then he stages his death to look like an accident. Maybe it mattered a lot to him that people not think he killed himself."

"A strong possibility," Wesley agreed. "He may have been involved in something he couldn't get out of, thus explaining the money wired to his bank account every month. Or he could have suffered from depression or from an intense personal loss that we know nothing of."

"Someone else could have deleted the files and taken any backup disks or printouts," I said. "Someone may have done this after he was already dead."

"Then this person had a key, knew codes and combinations," he said. "He knew Eddings wasn't home and wasn't going to be." He glanced up at me.

"Yes," I said.

"That's pretty complicated."

"This case is very complicated," I said, "but I can tell you with certainty that if Eddings were poisoned underwater with cyanide gas, he could not have done this to himself. And I want to know why he had so many guns. I want to know why the one he was carrying in his johnboat has a Birdsong coating and was loaded with KTWs."

Wesley glanced again at me, and his unflappability was hitting me hard. "Certainly, one could view his survivalist tendencies as an indicator of instability," he said.

"Or fear of being murdered," I said.

Then we went into that room. Submachine guns were on a rack on the wall, and pistols, revolvers and ammunition were inside the Browning safe that police had opened this morning. Ted Eddings had equipped a small bedroom with an arbor press, digital scale, case trimmer, reloading dies and everything else needed to keep him in cartridges. Copper tubing and primers were stored in a drawer. Gunpowder was in an old military case, and it seemed he had been fond of laser sights and spotting scopes.

"I think this shows a tilted mind-set." It was Lucy who spoke as she squatted before the safe, opening hard plastic gun cases. "I'd call all of this more than a little paranoid. It's like he thought an army was coming."

"Paranoia is healthy if there really is someone after you," I said.

"Me, I'm beginning to think the guy was wacky," Marino replied.

I did not care about their theories. "I smelled cyanide in the morgue," I reminded them as my patience wore thinner. "He didn't gas himself before going into the river, or he would have been dead when he hit the water."

"You smelled cyanide," Wesley said, pointedly. "No one else did, and we don't have tox results yet."

"What are you implying, that he drowned himself?" I stared at him.

"I don't know."

"I saw nothing to indicate drowning," I said.

"Do you always see indications in drownings?" he reasonably asked. "I thought drownings were notoriously difficult, explaining why expert witnesses from South Florida are often flown in to help with such cases."

"I began my career in South Florida and am considered an expert witness in drownings," I sharply said.

We continued arguing outside on the sidewalk by his car because I wanted him to take me home so we could finish our fight. The moon was vague, the nearest streetlight a block away, and we could not see each other well.

"For God's sake, Kay, I was not implying that you don't know what you're doing," he was saying.

"You most certainly were." I was standing by the driver's door as if the car were mine and I was about to leave in it. "You're picking on me. You're acting like an ass."

"We're investigating a death," he said in that steady tone of his. "This is not the time or place for anything to be taken personally."

"Well, let me tell you something, Benton, people aren't machines. They do take things personally."

"And that's really what this is all about." He moved beside me and unlocked the door. "You're reacting personally because of me. I'm not sure this was a good idea." Locks rushed up. "Maybe I shouldn't have come here today." He slid into the driver's seat. "But I felt it was important. I was trying to do the right thing and thought you would do the same."

I walked around to the other side and got in, and wondered why he had not opened my door when he usually did. Suddenly, I was very weary and afraid I might cry.

"It is important, and you did do the right thing," I said. "A man is dead. I not only believe he was murdered, but I think he might have been caught up in something bigger that I fear may be very ugly. I don't think he deleted his own computer files and disposed of all backups because that would imply he knew he was going to die."

"Yes. It would imply suicide."

"Which this case is not."

We looked at each other in the dark.

"I think someone entered his house late the night of his death."

"Someone he knew."

"Or someone who knew someone else who had access. Like a colleague or close friend, or a significant other. As for keys to get in, his are missing."

"You think this has to do with the New Zionists." He was beginning to mellow.

"I'm afraid of that. And someone is warning me to back off."

"That would implicate the Chesapeake police."

"Maybe not the entire department," I said. "Maybe just Roche."

"If what you're saying is true, he's superficial in this, an outer layer far removed from the core. His interest in you is a separate issue, I suspect."

"His only interest is to intimidate, to bully," I said. "And, therefore, I suspect it is related."

Wesley got quiet, looking out the windshield, and for a moment I indulged myself and stared at him.

Then he turned to me. "Kay, has Dr. Mant ever said anything about being threatened?"

"Not to me. But I don't know if he would say anything. Especially if he were frightened."

"Of what? That's what I'm having a very hard time imagining," he said as he started the car and pulled out onto the street. "If Eddings were linked to the New Zionists, then how could that possibly connect to Dr. Mant?"

I did not know, and was quiet as he drove.

He spoke again. "Any possibility your British colleague simply skipped town? Do you know for a fact that his mother died?"

I thought of my Tidewater morgue supervisor, who had quit before Christmas without giving notice or a reason. Then Mant suddenly had left, too.

"I know only what he told me," I said. "But I have no reason to think he is lying."

"When does your other deputy chief come back, the one out on maternity leave?"

"She just had her baby."

"Well, that's a little hard to fake," he said.

We were turning on Malvern, and the rain was tiny pinpricks against the glass. Welling up inside me were words I could not say, and when we turned on Cary Street I began to feel desperate. I wanted to tell Wesley that we had made the right decision, but ending a relationship doesn't end feelings. I wanted to inquire after Connie, his wife. I wanted to invite him into my home as I had done in the past, and ask him why he never called me anymore. Old Locke Lane was without light as we followed it toward the river, and he drove slowly in low gear.

"Are you going back to Fredericksburg tonight?" I asked.

He was silent, then said, "Connie and I are getting a divorce."

I made no reply.

"It's a long story and will probably be a rather long drawn-out messy thing. Thank God, at least, the kids are pretty much grown." He rolled down his window and the guard waved us through.

"Benton, I'm very sorry," I said, and his BMW was loud on my empty, wet street.

"Well, you probably could say I got what I deserved. She's been seeing another man for the better part of a year, and I was clueless. Some profiler I am, right?"

"Who is it?"

"He's a contractor in Fredericksburg and was doing some work on the house."

"Does she know about us?" I almost could not ask, for I had always liked Connie and was certain the truth would make her hate me.

We turned into my driveway and he did not answer until we had parked near my front door.

"I don't know." He took a deep breath and looked down at his hands on the wheel. "She's probably heard rumors, but she really doesn't listen to rumors, much less believe them." He paused. "She knows we've spent a lot of time together, taken trips, that sort of thing. But I really suspect she thinks that's solely because of work."

"I feel awful about all of this."

He said nothing.

"Are you still at home?" I asked.

"She wanted to move out," he replied. "She moved into an apartment where I guess she and Doug can regularly meet."

"That's the contractor's name."

His face was hard as he stared out the windshield. I reached over and gently took one of his hands.

"Look," I said quietly. "I want to help in any way I can. But you'll have to tell me what I can do."

He glanced at me, and for an instant his eyes shone with tears that I believed were for her. He still loved his wife, and though I understood, I did not want to see it.

"I can't let you do much for me." He cleared his throat. "Right now especially. For pretty much the next year. This guy she's with likes money and knows I have some, you know, from my family. I don't want to lose everything."

"I don't see how you can, in light of what she's done."

"It's complicated. I have to be careful. I want my children to still care about me, to respect me." He looked at me and withdrew his hand. "You know how I feel. Please try to just leave it at that."

"Did you know about her in December, when we decided to stop—"

He interrupted me, "Yes. I knew."

"I see." My voice was tight. "I wish you could have told me. It might have made it easier."

"I don't think anything could have made it easier."

"Good night, Benton," I said as I got out of his car, and I did not turn around to watch him drive away.

Inside, Lucy was playing Melissa Etheridge, and I was glad my niece was here and that there was music in the house. I forced myself to not think about him, as if I could walk into a different room in my mind and lock him out. Lucy was inside the kitchen, and I took my coat off and set my pocketbook on the counter.

"Everything okay?" She shut the refrigerator door with a shoulder and carried eggs to the sink.

"Actually, everything's pretty rotten," I said.

"What you need is something to eat, and as luck would have it, I'm cooking."

"Lucy"—I leaned against the counter—"if someone is trying to disguise Eddings's death as an accident or suicide, then I can see how subsequent threats or intrigue concerning my Norfolk office might make sense. But why would threats have been made to any member of my staff in the past? Your deductive skills are good. You tell me."

She was beating egg whites into a bowl and thawing a bagel in the microwave. Her nonfat routines were depressing, and I did not know how she kept them up.

"You don't know that anyone was threatened in the past," she matter-of-factly said.

"I realize I don't know, at least not yet." I had begun making Viennese coffee. "But I'm simply trying to reason this out. I'm looking for a motive and coming up empty-handed. Why don't you add a little onion, parsley and ground pepper to that? A pinch of salt can't hurt you, either."

"You want me to fix you one?" she asked as she whisked.

"I'm not very hungry. Maybe I'll eat soup later."

She glanced up at me. "Sorry everything's rotten."

I knew she referred to Wesley, and she knew I wasn't going to discuss him.

"Eddings's mother lives near here," I said. "I think I should talk to her."

"Tonight? At the last minute?" The whisk lightly clicked against the sides of the bowl.

"She very well may want to talk tonight, at the last minute," I said. "She's been told her son is dead and not much more."

"Yeah," Lucy muttered. "Happy New Year."

7

I did not have to ask anyone for a residential listing or telephone number because the dead reporter's mother was the only Eddings with a Windsor Farms address. According to the city directory, she lived on the lovely tree-lined street of Sulgrave, which was well known for wealthy estates and the sixteenth-century Tudor manors called Virginia House and Agecroft that in the 1920s had been shipped from England in crates. The night was still young when I called, but she sounded as if she had been asleep.

"Mrs. Eddings?" I said, and I told her who I was.

"I'm afraid I drifted off." She sounded frightened. "I'm sitting in my living room watching TV. Goodness, I don't even know what's on now. It was *My Brilliant Career* on PBS. Have you seen that?"

"Mrs. Eddings," I said again, "I have questions about your

son, Ted. I'm the medical examiner for his case. And I was hopeful we might talk. I live but a few blocks from you."

"Someone told me you did." Her thick southern voice got thicker with tears. "That you lived close by."

"Would now be a convenient time?" I asked after a pause.

"Well, I would appreciate it very much. And my name is Elizabeth Glenn," she said as she began to cry.

I reached Marino at his home, where his television was turned up so high I did not know how he could hear anything else. He was on the other line and clearly did not want to keep whoever it was on hold.

"Sure, see what you can find out," he said when I told him what I was about to do. "Me, I'm up to my ass right now. Got a situation down in Mosby Court that could turn into a riot."

"That's all we need," I said.

"I'm on my way over there. Otherwise I'd go with you."

We hung up and I dressed for the weather because I did not have a car. Lucy was on the phone in my office, talking to Janet, I suspected, based on her intense demeanor and quiet tone. I waved from the hallway and indicated by pointing at my watch I'd be back in about an hour. As I left my house and started walking in the cold, wet dark, my spirit began to crawl inside me like a creature trying to hide. Coping with the loved ones tragedy leaves behind remained one of the cruelest features of my career.

Over the years, I had experienced a multitude of reactions ranging from my being turned into a scapegoat to families begging me to somehow make the death untrue. I had seen people weep, wail, rant, rage and not react in the least, and throughout I was always the physician, always appropriately dispassionate yet kind, for that was what I was trained to be.

My own responses had to be mine. Those moments no one saw, not even when I was married, when I became expert at covering moods or crying in the shower. I remembered breaking out in hives one year and telling Tony I was allergic to plants, shellfish, the sulfite in red wine. My former husband was so easy because he did not want to hear.

Windsor Farms was eerily still as I entered it from the back, near the river. Fog clung to Victorian iron lamps reminiscent of England, and although windows were lighted in most of the stately homes, it did not seem anyone was up or out. Leaves were like soggy paper on pavement, rain lightly smacking and beginning to freeze. It occurred to me that I had foolishly walked out of my house with no umbrella.

When I reached the Sulgrave address, it was familiar, for I knew the judge who lived next door and had been to many of his parties. Three-story brick, the Eddings home was Federal-style with paired end chimneys, arched dormer windows and an elliptical fanlight over the paneled front door. To the left of the entry porch was the same stone lion that had been standing guard for years. I climbed slick steps, and had to ring the bell twice before a voice sounded faintly on the other side of thick wood.

"It's Dr. Scarpetta," I answered, and the door slowly opened.

"I thought it would be you." An anxious face peered out as the space got wider. "Please come in and get warm. It is a terrible night."

"It's getting very icy," I said as I stepped inside.

Mrs. Eddings was attractive in a well-bred, vain way, with refined features, and spun-white hair swept back from a high, smooth brow. She had dressed in a Black Watch suit and cashmere turtleneck sweater, as if she had been bravely receiving company all day. But her eyes could not hide her irrecoverable loss, and as she led me into the foyer, her gait was unsteady and I suspected she had been drinking.

"This is gorgeous," I said as she took my coat. "I've walked and driven past your house I don't know how many times and had no idea who lives here."

"And you live where?"

"Over there. Just west of Windsor Farms." I pointed. "My house is new. In fact, I just moved in last fall."

"Oh yes, I know where you are." She closed the closet door and led me down a hall. "I know quite a number of people over there."

The gathering room she showed me was a museum of antique Persian rugs, Tiffany lamps, and yew wood furniture in the style of Biedermeier. I sat on a black-upholstered couch that was lovely but stiff, and was already beginning to wonder how well mother had gotten along with son. The decors of both their dwellings painted portraits of people who could be stubborn and disconnected.

"Your son interviewed me a number of times," I began our conversation as we got seated.

"Oh, did he?" She tried to smile but her expression collapsed.

"I'm sorry. I know this is hard," I gently said as she tried to compose herself in her red leather chair. "Ted was someone I happened to like quite a lot. My staff liked him, too."

"Everyone likes Ted," she said. "From day one, he could charm. I remember the first big interview he got in Richmond." She stared into the fire, hands tightly clasped. "It was with Governor Meadows, and I'm sure you remember him. Ted got him to talk when no one else could. That was when everyone was saying the governor was using drugs and associating with immoral women."

"Oh, yes," I replied as if the same had never been said of other governors.

She stared off, her face distressed, and her hand trembled as she reached up to smooth her hair. "How could this happen? Oh Lord, how could he drown?"

"Mrs. Eddings, I don't think he did."

Startled, she stared at me with wide eyes. "Then what happened?"

"I'm not sure yet. There are tests to be done."

"What else could it be?" She began dabbing tears with a tissue. "The policeman who came to see me said it happened underwater. Ted was diving in the river with that contraption of his."

"There could be a number of possible causes," I answered. "A malfunction of the breathing apparatus he was using, for example. He could have been overcome by fumes. I don't know right this minute."

"I told him not to use that thing. I can't tell you how many times I begged him not to go off and dive with that thing."

"Then he had used it before."

"He loved to look for Civil War relics. He'd go diving almost anywhere with one of those metal detectors. I believe he found a few cannonballs in the James last year. I'm surprised you didn't know. He's written several stories about his adventures."

"Generally, divers have a partner with them, a buddy," I said. "Do you know who he usually went with?"

"Well, he may have taken someone with him now and then. I really don't know because he didn't discuss his friends with me very much."

"Did he ever say anything to you about going diving in the Elizabeth River to look for Civil War relics?" I asked.

"I don't know anything about him going there. He never mentioned it to me. I thought he was coming here today." She shut her eyes, brow furrowed, and her bosom deeply rose and fell as if there were not enough air in the room.

"What about these Civil War relics he collected?" I went on. "Do you know where he kept them?"

She did not respond.

"Mrs. Eddings," I went on, "we found nothing like that in his house. Not a single button, belt buckle or minié ball. Nor did we find a metal detector."

She was silent, hands shaking as she clutched the tissue hard.

"It is very important that we establish what your son might have been doing at the Inactive Ship Yard in Chesapeake," I spoke to her again. "He was diving in a classified area around Navy decommissioned ships and no one seems to know why. It's hard to imagine he was looking for Civil War relics there."

She stared at the fire and in a distant voice said, "Ted goes through phases. Once he collected butterflies. When he was ten. Then he gave them all away and started collecting gems. I remember he would pan for gold in the oddest places and pluck up garnets from the roadside with a pair of tweezers. He went from that to coins, and those he mostly spent because the Coke machine doesn't care if the quarter's pure silver or not. Baseball cards, stamps, girls. He never kept anything long. He told me he likes journalism because it's never the same."

I listened as she tragically went on.

"Why, I think he would have traded in his mother for a different one if that could have been arranged." A tear slid down her cheek. "I know he must have gotten so bored with me."

"Too bored to accept your financial help, Mrs. Eddings?" I delicately said.

She lifted her chin. "Now I believe you're getting a bit too personal."

"Yes, I am, and I regret that you have to be subjected to it. But I am a doctor, and right now, your son is my patient. It is my mission to do everything I can to determine what might have happened to him."

She took a deep, tremulous breath and fingered the top button of her jacket. I waited as she fought back tears.

"I sent him money every month. You know how inheritance taxes are, and Ted was accustomed to living beyond his means. I suppose his father and I are to blame." She could barely continue. "Life was not hard enough for my sons. I don't suppose life was very hard for me until Arthur passed on."

"What did your husband do?"

"He worked in tobacco. We met during the war when most of the world's cigarettes were made around here and you could find hardly a one, or stockings either."

Her reminiscing soothed her, and I did not interrupt.

"One night I went to a party at the Officers' Service Club at the Jefferson Hotel. Arthur was a captain in a unit of the Army called the Richmond Grays, and he could dance." She smiled. "Oh, he could dance like he breathed music and had it in his veins, and I spotted him right away. Our eyes needed to meet but once, and then we were never without each other."

She stared off, and the fire snapped and waved as if it had something important to say.

"Of course, that was part of the problem," she went on. "Arthur and I never stopped being absorbed with each other and I think the boys sometimes felt they were in the way." She was looking directly at me now. "I didn't even ask if you'd like tea or perhaps a touch of something stronger."

"Thank you. I'm fine. Was Ted close to his brother?"

"I already gave the policeman Jeff's number. What was his name? Martino or something. I actually found him rather rude. You know, a little Goldschlager is good on a night like this."

"No, thank you."

"I discovered it through Ted," she oddly went on as tears suddenly spilled down. "He found it when he was skiing out west and brought a bottle home. It tastes like liquid fire with a little cinnamon. That's what he said when he gave it to me. He was always bringing me little things."

"Did he ever bring you champagne?"

She delicately blew her nose.

"You said he was to have visited you today," I reminded her.

"He was supposed to come for lunch," she said.

"There is a very nice bottle of champagne in his refrigerator. It has a bow tied around it, and I'm wondering if this might have been something he had intended to bring when he came by for lunch today."

"Oh my." Her voice shook. "That must have been for some other celebration he planned. I don't drink champagne. It gives me a headache."

"We're looking for his computer disks," I said. "We're looking for any notes pertaining to what he might have been recently writing. Did he ever ask you to store anything for him here?"

"Some of his athletic equipment is in the attic but it's old as Methuselah." Her voice caught and she cleared it. "And papers from school."

"Are you aware of his having a safe deposit box, perhaps?"

"No." She shook her head.

"What about a friend he might have entrusted these things to?"

"I don't know about his friends," she said again as freezing rain clicked against glass.

"And he didn't mention any romantic interests? You're saying he had none?"

She pressed her lips tight.

"Please tell me if I am misunderstanding something."

"There was a girl he brought by some months back. I guess

it was in the summer and apparently she's some sort of scientist." She paused. "Seems he was doing a story or something, they met that way. We had a bit of a disagreement over her."

"Why?"

"She was attractive and one of these academic types. Maybe she's a professor. I can't recall but she's from overseas somewhere."

I waited, but she had nothing more to say.

"What was your disagreement?" I asked.

"I knew the minute I met her that she was not of good character, and she was not permitted in my home," Mrs. Eddings replied.

"Does she live in this area?" I asked.

"One would expect so, but I wouldn't know where she is."

"But he might have still been seeing her."

"I have no idea who Ted was seeing," she said, and I believed she was lying.

"Mrs. Eddings," I said, "by all appearances, your son was not home much."

She just looked at me.

"Did he have a housekeeper? For example, someone who took care of his plants?"

"I sent my housekeeper by when needed," she said. "Corian. Sometimes she brings him food. Ted can never bother with cooking."

"When was the last time she went by?"

"I don't know," she said, and I could tell she was getting weary of questions. "Some time before Christmas, I suspect, because she's had the flu."

"Did Corian ever mention to you what is in his house?"

"I guess you mean his guns," she said. "Just another something he started to collect a year or so back. That's all he wanted for his birthday—a gift certificate for one of those gun stores around here. As if a woman would dare walk into such a place."

It was pointless to probe further, for she had the single desire for her son to be alive. Beyond that, any activity or inquiry was simply an invasion she was determined to sidestep. At close to ten, I headed home, and almost slipped twice on vacant streets where it was too dark to see. The night was bitterly cold and filled with sharp wet sounds as ice coated trees and glazed the ground.

I felt discouraged because it did not seem anyone knew Eddings beyond what he had been like on the surface or in the past. I had learned he had collected coins and butterflies and had always been charming. He was an ambitious reporter with a limited attention span, and I thought how odd it was that I should be walking through his old neighborhood in such weather to talk about this man. I wondered what he would think could I tell him, and I felt very sad.

I did not want to chat with anyone when I walked into my house, but went straight to my room. I was warming my hands with hot water and washing my face when Lucy appeared in the doorway. I knew instantly that she was in one of her moods.

"Did you get enough to eat?" I looked at her in the mirror over the sink.

"I never get enough to eat," she irritably replied. "Someone named Danny from your Norfolk office called. He said the answering service was contacted about our cars."

For a moment my mind went blank. Then I remembered. "I gave the towing service the office number." I dried my face with a towel. "So I guess the answering service reached Danny at home."

"Whatever. He wants you to call." She stared at me in the mirror as if I had done something wrong.

"What is it?" I stared back.

"I've just got to get out of here."

"I'll try to get the cars here tomorrow," I said, stung.

I walked out of the bathroom, and she followed.

"I need to get back to UVA."

"Of course you do, Lucy," I said.

"You don't understand. I've got so much to do."

"I didn't realize your independent study or whatever it is had already started." I walked into the gathering room and headed for the bar.

"It doesn't matter if it's started. I've got a lot to set up. And I don't understand how you're going to get the cars here. Maybe Marino can take me to get mine."

"Marino is very busy and my plan is simple," I said. "Danny will drive my car to Richmond and he has a reliable friend who will drive your Suburban. Then Danny and his friend will take the bus back to Norfolk."

"What time?"

"That's the only snag. I can't permit Danny to do any of this until after hours, because he can't deliver my personal car on state time." I was opening a bottle of Chardonnay.

"Shit," Lucy impatiently said. "So I won't have transportation tomorrow, either?"

"I'm afraid neither of us will," I said.

"And what are you going to do, then?"

I handed her a glass of wine. "I'll be going into my office and probably spending a lot of time on the phone. Anything you might be able to do at the field office here?"

She shrugged. "I know a couple people who went through the Academy with me."

At the very least she could find another agent to take her to the gym so she could work off her ugly mood, I started to say, but held my tongue.

"I don't want wine." She set the glass down on the bar. "I think I'll just drink beer for a while."

"Why are you so angry?"

"I'm not angry." She got a Beck's Light out of the small refrigerator and popped off the cap.

"Do you want to sit down?"

"No," she said. "By the way, I've got the Book, so don't get alarmed when you don't find it in your briefcase."

"What do you mean, you have it?" I looked uneasily at her.

"I was reading it while you were out talking to Mrs. Eddings." She took a swallow of beer. "I thought it would be a good idea to go over it again in case there's something we didn't notice."

"I think you've looked at it quite enough," I flatly said. "In fact, I think all of us have."

"There's a lot of Old Testament-type stuff in there. I mean, it's not like it's satanic, really."

I watched her in silence as I wondered what was really going on in that incredibly complicated brain.

"I actually find it rather interesting, and believe it has power only if you allow it to have power. I don't allow it, so it doesn't bother me," she was saying.

I set down my glass. "Well, something certainly is."

"Only thing bothering me is I'm stranded and tired. So I guess I'll just go to bed," she said. "I hope you sleep well."

But I did not. Instead, I sat before the fire worrying about her, for I probably knew my niece better than anyone did. Perhaps she and Janet had simply had a fight and repairs would be made in the morning, or maybe she really did have too much to do, and not being able to return to Charlottesville was more of a problem than I knew.

I turned the fire off and checked the burglar alarm one more time to make certain it was armed, then I walked back to my bedroom and shut the door. Still, I could not sleep, so I sat up in lamplight listening to the weather as I studied the journal that had been printed by Eddings's fax machine. There were eighteen numbers dialed over the past two weeks, and all of them were curious and suggestive that he certainly had been home at least some of the time and doing something in his office.

What also struck me right away was that if he had worked at home, I would have expected numerous transmissions to the AP office downtown. But this was not the case. Since mid-December, he had faxed his office only twice, at least from the machine we had found at his house. This was simple enough to determine because he had entered a speed dial label for the wire service's fax number, so "AP DESK" appeared in the journal's identification column, along with less obvious labels like "NVSE," "DRMS,"

"CPT," and "LM." Three of those numbers had Tidewater, Central and Northern Virginia area codes and exchanges, while the area code for DRMS was Memphis, Tennessee.

I tried to sleep but information drifted past my eyes and questions spoke because I could not shut them off. I wondered who Eddings had been contacting in these different places, or if it mattered. But what I could not get away from was where he had died. I could still see his body suspended in that murky river, tethered by a useless hose caught on a rusting screw. I could feel his stiffness as I held him in my arms and swam him up with me. I had known before I had ever reached the surface that he had been dead many hours.

At three A.M. I sat up in bed and stared at the darkness. The house was quiet except for its usual shifting sounds, and I simply could not turn off my conscious mind. Reluctantly, I put my feet on the floor, my heart beating hard, as if it were startled that I should stir at such an hour. In my office I shut the door and wrote the following brief letter:

TO WHOM IT MAY CONCERN:
I realize this is a fax number, otherwise I would call in person. I need to know your identification, if possible, as your number has shown up on the printout of a recently deceased individual's fax machine. Please contact me at your earliest convenience. If you need verification of the authenticity of this communication, contact Captain Pete Marino of the Richmond Police Department.

I gave telephone numbers and signed my title and my name, and I faxed the letter to every speed dial listing in Eddings's journal, except, of course, the Associated Press. For a while I sat at my desk, staring rather glazed, as if my fax machine were going to solve this case immediately. But it remained silent as I read and waited. At the reasonable hour of six A.M., I called Marino.

"I take it there was no riot," I said after the phone banged and dropped and his voice mumbled over the line. "Good, you're awake," I added.

"What time is it?" He sounded as if he were in a stupor.

"It's time for you to rise and shine."

"We locked up maybe five people. The rest got quiet after that and went back inside. What are you doing awake?"

"I'm always awake. And by the way, I could use a ride to work today and I need groceries."

"Well, put on some coffee," he said. "I guess I'm coming over."

8

When he arrived, Lucy was still in bed and I was making fresh fruit salad and coffee. I let him in, dismayed again when I looked out at my street. Overnight, Richmond had turned to glass, and I had heard on the news that falling branches and trees had knocked down power lines in several sections of the city.

"Did you have any trouble?" I asked, shutting the front door.

"Depends on what kind you mean." Marino set down groceries, took off his coat and handed it to me.

"Driving."

"I got chains. But I was out till after midnight and I'm tired as hell."

"Come on. Let's get you some coffee."

"None of that unleaded shit."

"Guatemalan, and I promise it's leaded."

"Where's the kid?"

"Asleep."

"Yo. Must be nice." He yawned again.

We walked into the kitchen with its many windows. Through them the river was pewter and slow. Rocks were glazed, the woods a fantasy just beginning to sparkle in the wan morning light. Marino poured his own coffee, adding plenty of sugar and cream.

"You want some?" he asked.

"Black, please."

"I think by now you don't have to tell me."

"I never make assumptions," I said, getting plates out of a cabinet. "Especially about men, who seem to have a Mendelian trait which precludes them from remembering details important to women."

"Yeah, well, I could give you a list of things Doris never remembered, starting with using my tools and not putting them back," he said of his ex-wife.

I worked at the counter while he looked around as if he wanted to smoke. I wasn't going to let him.

"I guess Tony never fixed coffee for you," he said.

"Tony never did much of anything for me except try to get me pregnant."

"He didn't do a very good job unless you didn't want kids."

"Not with him I didn't."

"What about now?"

"I still don't want them with him. Here." I handed Marino a plate. "Let's sit."

"Wait a minute. This is it?"

"What else do you want?"

"Shit, Doc. This ain't food. And what the hell are these little green slices with black things."

"The kiwi fruit I told you to get. I'm sure you must have had it before," I patiently said. "I've got bagels in the freezer."

"Yeah, that'd be good. With cream cheese. You got any poppy-seed?"

"If you have a drug test today you'll come up positive for morphine."

"And don't give me any of the nonfat stuff. It's like eating paste."

"No, it's not," I said. "Paste is better."

I left off the butter, determined to make him live for a while. By now Marino and I were more than partners or even friends. We were dependent on each other in a way neither could explain.

"So tell me what all you did," he said as we sat at my breakfast table by a wide pane of glass. "I know you been up all night doing something." He took a large bite of bagel and reached for his juice.

I told him about my visit with Mrs. Eddings, and about the note I had written and sent to numbers belonging to places I did not know.

"It's weird he was faxing things everywhere but his office."

"He sent two faxes to his office," I reminded him.

"I need to talk to those people."

"Good luck. Remember, they're reporters."

"That's what I'm afraid of. To those drones, Eddings is just another story. Only thing they care about is what they're going to do with the info. The worse his death is, the better they like it."

"Well, I don't know. But I suspect whoever he associated with in that office is going to be extremely careful about what is said. I'm not sure I blame them. A death investigation is frightening to people who did not ask to be invited."

"What's the status of his tox?" Marino asked.

"Hopefully today," I said.

"Good. You get your verification it's cyanide, then maybe we can work this thing the way it ought to be worked. As it is, I'm trying to explain superstitions to the commander of A Squad and wondering what the hell I'm going to do about the Keystone Kops in Chesapeake. And I'm telling Wesley it's a homicide and he's asking for proof because he's on the spot, too."

The mention of his name was disturbing, and I looked out the window at unnavigable water moving thickly between big, dark rocks. The sun was lighting up gray clouds in the eastern part of the sky, and I heard the shower running in the back part of the house where Lucy was staying.

"Sounds like Sleeping Beauty's awake," Marino said. "She need a ride?"

"I think she's involved with the field office today. We should get going," I added, for staff meeting at my office was always at eight-thirty.

He helped gather dishes and we put them in the sink. Minutes later, I had on my coat, my medical bag and briefcase in hand, when my niece appeared in the foyer, hair wet, her robe pulled tight.

"I had a dream," she said in a depressed voice. "Someone shot us in our sleep. Nine-millimeter to the back of the head. They made it look like a robbery."

"Oh really?" Marino asked, pulling on rabbit-fur-lined gloves. "And where was yours truly? 'Cause that ain't going to happen if I'm in the house."

"You weren't here."

He gave her an odd look as he realized she was serious. "What the hell'd you eat last night?"

"It was like a movie. It must have gone on for hours." She looked at me, and her eyes were puffy and exhausted.

"Would you like to come to the office with me?" I asked.

"No, no. I'll be fine. The last thing I feel like being around right now is a bunch of dead bodies."

"You're going to get together with some of the agents you know in town?" I uneasily said.

"I don't know. We were going to work with closed-cycle oxygen respiration, but I just don't think I feel up to putting on a wet suit and getting in some indoor pool that stinks like chlorine. I think I'll just wait around for my car, then leave."

Marino and I didn't talk much as we drove downtown, his mighty tires gouging glazed streets with clanking teeth. I knew he was worried about Lucy. As much as he abused her, if anyone else tried to do the same Marino would destroy that person with his big bare hands. He had known her since she was ten. It was Marino who had taught her to drive a five-speed pickup truck and shoot a gun.

"Doc, I got to ask you something," he finally spoke as the

rhythm of chains slowed at the toll booth. "Do you think Lucy's doing okay?"

"Everyone has nightmares," I said.

"Hey, Bonita," he called to the toll taker as he handed his pass card out the window, "when you going to do something about this weather?"

"Don't you be blaming this on me, Cap'n." She returned his card, and the gate lifted. "You told me you're in charge."

Her mirthful voice followed us as we drove on, and I thought how sad it was that we lived in a day when even toll booth attendants had to wear plastic gloves for fear their flesh may come in contact with someone else's flesh. I wondered if we would reach a point when all of us lived in bubbles so we did not die of diseases like the Ebola virus and AIDS.

"I just think she's acting a little weird," Marino went on as his window rolled up. After a pause, he asked, "Where's Janet?"

"With her family in Aspen, I think."

He stared straight ahead and drove.

"After what happened at Dr. Mant's house, I don't blame Lucy for being a little rattled," I added.

"Hell, she's usually the one who looks for trouble," he said. "She doesn't get rattled. That's why the Bureau lets her hang out with HRT. You ain't allowed to get rattled when you're dealing with white supremacists and terrorists. You don't call in sick because you've had a friggin" bad dream."

Off the expressway, he took the Seventh Street exit into the old cobblestone lanes of Shockoe Slip, then turned north onto Fourteenth, where I went to work every day when I was in town. Virginia's Office of the Chief Medical Examiner, or OCME, was a squat stucco building with tiny dark windows that reminded me of unattractive, suspicious eyes. They overlooked slums to the east and the banking district to the west, and suspended overhead were highways and railroad tracks cutting through the sky.

Marino pulled into the back parking lot, where there was an impressive number of cars considering the condition of the roads. I got out in front of the shut bay door and used a key to enter another door to one side. Following the ramp intended for stretchers, I entered the morgue, and could hear the noise of people working down the hall. The autopsy suite was past the walk-in refrigerator, and doors were open wide. I walked in while Fielding, my deputy chief, removed various tubes and a catheter from the body of a young woman on the second table.

"You ice-skate in?" he asked and he did not seem surprised to see me.

"Close to it. I may have to borrow the wagon today. At the moment I'm without a car."

He leaned closer to his patient, frowning a bit as he studied the tattoo of a rattlesnake coiled around the dead woman's sagging left breast, its gaping mouth disturbingly aimed at her nipple.

"You tell me why the hell somebody gets something like this," Fielding said.

"I'd say the tattoo artist got the best end of that deal," I said. "Check the inside of her lower lip. She's probably got a tattoo there."

He pulled down her lower lip, and inside it in big crooked letters was *Fuck You*.

Fielding looked at me in astonishment. "How'd you know that?"

"The tattoos are homemade, she looks like a biker-type and my guess is she's no stranger to jail."

"Right on all counts." He grabbed a clean towel and wiped his face.

My body-building associate always looked as if he were about to split his scrubs, and he perspired while the rest of us were never quite warm. But he was a competent forensic pathologist. He was pleasant and caring, and I believed he was loyal.

"Possible overdose," he explained as he sketched the tattoo on a chart. "I guess her New Year was a little too happy."

"Jack," I said to him, "how many dealings have you had with the Chesapeake police?"

He continued to draw. "Very little."

"None recently?" I asked.

"I really don't think so. Why?" He glanced up at me.

"I had a rather odd encounter with one of their detectives."

"In connection with Eddings?" He began to rinse the body, and long dark hair flowed over bright steel.

"Right."

"You know, it's weird but Eddings had just called me. It couldn't have been more than a day before he died," Fielding said as he moved the hose.

"What did he want?" I asked.

"I was down here doing a case, so I never talked to him.

Now I wish I had." He climbed up a stepladder and began taking photographs with a Polaroid camera. "You in town long?"

"I don't know," I said.

"Well, if you need me to help out in Tidewater some, I will." The flash went off and he waited for the print. "I don't know if I told you, but Ginny's pregnant again and would probably love to get out of the house. And she likes the ocean. Tell me the name of the detective you're worried about, and I'll take care of him."

"I wish somebody would," I said.

The camera flashed again, and I thought about Mant's cottage and could not imagine putting Fielding and his wife in there or even nearby.

"It makes sense for you to stay here anyway," he added. "And hopefully Dr. Mant isn't going to stay in England forever."

"Thank you," I said to him with feeling. "Maybe if you could just commute several times a week."

"No problem. Could you hand me the Nikon?"

"Which one?"

"Uh, the N-50 with the single-reflex lens. I think it's in the cabinet over there." He pointed.

"We'll work out a schedule," I said as I got the camera for him. "But you and Ginny don't need to be in Dr. Mant's house, and you're going to have to trust me on that."

"You have a problem?" He ripped out another print and handed it down.

"Marino, Lucy and I started our New Year with slashed tires."

He lowered the camera and looked at me, shocked. "Shit. You think it was random?"

"No, I do not," I said.

I took the elevator up to the next floor and unlocked my office and the sight of Eddings's Christmas pepper surprised me like a blow. I could not leave it on the credenza, so I picked it up and then did not know where to move it. For a moment, I walked around, confused and upset, until I finally put it back where it had been, because I could not throw it out or subject some other member of my staff to its memories.

Looking through Rose's adjoining doorway, I was not surprised that she wasn't here yet. My secretary was advancing in years and did not like to drive downtown even on the nicest days. Hanging up my coat, I carefully looked around, satisfied that all seemed in order except for the cleaning job done by the custodial crew that came in after hours. But then, none of the sanitation engineers, as they were called by the state, wanted to work in this building. Few lasted long and none would go downstairs.

I had inherited my quarters from the previous chief, but beyond the paneling, nothing was as it had been back in those cigar-smoky days when forensic pathologists like Cagney nipped bourbon with cops and funeral home directors, and touched bodies with bare hands. My predecessor had not worried much about alternate light sources and DNA.

I remembered the first time I had been shown his space after he had died and I was being interviewed for his position. I had surveyed macho mementos he had proudly displayed, and when one of them turned out to be a silicone breast implant from a woman who had been raped and murdered, I had been tempted to stay in Miami.

I did not think the former chief would like his office now, for it was nonsmoking, and disrespect and sophomoric behavior were left outside the door. The oak furniture was not the state's but my own, and I had hidden the tile floor with a Sarouk prayer rug that was machine-made but bright. There were corn plants and a ficus tree, but I did not bother with art, because, like a psychiatrist, I wanted nothing provocative on my walls, and, frankly, I needed all the space I could find for filing cabinets and books. As for trophies, Cagney would not have been impressed with the toy cars, trucks and trains I used to help investigators reconstruct accidents.

I took several minutes to look through my in-basket, which was full of red-bordered death certificates for medical examiner cases and green-bordered ones for those that were not. Other reports also awaited my initialing, and a message on my computer screen told me I needed to check my electronic mail. All that could wait, I thought, and I walked back out into the hall to see who else was here. Only Cleta was, I discovered, when I reached the front office, but she was just who I needed to see.

"Dr. Scarpetta," she said, startled. "I didn't know you were here."

"I thought it was a good idea for me to return to Richmond right now," I said, pulling a chair close to her desk. "Dr. Fielding and I are going to try to cover Tidewater from here."

Cleta was from Florence, South Carolina, and wore a lot of makeup and her skirts too short because she believed that happiness was being pretty, which was something she would never be. In the midst of sorting grim photographs by case number, she sat straight in her chair, a magnifying glass in hand, bifocals on. Nearby was a sausage biscuit on a napkin that she probably had gotten from the cafeteria next door, and she was drinking Tab.

"Well, I think the roads are starting to melt," she let me know.

"Good." I smiled. "I'm glad you're here."

She seemed very pleased as she plucked more photographs out of the shallow box.

"Cleta," I said, "you remember Ted Eddings, don't you?"

"Oh yes, ma'am." She suddenly looked as if she might cry. "He was always so nice when he would come in here. I still can't believe it." She bit her lower lip.

"Dr. Fielding says Eddings called down here the end of last week," I said. "I'm wondering if you might remember that."

She nodded. "Yes, ma'am, I sure do. In fact, I can't stop thinking about it."

"Did he talk to you?"

"Yes."

"Can you remember what he said?"

"Well, he wanted to speak to Dr. Fielding, but his line was busy. So I asked if I could take a message, and we kidded around some. You know how he was." Her eyes got bright and her voice wavered. "He asked me if I was still eating so much maple syrup because I had to be eating plenty of it to talk like this. And he asked me out."

I listened as her cheeks turned red.

"Of course, he didn't mean it. He was always saying, you know, 'When are we going out on that date?' He didn't mean it," she said again.

"It's all right if he did," I kindly told her.

"Well, he already had a girlfriend."

"How do you know that?" I asked.

"He said he was going to bring her by sometime, and I got the impression he was pretty serious about her. I believe her name is Loren, but I don't know anything else about her."

I thought of Eddings engaging in personal conversations like this with my staff, and was even less surprised that he had seemed to gain access to me more easily than most reporters who called. I could not help but wonder if this same talent had led to his death, and I suspected it had.

"Did he ever mention to you what he wanted to talk to Dr. Fielding about?" I said as I got up.

She thought hard for a moment, absently rummaging through pictures the world should never see. "Wait a minute. Oh, I know. It was something about radiation. About what the findings would be if someone died from that."

"What kind of radiation?" I said.

"Well, I was thinking he was doing some sort of story on X-ray machines. You know, there's been a lot in the news lately because of all the people afraid of things like letter bombs."

I did not recall seeing anything in Eddings's house that

might indicate he was researching such a story. I returned to my office, and started on paperwork and began returning telephone calls. Hours later, I was eating a late lunch at my desk when Marino walked in.

"What's it doing out there?" I said, surprised to see him. "Would you like half a tuna-fish sandwich?"

Shutting both doors, he sat with his coat still on, and the look on his face frightened me. "Have you talked to Lucy?" he said.

"Not since I left the house." I put the sandwich down. "Why?"

"She called me"—he glanced at his watch—"roughly an hour ago. Wanted to know how to get in touch with Danny so she could call him about her car. And she sounded drunk."

I was silent for a moment, my eyes on his. Then I looked away. I did not ask him if he were certain because Marino knew about such matters, and Lucy's past was quite familiar to him.

"Should I go home?" I quietly asked.

"Naw. I think she's in some kind of mood and is blowing things off. At least she's got no car to drive."

I took a deep breath.

"Point is, I think she's safe at the moment. But I thought you should know, Doc."

"Thank you," I grimly said.

I had hoped my niece's proclivity to abuse alcohol was a problem she had left behind, for I had seen no worrisome signs since those early self-destructive days when she had driven drunk and almost died. If nothing else, her odd behavior at the house this morning in addition to what Marino had just revealed made me know that something was very wrong. I wasn't certain what to do.

"One other thing," he added as he got up. "You don't want her going back to the Academy like this."

"No," I said. "Of course not."

He left, and for a while I stayed behind shut doors, depressed, my thoughts like the sluggish river behind my home. I did not know if I was angry or frightened, but as I thought of the times I had offered wine to Lucy or gotten her a beer, I felt betrayed. Then I was almost desperate as I considered the magnitude of what she had accomplished, and what she had to lose, and suddenly other images came to me, too. I envisioned terrible scenes penned by a man who wanted to be a deity, and I knew that my niece with all her brilliance did not understand the darkness of that power. She did not understand malignancy the way I did.

I put my coat and gloves on, because I knew just where I should go. I was about to let the front office know I was leaving, when my phone rang, and I picked it up in the event it might be Lucy. But it was the Chesapeake police chief, who told me his name was Steels and that he had just moved here from Chicago.

"I'm sorry this is the way we have to meet," he said, and he sounded sincere. "But I need to talk to you about a detective of mine named Roche."

"I need to talk to you about him, too," I said. "Maybe you can explain to me exactly what his problem is."

"According to him, the problem's you," he said.

"That's ridiculous," I said, unable to restrain my anger. "To cut to the chase, Chief Steels, your detective is inappropriate, unprofessional and an obstruction in this investigation. He is banned from my morgue."

"You realize Internal Affairs is going to have to thoroughly investigate this," he said, "and I'm probably going to need you to come in at some point so we can talk to you."

"Exactly what is the accusation?"

"Sexual harassment."

"That's certainly popular these days," I ironically said. "However, I wasn't aware I had power over him, since he works for you, not me, and by definition, sexual harassment is about the abuse of power. But it's all moot since the roles are reversed in this case. Your detective is the one who made sexual advances toward me, and when they were not reciprocated, he's the one who became abusive."

Steels said after a pause, "Then it sounds to me like it's your word against his."

"No, what it sounds like is a lot of bullshit. And if he touches me one more time, I will get a warrant and have him arrested."

He was silent.

"Chief Steels," I went on, "I think what should be of glaring importance right now is a very frightening situation that is going on in your jurisdiction. Might we talk about Ted Eddings for a moment?"

He cleared his throat. "Certainly."

"You're familiar with the case?"

"Absolutely. I've been thoroughly briefed and am very familiar with it."

"Good. Then I'm sure you'll agree that we should investigate it to our fullest capacity."

"Well, I think we should look hard at everybody who dies, but in the Eddings case the answer's pretty plain to me."

I listened as I got only more furious.

"You may or may not know that he was into Civil War stuff—had a collection, and all. Apparently, there were some battles not so far from where he went diving, and it may be he was looking for artifacts like cannonballs."

I realized that Roche must have talked to Mrs. Eddings, or perhaps the chief had seen some of the newspaper articles Eddings supposedly had written about his underwater treasure hunts. I was no historian, but I knew enough to see the obvious problem with what was becoming a ridiculous theory.

I said to Steels, "The biggest battle on or near water in your area was between the *Merrimac* and the *Monitor*. And that was miles away in Hampton Roads. I have never heard of any battles in or near the part of the Elizabeth River where the shipyard is located."

"But Dr. Scarpetta, we really just don't know, do we?" he thoughtfully said. "Could be anything that was fired, any garbage dumped, and anybody killed at any place back then. It's not like there were television cameras or millions of reporters all over. Just Mathew Brady, and by the way, I'm a big fan of history and have read a lot about the Civil War. I'm personally of the belief that this guy, Eddings, went down in that shipyard so he could comb the river bottom for relics. He inhaled noxious gases from his machine and died, and whatever he had in his hands—like a metal detector—got lost in the silt."

"I am working this case as a possible homicide," I firmly said.

"And I don't agree with you, based on what I've been told."

"I expect the prosecutor will agree with me when I speak to her."

The chief said nothing to that.

"I should assume you don't intend to invite the Bureau's Criminal Investigative Analysis people into this," I added. "Since you have decided we're dealing with an accident."

"At this point, I see no reason in the world to bother the FBI. And I've told them that."

"Well, I see every reason," I answered, and it was all I could do not to hang up on him.

"Damn, damn, damn!" I muttered as I angrily grabbed my belongings and marched out the door.

Downstairs in the morgue office, I removed a set of keys from the wall, and I went outside to the parking lot and unlocked the driver's door of the dark blue station wagon we sometimes used to transport bodies. It was not as obvious as a hearse, but it wasn't what one might expect to see in a neighbor's driveway, either. Oversized, it had tinted windows obscured with blinds similar to those used by funeral homes, and in lieu of seats in back, the floor was covered with plywood fitted with fasteners to keep stretchers from sliding during transport. My morgue supervisor had hung several air fresheners from the rearview mirror, and the scent of cedar was cloying.

I opened my window part of the way and drove onto Main Street, grateful that by now roads were only wet, and rush-hour traffic not too bad. Damp, cold air felt good on my face, and I knew what I must do. It had been a while since I had stopped at church on my way home, for I thought to do this only when I was in crisis, when life had pushed me as far as I could go. At Three Chopt Road and Grove Avenue, I turned into the parking lot of Saint Bridget's, which was built of brick and slate and no longer kept its doors unlocked at night, because of what the world had become. But Alcoholics Anonymous met at this hour, and I always knew when I could get in and that I would not be bothered.

Entering through a side door, I blessed myself with holy water as I walked into the sanctuary with its statues of saints guarding the cross, and crucifixion scenes in brilliant stained glass. I chose the last row of pews, and I wished for candles to light, but that ritual had stopped here with Vatican II. Kneeling on the bench, I prayed for Ted Eddings and his mother. I prayed for Marino and Wesley. In my private, dark space, I prayed for my niece. Then I sat in silence with my eyes shut, and I felt my tension begin to ease.

At almost six P.M., I was about to leave when I paused in the narthex and saw the lighted doorway of the library down a hall. I wasn't certain why I was guided in that direction, but it did occur to me that an evil book might be countered by one that was holy, and a few moments with the catechism might be what the priest would prescribe. When I walked in, I found an older woman inside, returning books to shelves.

"Dr. Scarpetta?" she asked, and she seemed both surprised and pleased.

"Good evening." I was ashamed I did not remember her name.

"I'm Mrs. Edwards."

I remembered she was in charge of social services at the church, and trained converts in Catholicism, which some days I thought should include me since it was so rare I went to Mass. Small and slightly plump, she had never seen a convent but still inspired the same guilt in me that the good nuns had when I was young.

"I don't often see you here at this hour," she said.

"I just stopped by," I answered. "After work. I'm afraid I missed evening prayer."

"That was on Sunday."

"Of course."

"Well, I'm so glad I happened to see you on my way out." Her eyes lingered on my face and I knew she sensed my need.

I scanned bookcases.

"Might I help you find something?" she asked.

"A copy of the catechism," I said.

She crossed the room and pulled one off a shelf, and handed it to me. It was a large volume and I wondered if I had made a good decision, for I was very tired right now and I doubted Lucy was in a condition to read.

"Perhaps there is something I might help you with?" Her voice was kind.

"Maybe if I could speak to the priest for a few moments, that would be good," I said.

"Father O'Connor is making hospital visits." Her eyes continued searching. "Might I help you in some way?"

"Maybe you can."

"We can sit right here," she suggested.

We pulled chairs out from a plain wooden table reminiscent of ones I had sat at in parochial school when I was a girl in Miami. I suddenly remembered the wonder of what had awaited me on the pages of those books, for learning was what I loved, and any mental escape from home had been a blessing. Mrs. Edwards and I faced each other like friends, but the words were hard to say because it was rare I talked this frankly.

"I can't go into much detail because my difficulty relates to a case I am working," I began.

"I understand." She nodded.

"But suffice it to say that I have become exposed to a satanic-type bible. Not devil worship, per se, but something evil."

She did not react but continued to look me in the eye.

"And Lucy was, as well. Lucy is my twenty-three-year-old niece. She also read this manuscript."

"And you're having problems as a result?" Mrs. Edwards asked.

I took a deep breath and felt foolish. "I know this sounds rather weird."

"Of course it doesn't," she said. "We must never underestimate the power of evil, and we should avoid brushing up against it whenever we can."

"I can't always avoid that," I said. "It is evil that usually brings my patients to my door. But rarely do I have to look at documents like the one I'm talking about now. I've been having disturbing dreams, and my niece is acting erratically and has spent a lot of time with the Book. Mostly, I'm worried about her. That's why I'm here."

"'But continue thou in the things which thou hast learned and hast been assured of,'" she quoted to me. "It's really that simple." She smiled.

"I'm not certain I understand," I replied.

"Dr. Scarpetta, there is no cure for what you've just shared with me. I can't lay hands on you and push the darkness and bad dreams away. Father O'Connor can't, either. We have no ritual or ceremony that works. We can pray for you and, of course, we will. But what you and Lucy must do right now is return to your own faith. You need to do whatever it is that has given you strength in the past."

"That's why I came here today," I said again.

"Good. Tell Lucy to return to the religious community and pray. She should come to church."

That would be the day, I thought as I drove toward home, and my fears only intensified when I walked through my front door. It was not quite seven P.M. and Lucy was in bed.

"Are you asleep?" I sat next to her in the dark and placed my hand on her back. "Lucy?"

She did not answer and I was grateful that our cars had not arrived. I was afraid she might have tried to drive back to Charlottesville. I was so afraid she was about to repeat every terrible mistake she had ever made.

"Lucy?" I said again.

She slowly rolled over. "What?" she said.

"I'm just checking on you," I said in a hushed tone.

I saw her wipe her eyes and realized she was not asleep but crying.

"What is it?" I said.

"Nothing."

"I know it's something. And it's time we talk. You've not been yourself and I want to help."

She would not answer.

"Lucy, I will sit right here until you talk to me."

She was quiet some more, and I could see her eyelids move as she stared up at the ceiling. "Janet told them," she said. "She told her mom and dad. They argued with her, as if they know more about her feelings than she does. As if somehow she is wrong about herself."

Her voice was getting angrier and she worked her way up to a half-sitting position, stuffing pillows behind her back.

"They want her to go to counseling," she added.

"I'm sorry," I said. "I'm not sure I know what to say except that the problem lies with them and not with the two of you."

"I don't know what she's going to do. It's bad enough that we have to worry about the Bureau finding out."

"You have to be strong and true to who you are."

"Whoever that is. Some days I don't know." She got more upset. "I hate this. It's so hard. It's so unfair." She leaned her head against my shoulder. "Why couldn't I have been like you? Why couldn't it have been easy?"

"I'm not sure you want to be like me," I said. "And my life certainly isn't easy, and almost nothing that matters is easy. You and Janet can work things out if you are committed to do so. And if you truly love each other."

She took a deep breath and slowly blew out air.

"No more destructive behavior." I got up from her bed in the shadows of her room. "Where's the Book?"

"On the desk," she said.

"In my office?"

"Yes. I put it there."

We looked at each other, and her eyes shone. She sniffed loudly and blew her nose.

"Do you understand why it's not good to dwell on something like that?" I asked.

"Look what you have to dwell on all the time. It goes with the turf."

"No," I said, "what goes with the turf is knowing where to step and where not to stand. You must respect an enemy's power as much as you despise it. Otherwise, you will lose, Lucy. You had better learn this now."

"I understand," she quietly said as she reached for the catechism I had set on the foot of the bed. "What is this, and do I have to read it all tonight?"

"Something I picked up for you at church. I thought you might like to look at it."

"Forget church," she said.

"Why?"

"Because it's forgotten me. It thinks people like me are aberrant, as if I should go to hell or jail for the way I am. That's what I'm talking about. You don't know what it's like to be isolated."

"Lucy, I've been isolated most of my life. You don't even know what discrimination is until you're one of only three women in your medical school class. Or in law school, the men won't share their notes if you're sick and miss class. That's why I don't get sick. That's why I don't get drunk and hide in bed." I sounded hard because I knew I needed to be.

"This is different," she said.

"I think you want to believe it's different so you can make excuses and feel sorry for yourself," I said. "It seems to me that the person doing all of the forgetting and rejecting here is you. It's not the church. It's not society. It's not even Janet's parents, who simply may not understand. I thought you were stronger than this."

"I am strong."

"Well, I've had enough," I said. "Don't you come to my house and get drunk and pull the covers over your head so that I worry about you all day. And then when I try to help, you push me and everyone else away."

She was silent as she stared at me. Finally she said, "Did you really go to church because of me?"

"I went because of me," I said. "But you were the main topic of conversation."

She threw the covers off. "'A person's chief end is to glorify God and enjoy God forever,'" she said as she got up.

I paused in her doorway.

"Catechism. Using inclusive language, of course. I had a religion course at UVA. Do you want dinner?"

"What would you like?" I said.

"Whatever's easy." She came over and hugged me. "Aunt Kay, I'm sorry," she said.

In the kitchen I opened the freezer first and was not inspired by anything I saw. Next I looked inside the refrigerator, but my appetite had gone into hiding along with my peace of mind. I ate a banana and made a pot of coffee. At half past eight, the base station on the counter startled me.

"Unit six hundred to base station one," Marino's voice came over the air.

I picked up the microphone and answered him, "Base station one."

"Can you call me at a number?"

"Give it to me," I said, and I had a bad feeling.

It was possible the radio frequency used by my office could be monitored, and whenever a case was especially sensitive, the detectives tried to keep all of us off the air. The number Marino gave me was for a pay phone.

When he answered, he said, "Sorry, I didn't have any change."

"What's going on?" I didn't waste time.

"I'm skipping the M.E. on call because I knew you'd want us to get hold of you first."

"What is it?"

"Shit, Doc, I'm really sorry. But we've got Danny."

"Danny?" I said in confusion.

"Danny Webster. From your Norfolk office."

"What do you mean you've got him?" I was gripped by fear. "What did he do?" I imagined he had gotten arrested driving my car. Or maybe he had wrecked it.

Marino said, "Doc, he's dead."

Then there was silence on his end and mine.

"Oh God." I leaned against the counter and shut my eyes. "Oh my God," I said. "What happened?"

"Look, I think the best thing is for you to get down here."

"Where are you?"

"Sugar Bottom, where the old train tunnel is. Your car's about a block uphill at Libby Hill Park."

I asked nothing further but told Lucy I was leaving and probably would not be home until late. I grabbed my medical bag and my pistol, for I was familiar with the skid row part of town where the tunnel was, and I could not imagine what might have lured Danny there. He and his friend were to have driven my car and Lucy's Suburban to my office, where my administrator was to meet them in back and give them a ride to the bus station. Certainly, Church Hill was not far from the OCME, but I could not imagine why Danny would have driven anywhere in my Mercedes other than where he knew he was to be. He did not seem the type to abuse my trust.

I drove swiftly along West Cary Street, passing huge brick homes with roofs of copper and slate, and entrances barricaded by tall black wrought-iron gates. It seemed surreal to be speeding in the morgue wagon through this elegant part of the city while one of my employees lay dead, and I fretted over leaving Lucy alone again. I could not remember if I had armed the alarm system and turned the motion sensors off on my way out. My hands were shaking and I wished I could smoke.

Libby Hill Park was on one of Richmond's seven hills in an area where real estate was now considered prime. Century-old row houses and Greek Revival homes had been brilliantly restored by people bold enough to reclaim a historic section of the city from the clutches of decay and crime. For most residents, the chance they took had turned out fine, but I knew I could not live near housing projects and depressed areas where the major industry was drugs. I did not want to work cases in my neighborhood.

Police cruisers with lights throbbing red and blue lined both sides of Franklin Street. The night was very dark, and I could barely make out the octagonal bandstand or the bronze soldier on his tall granite pedestal facing the James. My Mercedes was surrounded by officers and a television crew, and people had emerged on wide porches to watch. As I slowly drove past, I could not tell if my car had been damaged, but the driver's door was open, the interior light on.

East past 29th Street, the road sloped down to a low-lying section known as Sugar Bottom, named for prostitutes once kept in business by Virginia gentlemen, or maybe it was for moonshine. I wasn't sure of the lore. Restored homes abruptly turned into slumlord apartments and leaning tarpaper shacks, and off the pavement, midway down the steep hill, were woods thick and dense where the C&O tunnel had collapsed in the twenties.

I remembered flying over this area in a state police helicopter once, and the tunnel's black opening had peeked out of trees at me, its railroad bed a muddy scar leading to the river. I thought of the train cars and laborers supposedly still sealed inside, and, again, I could not imagine why Danny would have come here willingly. If nothing else, he would have worried about his injured knee. Pulling over, I parked as close to Marino's Ford as I could, and instantly was spotted by reporters.

"Dr. Scarpetta, is it true that's your car up the hill?" asked a woman journalist as she hurried to my side. "I understand the Mercedes is registered to you. What color is it? Is it black?" she persisted when I did not reply.

"Can you explain how it got there?" A man pushed a microphone close to my face.

"Did you drive it there?" asked someone else.

"Was it stolen from you? Did the victim steal it from you? Do you think this is about drugs?"

Voices folded into each other because no one would wait his turn and I would not speak. When several uniformed officers realized I had arrived, they loudly intervened.

"Hey, get back."

"Now. You heard me."

"Let the lady through."

"Come on. We got a crime scene to work here. I hope that's all right with you."

Marino was suddenly holding on to my arm. "Bunch of squirrels," he said as he glared at them. "Be real careful where you step. We got to go through the woods almost all the way to where the tunnel is. What kind of shoes you got on?"

"I'll be all right."

There was a path, and it was long and led steeply down from the street. Lights had been set up to illuminate the way, and they cut a swath like the moon on a dangerous bay. On the margins, woods dissolved into blackness stirred by a subtle wind.

"Be real careful," he said again. "It's muddy and there's shit all over the place."

"What shit?" I asked.

I turned on my flashlight and directed it straight down at the narrow muddy path of broken glass, rotting paper, and discarded shoes that glinted and glowed a washed-out white amid brambles and winter trees.

"The neighbors have been trying to turn this into a landfill," he said.

"He could not have gotten down here with his bad knee," I said. "What's the best way to approach this?"

"On my arm."

"No. I need to look at this alone."

"Well, you're not going down there alone. We don't know if someone else might still be down there somewhere."

"There's blood there." I pointed the flashlight, and several large drops glistened on dead leaves about six feet down from where I was.

"There's a lot of it up here."

"Any up by the street?"

"No. It looks like it pretty much starts right here. But we've found some on the path going all the way down to where he is."

"All right. Let's do it." I looked around and began careful steps, Marino's heavier ones behind me.

Police had run bright yellow tape from tree to tree, securing as much of the area as possible, for right now we did not know how big this scene might be. I could not see the body until I emerged from the woods into a clearing where the old railroad bed led to the river south of me and disappeared into the tunnel's yawning mouth to the west. Danny Webster lay half on his back, half on his side in an awkward tangle of arms and legs. A large puddle of blood was beneath his head. I slowly explored him with the flashlight and saw an abundance of dirt and grass on his sweater and jeans, and bits of leaves and other debris clung to his blood-matted hair.

"He rolled down the hill," I said as I noted that several straps had come loose in his bright red brace, and debris was caught in the Velcro. "He was already dead or almost dead when he came to rest in this position."

"Yeah, I think it's pretty clear he was shot up there," Marino said. "My first question was whether he bled while he maybe tried to get away. And he makes it about this far, then collapses and rolls the rest of the way."

"Or maybe he was made to think he was being given a chance to get away." Emotion crept into my voice. "You see this knee brace he has on? Do you have any idea how slowly he would have moved were he trying to get down this path? Do you know what it's like to inch your way along on a bad leg?"

"So some asshole was shooting fish in a barrel," Marino said.

I did not answer him as I directed the light at grass and trash leading up to the street. Drops of blood glistened dark red on a flattened milk carton whitened by weather and time.

"What about his wallet?" I asked.

"It was in his back pocket. Eleven bucks and charge cards still in it," Marino said, his eyes constantly moving.

I took photographs, then knelt by the body and turned it so I could get a better look at the back of Danny's ruined head. I felt his neck, and he was still warm, the blood beneath him coagulating. I opened my medical bag.

"Here." I unfolded a plastic sheet and gave it to Marino. "Hold this up while I take his temperature."

He shielded the body from any eyes but ours as I pulled down jeans and undershorts, finding that both were soiled. Although it was not uncommon for people to urinate and defecate at the instant of death, sometimes this was the body's response to terror.

"You got any idea if he fooled around with drugs?" Marino asked.

"I have no reason to think so," I said. "But I have no idea."

"For example, he ever look like he lived beyond his means? I mean, how much did he earn?"

"He earned about twenty-one thousand dollars a year. I don't know if he lived beyond his means. He still lived at home."

The body temperature was 94.5, and I set the thermometer on top of my bag to get a reading of the ambient air. I moved arms and legs, and rigor mortis had started only in small muscles like his fingers and eyes. For the most part, Danny was still warm and limber as in life, and as I bent close to him I could smell his cologne and knew I would recognize it forever. Making sure the sheet was completely under him, I turned him on his back, and more blood spilled as I began looking for other wounds.

"What time did you get the call?" I asked Marino, who was moving slowly near the tunnel, probing its tangled growths of vines and brush with his light.

"One of the neighbors heard a gunshot coming from this area and dialed 911 at seven-oh-five P.M. We found your car and him maybe fifteen minutes after that. So we're talking about two hours ago. Does that work with what you're finding?"

"It's almost freezing out. He's heavily clothed and he's lost about four degrees. Yes, that works. How about handing me those bags over there. Do we know what happened to the friend who was supposed to be driving Lucy's Suburban?"

I slipped the brown paper bags over the hands and secured them at the wrist with rubber bands to preserve fragile evidence like gunshot residue, or fibers or flesh beneath fingernails, supposing he had struggled with his assailant. But I did not think he had. Whatever had happened, I suspected Danny had done exactly as he had been told.

"At the present time we don't know anything about whoever his friend is," Marino said. "I can send a unit down to your office to check."

"I think that's a good idea. We don't know that the friend isn't somehow connected to this."

"One hundred," Marino said into his portable radio as I began taking photographs again.

"One hundred," the dispatcher came back.

"Ten-five any unit that might be in the area of the medical examiner's office at Fourteenth and Franklin."

Danny had been shot from behind, the wound close range, if not contact. I started to ask Marino about cartridge cases when I heard a noise I knew all too well.

"Oh no," I said as the beating sound got louder. "Marino, don't let them get near."

But it was too late, and we looked up as a news helicopter

appeared and began circling low. Its searchlight swept the tunnel and the cold, hard ground where I was on my knees, brains and blood all over my hands. I shielded my eyes from the blinding glare as leaves and dirt stormed and bare trees rocked. I could not hear what Marino yelled as he furiously waved his flashlight at the sky while I shielded the body with my own as best I could.

I enclosed Danny's head in a plastic bag and covered him with a sheet while the crew for Channel 7 destroyed the scene because they were ignorant or did not care, or maybe both. The helicopter's passenger door had been removed, and the cameraman hung out in the night as the light nailed me for the eleven o'clock news. Then the blades began their thunderous retreat.

"Goddamnsonofabitch!" Marino was screaming as he shook his fist after them. "I ought to shoot your ass out of the air!"

9

While a car was dispatched there, I zipped the body inside a pouch, and when I stood I felt faint. For an instant I had to steady myself as my face got cold and I could not see.

"The squad can move him," I told Marino. "Can't someone get those goddamn television cameras out of here?"

Their bright lights floated like satellites up on the dark street as they waited for us to emerge. He gave me a look because we both knew nobody could do a thing about reporters or what they used to record us. As long as they did not interfere with the scene, they could do as they pleased, especially if they were in helicopters we could not stop or catch.

"You going to transport him yourself?" he asked me.

"No. A squad's already there," I said. "And we need some help getting him back up there. Tell them to come on now."

He got on the radio as our flashlights continued to lick over trash and leaves and potholes filled with muddy water.

Then Marino said to me, "I'm going to keep a few guys out here poking around for a while. Unless the perp collected his cartridge case, it's got to be out here somewhere." He looked up the hill. "Problem is, some of those mothers can eject a long way and that goddamn chopper blew stuff all the hell over the place."

Within minutes, paramedics were coming down with a stretcher, feet crunching broken glass, metal clanging. We waited until they had lifted the body, and I probed the ground where it had been. I stared into the black opening of a tunnel that long ago had been dug into a mountainside too soft to support it, and I moved closer until I was just inside its mouth. A wall sealed it deep inside, and whitewash on bricks glinted in my light. Rusting railroad spikes protruded from rotting ties covered with mud, and scattered about were old tires and bottles.

"Doc, there's nothing in there." Marino was picking his way right behind me. "Shit." He almost slipped. "We've already looked."

"Well, obviously, he couldn't have escaped through here," I said as my light discovered cobblestones and dead weeds. "And no one could hide in here. And your average person shouldn't have known about this place, either."

"Come on." Marino's voice was gentle but firm as he touched my arm.

"This wasn't picked randomly. Not many people around here even know where this is." My light moved more. "This was someone who knew exactly what he was doing."

"Doc," he said as water dripped, "this ain't safe."

"I doubt Danny knew about this place. This was premeditated and cold-blooded." My voice echoed off old, dark walls.

Marino held my arm this time, and I did not resist him. "You've done all you can do here. Let's go."

Mud sucked at my boots and oozed over his black military shoes as we followed the rotting railroad bed back out into the night. Together, we climbed up the littered hillside, carefully stepping around blood spilled when Danny's body had been rolled down the steep slope like garbage. Much of it had been displaced by the helicopter's violent wind, and that would one day matter if a defense attorney thought it did. I averted my face from the glare of cameras and flashing strobes. Marino and I got out of the way, and we did not talk to anyone.

"I want to see my car," I said to him as his unit number blared.

"One hundred," he answered, holding the radio close to his mouth.

"Go ahead, one-seventeen," the dispatcher said to somebody else.

"I checked the lot front and back, Captain," Unit 117 said to Marino. "No sign of the vehicle you described."

"Ten-four." Marino lowered the radio and looked very annoyed. "Lucy's Suburban ain't at your office. I don't get it," he said to me. "None of this is making sense."

We began walking back to Libby Hill Park because it really wasn't far, and we wanted to talk.

"What it's looking like to me is Danny might have picked somebody up," Marino said as he lit a cigarette. "Sure sounds like it could be drugs."

"He wouldn't do that when he was delivering my car," I said, and I knew I sounded naive. "He wouldn't pick anybody up."

Marino turned to me. "Come on," he said. "You don't know that."

"I've never had any reason to think he was irresponsible or into drugs or anything else."

"Well, I think it's obvious he was into an alternative life, as they say."

"I don't know that at all." I was tired of that talk.

"You better find out because you got a lot of blood on you."

"These days I worry about that no matter who it is."

"Look, what I'm saying is people you know do disappointing things," he went on as the lights of the city spread below us. "And sometimes people you don't know very well are worse than ones you don't know at all. You trusted Danny because you liked him and thought he did a good job. But he could have been into anything behind the scenes, and you weren't going to know."

I did not reply. What he said was true.

"He's a nice-looking kid, a pretty boy. And now he's driving this unbelievable ride. The best could have been tempted to maybe do a little trolling before turning in the boss's ride. Or maybe he just wanted to score a little dope."

I was more concerned that Danny had fallen prey to an

attempted carjacking, and I pointed out that there had been a rash of them downtown and in this area.

"Maybe," Marino said as my car came into view. "But your ride's still here. Why do you walk someone down the street and shoot them, and leave the car right where it is? Why not steal it? Maybe we should be worried about a gay bashing. You thought about that?"

We had arrived at my Mercedes, and reporters took more photographs and asked more questions as if this were the crime of all time. We ignored them as we moved around to the open driver's door and looked inside my S–320. I scanned armrests, ashtrays, dashboard and saddle leather upholstery, and saw nothing out of place. I saw no sign of a struggle, but the floor mat on the passenger's side was dirty. I noted the faint impressions left by shoes.

"This was the way it was found?" I asked. "What about the door being opened?"

"We opened the door. It was unlocked," Marino said.

"Nobody got inside?"

"No."

"This wasn't there before." I pointed to the floor mat.

"What?" Marino asked.

"See those shoe impressions and the dirt?" I spoke quietly so reporters could not hear. "There shouldn't have been anybody in the passenger's seat. Not while Danny was driving, and not earlier when it was being repaired at Virginia Beach."

"What about Lucy?"

"No. She hasn't ridden with me recently. I can't think of anybody who has since it was cleaned last."

"Don't worry, we're going to vacuum everything." He looked away from me and reluctantly added, "You know we're going to have to impound it, Doc."

"I understand," I said, and we started walking back to the street near the tunnel, where we had parked.

"I'm wondering if Danny was familiar with Richmond," Marino said.

"He's been to my office before," I replied, and my soul felt heavy. "In fact, when he was first hired, he did a week's internship with us. I don't remember where he stayed, but I think it was the Comfort Inn on Broad Street."

We walked in silence for a moment, and I added, "Obviously, he knew the area around my office."

"Yeah, and that includes here since your office is only about fifteen blocks from here."

Something occurred to me. "We don't know that he didn't just come up here tonight to get something to eat before the bus ride home. How do we know he wasn't just doing something mundane like that?"

Our cars were near several cruisers and a crime scene van, and the reporters had gone. I unlocked the station wagon door and got in. Marino stood with his hands in his pockets, a suspicious expression on his face because he knew me so well.

"You aren't posting him tonight, are you?" he said.

"No." It wasn't necessary and I wouldn't put myself through it.

"And you don't want to go home. I can tell."

"There are things to do," I said. "The longer we wait, the more we might lose."

"Which places do you want to try?" he asked, because he knew what it was like to have someone you worked with killed.

"Well, there's a number of places to eat right around here. Millie's, for example."

"Nope. Too high-dollar. Same with Patrick Henry's and most of the joints in the Slip and Shockoe Bottom. Remember, Danny's not going to have a lot of money unless he's getting it from places we don't know about."

"Let's assume he's getting nothing from anywhere," I said. "Let's assume he wanted something that was a straight shot from my office, so he stayed on Broad Street."

"Poe's, which isn't on Broad, but is very close to Libby Hill Park. And of course there's the Cafe," he said.

"That's what I would say, too," I agreed.

When we walked into Poe's, the manager was ringing up the check of the last customer for the night. We waited what seemed a long time, only to be told that dinner had been slow and no one resembling Danny had come in. Returning to our cars, we continued east on Broad to the Hill Cafe at 28th Street, and my pulse picked up when I realized the restaurant was but one street down from where my Mercedes had been found.

Known for its Bloody Marys and chili, the cafe was on the corner, and over the years had been a favorite hangout for cops. So I had been here many times, usually with Marino. It was a true neighborhood bar, and at this hour, tables were still full, smoke thick in the air, the television loudly playing old Howie Long clips on ESPN. Daigo was drying glasses behind the bar when she saw Marino and gave him a toothy grin.

"Now what you doing in here so late?" she said as if it had never happened before. "Where were you earlier when things were popping?"

"So tell me," Marino said to her, "in the joint that makes the best steak sandwich in town, how's business been tonight?" He moved closer so others could not hear what he had to say.

Daigo was a wiry black woman, and she was eyeing me as if she had seen me somewhere before. "They were crawling in from everywhere earlier," she said. "I thought I was going to drop. Can I get something for you and your friend, Captain?"

"Maybe," he said. "You know the doc here, don't ya?"

She frowned and then recognition gleamed in her eyes. "I knew I seen you in here before. With him. You two married yet?" She laughed as if this were the funniest thing she had ever said.

"Listen, Daigo," Marino went on, "we're wondering if a kid might have come in here today. White male, slender, long dark hair, real nice-looking. Would have been wearing a leather jacket, jeans, a sweater, tennis shoes, and a bright red knee brace. About twenty-five years old and driving a new black Mercedes-Benz with a lot of antennas on it."

Her eyes narrowed and her face got grim as Marino continued to talk, the dish towel limp in her hand. I suspected the police had asked her questions in the past about other unpleasant matters, and I could tell by the set of her mouth that she had no use for lazy, bad people who felt nothing when they ruined decent lives.

"Oh, I know exactly who you mean," she said.

Her words had the effect of a fired gun. She had our complete attention, both of us startled.

"He came in, I guess it was around five, 'cause it was still early," she said. "You know, there were some in here drinking beer just like always. But not too many in for dinner yet. He sat right over there."

She pointed at an empty table beneath a hanging spider plant all the way in back, where there was a painting of a rooster on the white brick wall. As I stared at the table where Danny had eaten last while in this city because of me, I saw him in my mind. He was alive and helpful with his clean features and shiny long hair, and then he was bloody and muddy on a dark hillside strewn with garbage. My chest hurt and, for a moment, I had to look away. I had to do something else with my eyes.

When I was more composed, I turned to Daigo and said, "He worked for me at the medical examiner's office. His name was Danny Webster."

She looked at me a long time, my meaning very clear. "Uh-oh," she said in a low voice. "That's him. Oh sweet Jesus, I can't believe it. It's been all over the news, people in here talking about it all night 'cause it's just down the street."

"Yes," I said.

She looked at Marino as if pleading with him. "He was just a boy. Come in here not minding no one, and all he did was eat his sailor sandwich and then someone kills him! I tell you"—she angrily wiped down the counter—"there's too much meanness. Too damn much! I'm sick of it. You understand me? People just kill like it's nothing."

Several diners nearby overheard our conversation, but they continued their own without stares or asides. Marino was in uniform. He clearly was the brass, and that tended to inspire people to mind their own affairs. We waited until Daigo had sufficiently vented her spleen, and we found a table in the quietest corner of the bar. Then she nodded for a waitress to stop by.

"What you want, sugar?" Daigo asked me.

I did not think I could ever eat again, and ordered herbal tea, but she would not hear of that.

"I tell you what, you bring the chief here a bowl of my bread pudding with Jack Daniel's sauce; don't worry, the whiskey's cooked off," she said, and she was the doctor now. "And a cup of strong coffee. Captain?" She looked at Marino. "You want your usual, honey? Uh-huh," she said before he could respond. "That will be one steak sandwich medium rare, grilled onions, extra fries. And he likes A.1., ketchup, mustard, mayo. No dessert. We want to keep this man alive."

"You mind?" Marino got out his cigarettes, as if he needed one more thing that might kill him this day.

Daigo lit up a cigarette, too, and told us more about what she remembered, which was everything because the Hill Cafe was the sort of bar where people noticed strangers. Danny, she said, had stayed less than an hour. He had come and gone alone, and it had not appeared that he was expecting anyone to join him. He had seemed mindful of the time because he frequently checked his watch, and he had ordered a sailor sandwich with fries and a Pepsi. Danny Webster's last meal had cost him six dollars and twenty-seven cents. His waitress was named Cissy, and he had tipped her a dollar.

"And you didn't see anybody in the area that made your antenna go up? Not at any point today?" Marino asked.

Daigo shook her head. "No, sir. Now that doesn't mean there wasn't some son of a bitch hanging out somewhere on the street. 'Cause they're out there. You don't have to go far to find 'em. But if there was somebody, I didn't see him. Nobody who came in here complained about anybody out there like that, either."

"Well, we need to check with your customers, as many as we can," Marino said. "Maybe a car was noticed around the time Danny went out."

"We got charge receipts." She plucked at her hair and by now it was looking wild. "Most people who been in here we know anyhow."

We were about to leave but there was one more detail I needed to know. "Daigo," I asked, "did he take anything with him to go?"

She looked perplexed and got up from the table. "Let me ask."

Marino crushed out another cigarette, and his face was deep red.

"Are you all right?" I said.

He mopped his face with a napkin. "It's hot as shit in here."

"He took his fries," Daigo announced when she got back. "Cissy says he ate his sandwich and slaw but she wrapped almost all of his fries. Plus when he got to the register, he bought a jumbo pack of gum."

"What kind?" I asked.

"She's pretty sure it was Dentyne."

As Marino and I stepped outside, he loosened the neck of his white uniform shirt and yanked off his tie. "Damn, some days I wish I'd never left A-Squad," he said, for when he had commanded detectives it had been in street clothes. "I don't care who's watching," he muttered. "I'm about to die."

"Please tell me if you're serious," I said.

"Don't worry, I'm not ready for one of your tables yet. I just ate too much."

"Yes, you did," I said. "And you smoked too much, too. And that's what prepares people for my tables, goddamn it. Don't you even think about dying. I'm tired of people dying."

We had reached my station wagon and he was staring at me, searching for anything I might not want him to see. "Are you okay?"

"What do you think? Danny worked for me." My hand shook as I fumbled with the key. "He seemed nice and decent. It seemed he always tried to do what was right. He was driving my car here from Virginia Beach because I asked him to and now he's missing the back of his head. How the hell do you think I feel?"

"I think you feel like this is somehow your fault."

"And maybe it is."

We stood in the dark, looking at each other.

"No, it's not," he said. "It's the fault of the asshole who pulled the trigger. You had nothing in the world to do with that. But if it was me, I'd feel the same way."

"My God," I suddenly said.

"What?" He was alarmed, and he looked around as if I had spotted something.

"His doggie bag. What happened to it? It wasn't inside my Mercedes. There was nothing in there that I could see. Not even a gum wrapper," I said.

"Damn, you're right. And I didn't see nothing on the street where your ride was parked. Nothing with the body or anywhere at the scene, either."

There was one place no one had looked, and it was right where we were, on this street by the restaurant. So Marino and I got out flashlights again and prowled. We looked along Broad Street, but it was on 28th near the curb where we found the small white bag as a large dog began barking from a yard. The bag's location suggested that Danny had parked my car as close to the cafe as possible in an area where buildings and trees cast dense shadows and lights were few.

"You got a couple pencils or pens inside your purse?" Marino squatted by what we suspected might be the remains of Danny's dinner.

I found one pen and a long-handled comb, which I gave to him. Using these simple instruments, he opened the bag without touching it as he probed. Inside were cold French fries wrapped in foil and a jumbo pack of Dentyne gum. The sight of them was jolting and told a terrible story. Danny had been confronted as he had walked out of the cafe to my car. Perhaps someone emerged from shadows and pulled a gun as Danny was unlocking the door. We did not know, but it seemed likely he was forced to drive a street away, where he was walked to a remote wooded hillside to die.

"I wish that damn dog would shut up," Marino said as he stood. "Don't go anywhere. I'll be right back."

He crossed the street to his car and opened the trunk. When he returned, he was carrying the usual large brown paper bag police used for evidence. While I held it open, he maneuvered the comb and pencils to drop Danny's leftovers inside.

"I know I should take this into the property room, but they don't like food in there. Besides, there's no fridge." Paper crackled as he folded shut the top of the evidence bag.

Our feet made scuffing noises on pavement as we walked.

"Hell, it's colder than any refrigerator out here," he went on. "If we get any prints they'll probably be his. But I'll get the labs to check anyway."

He locked the bag inside his trunk, where I knew he had stored evidence many times before. Marino's reluctance to follow departmental rules went beyond his dress.

I looked around the dark street lined with cars. "Whatever happened started right here," I said.

Marino was silent as he looked around, too. Then he asked, "You think it was your Benz? You think that was the motive?"

"I don't know," I replied.

"Well, it could be robbery. The car made him look rich even if he wasn't."

I was overwhelmed by guilt again.

"But I still think he might have met someone he wanted to pick up."

"Maybe it would be easier if he had been up to no good," I said. "Maybe it would be easier for all of us because then we could blame him for being killed."

Marino was silent as he looked at me. "Go home and get some sleep. You want me to follow you?"

"Thank you. I'll be fine."

But I wasn't, really. The drive was longer and darker than I remembered, and I felt unusually unskilled at everything I tried to do. Even rolling down the window at the toll booth and finding the right change was hard. Then the token I tossed missed the bin, and when someone behind me honked, I jumped. I was so out of sorts I could think of nothing that might calm me down, not even whiskey. I returned to my neighborhood at nearly one A.M., and the guard who let me through was grim, and I expected he had heard the news, too, and knew where I had been. When I pulled up to my house, I was stunned to see Lucy's Suburban parked in the drive.

She was up and seemed recovered, sitting in the gathering room. The fire was on, and she had a blanket over her legs, and on TV, Robin Williams was hilarious at the Met.

"What happened?" I sat in a chair nearby. "How did your car get here?"

She had glasses on and was reading some sort of manual

that had been published by the FBI. "Your answering service called," she said. "This guy who was driving my car arrived at your office downtown and your assistant never showed up. What's his name, Danny? So the guy in my car calls, and next thing the phone's ringing here. I had him drive to the guard booth, and that's where I met him."

"But what happened?" I asked again. "I don't even know the name of this person. He was supposed to be an acquaintance of Danny's. Danny was driving my car. They were supposed to park both vehicles behind my office." I stopped and simply stared. "Lucy, do you have any idea what's going on? Do you know why I'm home so late?"

She picked up the remote control and turned the television off. "All I know is you got called out on a case. That's what you said to me right before you left."

So I told her. I told her who Danny was and that he was dead, and I explained about my car. I gave her every detail.

"Lucy, do you have any idea who this person was who dropped off your car?" I then said.

"I don't know." She was sitting up now. "Some Hispanic guy named Rick. He had an earring, short hair and looked maybe twenty-two, twenty-three. He was very polite, nice."

"Where is he now?" I said. "You didn't just take your car from him."

"Oh no. I drove him to the bus station, which George gave me directions to."

"George?"

"The guard on duty at the time. At the guard gate. I guess this would have been close to nine."

"Then Rick's gone back to Norfolk."

"I don't know what he's done," she said. "He told me as we were driving that he was certain Danny would show up. He probably has no idea."

"God. Let's hope he doesn't unless he heard it on the news. Let's hope he wasn't there," I said.

The thought of Lucy alone with this stranger in her car filled me with terror, and in my mind I saw Danny's head. I felt shattered bone beneath gloves slippery with his blood.

"Rick's considered a suspect?" She was surprised.

"At the moment, just about anybody is."

I picked up the phone at the bar. Marino had just gotten home, too, and before I could say anything, he butted in.

"We found the cartridge case."

"Great," I said, relieved. "Where?"

"If you're on the road looking down toward the tunnel, it was in a bunch of undergrowth about ten feet to the right of the path where the blood starts."

"A right port ejector," I said.

"Had to be, unless both Danny and his killer were going downhill backwards. And this asshole meant business. He was shooting a forty-five. The ammo's Winchester."

"Overkill," I said.

"You got that right. Someone wanted to make sure he was dead."

"Marino," I said, "Lucy met Danny's friend tonight."

"You mean the guy driving her car?"

"Yes," and I explained what I knew.

"Maybe this thing's making a little more sense," he said.

"The two of them got separated on the road, but in Danny's mind it didn't matter because he'd given his pal directions and a phone number."

"Can someone try to find out who Rick is before he disappears? Maybe intercept him when he gets off the bus?" I asked.

"I'll call Norfolk P.D. I got to anyway because somebody's got to go over to Danny's house and notify his family before they hear about this from the media."

"His family lives in Chesapeake," I told him the bad news, and I knew I would need to talk to them, too.

"Shit," Marino said.

"Don't talk to Detective Roche about any of this, and I don't want him anywhere near Danny's family."

"Don't worry. And you'd better get hold of Dr. Mant."

I tried the number for his mother's flat in London, but there was no answer, and I left an urgent message. There were so many calls to make, and I was drained. I sat next to Lucy on the couch.

"How are you doing?"

"Well, I looked at the catechism but I don't think I'm ready to be confirmed."

"I hope someday you will be."

"I have a headache that won't go away."

"You deserve one."

"You're absolutely right." She rubbed her temples.

"Why do you do it after all you've been through?" I could not help but ask.

"I don't always know why. Maybe because I have to be

such a tight-ass all the time. Same thing with a lot of the agents. We run and lift and do everything right. Then we blow it off on Friday night."

"Well, at least you were in a safe place to do that this time."

"Don't you ever lose control?" She met my eyes. "Because I've never seen it."

"I've never wanted you to see it," I said. "That's all you ever saw with your mother, and you've needed someone to feel safe with."

"But you didn't answer my question." She held my gaze.

"What? Have I ever been drunk?"

She nodded.

"It isn't something to be proud of, and I'm going to bed." I got up.

"More than once?" Her voice followed me as I walked off.

I stopped in the doorway and faced her. "Lucy, throughout my long, hard life there isn't much I haven't done. And I have never judged you for anything you've done. I've only worried when I thought your behavior placed you in harm's way." I spoke in understatements yet again.

"Are you worried about me now?"

I smiled a little. "I will worry about you for the rest of my life."

I went to my room and shut the door. I placed my Browning by my bed, and took a Benadryl because otherwise I would not sleep the few hours that were left. When I awakened at dawn, I was sitting up with the lamp on, the latest *Journal of the American Bar Association* still in my lap. I got up and walked out into the hall, where I was surprised to find Lucy's door open, her bed unmade. She was not in the gathering room on the couch, and I hurried into the dining room at the front of the house. I stared out windows at an empty expanse of frosted brick pavers and grass, and it was obvious the Suburban had been gone for some time.

"Lucy," I muttered as if she could hear me. "Damn you, Lucy," I said.

10

I was ten minutes late for the staff meeting, which was unusual, but no one commented or seemed to care. The murder of Danny Webster was heavy in the air, as if tragedy might suddenly rain down on us all. My staff was slow-moving and stunned, no one thinking very clearly. After all these years, Rose had brought me coffee and had forgotten I drink it black.

The conference room, which had been recently refurbished, seemed very cozy with its deep blue carpet, long new table and dark paneling. But anatomical models on tables and the human skeleton beneath his plastic shroud were reminders of the hard realities discussed in here. Of course, there were no windows, and art consisted of portraits of previous chiefs, all of them men who stared sternly down at us from the walls.

Seated on either side of me this morning were my chief and assistant chief administrators, and the chief toxicologist from the Division of Forensic Science upstairs. Fielding, to my left, was eating plain yogurt with a plastic spoon, while next to him sat the assistant chief and the new fellow, who was a woman.

"I know you've heard the terrible news about Danny Webster," I somberly proceeded from the head of the table, where I always sat. "Needless to say, it is impossible to describe how a senseless death like this affects each one of us."

"Dr. Scarpetta," said the assistant chief, "is there anything new?"

"At the moment we know the following," I said, and I repeated all that I knew. "It appeared at the scene last night that he had at least one gunshot wound to the back of the head," I concluded.

"What about cartridge cases?" Fielding asked.

"Police recovered one in woods not too far from the street."

"So he was shot there at Sugar Bottom versus in or near the car."

"It does not appear he was shot inside or near the car," I said.

"Inside whose car?" asked the fellow, who had gone to medical school late in life and was far too serious.

"Inside my car. The Mercedes."

The fellow seemed very confused until I explained the scenario again. Then she made a rather salient comment. "Is there any possibility you were the intended victim?"

"Jesus," Fielding irritably said as he set down the yogurt cup. "You shouldn't even say something like that."

"Reality isn't always pleasant," said the fellow, who was

very smart and just as tedious. "I'm simply suggesting that if Dr. Scarpetta's car was parked outside a restaurant she has gone to numerous times before, maybe someone was waiting for her and got surprised. Or maybe someone was following and didn't know it wasn't her inside, since it was dark by the time Danny was on the road heading here."

"Let's move on to this morning's other cases," I said, as I took a sip of Rose's saccharine coffee whitened with nondairy creamer.

Fielding moved the call sheet in front of him and in his usual impatient Northern tone went down the list. In addition to Danny, there were three autopsies. One was a fire death, another a prisoner with a history of heart disease, and a seventy-year-old woman with a defibrillator and pacemaker.

"She has a history of depression, mostly over her heart problems," Fielding was saying, "and this morning at about three o'clock her husband heard her get out of bed. Apparently she went into the den and shot herself in the chest."

Possible views were of other poor souls who during the night had died from myocardial infarcts and wrecks in cars. I turned down an elderly woman who clearly was a victim of cancer, and an indigent man who had succumbed to his coronary disease. Finally, we pushed back chairs and I went downstairs. My staff was respectful of my space and did not question what I was going through. No one spoke in the elevator as I stared straight ahead at shut doors, and in the locker room we put on gowns and washed our hands in silence. I was pulling on shoe covers and gloves when Fielding got close to me and spoke in my ear.

"Why don't you let me take care of him." His eyes were earnest on mine.

"I'll handle it," I said. "But thank you."

"Dr. Scarpetta, don't put yourself through it, you know? I wasn't here the week he came in. I never met him."

"It's okay, Jack." I walked away.

This was not the first time I had autopsied a person I knew, and most police and even the other doctors did not always understand. They argued that the findings were more objective if someone else did the case, and this simply wasn't true as long as there were witnesses. Certainly, I had not known Danny intimately or for long, but he had worked for me, and in a way had died for me. I would give him the best that I had.

He was on a gurney parked next to table one, where I usually did my cases, and the sight of him this morning was worse and hit me with staggering force. He was cold and in full rigor, as if what had been human in him had given up during the night, after I had left him. Dried blood smeared his face, and his lips were parted as if he had tried to speak when life had fled from him. His eyes stared the slitted dull stare of the dead, and I saw his red brace and remembered him mopping the floor. I remembered his cheerfulness, and the sad look on his face when he talked about Ted Eddings and other young people suddenly gone.

"Jack." I motioned for Fielding.

He almost trotted to my side. "Yes, ma'am," he said.

"I'm going to take you up on your offer." I began labeling test tubes on a surgical cart. "I could use your help if you're sure you're up to it."

"What do you want me to do?"

"We'll do him together."

"Not a problem. You want me to scribe?"

"Let's photograph him as he is but let's cover the table with a sheet first," I said.

Danny's case number was ME–3096, which meant he was the thirtieth case of the new year in the central district of Virginia. After hours of refrigeration he was not cooperative, and when we lifted him onto the table, arms and legs loudly banged against stainless steel as if protesting what we were about to do. We removed dirty, bloody clothing. Arms resisted coming out of sleeves, and tight-fitting jeans were stubborn. I dipped my hands in pockets, and came up with twenty-seven cents in change, a Chap Stick and a ring of keys.

"That's weird," I said as we folded garments and placed them on top of the gurney covered by a disposable sheet. "What happened to my car key?"

"Was it one of those remote-control ones?"

"Right." Velcro ripped as I removed the knee brace.

"And obviously, it wasn't anywhere at the scene."

"We didn't find it. And since it wasn't in the ignition, I assumed Danny would have had it." I was pulling off thick athletic socks.

"Well, I guess the killer could have taken it, or it could have gotten lost."

I thought of the helicopter making a bigger mess, and I had heard that Marino had been on the news. He was shaking his fist and yelling for all the world to see, and I was there, too.

"Okay, he's got tattoos." Fielding picked up the clipboard.

Danny had a pair of dice inked into the top of his feet.

"Snake eyes," Fielding said. "Ouch, that must have hurt."

I found a faint scar from an appendectomy, and another old one on Danny's left knee that may have come from an accident when he was a child. On his right knee, scars from recent arthroscopic surgery were purple, the muscles in that leg showing minimal atrophy. I collected samples of his fingernails and hair, and at a glance saw nothing indicative of a struggle. I saw no reason to assume he had resisted whomever he had encountered outside the Hill Cafe when he had dropped his bag of leftovers.

"Let's turn him," I said.

Fielding held the legs while I gripped my hands under the arms. We got him on his belly and I used a lens and a strong light to examine the back of his head. Long dark hair was tangled with clotted blood and debris, and I palpated the scalp some more.

"I need to shave this here so I can be sure. But it looks like we've got a contact gunshot wound behind his right ear. Where are his films?"

"They should be ready." Fielding looked around.

"We need to reconstruct this."

"Shit." He helped me hold together what was a profound stellate wound that looked more like an exit, because it was so huge.

"It's definitely an entrance," I said as I used a scalpel blade to carefully shave that part of the scalp. "See, we've got a faint muzzle mark up here. Very faint. Right there." I traced it with a gloved bloody finger. "This is very destructive. Almost like a rifle."

"Forty-five?"

"A half-inch hole," I said almost to myself as I used a ruler. "Yes, that's definitely consistent with a forty-five."

I was removing the skull cap in pieces to look at the brain when the autopsy technician appeared and slapped films on a nearby light box. The bright white shape of the bullet was lodged in the frontal sinus, three inches from the top of the head.

"My God," I muttered as I stared at it.

"What the hell is that?" Fielding asked as both of us left the table to get closer.

The deformed bullet was big with sharp petals folded back like a claw.

"Hydra-Shok doesn't do that," my deputy chief said.

"No, it does not. This is some kind of special high-performance ammo."

"Maybe Starfire or Golden Sabre?"

"Like that, yes," I answered, and I had never seen this ammunition in the morgue. "But I'm thinking Black Talon because the cartridge case recovered isn't PMC or Remington. It's Winchester. And Winchester made Black Talon until it was taken off the market."

"Winchester makes Silvertip."

"This is definitely not Silvertip," I replied. "You ever seen a Black Talon?"

"Only in magazines."

"Black-coated, brass-jacketed with a notched hollow point

that blossoms like this. See the points." I showed him on the film. "Unbelievably destructive. It goes through you like a buzz saw. Great for law enforcement but a nightmare if in the wrong hands."

"Jesus," Fielding said, amazed. "It looks like a damn octopus."

I pulled off latex gloves and replaced them with ones made of a tightly woven cloth, for ammunition like Black Talon was dangerous in the ER and the morgue. It was a bigger threat than a needle stick, and I did not know if Danny had hepatitis or AIDS. I did not want to cut myself on the jagged metal that had killed him so his assailant could end up taking two lives instead of one.

Fielding put on a pair of blue Nitrile gloves, which were sturdier than latex, but not good enough.

"You can wear those for scribing," I said. "But that's it."

"That bad?"

"Yes," I said, plugging in the autopsy saw. "You wear those and handle this and you're going to get cut."

"This doesn't seem like a carjacking. This seems like someone who was very serious."

"Believe me," I raised my voice above the loud whine of the saw, "it doesn't get any more serious than this."

The story told by what lay beneath the scalp only got worse. The bullet had shattered the temporal, occipital, parietal and frontal bones of the skull. In fact, had it not lost its energy fragmenting the thick petrous ridge, the twisted claw would have exited, and we would have lost what was a very important piece of evidence. As for the brain, what the Black Talon had done to it was awful. The explosion of gas and shredding caused by copper and lead had plowed a terrible path through the miraculous matter that had made Danny who he was. I rinsed the bullet, then cleaned it thoroughly in a weak solution of Clorox, because body fluids can be infectious and are notorious for oxidizing metal evidence.

At almost noon, I double-bagged it in plastic envelopes and carried it upstairs to the firearms lab, where weapons of every sort were tagged and deposited on countertops, or wrapped in brown paper bags. There were knives to be examined for tool marks, submachine guns and even a sword. Henry Frost, who was new to Richmond but well known in his field, was staring into a computer screen.

"Has Marino been up here?" I asked him as I walked in.

Frost looked up, hazel eyes focusing, as if he had just arrived from some distant place where I had never been. "About two hours ago." He tapped several keys.

"Then he gave you the cartridge case." I moved beside his chair.

"I'm working on it now," he said. "The word is, this case is a number-one priority."

Frost, I guessed, was about my age and had been divorced at least twice. He was attractive and athletic, with well-proportioned features and short black hair. According to the typical legends people always claimed about their peers, he ran marathons, was an expert in whitewater rafting, and could shoot a fly off an elephant at a hundred paces. What I did know from personal observation was that he loved his trade better than any woman, and there was nothing he would rather talk about than guns.

"You've entered the forty-five?" I asked him.

"We don't know for a fact it's connected to the crime, do we?" He glanced at me.

"No," I said. "We don't know for a fact." I spotted a chair with wheels close by and pulled it over. "The cartridge case was found about ten feet from where we believe he was shot. In the woods. It's clean. It looks new. And I've got this." I dipped into a pocket of my lab coat and withdrew the envelope containing the Black Talon bullet.

"Wow," he said.

"Consistent with a Winchester forty-five?"

"Man alive. There is always a first time." He opened the envelope and was suddenly excited. "I'll measure lands and grooves and tell you in a minute whether it's a forty-five."

He moved before the comparison microscope and used the Air Gap method to fix the bullet to the stage, which meant he used wax so he didn't leave any marks on metal that weren't already there.

"Okay," he talked without looking up, "the rifling is to the left, and we've got six lands and grooves." He began measuring with micrometer jaws. "Land impressions are point oh-seven-four. Groove impressions are point one-five-three. I'm going to enter that into the GRC," he said, referring to the FBI's computerized General Rifling Characteristics. "Now let's determine the caliber," he spoke abstractedly as he typed.

While the computer raced through its databases, Frost checked the bullet with a vernier measuring device. Unsurprisingly, what he found was that the caliber of the Black Talon was .45, and then the GRC came back with a list of twelve brands of firearms that could have fired it. All, except Sig Sauer and several Colts, were military pistols.

"What about the cartridge case?" I said. "Do we know anything about it?"

"I've got it on live video but I haven't run it yet."

He returned to the chair where I had found him when I had first come in and began typing on a workstation connected by modem to an FBI firearms evidence imaging system called DRUGFIRE. The application was part of the massive Crime Analysis Information Network known as CAIN, which Lucy had developed, and the point was to link firearms-related crimes. Succinctly put, I wanted to know if the gun that had killed Danny might have killed or maimed before, especially since the type of ammunition hinted that the assailant was no novice.

The workstation was simple, with its 486 turbo PC connected to a video camera and comparison microscope that made it possible to capture images in real time and in color on a twenty-inch screen. Frost went into another menu and the video display was suddenly filled with a checkerboard of silvery disks representing other .45 cartridge cases, each with unique impressions. The breech face of the Winchester .45 connected to my case was on the top left-hand side, and I could see every mark made by breech block, firing pin, ejector or any other metal part of the gun that had fired the round into Danny's head.

"Yours had a big drag to the left." Frost showed me what looked like a tail coming out of the circular dent left by the firing pin. "And there's this other mark here, also to the left." He touched the screen with his finger.

"Ejector?" I said.

"Nope, I'd say that's from the firing pin bouncing back."

"Unusual?"

"Well, I'd just say it's unique to this weapon," he replied as he stared. "So we can run this if you want."

"Let's."

He pulled up another screen and entered the information he had, such as the hemispherical shape the firing pin had impressed in the soft metal of the primer, and the direction of twist and parallel striation of the microscopic characteristics of the breech face. We did not enter anything about the bullet I had recovered from Danny's brain, for we could not prove that the Black Talon and the cartridge case were related, no matter how much we might suspect it. The examination of those two items of evidence was really unrelated, for lands and grooves and firing pin impressions are as different as fingerprints and footwear. All one can hope is that the stories the witnesses tell are the same.

Amazingly, in this case they were. When Frost executed his search, we had to wait only a minute or two before DRUGFIRE let us know that it had several candidates that might match the small, nickel-plated cylinder found ten feet from Danny's blood.

"Let's see what we've got here." Frost talked to himself as he positioned the top of the list on his screen. "This is your front runner." He dragged his finger across the glass. "No contest. This one's way ahead of the pack."

"A Sig forty-five P220," I said, looking at him in astonishment. "The cartridge case is matching with a weapon versus another cartridge case?"

"Yes. Damn if it isn't. Je-sus Christ."

"Let me make sure I understand this." I could not believe what I was seeing. "You wouldn't have the characteristics of a firearm entered into DRUGFIRE unless that firearm had been turned in to a lab. By the police, for some reason."

"That's how it's done," Frost agreed as he began to print screens. "This Sig forty-five that's in the computer is coming up as the same one that fired the cartridge found near Danny Webster's body. That much we know right this second. What I've got to do is pull the actual cartridge case from the test fire done when we originally got the gun." He stood.

I did not move as I continued staring at the list in DRUGFIRE with its symbols and abbreviations that told us about this pistol. It left recoil and drag marks, or its fingerprints, on the cartridge cases of every round it spent. I thought of Ted Eddings's stiff body in the cold waters of the Elizabeth River. I thought of Danny dead near a tunnel that no longer led anywhere.

"Then this gun somehow got back out on the street," I said.

Frost pursed his lips as he opened file drawers. "It would appear that way. But I really don't know the details of why it was entered into the system to begin with." Still rooting around, he added, "I believe the police department that originally turned the weapon in to us was Henrico County. Let's see, where's CVA5471? We are seriously running out of room in this place."

"This was submitted last fall." I noted the date on the computer screen. "September twenty-ninth."

"Right. That should be the date the form was completed."

"Do you know why the police turned the gun in?"

"You'd have to call them," Frost said.

"Let's get Marino on it now."

"Good idea."

I called Marino's pager as Frost pulled a file folder. Inside was the usual clear plastic envelope that we used to store the thousands of cartridge cases and shotgun shells that came through Virginia's labs every year.

"Here we go," he said.

"You have any Sig P220s in here?" I got up, too.

"One. It should be on the rack with the other forty-five auto loads."

While he mounted his test-fire cartridge case on the microscope's stage, I walked into a room that was either a nightmare or a toy store, depending on your point of view. Walls were pegboards crowded with pistols, revolvers, and Tec-11s and Tec-9s. It was depressing to think how many deaths were represented by the weapons in this one cramped room, and how many of the cases had been mine. The Sig Sauer P220 was black, and looked so much like the nine-millimeter carried by Richmond police that at a glance I could not have told them apart. Of course, on close inspection, the .45 was somewhat bigger, and I suspected its muzzle mark might be different, too.

"Where's the ink pad?" I asked Frost as he leaned over the microscope, lining up both cartridge cases so he could physically compare them side by side.

"In my top desk drawer," he said as the telephone rang. "Towards the back."

I got out the small tin of fingerprint ink and unfolded a snowy clean cotton twill cloth, which I placed on a thin, soft plastic pad. Frost picked up the phone.

"Hey, Bud. We got a hit on DRUGFIRE," he said, and I knew he was talking to Marino. "Can you run something down?"

He proceeded to tell Marino what he knew. Then Frost said to me as he hung up, "He's going to check with Henrico even as we speak."

"Good," I abstractedly said as I pressed the pistol's barrel into the ink, and then onto the cloth.

"These are definitely distinctive," I said right off as I studied several blackened muzzle marks that clearly showed the combat pistol's front sight blade, recoil guide and shape of the slide.

"You think we could identify that specific type of pistol?" he asked, and he was peering into the microscope again.

"On a contact wound, theoretically, we could," I said. "The obvious problem is that a forty-five loaded with high-performance ammunition is so incredibly destructive, you aren't likely to find a good pattern, not on the head."

This had been true in Danny's case, even after I had conjured up my plastic surgery skills to reconstruct the entrance wound as best I could. But as I compared the cloth to diagrams and photographs I had made downstairs in the morgue, I found nothing inconsistent with a Sig P220 being the murder weapon. In fact, I thought I might have matched a sight mark protruding from the margin of the entrance.

"This is our confirmation," Frost said, adjusting the focus as he continued staring into the comparison microscope.

We both turned at the sound of someone running down the hall.

"You want to see?" he asked.

"Yes, I do," I said as yet another person ran past, keys jingling madly from a belt.

"What the hell?" Frost got up, frowning toward the door.

Voices had gotten louder outside in the hall, and now people were hurrying by, but going the other way. Frost and I stepped outside the lab at the same moment several security guards rushed past, heading for their station. Scientists in lab coats stood in doorways casting about. Everyone was asking everyone else what was going on, when suddenly the fire alarm hammered overhead and red lights in the ceiling flashed.

"What the hell is this, a fire drill?" Frost yelled.

"There isn't one scheduled." I held my hands over my ears as people ran.

"Does that mean there's a fire?" He looked stunned.

I glanced up at sprinkler heads in the ceilings, and said, "We've got to get out of here."

I ran downstairs and had just pushed through doors into the hall on my floor when a violent white storm of cool halon gas blasted from the ceiling. It sounded as if I were surrounded by huge cymbals being beaten madly with a million sticks as I dashed in and out of rooms. Fielding was gone, and every other office I checked had been evacuated so fast that drawers were left open, and slide displays and microscopes were on. Cool clouds rolled over me, and I had the surreal sensation I was flying through a hurricane in the middle of an air raid. I dashed into the library, the restrooms, and when I was satisfied that everyone was safely out, I ran down the hall and pushed my way out of the front doors. For a moment, I stood to catch my breath and let my heart slow down.

The procedure for alarms and drills was as rigidly structured as most routines in the state. I knew I would find my staff gathered on the second floor of the Monroe Tower parking deck across Franklin Street. By now, all Consolidated Lab employees should be in their designated spots, except for section chiefs and agency heads, and of those, it seemed, I was the last to leave, except for the director of general services, who was in charge of my building. He was briskly crossing the street in front of me, a hard hat tucked under his arm. When I called out to him, he turned around and squinted as if he did not know me at all.

"What in God's name is going on?" I asked as I caught up with him and we crossed to the sidewalk.

"What's going on is you better not have requested anything extra in your budget this year." He was an old man who was always well dressed and unpleasant. Today he was in a rage.

I stared at the building and saw no smoke as fire trucks screamed and blared several streets away.

"Some jackass tripped the damn deluge system, which doesn't stop until all the chemicals are dumped." He glared at me as if I were to blame. "I had the damn thing set on a delay to prevent this very thing."

"Which wasn't going to help if there was a chemical fire or explosion in a lab," I couldn't resist pointing out, because most of his decisions were about this bad. "You don't want a thirty-second delay when something like that happens."

"Well, something like that didn't happen. Do you have any idea how much this is going to cost?"

I thought of the paperwork on my desk and other important items flung far and wide and possibly damaged. "Why would anyone trip the system?" I asked.

"Look, at the moment I'm about as informed as you are."

"But thousands of gallons of chemicals have been dumped over all of my offices, and the morgue and the anatomical division." We climbed stairs, my frustration becoming harder to contain.

"You won't know it was even there." He rudely waved off the remark. "It disappears like a vapor."

"It's sprayed all over bodies we are autopsying, including several homicides. Let's hope a defense attorney never brings that up in court."

"What you'd better hope is that somehow we can pay for this. To refill those halon tanks, we're talking several hundred thousand dollars. That's what ought to make you stay awake at night."

The second level of the parking deck was crowded with hundreds of state employees on an unexpected break. Ordinarily, drills and false alarms were an invitation to play, and people were in good moods as long as the weather was nice. But no one was relaxed this day. It was cold and gray, and people were talking in excited voices. The director abruptly walked off to speak to one of his henchmen, and I began to look around. I had just spotted my staff when I felt a hand on my arm.

"Geez, what's the matter?" Marino asked when I jumped. "You got post-traumatic stress syndrome?"

"I'm sure I do," I said. "Were you in the building?"

"Nope, but not far away. I heard about your full fire alarm on the radio and thought I'd check it out."

He hitched up his police belt with all its heavy gear, his eyes roaming the crowd. "You mind telling me what the hell's going on? You finally have a case of spontaneous combustion?"

"I don't know exactly what's going on. But what I've been told is that someone apparently tripped a false alarm that set off the deluge system throughout the entire building. Why are you here?"

"I see Fielding way over there." Marino nodded. "And Rose. They're all together. You look cold as shit."

"You were just in the area?" I asked, because when he was evasive, I knew something was up.

"I could hear the damn alarm all the way on Broad Street," he said.

As if on cue, the awful clanging across the street suddenly stopped. I stepped closer to the parking deck wall and looked over the top of it as I worried more about what I would find when all of us were allowed to return to the building. Fire trucks rumbled loudly in parking lots, and firefighters in protective gear were entering through several different doors.

"When I saw what was going on," he added, "I figured you'd be up here. So I thought I'd check on you."

"You figured right," I said, and my fingernails had turned blue. "You know anything about this Henrico case, the forty-five cartridge case that seems to have been fired by the same Sig P220 that killed Danny?" I asked as I continued to lean against the cold concrete wall and stare out at the city.

"What makes you think I'd find anything out that fast?"

"Because everybody's scared of you."

"Yeah, well they sure as hell should be."

Marino moved closer to me. He leaned against the wall, only facing the other way, for he did not like having his back to people, and this had nothing to do with manners. He adjusted his belt again and crossed his arms at his chest. He avoided my eyes, and I could tell he was angry.

"On December eleventh," he said, "Henrico had a traffic stop at 64 and Mechanicsville Turnpike. As the Henrico officer approached the car, the subject got out and ran, and the officer pursued on foot. This was at night." He got out his cigarettes. "The foot pursuit crossed the county line into the city, eventually ending in Whitcomb Court." He fired his lighter. "No one's real sure what happened, but at some point during all this, the officer lost his gun."

It took a moment for me to remember that several years ago the Henrico County Police Department had switched from nine-millimeters to Sig Sauer P220 .45 caliber pistols.

"And that's the pistol in question?" I uneasily asked.

"Yup." He inhaled smoke. "You see, Henrico's got this policy. Every Sig gets entered into DRUGFIRE in the event this very thing happens."

"I didn't know that."

"Right. Cops lose their guns and have them stolen like anybody else. So it's not a bad thing to track them after they're gone, in case they're used in the commission of crimes."

"Then the gun that killed Danny is the one this Henrico officer lost," I wanted to make sure.

"It would appear that way."

"It was lost in the projects about a month ago," I went on. "And now it's been used for murder. It was used on Danny."

Marino turned toward me, flicking an ash. "At least it wasn't you in the car outside the Hill Cafe."

There was nothing I could say.

"That area of town ain't exactly far from Whitcomb Court and other bad neighborhoods," he said. "So we could be talking about a carjacking, after all."

"No." I still would not accept that. "My car wasn't taken."

"Something could have happened to make the squirrel change his mind," he said.

I did not respond.

"It could have been anything. A neighbor turns a light on. A siren sounds somewhere. Someone's burglar alarm accidentally goes off. Maybe he got spooked after shooting Danny and didn't finish what he started."

"He didn't have to shoot him." I watched traffic slowly rolling past on the street below. "He could have just stolen my Mercedes outside the cafe. Why drive him off and walk him down the hill into the woods?" My voice got harder. "Why do all of that for a car you don't end up taking?"

"Things happen," he said again. "I don't know."

"What about the tow lot in Virginia Beach," I said. "Has anybody checked with them?"

"Danny picked up your ride around three-thirty, which is the time they told you it would be ready."

"What do you mean, the time they told me?"

"The time they told you when you called."

I looked at him and said, "I never called."

He flicked an ash. "They said you did."

"No." I shook my head. "Danny called. That was his job. He dealt with them and my office's answering service."

"Well, someone who claimed to be Dr. Scarpetta called. Maybe Lucy?"

"I seriously doubt she would say she was me. Was this person who called a woman?"

He hesitated. "Good question. But you probably should ask Lucy, just to make sure she didn't call."

Firefighters were emerging from the building, and I knew that soon we would be allowed to return to our offices. We would spend the rest of the day checking everything, speculating and complaining as we hoped that no more cases came in.

"The ammo's the thing that's really eating at me," Marino then said.

"Frost should be back in his lab within the hour," I said, but Marino did not seem to care.

"I'll call him. I'm not going up there in all this mess."

I could tell he did not want to leave me and his mind was on more than this case.

"Something's troubling you," I said.

"Yeah, Doc. Something always is."

"What this time?"

He got out his pack of Marlboros again, and I thought of my mother, whose constant companion now was an oxygen tank, because she once had been as bad as him.

"Don't look at me like that," he warned as he fished for his lighter again.

"I don't want you to kill yourself. And today you seem to be really trying."

"We're all going to die."

"Attention," blared a fire truck's P.A. system. "This is the Richmond Fire Department. The emergency has ended. You may reenter the building," sounded the mechanical broadcast with its jarring repetitive beeps and monotonous tones. "Attention. The emergency has ended. You may reenter the building . . ."

"Me," Marino went on, unmindful of the commotion, "I want to croak while I'm drinking beer, eating nachos with chili and sour cream, smoking, downing shots of Jack Black and watching the game."

"You may as well have sex while you're at it." I did not smile, for I found nothing amusing about his health risks.

"Doris cured me of sex." Marino was serious, too, as he referred to the woman he had been married to most of his life.

"When did you hear from her last?" I asked, as I realized she was probably the explanation for his mood.

He moved away from the wall and smoothed back his thinning hair. He tugged at his belt again, as if he hated the accoutrements of his profession and the layers of fat that had rudely inserted themselves into his life. I had seen photographs of him when he was a New York cop astride a motorcycle or horse, when he had been powerful and lean, with thick dark hair and tall leather boots. There had been a day when Doris must have found Pete Marino handsome.

"Last night. You know, she calls now and then. Mostly to talk about Rocky," he said of their son.

Marino was scanning state employees as they began to make their way toward the stairs. He stretched his fingers and arms, then took in a large volume of air. He rubbed the back of his neck as people exited the parking deck, most of them cold and cranky and trying to salvage what a false alarm had done to their day.

"What does she want from you?" I felt compelled to ask.

He looked around some more. "Well, it seems she's gotten married," he said. "That's the headline of the day."

I was quite taken aback. "Marino," I quietly said. "I'm so sorry."

"Her and the drone with the big car with leather seats. Don't you love it? One minute she leaves. Then she wants me back. Then Molly quits dating me. Then Doris gets married, just like that."

"I'm sorry," I said again.

"You better get back inside before you catch pneumonia," he said. "I got to get back to the precinct and call Wesley about what's going on. He's going to want to know about the gun, and to be honest with you"—he glanced over at me as we walked—"I know what the Bureau's going to say."

"They're going to say that Danny's death is random," I said.

"And I'm not so sure that ain't exactly right. It's looking

more like Danny might have been trying to score a little crack or something and ran into the wrong guy who happened to have found a policeman's gun."

"I still don't believe that," I said.

We crossed Franklin Street, and I looked down it to the north, where the imposing old Gothic red brick train station with its clock tower blocked my view of Church Hill. Danny had strayed very little from the area where he was supposed to have been last night when he was to deliver my car. I had found nothing that might hint he intended to do drugs. I had found no physical indication that he used drugs, for that matter. Of course, his toxicology reports were not in, yet, although I did know he had not been drinking.

"By the way," Marino said as he unlocked his Ford. "I stopped by the substation at Seventh and Duval, and you should get your Mercedes back this afternoon."

"They've already processed it?"

"Oh yeah. We did that last night and had everything in by the time the labs opened this morning 'cause I've made it clear we ain't shitting around with this case. Everything else moves to the back of the line."

"What did you find?" I asked, and the thought of my car and what had happened inside it was almost more than I could stand.

"Prints, we don't know whose. We got vacuumings. That's really it." He climbed in and left the door open. "Anyway, I'll make sure it's here so you have a way home."

I thanked him, but as I walked inside my building, I knew

I could not drive that car. I knew I could not drive it ever. I did not believe I could even unlock its doors or sit inside it again.

Cleta was mopping the lobby while the receptionist wiped down furniture with towels, and I tried explaining to them that this wasn't necessary. The point of an inert gas like halon, I patiently said, was that it did not damage paper or sensitive instruments.

"It evaporates and doesn't leave a residue," I promised. "You don't have to clean up. But paintings on the walls will need to be straightened, and it looks like Megan's desk is a terrible mess."

In the receptionist's area, requests for anatomical donations and a variety of other forms were scattered all over the floor.

"I still think some of it smells funny," Megan said.

"Yeah, magazines, that's what you smell, you goofball," said Cleta. "They always have a funny smell." She asked me, "What about the computers?"

"They shouldn't be affected in the least," I said. "What worries me more are the floors that you're getting wet. Let's go ahead and dry them off so nobody slips."

With a growing sense of hopelessness, I carefully walked over slippery tile while they mopped and wiped. As my office came in sight, I braced myself, then stopped inside my doorway. My secretary was already at work inside.

"Okay," I said to Rose. "How bad is it?"

"Not a problem except some of your paperwork's blown

to Oz. I've already straightened out your plants." She was an imperious woman old enough to retire, and she peered at me over reading glasses. "You've always wanted to keep your in and out baskets empty, well, now they are."

Wherever I looked, death certificates, call sheets and autopsy reports had blown about like autumn leaves. They were on the floor, in bookshelves and caught in the branches of my ficus tree.

"I also believe you shouldn't assume that just because you can't see something doesn't mean it's not a problem. So I think you ought to let this paperwork air out. I'm going to rig up a clothesline here with paper clips." She talked as she worked, and gray hair strayed from her French twist.

"I don't think we're going to need anything like that," I started the same old speech again. "Halon disappears when it dries."

"I noticed you never got your hard hat off the shelf."

"I didn't have time," I said.

"Too bad we don't have windows." Rose said this at least once a week.

"Really, all we need to do is pick things up," I said. "You're paranoid, every last one of you."

"You ever been gassed by this stuff before?"

"No," I said.

"Uh-huh," she said as she set a stack of towels nearby. "Then we can't be too careful."

I sat at my desk and opened the top drawer, where I pulled out several boxes of paper clips. Despair fluttered in my breast and I feared I would dissolve right there. My secretary knew me better than my mother, and she caught my every expression, but she did not stop working.

After a long silence, she said, "Dr. Scarpetta, why don't you go home? I'll take care of this."

"Rose, we will take care of this together," I stubbornly replied.

"I can't believe that stupid security guard."

"What security guard?" I stopped what I was doing and looked at her.

"The one who set off the system because he thought we were going to have some sort of radioactive meltdown upstairs."

I stared at her as she lifted a death certificate from the carpet. With paper clips, she hung it from the twine while I continued to rearrange the top of my desk.

"What in the world are you talking about?" I asked.

"That's all I know. They were discussing it on the parking deck." She pressed the small of her back and looked around. "I can't get over how fast this stuff dries. It's like something out of a science fiction movie." She hung another death certificate. "I think this is going to work out just fine."

I did not comment as I thought again of my car. I was honestly terrified of seeing it, and I covered my face with my hands. Rose did not quite know what to do because she had never seen me cry.

"Can I get you some coffee?" she asked.

I shook my head.

"This is like a big windstorm blew through. Tomorrow it will be like it never happened." She tried to make me feel better.

I was grateful when I heard her leave. She quietly shut both of my doors, and I leaned back in my chair and was spent. I picked up the phone and tried Marino's number, but he was not in, so I looked up McGeorge Mercedes and hoped that Walter wasn't off somewhere.

He wasn't.

"Walter? It's Dr. Scarpetta," I said with no preamble. "Can you please come get my car?" I faltered, "I guess I need to explain."

"No explanation necessary. How much was it damaged?" he asked, and he clearly had been following the news.

"For me it's totaled," I said. "For someone else, it's as good as new."

"I understand and I don't blame you," he said. "What do you want to do?"

"Can you trade it for something right now?"

"I got almost the identical car. But it's used."

"How used?"

"Barely. It belonged to my wife. An S-500, black with saddle interior."

"Can you have someone drive it to my parking space in back and we'll swap?"

"My dear, I'm on the way."

He arrived at half past five, when it was already dark out, which was a good time for a salesman to show a used car to someone as desperate as me. But, in truth, I had dealt with Walter for years and really would have bought the car sight unseen because I trusted him that much. He was a very distinguished-looking man with an immaculate mustache and close-cropped hair. He dressed better than most lawyers I knew, and wore a gold Medic Alert bracelet because he was allergic to bees.

"I'm really sorry about all this," he said as I cleaned out my trunk.

"I'm sorry about it, too." I made no attempt at being friendly or hiding my mood. "Here is one key. Consider the other one lost. And what I'd like to do, if you don't mind, is to drive off this minute. I don't want to see you get into my car. I just want to leave. We'll worry about the radio equipment later."

"I understand. We'll get into the details another time."

I did not care about them at all. At the moment I was not interested in the cost-effectiveness of what I had just done, or if it was true that the condition of this car was as good as the one I had traded away. I could have been driving a cement truck and that would have been fine. Pushing a button on the console, I locked the doors and tucked my pistol between the seats.

I drove south on Fourteenth Street and turned off on Canal toward the interstate I usually took home, and several exits later I got off and turned around. I wanted to follow the route I suspected Danny had taken last night, and if he were coming from Norfolk he would have taken 64 West. The easiest exit for him would have been the one for the Medical College of Virginia, for this would have brought him almost to the OCME. But I did not think this was what he had done.

By the time he reached Richmond, he would have been

thinking about food, and there was nothing much to interest him close to my office. Danny obviously would have known that since he had spent time with us before. I suspected he had exited at Fifth Street, as I was doing now, and had followed it to Broad. It was very dark as I passed construction and empty lots that would soon be Virginia's Biomedical Research Park, where my division would be moved one day.

Several police cruisers quietly floated past, and I stopped behind one of them at a traffic light next to the Marriott. I watched the officer ahead as he turned on an interior light and wrote something on a metal clipboard. He was very young with light blond hair, and he unhooked the microphone of his radio and began to speak. I could see his lips move as he gazed out at the dark shape of the mini-precinct on the corner. He got off the air and sipped from a 7-Eleven cup, and I knew he had not been a cop long, because he had not read his surroundings. He did not seem aware that he was being watched.

I moved on and turned left on Broad, past a Rite Aid and the old Miller & Rhoads department store that had permanently closed its doors as fewer people shopped downtown. The old city hall was a granite Gothic fortress on one side of the street, and then on the other was the campus of MCV, which may have been familiar to me, but not to Danny. I doubted he would have known about The Skull & Bones, where medical staff and students ate. I doubted he would have known where to park my car around here.

I believed he had done what anyone would do if he were relatively unfamiliar with a city and driving his boss's expensive car. He would have driven straight and stopped at the first decent place he found. That, quite literally, was the Hill Cafe. I circled the block, as he had to have done to park southbound, where we had found his bag of leftovers. Pulling over beneath that magnificent magnolia tree, I got out as I slid the pistol into a pocket of my coat. Instantly, the barking behind the chain-link fence began again. The dog sounded big and as if we had a history that had filled him with hate. Lights went on in the upstairs of his owner's small home.

Crossing the street, I entered the cafe, which was typically busy and loud. Daigo was mixing whiskey sours and did not notice me until I was pulling out a chair at the bar.

"You look like you need something strong tonight, honey," she said, dropping an orange slice and a cherry into each glass.

"I do but I'm working," I said, and the dog's barking had stopped.

"That's the problem with you and the Captain, both. You're always working." She caught a waiter's eye.

He came over and got the drinks, and Daigo started on the next order.

"Are you aware of the dog directly across the street from you? Across Twenty-eighth Street?" I asked in a quiet voice.

"You must mean Outlaw. Least that's what I call that son of a bitch dog. You have any idea how many customers that mangy thing's scared off from here?" She glanced at me as she angrily sliced a lime. "You know he's half shepherd and half wolf," she went on before I could reply. "He bother you or something?"

"It's just that his barking is very fierce and loud, and I'm wondering if he might have barked after Danny Webster left here last night. Especially since we are suspicious he was parked under the magnolia tree, which is in the dog's yard."

"Well, that damn dog barks all the time."

"Then you don't remember, not that I would expect you—"

She cut me off as she read an order and popped open a beer, "Course I remember. Like I said, he barks all the time. Wasn't no different with that poor boy. Outlaw barked up a storm when he went out. That damn dog barks at the wind."

"What about before Danny went out?" I asked.

She paused to think, then her eyes lit up. "Well, now that you mention it, it seems like the barking was pretty constant early in the evening. In fact, I made a comment about it, said it was driving me crazy and I had half a mind to call the damn thing's owner."

"What about other customers?" I asked. "Did many other people come in while Danny was in here?"

"No." Of that she was sure. "First of all, he came in early. Other than the usual barflies, there was no one here when he arrived. Fact is, I don't remember anybody coming in to eat until at least seven. And by then he'd already left."

"And how long did the dog bark after he left?"

"On and off the rest of the night, like he always does."

"On and off but not solidly."

"No one would take that all night. Not solidly." She eyed me shrewdly. "Now if you're wondering if that dog was barking because somebody was out there waiting for that boy"—she pointed her knife at me—"I don't think so. The kind of riffraff that would show up here is going to run like hell when that dog starts in. That's why they have him. Those people over there." She pointed with her knife again.

I thought again of the stolen Sig used to shoot Danny, and of where the officer had lost it, and I knew exactly what Daigo meant. The average street criminal would be afraid of a big, loud dog and the attention its barking might bring. I thanked her and walked back outside. For a moment I stood on the sidewalk and surveyed smudges of gas lamps set far apart along narrow, dark streets. Spaces between buildings and homes were thick with shadows, and anyone could wait in them and not be seen.

I looked across at my new car, and the small yard beyond it where the dog lay in wait. He was silent just now, and I walked north on the sidewalk for several yards to see what he might do. But he did not seem interested until I neared his yard. Then I heard the low, evil growling that raised the hair on the back of my neck. By the time I was unlocking my car door, he was on his hind legs, barking and shaking the fence.

"You're just guarding your turf, aren't you, boy?" I said. "I wish you could tell me what you saw last night."

I looked at the small house as an upstairs window suddenly slid up.

"Bozo, shut up!" yelled a fat man with tousled hair. "Shut up, you stupid mutt!" The window slammed shut.

"All right, Bozo," I said to the dog who was not really

called Outlaw, unfortunately for him. "I'm leaving you alone now." I looked around one last time and got into my car.

The drive from Daigo's restaurant to the restored area on Franklin where police had found my former car took less than three minutes if one were driving the posted speed. I turned around at the hill leading to Sugar Bottom, for to drive down there, especially in a Mercedes, was out of the question. That thought led to another.

I wondered why the assailant would have chosen to remain on foot in a restored area with a Neighborhood Watch program as widely publicized as the one here. Church Hill published its own newsletter, and residents looked out their windows and did not hesitate to call the cops, especially after shots had been fired. It seemed it might have been safer to have casually returned to my car and driven a safe distance away.

Yet the killer did not do this, and I wondered if he knew this area's landmarks but not the culture because he really was not from here. I wondered if he had not taken my car because his own was parked nearby and mine was of no interest. He didn't need it for money or to get away. That theory made sense if Danny had been followed instead of happened upon. While he was eating dinner, his assailant could have parked, then returned to the cafe on foot and waited in the dark near the Mercedes while the dog barked.

I was passing my building on Franklin when my pager vibrated against my side. I slipped it off and turned on its light so I could see. I had neither radio nor phone yet, and made a quick decision to turn into the OCME back parking lot. Letting myself in through a side door, I entered our security code, walked into the morgue and took the elevator upstairs. Traces of the day's false alarm had vanished, but Rose's death certificates suspended in air were an eerie display. Sitting behind my desk, I returned Marino's page.

"Where the hell are you?" he said right off.

"The office," I said, staring up at the clock.

"Well, I think that's the last place you ought to be right now. And I bet you're alone. You eaten yet?"

"What do you mean, this is the last place I should be right now?"

"Let's meet and I'll explain."

We agreed to go to the Linden Row Inn, which was downtown and private. I took my time because Marino lived on the other side of the river, but he was quick. When I arrived, he was sitting at a table before the fire in the parlor. Off duty, he was drinking a beer. The bartender was a quaint older man in a black bow tie, and he was carrying in a big bucket of ice while Pachelbel played.

"What is it?" I said to Marino as I sat. "What's happened now?"

He was dressed in a black golf shirt, and his belly strained against the knitted fabric and flowed roundly over the waistband of his jeans. The ashtray was already littered with cigarette butts, and I suspected the beer he was drinking wasn't his first or last.

"Would you like to hear the story of your false alarm this afternoon, or has someone gotten to you first?" He lifted the mug to his lips.

"No one has gotten to me about much of anything.

Although I've heard a rumor about some radioactivity scare," I said as the bartender appeared with fruit and cheese. "Pellegrino with lemon, please," I ordered.

"Apparently, it's more than a rumor," Marino said.

"What?" I gave him a frown. "And why would you know more about what's going on inside my building than I do?"

"Because this radioactive situation has to do with evidence in a city homicide case." He took another swallow of beer. "Danny Webster's homicide, to be exact."

He allowed me a moment to grasp what he had just said, but my limits were unwilling to stretch.

"Are you implying that Danny's body was radioactive?" I asked as if he were crazy.

"No. But the debris we vacuumed from the inside of your car apparently is. And I'm telling you, the guys that did the processing are scared shitless, and I'm not happy about it either because I poked around inside your ride, too. That's one thing I got a big damn problem with like some people do with spiders and snakes. It's like these guys who got exposed to Agent Orange in Nam, and now they're dying of cancer."

The expression on my face now was incredulous. "You're talking about the front seat passenger's side of my black Mercedes?"

"Yeah, and if I were you, I wouldn't drive it anymore. How do you know that shit won't get to you over a long time?"

"I won't be driving that car anymore," I said. "Don't worry. But who told you the vacuumings were radioactive?"

"The lady who runs that SEM thing."

"The scanning electron microscope."

"Yeah. It picked up uranium, which set the Geiger counter off. Which I'm told has never happened before."

"I'm sure it hasn't."

"So next we have a panic on the part of security, which are right down the hall, as you know," he went on. "And this one guard makes the executive decision to evacuate the building. Only problem is, he forgets that when he breaks the glass on the little red box and yanks the handle, he's also going to set off the deluge system."

"To my knowledge," I said, "it's never been used. I could see how someone might forget. In fact, he might not even have known about it." I thought of the director of general services, and I knew what his attitude would be. "Good God. All this happened because of my car. In a sense, because of me."

"No, Doc." Marino met my eyes and his face was hard. "It all happened because some asshole killed Danny. How many times I got to tell you that?"

"I think I'd like a glass of wine."

"Quit blaming yourself. I know what you're doing. I know how you get."

I searched for the bartender, and the fire was beginning to feel too hot. Four people had sat nearby and they were talking loudly about the "enchanted garden" in the Inn's courtyard where Edgar Allan Poe used to play when he was a boy in Richmond.

"He wrote about it in one of his poems," a woman was saying.

"They say the crab cakes are good here."

"I don't like it when you get like this," Marino went on, leaning closer to me and pointing a finger. "Next thing I know you're doing things on your own, and me? I don't sleep."

The bartender saw me and made a quick detour in our direction. I changed my mind about Chardonnay and ordered Scotch as I took off my jacket and draped it over a chair. I was perspiring and uncomfortable in my skin.

"Give me one of your Marlboros," I said to Marino.

His lips parted as he stared at me, shocked.

"Please." I held out my hand.

"Oh no you don't." He was adamant.

"I'll make a deal with you. I'll smoke one and you'll smoke one and then both of us will quit."

He hesitated. "You ain't serious."

"The hell I'm not."

"I don't see anything in it for me."

"Except being alive. If it's not too late."

"Thank you. But no deal." Picking up his pack, he knocked out a cigarette for each of us, his lighter in hand.

"How long has it been?"

"I don't know. Maybe three years." The cigarette tasted bland, but holding it with my lips felt wonderful, as if lips had been created for such a fit.

The first hit cut my lungs like a blade, and I was instantly lightheaded. I felt as I had when I smoked my first Camel at the age of sixteen. Then nicotine enveloped my brain, just as it had back then, and the world spun more slowly and my thoughts coalesced.

"God, I have missed this," I mourned as I tapped an ash.

"So don't nag me anymore."

"Someone needs to."

"Hey, it's not like it's marijuana or something."

"I haven't smoked that. But if it wasn't illegal, maybe today I would."

"Shit. Now you're beginning to scare me."

I inhaled one last time and put the cigarette out while Marino watched me with a weird expression on his face. He always slightly panicked if I acted in a way he did not know.

"Listen." I got down to business. "I think Danny was followed last night, that his death isn't a random crime motivated by robbery, gay bashing or drugs. I think his killer waited for him, maybe as long as an hour, then confronted him as he returned to my car in the dark shadows near the magnolia tree on Twenty-eight Street. You know that dog, the one who lives right there? He barked the entire time Danny was inside the Hill Cafe, according to Daigo."

Marino regarded me in silence for a moment. "See, that's what I was just saying. You went there tonight."

"Yes, I did."

His jaw muscles bunched as he looked away. "That's exactly what I mean."

"Daigo remembers the dog barking nonstop."

He said nothing.

"I was there earlier and the dog doesn't bark unless you get close to his property. Then he goes berserk. Do you understand what I'm saying?"

His eyes came back to me. "Who's going to hang out there for an hour when a dog's acting like that? Come on, Doc."

"Not your average killer," I answered as my drink appeared. "That's my point."

I waited until the bartender served us, and after he was gone from our table I said, "I think Danny may have been a professional hit."

"Okay." He drained his beer. "Why? What the hell did that kid know? Unless he was into drugs or some type of organized crime."

"What he was into was Tidewater," I said. "He lived there. He worked in my office there. He was at least peripherally involved in the Eddings case, and we know whoever killed Eddings was very sophisticated. That, too, was premeditated and carefully planned."

Marino was thoughtfully rubbing his face. "So you're convinced there's a connection."

"I think nobody wanted us to know there was. I think whoever is behind this assumed he would look like a carjacking gone bad or some other street crime."

"Yeah, and that's what everybody still thinks."

"Not everybody." I held his eyes. "Absolutely, not everybody."

"And you're convinced Danny was the intended victim, saying this was a professional hit."

"It could have been me. It could have been him to scare me," I said. "We may never know."

"You got tox yet on Eddings?" He motioned for another round.

"You know what today was like. Hopefully, I'll know something tomorrow. Tell me what's going on with Chesapeake."

He shrugged. "Don't got a clue."

"How can you not have a clue?" I impatiently said. "They must have three hundred officers. Isn't anybody working on Ted Eddings's death?"

"Doesn't matter if they have three thousand officers. All you need is one division screwed up, and in this instance it's homicide. So that's a barricade we can't get around because Detective Roche is still on the case."

"I don't understand it," I said.

"Yeah, well, he's still on your case, too."

I didn't listen for he wasn't worth my time.

"I'd watch my back, if I were you." He met my eyes. "I wouldn't take it lightly." He paused. "You know how cops talk, so I hear things. And there's a rumor being spread out there that you hit on Roche, and his chief's going to try to get the governor to fire you."

"People can gossip about whatever they like," I impatiently said.

"Well, part of the problem is they look at him and how young he is, and some people don't have a hard time imagining that you might be attracted." He hesitated, and I could tell he despised Roche and wanted to maim him at the very least. "I hate to tell you," Marino added, "but you'd be a whole lot better off if he wasn't good-looking."

"Harassment is not about how people look, Marino. But he has no case, and I'm not worried about it."

"Point is, he wants to hurt you, Doc, and he's already

trying hard. One way or another he's going to screw you, if he can."

"He can wait in line with all the other people who want to."

"The person who called the tow lot in Virginia Beach and said they was you was a man." He stared at me. "Just so you know."

"Danny wouldn't have done that," was all I could say.

"I wouldn't think so. But maybe Roche would," Marino replied.

"What are you doing tomorrow?"

He sighed. "I don't have time to tell you."

"We may need to make a trip to Charlottesville."

"What for?" He frowned. "Don't tell me Lucy's still acting screwy."

"That's not why we need to go. But maybe we'll see her, too," I said.

11

The next morning, I made evidence rounds, and my first stop was the Scanning Electron Microscopy lab where I found forensic scientist Betsy Eckles sputter-coating a square of tire rubber. She was sitting with her back to me, and I watched her mount the sample on a platform, which would next go into a vacuum chamber of glass so it could be coated by atomic particles of gold. I noted the cut in the center of the rubber, and thought it looked familiar, but couldn't be sure.

"Good morning," I said.

She turned around from her intimidating console of pressure gauges, dials, and digital microscopes that built images in pixels instead of lines on video screens. Graying and trim in a long lab coat, she seemed more harried than usual this Thursday.

"Oh, good morning, Dr. Scarpetta," she said as she placed the sample of punctured rubber into the chamber.

"Slashed tires?" I asked.

"Firearms asked me to coat the sample. They said it had to be done right now. Don't ask me why."

She was not happy about it in the least, for this was an unusual response to what was generally not considered a serious crime. I did not understand why it would be a priority today when labs were backed up to the moon, but this was not why I was here.

"I came to talk to you about the uranium," I said.

"That's the first time I've ever found anything like that." She was opening a plastic envelope. "We're talking twenty-two years."

"We need to know which isotope of uranium we're dealing with," I said.

"I agree, and since this has never come up before, I'm not sure where to do that. But I can't do it here."

Using double sticky tape, she began mounting what looked like particles of dirt on a stub that would go into a storage vial. She got vacuumings every day and was never caught up.

"Where is the radioactive sample now?" I asked.

"Right where I left it. I haven't opened that chamber back up and don't think I want to."

"May I see what we've got?"

"Absolutely."

She moved to another digitalized scope, turned on the monitor, and it filled with a black universe scattered with stars of different sizes and shapes. Some were a very bright white while others were dim, and all were invisible to the unaided eye.

"I'm zooming it up to three thousand," she said as she turned dials. "You want it higher?"

"I think this will do the trick," I replied.

We stared at what could have been a scene from inside an observatory. Metal spheres looked like three-dimensional planets surrounded by smaller moons and stars.

"That's what came out of your car," she let me know. "The bright particles are uranium. Duller ones are iron oxide, like you find in soil. Plus there's aluminum, which is used in just about everything these days. And silicon, or sand."

"Very typical for what someone might have on the bottom of his shoes," I said. "Except for the uranium."

"And there's something else I'll point out," she went on. "The uranium has two shapes. The lobed or spherical, which resulted from some process in which the uranium was molten. But here." She pointed. "We have irregular shapes with sharp edges, meaning these came from a process involving a machine."

"CP&L would use uranium for their nuclear power plants." I referred to Commonwealth Power & Light, which supplied electricity for all of Virginia and some areas of North Carolina.

"Yes, they would."

"Any other business around here that might?" I asked.

She thought for a minute. "There are no mines around here or processing plants. Well, there's the reactor at UVA, but I think that's mainly for teaching."

I continued to stare at the small storm of radioactive material that had been tracked into my car by whoever had killed Danny. I thought of the Black Talon bullet with its savage claws, and the weird phone call I had gotten in Sandbridge which was followed by someone climbing over my wall. I believed Eddings was somehow the common link, and that was because of his interest in the New Zionists.

"Look," I said to Eckles, "just because a Geiger counter's gone off doesn't mean the radioactivity is harmful. And, in fact, uranium isn't harmful."

"The problem is we don't have a precedent for something like this," she said.

I patiently explained, "It's very simple. This material is evidence in a homicide investigation. I am the medical examiner in that case, and it is Captain Marino's jurisdiction. What you need to do is receipt this vacuuming to Marino and me. We will drive it to UVA and have the nuclear physicist there determine which isotope it is."

Of course, this could not be accomplished without a telephone conference that included the director of the Bureau of Forensic Science, along with the health commissioner, who was my direct boss. They worried about a possible conflict of interest because the uranium had been found in my car, and, of course, Danny had worked for me. When I pointed out that I was not a suspect in the case, they were appeased, and in the end, relieved to have this radioactive sample taken off their hands.

I returned to the SEM lab and Eckles opened that frightful chamber while I slipped on cotton gloves. Carefully, I removed the sticky tape from its stub and tucked it inside a plastic bag, which I sealed and labeled. Before I left her floor, I stopped by Firearms, where Frost was seated before a comparison microscope, examining an old military bayonet on top of a stage. I asked him about the punctured rubber he was having sputter-coated with gold, because I had a feeling.

"We've got a possible suspect in your tire-slashing case," he said, adjusting the focus as he moved the blade.

"This bayonet?" I knew the answer before I asked.

"That's right. It was just turned in this morning."

"By whom?" I said as my suspicions grew.

He looked at a folded paper bag on a nearby table. I saw the case number and date, and the last name "Roche."

"Chesapeake," Frost replied.

"Do you know anything about where it came from?" I felt enraged.

"The trunk of a car. That's all I was told. Apparently, there's a hellfire rush on it for some reason."

I went upstairs to Toxicology because it was a last round I certainly needed to make. But my mood was bad, and I was not cheered when I finally found someone home who could confirm what my nose had told me in the Norfolk morgue. Dr. Rathbone was a big, older man whose hair was still very black. I found him at his desk signing lab reports.

"I just called you." He looked up at me. "How was your New Year?"

"It was new and different. How about you?"

"I got a son in Utah, so we were there. I swear I'd move if I could find a job, but I reckon Mormons don't have much use for my trade."

"I think your trade is good anywhere," I said. "And I

assume you've got results on the Eddings case," I added as I thought of the bayonet.

"The concentration of cyanide in his blood sample is point five milligrams per liter, which is lethal, as you know." He continued signing his name.

"What about the hookah's intake valve and tubes and so on?"

"Inconclusive."

I was not surprised, nor did it really matter since there was now no doubt that Eddings had been poisoned with cyanide gas, his manner of death unequivocally a homicide. I knew the prosecutor in Chesapeake and stopped by my office long enough to give her a call so she could encourage the police to do the right thing.

"You shouldn't have to ring me up for that," she said.

"You're right, I shouldn't."

"Don't give it another thought." She sounded angry. "What a bunch of idiots. Has the FBI gotten into this one at all?"

"Chesapeake doesn't need their help."

"Oh good. I guess they work homicidal cyanide gas poisonings in diving deaths all the time. I'll get back to you."

Hanging up, I collected coat and bag, and walked out into what was becoming a beautiful day. Marino's car was parked on the side of Franklin Street, and he was sitting inside with the engine running and his window down. As I headed toward him he opened his door and released the trunk.

"Where is it?" he said.

I held up a manila envelope, and he looked shocked.

"That's all you've got it in?" he exclaimed, eyes wide.

"I thought you'd at least put it in one of those metal paint cans."

"Don't be ridiculous," I said. "You could hold uranium in your bare hand and it wouldn't hurt you."

I shut the envelope inside the trunk.

"Then how come the Geiger counter went off?" he continued arguing as I climbed in. "It went off because the friggin" shit is radioactive, right?"

"Without a doubt, uranium is radioactive, but, by itself, not very, because it is decaying at such a slow rate. Plus, the sample in your trunk is extremely small."

"Look, a little radioactive is like a little pregnant or a little dead, in my opinion. And if you ain't worried about it how come you sold your Benz?"

"That's not why I sold it."

"I don't want to be rayed, if it's all the same to you," he irritably said.

"You're not going to be rayed."

But he railed on, "I can't believe you'd expose me and my car to uranium."

"Marino," I tried again, "a lot of my patients come into the morgue with very grim diseases like tuberculosis, hepatitis, meningitis, AIDS. And you've been present for their autopsies, and you've always been safe with me."

He drove fast along the interstate, cutting in and out of traffic.

"I should think that you would know by now that I would never deliberately place you in harm's way," I added.

"Deliberately is right. Maybe you're into something you

don't know about," he said. "When was the last time you had a radioactive case?"

"In the first place," I explained, "the case itself is not radioactive, only some microscopic debris associated with it is. And secondly, I do know about radioactivity. I know about X-rays, MRIs and isotopes like cobalt, iodine and technetium that are used to treat cancer. Physicians learn about a lot of things, including radiation sickness. Would you please slow down and choose a lane?"

I stared at him with growing alarm as he eased up on the accelerator. Sweat was beaded on top of his head and rolling down his temples, his face dark red. With jaw muscles clenched, he gripped the steering wheel hard, his breathing labored.

"Pull over," I demanded.

He did not respond.

"Marino, pull over. Now," I repeated in a tone he knew not to resist.

The shoulder was wide and paved on this stretch of 64, and without a word I got out and walked around to his side of the car. I motioned with my thumb for him to get out, and he did. The back of his uniform was soaking wet and I could see the outline of his undershirt through it.

"I think I must be getting the flu," he said.

I adjusted the seat and mirrors.

"I don't know what's wrong with me." He mopped his face with a handkerchief.

"You're having a panic attack," I said. "Take deep breaths and try to calm down. Bend over and touch your toes. Go limp, relax."

"Anybody sees you driving a city car, my ass is on report," he said, pulling the shoulder harness across his chest.

"Right now the city should be grateful that you're not driving anything," I said. "You shouldn't be operating any machinery at this moment. In fact, you should probably be sitting in a psychiatrist's office." I looked over at him and sensed his shame.

"I don't know what's wrong," he mumbled, staring out his window.

"Are you still upset about Doris?"

"I don't know if I ever told you about one of the last big fights she and I had before she left." He mopped his face again. "It was about these damn dishes she got at a yard sale. I mean, she'd been thinking about getting new dishes for a long time, right? And I come home from work one night and here's this big set of blaze orange dishes spread out on the dining-room table." He looked at me. "You ever heard of Fiesta Ware?"

"Vaguely."

"Well, there was something in the glaze of this particular line that I come to find out will set a Geiger counter off."

"It doesn't take much radioactivity to set a Geiger counter off." I made that point again.

"Well, there'd been stories written about the stuff, which had been taken off the market," he went on. "Doris wouldn't listen. She thought I was overreacting."

"And you probably were."

"Look, some people are phobic of all kinds of things. Me, it's radiation. You know how much I hate even being in the

X-ray room with you, and when I turn on the microwave, I leave the kitchen. So I packed up all the dishes and dumped them without telling her where."

He got quiet and wiped his face again. He cleared his throat several times.

Then he said, "A month later she left."

"Listen," I softened my voice, "I wouldn't want to eat off those dishes, either. Even though I know better. I understand fear, and fear isn't always rational."

"Yeah, Doc, well maybe in my case it is." He opened his window a crack. "I'm afraid of dying. Every morning I get up and think about it, if you want to know. Every day I think I'm going to stroke out or be told I got cancer. I dread going to bed because I'm afraid I'll die in my sleep." He paused, and it was with great difficulty that he added, "That's the real reason Molly stopped seeing me, if you want to know."

"That wasn't a very kind reason." What he just said hurt me.

"Well"—he got more uncomfortable—"she's a lot younger than me. And part of the way I feel these days is I don't want to do anything that might exert myself."

"Then you're afraid of having sex."

"Shit," he said, "why don't you just wave it like a flag."

"Marino, I'm a doctor. All I want to do is help, if I can."

"Molly said I made her feel rejected," he went on.

"And you probably did. How long have you had this problem?"

"I don't know, Thanksgiving."

"Did something happen?"

He hesitated again. "Well, you know I've been off my medicine."

"Which medication? Your adrenergic blocker or the finasteride? And no, I didn't know."

"Both."

"Now why would you do anything that foolish?"

"Because when I'm on it nothing works right," he blurted out. "I quit taking it when I started dating Molly. Then I started again around Thanksgiving after I had a checkup and my blood pressure was really up there and my prostate was getting bad again. It scared me."

"No woman is worth dying for," I said. "And what this is all about is depression, which you're a perfect candidate for, by the way."

"Yeah, it's depressing when you can't do it. You don't understand."

"Of course, I understand. It's depressing when your body fails you, when you get older and have other stressors in your life like change. And you've had a lot of change in the past few years."

"No, what's depressing," he said, and his voice was getting louder, "is when you can't get it up. And then sometimes you get it up and it won't go down. And you can't pee when you feel like you got to go, and other times you go when you don't feel like it. And then there's the whole problem of not being in the mood when you got a girlfriend almost young enough to be your daughter." He was glaring at me, veins standing out in his neck. "Yeah, I'm depressed. You're fucking right I am!"

"Please don't be angry with me."

He looked away, breathing hard.

"I want you to make appointments with your cardiologist and your urologist," I said.

"Uh-uh. No way." He shook his head. "This damn new healthcare plan I'm on has me assigned to a woman urologist. I can't go in there and tell a woman all this shit."

"Why not? You just told me."

He fell silent, staring out the window. He looked in the side mirror and said, "By the way, some drone in a gold Lexus has been behind us since Richmond."

I looked in the rearview mirror. The car was a newer model and the person driving was talking on the phone.

"Do you think we're being followed?" I asked.

"Hell if I know, but I wouldn't want to pay his damn phone bill."

We were close to Charlottesville, and the gentle landscape we had left had rounded into western hills that were winter-gray between evergreens. The air was colder and there was more snow, although the interstate was dry. I asked Marino if we could turn the scanner off because I was tired of hearing police chatter, and I took 29 North toward the University of Virginia.

For a while, the scenery was sheer rocky faces interspersed with trees spreading from woods to roadsides. Then we reached the outer limits of the campus, and blocks were crowded with places for pizzas and subs, convenience stores and filling stations. The university was still on Christmas break, but my niece was not the only person in the world to ignore that fact. At Scott Stadium, I turned on Maury Avenue, where students perched on benches and rode by on bikes, wearing backpacks or holding satchels that seemed full of work. There were plenty of cars.

"You ever been to a game here?" Marino had perked up.

"I can't say that I have."

"Now that ought to be against the law. You have a niece going here and you never once saw the Hoos? What'd you do when you came to town? I mean, what did you and Lucy do?"

In fact, we had done very little. Our time together generally was spent taking long walks on the campus or talking inside her room on the Lawn. Of course we had many dinners at restaurants like The Ivy and Boar's Head, and I had met her professors and even gone to class. But I did not see friends, what few of them she had. They, like the places where she met them, were not something shared with me.

I realized Marino was still talking.

"I'll never forget when I saw him play," he was saying.

"I'm sorry," I said.

"Can you imagine being seven feet tall? You know he lives in Richmond now."

"Let's see." I studied buildings we were passing. "We want the School of Engineering, which starts right here. But we need Mechanical, Aerospace and Nuclear Engineering."

I slowed down as a brick building with white trim came in sight, and then I saw the sign. Parking was not hard to find, but Dr. Alfred Matthews was. He had promised to meet me in his office at eleven-thirty, but apparently had forgotten.

"Then where the hell is he?" asked Marino, who was still worried about what was in his trunk.

"The reactor facility." I got back in the car.

"Oh great."

It was really called the High Energy Physics Lab, and was on top of a mountain that was also shared by an observatory. The university's nuclear reactor was a large silo made of brick. It was surrounded by woods that were fenced in, and Marino was acting phobic again.

"Come on. You'll find this interesting." I opened my door.

"I got no interest in this at all."

"Okay. Then you stay here and I'll go in."

"You won't get an argument out of me," he replied.

I retrieved the sample from the trunk, and at the facility's main entrance, I rang a bell and someone released a lock. Inside was a small lobby where I told a young man behind glass that I was looking for Dr. Matthews. A list was checked and I was informed that the head of the physics department, whom I knew only in a limited way, was this moment by the reactor's pool. The young man then picked up an in-house phone while sliding out a visitor's pass and a detector for radiation. I clipped them to my jacket, and he left his station to escort me through a heavy steel door beneath a red light sign that indicated the reactor was on.

The room was windowless with high tile walls, and every object I saw was marked with a bright yellow radioactive tag. At one end of the lighted pool, Cerenkov radiation caused the water to glow a fantastic blue as unstable atoms spontaneously disintegrated in the fuel assembly twenty feet down.

Dr. Matthews was conferring with a student who, I gathered as I heard them talk, was using cobalt instead of an autoclave to sterilize micropipettes used for in vitro fertilization.

"I thought you were coming tomorrow," the nuclear physicist said to me, a distressed expression on his face.

"No, it was today. But thank you for seeing me at all. I have the sample with me." I held up the envelope.

"Okay, George," he said to the young man. "Will you be all right?"

"Yes, sir. Thanks."

"Come on," Matthews said to me. "We'll take it down there now and get started. Do you know how much you've got here?"

"I don't know exactly."

"If we've got enough, we can do it while you wait."

Beyond a heavy door, we turned left and paused at a tall box that monitored the radiation of our hands and feet. We passed with bright green colors and went on to stairs that led to the neutron radiography lab, which was in a basement of machine shops and forklifts, and big black barrels containing low-level nuclear waste waiting to be shipped. There was emergency equipment at almost every turn, and a control room locked inside a cage. Most remote to all of this was the low background counting room. Built of thick windowless concrete, it was stocked with fifty-gallon canisters of liquid nitrogen, and germanium detectors and amplifiers, and bricks made of lead.

The process for identifying my sample was surprisingly simple. Matthews, wearing no special protection other than lab coat and gloves, placed the piece of sticky tape into a tube, which he then set inside a two-foot-long aluminum container housing the germanium crystal. Finally, he stacked lead bricks on every side to shield the sample from background radiation.

Activating the process required a simple computer command, and a counter on the canister began measuring radioactivity so it could tell us which isotope we had. This was all rather strange to see, for I was accustomed to arcane instruments like scanning electron microscopes and gas chromatographs. This detector, on the other hand, was a rather formless house of lead cooled by liquid nitrogen, and did not seem capable of intelligent thought.

"Now, if you'll just sign this evidence receipt," I said, "I'll be on my way."

"It could take an hour or two. It's hard to say," he answered.

He signed the form and I gave him a copy.

"I'll stop by after I check on Lucy."

"Come on, I'll escort you up to make sure you don't set anything off. How is she?" he asked as we passed detectors without a complaint. "Did she ever go on to MIT?"

"She did do an internship there last fall," I said. "In robotics. You know, she's back here. For at least a month."

"I didn't know. That's wonderful. Studying what?"

"Virtual reality, I think she said."

Matthews looked perplexed for a moment. "Didn't she take that when she was here?"

"I expect this is more advanced."

"I expect it would have to be." He smiled. "I wish I had at least one of her in every class."

Lucy had probably been the only non-physics major at UVA to take a course in nuclear design for fun. I walked outside, and Marino was leaning against the car, smoking.

"So what now?" he said, and he still looked glum.

"I thought I'd surprise my niece and take her to lunch. You're more than welcome to join us."

"I'm going to drop by the E"on station down the street and use the pay phone," he said. "I got some calls to make."

12

He drove me to the rotunda, brilliant white in sunlight and my favorite building Thomas Jefferson had designed. I followed old brick colonnaded walkways beneath ancient trees, where Federal pavilions formed two rows of privileged housing known as the Lawn.

Living here was an award for academic achievement, yet it might have been considered a dubious honor by some. Showers and toilets were located in another building in back, the sparsely furnished rooms not necessarily intended for comfort. Yet I had never heard Lucy complain, for she had truly loved her life at UVA.

She was staying on the West Lawn in Pavilion III, with its Corinthian capitals of Carrara marble that had been carved in Italy. Wooden shutters outside room 11 were drawn, the morning paper still on the mat, and I wondered, perplexed, if she had not gotten up yet. I rapped on the door several times and heard someone stirring.

"Who is it?" my niece's voice called out.

"It's me," I said.

There was a pause, then a surprised, "Aunt Kay?"

"Are you going to open the door?" My good mood was fading fast for she did not sound pleased.

"Uh, hold on a minute. I'm coming."

The door unlocked and opened.

"Hi," she said as she let me in.

"I hope I didn't wake you up." I handed her the newspaper.

"Oh, T.C. gets that," she said, referring to the friend who really belonged to this room. "She forgot to cancel it before she left for Germany. I never get around to reading it."

I entered an apartment not so different from where I had visited my niece last year. The space was small with bed and sink, and crowded bookcases. Heart of pine floors were bare, with no art on whitewashed walls except a single poster of Anthony Hopkins in *Shadowlands*. Lucy's technical pre-occupations had taken over tables, desk and even several chairs. Other equipment, like the fax machine and what looked like a small robot, was out cold on the floor.

Additional telephone lines had been installed, and these were connected to modems winking with green lights. But I did not get the impression that my niece was living here alone, for on the sink were two toothbrushes, and solution for contact lenses that she did not wear. Both sides of the twin bed were unmade, and on top of it was a briefcase I did not recognize, either.

"Here." She lifted a printer off a chair and put me close to the fire. "Sorry everything's such a mess." She wore a bright orange UVA sweatshirt and jeans, and her hair was wet. "I can heat up some water," she said, and she was very distracted.

"If you're offering tea, I accept," I said.

I watched her closely as she filled a pot with water and plugged it in. Nearby, on a dresser top, were FBI credentials, a pistol, and car keys. I spotted file folders and pieces of paper scribbled with notes, and I spotted unfamiliar clothing hanging inside the closet.

"Tell me about T.C.," I said.

Lucy opened a tea bag. "A German major. She's spending the next six weeks in Munich. So she said I could stay here."

"That was very nice of her. Would you like me to help you pack up her things or at least make room for yours?"

"You don't need to do any work at all right now."

I glanced toward the window, hearing someone.

"You still take your tea black?" Lucy said.

The fire crackled, smoking wood shifted, and I wasn't surprised when the door opened and another woman walked in. But I was not expecting Janet, and she was not expecting me.

"Dr. Scarpetta," she said in surprise as she glanced at Lucy. "How great of you to drop by."

She was carrying shower items, a baseball cap pulled over wet hair that was almost to her shoulders. Dressed in sweats and tennis shoes, she was lovely and healthy, and like Lucy, seemed even younger because she was on a university campus again.

"Please join us," Lucy said to her as she handed me a mug of tea.

"We were out running." Janet smiled. "Sorry about the hair. So what brings you here?" she asked as she sat on the floor.

"I need some help with a case," was all I said. "Are you taking this virtual reality course too?" I studied both of their faces.

"Right," Janet said. "Lucy and I are here together. As you may or may not know, I was transferred to the Washington Field Office late last year."

"Lucy mentioned it."

"I've been assigned to white-collar crime," she went on. "Especially anything that might be related to a violation of the IOC."

"Which is?" I asked.

It was Lucy who replied as she sat next to me, "Interception of Communication statute. We've got the only group in the country with experts who can handle these cases."

"Then the Bureau has sent both of you here for training because of this group." I tried to understand. "But I guess I don't see what virtual reality might have to do with hackers breaking into major databases," I added.

Janet was silent as she took off her cap and combed her hair, staring into the fire. I could tell she was very uncomfortable, and I wondered how much of it had to do with what had happened in Aspen over the holidays. My niece moved to the hearth and sat facing me.

"We're not here for a class, Aunt Kay," she said with quiet seriousness. "That's how it's supposed to look to everybody else. Now, I'm going to tell you this when I shouldn't, but it's too late for any more lies."

"You don't have to tell me," I said. "I understand."

"No." Her eyes were intense. "I want you to understand what's going on. And to give you a quick, dirty summary, last fall Commonwealth Power & Light began experiencing problems when what appeared to be a hacker started getting inside their computer system. The attempts were frequent—sometimes four or five times a day. But there was no success in identifying this individual until he left tracks in an audit log after accessing and printing customer billing information. We were called, and remotely we managed to trace the perpetrator to UVA."

"Then you haven't caught whoever it is," I said.

"No." It was Janet who spoke. "We interviewed the graduate student whose I.D. it was, but he definitely isn't the hacker. We have reasons to be very sure of that."

"Point is," said Lucy, "several other I.D.s have been stolen from students here since, and the perpetrator was also trying to access CP&L along with the university computer and one in Pittsburgh."

"Was?" I asked.

"Actually, he's been pretty quiet lately, which makes it harder for us," Janet said. "Mostly, we've been chasing him through the university computer."

"Right," Lucy said. "We haven't tracked him in CP&L's computer for almost a week. I figure because of the holidays."

"Why might someone be doing this?" I asked. "Do you have a theory?"

"A power trip, no pun intended," Janet simply said. "Maybe so he can turn lights on and off throughout Virginia and the Carolinas. Who knows?"

"But what we believe is that whoever's doing it is on campus, and is getting in via the Internet and another link called Telnet," Lucy said, adding confidently, "We'll get him."

"You mind if I ask why all the secrecy?" I said to my niece. "Could you not just tell me you were on a case you couldn't discuss?"

She hesitated before responding. "You're on the faculty here, Aunt Kay."

This was true, and I had not even thought of that. Though I was only a visiting professor in pathology and legal medicine, I decided Lucy's point was well taken, and I supposed I did not blame her for keeping this from me for yet another reason. She wanted her independence, especially in this place where for the duration of her undergraduate studies it had been well known that she was related to me.

I looked at her. "Is this why you left Richmond so abruptly the other night?"

"I got paged."

"By me," Janet said. "I was flying in from Aspen, got delayed, et cetera. Lucy picked me up at the airport and we came back here."

"And were there any other attempted break-ins over the holidays?"

"Some. The system is constantly being monitored," Lucy said. "We're not alone in this by any means. We've just been assigned an undercover post here so we can do some hands-on detective work."

"Why don't you walk me to the Rotunda." I got up, and so did they. "Marino should be back with the car." I hugged Janet and her hair smelled like lemon. "You take care and come see me more often," I said to her. "I consider you family. Lord knows it's about time I had some help in taking care of this one." I smiled as I put my arm around Lucy.

Outside in the sun, the afternoon was warm enough for only sweaters, and I wished I could stay longer. Lucy did not linger during our brief walk, and I could tell she was anxious about anyone seeing us together.

"It's just like the old days," I said lightly to hide my hurt.

"How's that?" she asked.

"Your ambivalence about being seen with me."

"That's not true. I used to be proud of it."

"And now you're not," I said with irony.

"Maybe I'd like you to feel proud to be seen with me," she said. "Instead of it always the other way. That's what I meant."

"I am proud of you and always have been, even when you were such a mess that sometimes I wanted to lock you in the basement."

"I believe that's called child abuse."

"No, the jury would vote for aunt abuse in your case. Trust me," I said. "And I'm glad you and Janet seem to be getting along. I'm glad she's back from Aspen and the two of you are together."

My niece stopped and looked at me, squinting in the sun. "Thanks for what you said to her. Right now, especially, that meant a lot."

"I spoke the truth, that's all," I said. "Maybe someday her family will speak it, too."

We were in sight of Marino's car, and he was sitting in it, as usual, and puffing away.

Lucy walked up to his door. "Hey, Pete," she said, "you need to wash your ride."

"No, I don't," he grumbled as he immediately tossed the cigarette and got out.

He looked around, and the sight of him hitching up his pants and inspecting his car because he could not help himself was too much. Lucy and I both laughed, and then he tried not to smile. In truth, he secretly enjoyed it when we teased. We bantered a little bit more, and then Lucy left as a late-model gold Lexus with tinted glass drove past. It was the same one we had seen earlier on the road, but the driver was obliterated by glare.

"This is beginning to get on my nerves." Marino's eyes followed the car.

"Maybe you should run the plate number," I stated the obvious.

"Oh, I already done that." He started the car and began backing. "DMV's down."

DMV was the Department of Motor Vehicles computer, and it was down a lot, it seemed. We headed back up to the reactor facility, and when we got there, Marino again refused to go inside. So I left him in the parking lot, and this time the young man in the control room behind glass told me I could enter unescorted.

"He's down in the basement," he said with eyes on his computer screen.

I found Matthews in the low background counting room again, sitting before a computer screen displaying a spectrum in black and white.

"Oh, hello," he said, when he realized I was beside him.

"Looks like you've had some luck," I said. "Although I'm not sure what I'm seeing. And I might be too early."

"No, no, you're not too early. These vertical lines here indicate the energies of the significant gamma rays detected. One line equals one energy. But most of the lines we're seeing here are for background radiation." He showed me on the screen. "You know, even the lead bricks don't get rid of all of that."

I sat next to him.

"I guess what I'm trying to show you, Dr. Scarpetta, is that the sample you brought in isn't giving off high-energy gamma rays when it decays. If you look here on this energy spectrum" —he was staring at the screen—"it looks like this characteristic gamma ray on the spectrum is for uranium two-thirty-five." He tapped a spike on the glass.

"Okay," I said. "And what does that mean?"

"That's the good stuff." He looked over at me.

"Such as is used in nuclear reactors," I said.

"Exactly. That's what we use to make fuel pellets or rods.

But as you probably know, only point three percent of uranium is two-thirty-five. The rest is depleted."

"Right. The rest is uranium two-thirty-eight," I said.

"And that's what we've got here."

"If it isn't giving off high-energy gamma rays," I said. "How can you tell that from this energy spectrum?"

"Because what the germanium crystal is detecting is uranium two-thirty-five. And since the percentage of it is so low, this indicates that the sample we're dealing with must be depleted uranium."

"It couldn't be spent fuel from a reactor," I thought out loud.

"No, it couldn't," he said. "There's no fission material mixed in with your sample. No strontium, cesium, iodine, barium. You would have already seen those with SEM."

"No isotopes like that came up," I agreed. "Only uranium and other nonessential elements that you might expect with soil tracked in on the bottom of someone's shoes."

I looked at peaks and valleys of what could have been a scary cardiogram while Matthews made notes.

"Would you like printouts of all of this?" he asked.

"Please. What is depleted uranium used for?"

"Generally, it's worthless." He hit several keys.

"If it didn't come from a nuclear power plant, then from where?"

"Most likely a facility that does isotopic separation."

"Such as Oak Ridge, Tennessee," I suggested.

"Well, they don't do that anymore. But they certainly did for decades, and they must have warehouses of uranium metal.

Now there also are plants in Portsmouth, Ohio, and Paducah, Kentucky."

"Dr. Matthews," I said. "It appears someone had depleted uranium metal on the bottom of his shoes and tracked it into a car. Can you give me any logical explanation as to how or why?"

"No." His expression was blank. "I don't think I can."

I thought of the jagged and spherical shapes the scanning electron microscope had revealed to me, and tried again. "Why would someone melt uranium two-thirty-eight? Why would they shape it with a machine?"

Still, he did not seem to have a clue.

"Is depleted uranium used for anything at all?" I then asked.

"In general, big industry doesn't use uranium metal," he answered. "Not even in nuclear power plants, because in those the fuel rods or pellets are uranium oxide, a ceramic."

"Then maybe I should ask what depleted uranium metal could, in theory, be used for," I restated.

"At one time there was some talk by the Defense Department about using it for armor plating on tanks. And it's been suggested that it could be used to make bullets or other types of projectiles. Let's see. I guess the only other thing we know that it's good for is shielding radioactive material."

"What sort of radioactive material?" I said as my adrenal glands woke up. "Spent fuel assemblies, for example?"

"That would be the idea if we knew how to get rid of nuclear waste in this country," he wryly said. "You see, if we could remove it to be buried a thousand feet beneath Yucca

Mountain, Nevada, for example, then U-238 could be used to line the casks needed for transport."

"In other words," I said, "if the spent assemblies are to be removed from a nuclear power plant, they will have to be put in something, and depleted uranium is a better shield than lead."

He said this was precisely what he meant, and receipted my sample back to me, because it was evidence and one day could end up in court. So I could not leave it here, even though I knew how Marino would feel when I returned it to his trunk. I found him walking around, his sunglasses on.

"What now?" he said.

"Please pop the trunk."

He reached inside the car and pulled a release as he said, "I'm telling you right now, that it ain't going in no evidence locker in my precinct or at HQ. No one's going to cooperate, even if I wanted them to."

"It has to be stored," I simply said. "There's a twelve-pack of beer in here."

"So I didn't want to have to bother stopping for it later."

"One of these days you're going to get in trouble." I shut the trunk of his city-owned police car.

"Well, how about you store the uranium at your office," he said.

"Fine." I got in. "I can do that."

"So, how was it?" he asked, starting the engine.

I gave him a summary, leaving out as much scientific detail as I could.

"You're telling me that someone tracked nuclear waste into your Benz?" he asked, baffled.

"That's the way it appears. I need to stop by and talk to Lucy again."

"Why? What's she got to do with it?"

"I don't know that she does," I said as he drove down the mountain. "I have a rather wild idea."

"I hate it when you get those."

Janet looked worried when I was back at their door, this time with Marino.

"Is everything all right?" she asked, letting us in.

"I think I need your help," I said. "Strike that. What I mean is that both of us do."

Lucy was sitting on the bed, a notebook open in her lap. She looked at Marino. "Fire away. But we charge for consultations."

He sat by the fire, while I took a chair close to him.

"This person who has been getting into CP&L's computer," I said. "Do we know what else he has gotten into besides customer billing?"

"I can't say we know everything," Lucy replied. "But the billing is a certainty, and customer info is in general."

"Meaning what?" Marino asked.

"Meaning that the information about customers includes billing addresses, phone numbers, special services, energy-use averaging, and some customers are part of a stock-sharing program—"

"Let's talk about stock sharing," I stopped her. "I'm involved in that program. Part of my check every month buys stock in CP&L, and therefore the company has some financial information on me, including my bank account and social security numbers." I paused, thinking. "Could that sort of thing be important to this hacker?"

"Theoretically, it could," Lucy said. "Because you've got to remember that a huge database like CP&L's isn't going to reside in any one place. They've got other systems with gateways leading to them, which might explain the hacker's interest in the mainframe in Pittsburgh."

"Maybe it explains something to you," said Marino, who always got impatient with Lucy's computer talk. "But it don't explain shit to me."

"If you think of the gateways as major corridors on a map—like I-95, for example," she patiently said, "then if you go from one to the other, theoretically you could start cruising the global web. You could pretty much get into anything you want."

"Like what?" he asked. "Give me an example that I can relate to."

She rested the notebook in her lap and shrugged. "If I broke into the Pittsburgh computer, my next stop would be at AT&T."

"That computer's a gateway into the telephone system?" I asked.

"It's one of them. And that's one of the suspicions Jan and I have been working on—that this hacker's trying to figure out ways to steal electricity and phone time."

"Of course, at the moment this is just a theory," Janet said. "So far, nothing has come up that might tell us what the hacker's motive is. But from the FBI's perspective, the break-ins are against the law. That's what counts."

"Do you know which CP&L customer records were accessed?" I asked.

"We know that this person has access to all customers," Lucy replied. "And we're talking millions. But as for individual records that we know were looked at in more detail, those were few. And we have them."

"I'm wondering if I could see them," I said.

Lucy and Janet paused.

"What for?" Marino asked as he continued to stare at me. "What are you getting at, Doc?"

"I'm getting at that uranium fuels nuclear power plants, and CP&L has two nuclear power plants in Virginia and one in Delaware. Their mainframe is being broken into. Ted Eddings called my office with radioactivity questions. In his home PC he had all sorts of files on North Korea and suspicions that they were attempting to manufacture weapons-grade plutonium in a nuclear reactor."

"And the minute we start looking into anything in Sandbridge we get a prowler," Lucy added. "Then someone slashes our tires and Detective Roche threatens you. Now Danny Webster comes to Richmond and ends up dead and it appears that whoever killed him tracked uranium into your car." She looked at me. "Tell me what you need to see."

I did not require a complete customer list, for that would be virtually all of Virginia, including my office and me. But I was interested in any detailed billing records that were accessed, and what I was shown was curious but short. Out of five names, I recognized all but one.

"Does anybody know who Joshua Hayes is? He has a post office box in Suffolk," I said.

"All we know so far," said Janet, "is that he's a farmer."

"All right," I moved on. "We've got Brett West, who is an executive at CP&L. I can't remember his title." I looked at the printout.

"Executive Vice President in charge of Operations," Janet said.

"He lives in one of those brick mansions near you, Doc," Marino said. "In Windsor Farms."

"He used to. If you study his billing address," Janet pointed out, "you'll see it changed as of last October. It appears he moved to Williamsburg."

There were two other CP&L executives whose records had been perused by whoever was illegally prowling the Internet. One was the CEO, the other the president. But it was the identity of the fifth electronic victim that truly frightened me.

"Captain Green." I stared at Marino, stunned.

His face was vague. "I got no idea who you're talking about."

"He was present at the Inactive Ship Yard when I got Eddings's body out of the water," I said. "He's with Navy Investigative Services."

"I hear you." Marino's face darkened, and Lucy and Janet's IOC case dramatically shifted before their eyes.

"Maybe it's not surprising this person breaking in would

be curious about the highest-ranking officials of the corporation he's violating, but I don't see how NIS fits in," Janet said.

"I'm not sure I want to know how it might," I said. "But if what Lucy has to say about gateways is relevant, then maybe the final stop for this hacker is certain people's telephone records."

"Why?" Marino asked.

"To see who they were calling." I paused. "The sort of information a reporter might be interested in, for example."

Getting up from the chair, I began to pace about as fear tingled along my nerves. I thought of Eddings poisoned in his boat, of Black Talons and uranium, and I remembered that Joel Hand's farm was in Tidewater somewhere.

"This person named Dwain Shapiro who owned the bible you found in Eddings's house," I said to Marino. "He allegedly died in a carjacking. Do we have any further information on that?"

"Right now we don't."

"Danny's death could have been signed out as the same sort of thing," I said.

"Or yours could have. Especially because of the type of car. If this were a hit, maybe the assailant didn't know that Dr. Scarpetta isn't a man," Janet said. "Maybe the gunman was cocky and only knew what you would be driving."

I stopped by the hearth as she went on.

"Or maybe the killer didn't figure out Danny wasn't you until it was too late. Then Danny had to be dealt with."

"Why me?" I said. "What would be the motive?"

It was Lucy who replied. "Obviously, they think you know something."

"They?"

"Maybe the New Zionists. The same reason they killed Ted Eddings," she said. "They thought he knew something or was going to expose something."

I looked at my niece and Janet as my anxieties got more inflamed.

"For God's sake," I said to them with feeling, "don't do anything more on this until you talk to Benton or someone. Damn! I don't want them thinking you know something, too."

But I knew Lucy, at least, would not listen. She would be on her keyboard with renewed vigor the moment I shut the door.

"Janet?" I held the gaze of my only hope for their playing it safe. "Your hacker is very possibly connected to people being murdered."

"Dr. Scarpetta," she said. "I understand."

Marino and I left UVA, and the gold Lexus we had already seen twice this day was behind us all the way back to Richmond. Marino drove with his eyes constantly on his mirrors. He was sweating and mad because the DMV computer wasn't up yet, and the plate number he had called in was taking forever to come back. The person behind us in the car was young and white. He wore dark glasses and a cap.

"He doesn't care if you know who he is," I said. "If he cared, he wouldn't be so obvious, Marino. This is just one more intimidation attempt."

"Yeah, well, let's see who intimidates who," he said, slowing down.

He stared in the rearview mirror again, slowing more, and the car got closer. Suddenly, he hit his brakes hard. I didn't know who was more shocked, our tailgater or me, as the Lexus's brakes screeched, horns blaring all around, and the car clipped the rear end of Marino's Ford.

"Uh-oh," he said. "Looks like someone's just rear-ended a policeman."

He got out and subtly unsnapped his holster while I looked on in disbelief. I slipped out my pistol and dropped it in a pocket of my coat as I decided I should get out, too, since I had no idea what was about to happen. Marino was by the Lexus's driver's door, watching the traffic at his back as he talked into his portable radio.

"Keep your hands where I can see them at all times," he ordered the driver again in a loud, authoritative voice. "Now I want you to give me your driver's license. Slow."

I was on the other side of the car, near the passenger's door, and I knew who the offender was before Marino saw the license, and the photograph on it.

"Well, well, Detective Roche," Marino raised his voice above the rush of traffic. "Fancy we should run into you. Or vice versa." His tone turned hard. "Get out of the car. Now. You got any firearms on you?"

"It's between the seats. In plain view," he said, coldly.

Then Roche slowly got out of the car. He was tall and slender in fatigue pants, a denim jacket, boots and a large black dive watch. Marino turned him around and ordered him again to keep his hands in plain view. I stood where I was while Roche's sunglasses fixed on me, his mouth smug.

"So tell me, Detective Cock-Roche," Marino said, "who you snitching for today? Might it be Captain Green you've been talking to on your portable phone? You been telling him everywhere we've been going today and what we're doing, and how much you've been scaring our asses as we spot you in our mirrors? Or are you obvious just because you're a dumb shit?"

Roche said nothing, his face hard.

"Is that what you did to Danny, too? You called the tow lot and said you were the doc and wanted to know about your car. Then you passed the info down the line, only it just so happened it wasn't the doc driving that night. And now a kid's missing half his head because some soldier of fortune didn't know the doc ain't a man or maybe mistook Danny for a medical examiner."

"You can't prove anything," Roche said with the same mocking smile.

"We'll see how much I can prove when I get hold of your cellular phone bills." Marino moved closer so Roche could feel his big presence, his belly almost touching him. "And when I find something, you're going to have a lot more to worry about than a driving penalty. At the very least I'm going to nail your pretty ass for being an accomplice to murder prior to the fact. That ought to get you about fifty years.

"In the meantime"—Marino jabbed a thick finger at his face—"I'd better never see you even within a mile of me again. And I wouldn't recommend you getting anywhere close to the doc, either. You've never seen her when she gets irritated."

Marino lifted his radio and got back on the air to check the status of getting an officer to the scene, and even as his request was broadcast again, a cruiser appeared on 64. It pulled in behind us on the shoulder, and a uniformed female sergeant from Richmond P.D. got out. She walked our way with purpose, her hand discreetly near her gun.

"Captain, good afternoon." She adjusted the volume on the radio on her belt. "What seems to be the problem?"

"Well, Sergeant Schroeder, it seems this person's been tailgating me for the better part of the day," Marino said. "And unfortunately, when I was forced to apply my brakes due to a white dog running in front of my vehicle, he struck me from the rear."

"Was this the same white dog?" the sergeant asked without a trace of a smile.

"Looked like the same one we've had problems with."

They went on with what must have been the oldest police joke, for when it came to single-car accidents, it seemed a ubiquitous white canine was always to blame. It darted in front of vehicles and then was gone until it darted in front of the next bad driver and again got blamed.

"He has at least one firearm inside his vehicle," Marino added in his most serious police tone. "I want him thoroughly searched before we get him inside."

"All right, sir, you need to spread your arms and legs."

"I'm a cop," Roche snapped.

"Yes, sir, so you should know exactly what I'm doing," Sergeant Schroeder matter-of-factly stated.

She patted him down, and discovered an ankle holster on his inner left leg.

"Now ain't that sweet," Marino said.

"Sir," the sergeant said a little more loudly as another unmarked unit pulled up, "I'm going to have to ask you to remove the pistol from your ankle holster and place it inside your vehicle."

A deputy chief got out, resplendent in patent leather, navy and brass, and not exactly thrilled to be on the scene. But it was procedure to call him whenever a captain was involved in any police matter, no matter how small. He silently looked on as Roche removed a Colt .380 from the black nylon holster. He locked it inside the Lexus and was red with rage as he was placed in the back of the patrol car. The sergeant and deputy chief interviewed him and Marino while I waited inside the damaged Ford.

"Now what happens?" I asked Marino when he returned.

"He'll be charged with following too close and be released on a Virginia Uniform Summons." He buckled up and seemed pleased.

"That's it?"

"Yup. Except court. The good news is, I ruined his day. The better news is now we got something to investigate that may eventually send his ass to Mecklenburg where, as sweet-looking as he is, he'll have lots of friends."

"Did you know it was him before he hit us?" I asked.

"Nope. I had no idea." We pulled back out into traffic.

"And what did he say when he was questioned?"

"What you'd expect. I stopped suddenly."

"Well, you did."

"And by law it's all right to do that."

"What about following us? Did he have an explanation?"

"He's been out all day running errands and sightseeing. He doesn't know what we're talking about."

"I see. If you're going to run errands, you need to bring along at least two guns."

"You want to tell me how the hell he can afford a car like that?" Marino glanced over at me. "He probably doesn't make half what I do, and that Lexus he's got probably cost close to fifty grand."

"The Colt he was carrying isn't cheap, either," I said. "He's getting money from somewhere."

"Snitches always do."

"That's all you think he is?"

"Yeah, for the most part. I think he's been doing shit work, probably for Green."

The radio suddenly interrupted us with the loud blare of an alert tone, and then we were given answers that were even worse than any we might have feared.

"All units be advised that we have just received a teletype from state police that gives the following information," a dispatcher repeated. "The nuclear power plant at Old Point has been taken over by terrorists. Shots have been fired and there are fatalities."

I was shocked speechless as the message went on and on.

"The chief of police has ordered that the department move

to emergency plan A. Until further notice all day-shift units will remain on their posts. Updates will follow. All division commanders will report to the command post at the police academy immediately."

"Hell no," Marino said as he slammed the accelerator to the floor. "We're going to your office."

13

The invasion of the Old Point nuclear power plant had happened swiftly and horrifically, and in disbelief we listened to the news while Marino sped through town. We did not utter a sound as an almost hysterical reporter at the scene rambled in a voice several octaves above what it usually was.

"Old Point nuclear power plant has been seized by terrorists," he repeated. "This happened about forty-five minutes ago when a bus carrying at least twenty men posing as CP&L employees stormed the main administration building. It is believed that at least three civilians are dead." His voice was shaking and we could hear helicopters overhead. "I can see police vehicles and fire trucks everywhere, but they can't get close. Oh my God, this is awful . . ."

Marino parked on the side of the street by my building. For a while we could not move as we listened to the same information again and again. It did not seem real, for less than a hundred miles from Old Point, here in Richmond, the afternoon was bright. Traffic was normal and people walked along sidewalks as if nothing had happened. My eyes stared without focusing, my thoughts flying through lists of what I must do.

"Come on, Doc." Marino cut the engine off. "Let's go inside. I got to use the phone and get hold of one of my lieutenants. I've got to get things mobilized in case the lights go out in Richmond, or worse."

I had my own mobilizing to do, and started with assembling everyone in the conference room, where I declared a statewide emergency.

"Each district must be on standby and ready to implement their part of the disaster plan," I announced to everyone in the room. "A nuclear disaster could affect all districts. Obviously, Tidewater is the most imperiled and the least covered. Dr. Fielding," I said to my deputy chief, "I'd like to put you in charge of Tidewater and make you acting chief when I can't be there."

"I'll do the best I can," he said bravely, although no one of sound mind would want the assignment I just gave him.

"Now, I won't always know where I'm going to be throughout this," I said to other anxious faces. "Business goes on as usual here, but I want any bodies brought here. Any bodies from Old Point, I'm saying, starting with the shooting fatalities."

"What about other Tidewater cases?" Fielding wanted to know.

"Routine cases are done as usual. I understand we do have another autopsy technician to fill in until we can find a permanent replacement."

"Any chance these bodies you want here might be contaminated?" my administrator asked, and he had always been a worrier.

"So far we're talking about shooting victims," I said.

"And they couldn't be."

"No."

"But what about later?" he went on.

"Mild contamination isn't a problem," I said. "We just scrub the bodies and get rid of the soapy water and clothes. Acute exposure to radiation is another matter, especially if the bodies are badly burned, if debris is burned into them, as it was in Chernobyl. Those bodies will need to be shielded in a special refrigerated truck, and all exposed personnel will wear lead-lined suits."

"Those bodies we'll cremate?"

"I would recommend that. Which is another reason why they need to come here to Richmond. We can use the crematorium in the anatomical division."

Marino stuck his head inside the conference room. "Doc?" He motioned me out.

I got up and we spoke in the hall.

"Benton wants us at Quantico now," he said.

"Well, it won't be now," I said.

I glanced back at the conference room. Through the doorway I could see Fielding making some point, while one of the other doctors looked tense and unhappy.

"You got an overnight bag with you?" Marino went on, and he knew I always kept one here.

"Is this really necessary?" I complained.

"I'd tell you if it wasn't."

"Give me just fifteen minutes to finish up this meeting."

I brought confusion and fear to closure as best I could, and told the other doctors I could be gone for days because I'd just been summoned to Quantico. But I would wear my pager. Then Marino and I took my car instead of his, since he had already made arrangements for repairs to the bumper Roche had hit. We sped north on 95 with the radio on, and by now we had heard the story so many times we knew it as well as the reporters.

In the past two hours, no one else had died at Old Point, at least not that anybody knew of, and the terrorists had let dozens of people go. These fortunate ones had been allowed to leave in twos and threes, according to the news. Emergency medical personnel, state police and the FBI intercepted them for examinations and interviews.

We arrived at Quantico at almost five, and Marines in camouflage were vigorously blasting the rapid approach of night. They were crowded in trucks and behind sandbags on the range, and when we passed close to a knot of them gathered by the road, I was pained by their young faces. I rounded a bend, where tall tan brick buildings suddenly rose above trees. The complex did not look military, and, in fact, could have been a university were it not for the rooftops of antennae. A road leading to it stopped midway at an entrance gate where tire shredders bared teeth to people going the wrong way.

An armed guard emerged from his booth and smiled because we were no strangers, and he let us through. We parked in the big lot across from the tallest building, called Jefferson, which was basically the Academy's self-contained downtown. Inside were the post office, the indoor range, dining hall, and PX, with upper floors for dormitory rooms, including security suites for protected witnesses and spies.

New agents in khaki and dark blue were honing weapons in the gun-cleaning room. It seemed I had smelled the solvents all of my life, and could hear in my mind compressed air blasting through barrels and other parts whenever I wanted to. My history had become entwined with this place. There was scarcely a corner that did not evoke emotion, for I had been in love here, and had brought into this building my most terrible cases. I had taught and consulted in their classrooms, and inadvertently given them my niece.

"God knows what we're about to walk into," Marino said as we got on the elevator.

"We'll just take it one inch at a time," I said as the new agents in their FBI caps vanished behind shutting steel doors.

He pressed the button for the lower level, which had been intended as Hoover's bomb shelter in a different age. The profiling unit, as the world still called it, was sixty feet below ground, with no windows or any other relief from the horrors it found. I frankly had never understood how Wesley could endure it year after year, for whenever I sat in consultations that lasted more than a day, I was crazed. I had to walk or drive my car. I had to get away.

"An inch at a time?" Marino repeated as the elevator

stopped. "There ain't no inch or mile that's going to help this scenario. We're a day late and a dollar short. We started putting the pieces together after the game was goddamn over."

"It isn't over," I said.

We walked past the receptionist and around a corner, where a hallway led to the unit chief's office.

"Yeah, well, let's hope it don't end with a bang. Shit. If only we had figured it out sooner." His stride was long and angry.

"Marino, we couldn't have known. There isn't a way."

"Well, I think we should have figured out something sooner. Like in Sandbridge, when you got the weird phone call and then everything else."

"Oh for God's sake," I said. "What? A phone call should have tipped us off that terrorists were about to seize a nuclear power plant?"

Wesley's secretary was new and I could not remember her name.

"Good afternoon," I said to her. "Is he in?"

"May I tell him who you are?" she asked with a smile.

We told her, and were patient as she rang him. They did not speak long.

When she looked back at us she said, "You may go in."

Wesley was behind his desk, and when we walked in he stood. He was typically preoccupied and somber in a gray herringbone suit and black and gray tie.

"We can go in the conference room," he said.

"Why?" Marino took a chair. "You got some other people coming?"

"Actually, I do," he replied.

I stood where I was and would not give him my eyes any longer than was polite.

"I'll tell you what," he reconsidered. "We can stay in here. Hold on." He walked to the door. "Emily, can you find another chair?"

We got settled while she brought one in, and Wesley was having a hard time keeping his thoughts in one place and making decisions. I knew what he was like when he was overwhelmed. I knew when he was unnerved.

"You know what's going on," he said as if we did.

"We know what everybody else does," I replied. "We've heard the same news on the radio probably a hundred times."

"So how about starting from the beginning," Marino said.

"CP&L has a district office in Suffolk," Wesley began. "At least twenty people left there this afternoon in a bus for an alleged in-service in the mock control room of the Old Point plant. They were men, white, thirties to early forties, posing as employees, which they obviously are not. And they managed to get into the main building where the control room is located."

"They were armed," I said.

"Yes. When it was time for them to go through the X-ray machines and other detectors at the main building, they pulled out semiautomatic weapons. As you know, people have been killed—we think at least three CP&L employees, including a nuclear physicist who just happened to be paying a site visit today and was going through security at the wrong time."

"What are their demands?" I asked, and I wondered how much Wesley had known and for how long. "Have they said what they want?"

He met my eyes. "That's what worries us the most. We don't know what they want."

"But they're letting people go," Marino said.

"I know. And that worries me, too," Wesley stated. "Terrorists generally don't do that." His telephone rang. "This is different." He picked up the receiver. "Yes," he said. "Good. Send him in."

Major General Lynwood Sessions was in the uniform of the Navy he served when he entered the office and shook hands with each of us. He was black, maybe forty-five and handsome in a way that was not to be dismissed. He did not take off his jacket or even loosen a button as he formally took a chair and set a fat briefcase beside him.

"General, thank you for coming," Wesley began.

"I wish it were for a happier reason," he said as he bent over to get out a file folder and legal pad.

"Don't we all," Wesley said. "This is Captain Pete Marino with Richmond, and Dr. Kay Scarpetta, the chief medical examiner of Virginia." He looked at me and held my gaze. "They work with us. Dr. Scarpetta, as a matter of fact, is the medical examiner in the cases that we believe are related to what is happening today."

General Sessions nodded and made no comment.

Wesley said to Marino and me, "Let me try to tell you what we know beyond the immediate crisis. We have reason to believe that vessels in the Inactive Ship Yard are being sold to countries that should not have them. This includes Iran, Iraq, Libya, North Korea, Algeria."

"What sort of vessels?" Marino asked.

"Mainly submarines. We also suspect that this shipyard is buying vessels from places like Russia and then reselling them."

"And why have we not been told this before?" I asked.

Wesley hesitated. "No one had proof."

"Ted Eddings was diving in the Inactive Yard when he died," I said. "He was near a submarine."

No one replied.

Then the general said, "He was a reporter. It's been suggested that he might have been looking for Civil War relics."

"And what was Danny doing?" I measured my words because I was getting tired of this. "Exploring a historic train tunnel in Richmond?"

"It's hard to know what Danny Webster was into," he said. "But I understand the Chesapeake police found a bayonet in the trunk of his car, and it is consistent with the tool marks left on your slashed tires."

I looked a long time at him. "I don't know where you got your information, but if what you've said is true, then I suspect Detective Roche turned that evidence in."

"I believe he turned in the bayonet, yes."

"I believe all of us in this room can be trusted." I kept my eyes on his. "If there is a nuclear disaster, I am mandated by law to take care of the dead. There are already too many dead at Old Point." I paused. "General Sessions, now would be a very good time to tell the truth."

The men were silent for a moment.

Then the general said, "NAVSEA has been concerned about that shipyard for a while."

"NAVSEA? What the hell is that?" Marino asked.

"Naval Sea Systems Command," he said. "They're the people responsible for making certain that shipyards like the one in question abide by the appropriate standards."

"Eddings had the label N-V-S-E programmed into his fax machine," I said. "Was he in communication with them?"

"He had asked questions," General Sessions said. "We were aware of Mr. Eddings. But we could not give him the answers he wanted. Just as we could not answer you, Dr. Scarpetta, when you sent us a fax asking who we were." His face was inscrutable. "I'm certain you can understand that."

"What is D-R-M-S out of Memphis?" I then asked.

"Another fax number that Eddings called, as did you," he said. "Defense Reutilization Marketing Service. They handle all surplus sales, which must be approved by NAVSEA."

"This is making sense," I said. "I can see why Eddings would have been in touch with these people. He was on to what was happening at the Inactive Yard, that the Navy's standards were being violated in a rather shocking way. And he was probing for his story."

"Tell me more about these standards," Marino said. "Exactly what is the shipyard supposed to abide by?"

"I'll give you an example. If Jacksonville wants the *Saratoga* or some other aircraft carrier, then NAVSEA makes certain that any work done to it meets the Navy's standards."

"Like in what way?"

"For example, the city has to have the five million it will take to fix it up, and the two million for maintenance each year. And the water in the harbor must be at least thirty feet deep. On the other hand, where the ship is moored, someone from NAVSEA, probably a civilian, is going to appear about once a month and inspect the work being done to the vessel."

"And this has been happening at the Inactive Ship Yard?" I asked.

"Well, right now, we're not sure of the civilian doing it." The general looked straight at me.

Then it was Wesley who spoke, "That's the problem. There are civilians everywhere, some of them mercenaries who would buy or sell anything with absolute reckless disregard for national security. As you know, a civilian company runs the Inactive Yard. It inspects the ships being sold to cities or for salvage."

"What about the submarine in there now, the *Exploiter*?" I asked. "The one I saw when I recovered Eddings's body?"

"A Zulu V class ballistic missile sub. Ten torpedo tubes plus two missile tubes. It was made from 1955 to 1957," General Sessions said. "Since the sixties, all subs built in the U.S. are nuclear-powered."

"So the sub we're talking about is old," Marino said. "It's not nuclear."

The general replied, "It couldn't be nuclear-powered. But you can put any type of warhead on a missile or torpedo you want."

"Are you saying that the sub I dove near might be retrofitted to fire nuclear weapons?" I asked as this frightening specter just loomed bigger.

"Dr. Scarpetta," the general said as he leaned closer to me. "We're not assuming that sub has been retrofitted here in the United States. All that was needed was for it to be brought back up to speed and sent out to sea where it might be intercepted by a principality that should not have it. Work could be done there. But what Iraq or Algeria cannot do for themselves on their own soil is produce weapons-grade plutonium."

"And where is that going to come from?" Marino asked. "It's not like you can get that from a power plant. And if the terrorists think otherwise, then I guess we're dealing with a bunch of redneck dumb shits."

"It would be extremely hard, if not close to impossible, to get plutonium from Old Point," I agreed.

"An anarchist like Joel Hand doesn't think about how hard it might be," Wesley said.

"And it is possible," Sessions added. "For about two months after new fuel rods have been placed in a reactor, there is a window in which you can get plutonium."

"How often are the rods replaced?" Marino asked.

"Old Point replaces one-third of them every fifteen months. That's eighty assemblies, or about three atom bombs if you shut down the reactors and get the assemblies out during that two-month window."

"Then Hand had to know the schedule," I said.

"Oh, yes."

I thought of the telephone records of CP&L executives that someone like Eddings might have illegally accessed.

"So someone was on the take," I said.

"We think we know who. One high-ranking officer, really," Sessions said. "Someone who had a lot of say in the decision to locate the CP&L field office on property adjacent to Hand's farm."

"A farm belonging to Joshua Hayes?"

"Yes."

"Shit," Marino said. "Hand had to be planning this for years, and he sure as hell was getting a lot of bucks from somewhere."

"No question about either," the general agreed. "Something like this would have to be planned for years, and someone was paying for it."

"You need to remember that for a fanatic like Hand," Wesley said, "what he is engaged in is a religious war of eternal significance. He can afford to be patient."

"General Sessions," I went on, "if the submarine we're speaking of is destined for a distant port, might NAVSEA know that?"

"Absolutely."

"How?" Marino wanted to know.

"A number of things," he said. "For example, when ships are stored at the Inactive Yard, their missile and torpedo tubes are covered with steel plates outside the hull. And a plate is welded over the shaft inside the ship so the screw is fixed. Obviously, all guns and communications are removed."

"Meaning that a violation of at least some of these regulations could be inspected from the outside," I said. "You could tell by looking at the vessel if you were near it in the water."

He looked at me and caught my meaning precisely. "Yes, you could tell."

"You could dive around this sub and find that the torpedo tubes, for example, are not sealed. You might even be able to tell that the screw was not welded."

"Yes," he said again. "All of that you could tell."

"That's what Ted Eddings was doing."

"I'm afraid so." It was Wesley who spoke. "Divers recovered his camera and we've looked at the film, which had only three exposures. All blurred images of the *Exploiter*'s screw. So it doesn't appear he was in the water long before he died."

"And where is that submarine now?" I asked.

The general paused. "You might say that we're in subtle pursuit of it."

"Then it's gone."

"I'm afraid it left port about the same time the nuclear power plant was stormed."

I looked at the three men. "Well, I certainly think we know why Eddings had gotten increasingly paranoid about self-protection."

"Someone must have set him up," Marino said. "You can't just decide at the last minute to poison someone with cyanide gas."

"His was a premeditated murder committed by someone he must have trusted," Wesley said. "He wouldn't have told just anybody what he was doing that night."

I thought of another label in Eddings's fax machine. CPT could stand for captain, and I mentioned Captain Green's name to them.

"Well, Eddings must have had at least one inside source for his story," was Wesley's comment. "Someone was leaking information to him and I suspect this same someone set him up or at least assisted in it." He looked at me. "And we know from his phone bills that over the past few months, he had quite a lot of communication with Green, by phone and fax, that seems to have begun last fall when Eddings did a rather harmless profile on the shipyard."

"Then he started digging too deep," I said.

"His curiosity was actually helpful to us," General Sessions said. "We started digging deeper, too. We've been investigating this situation longer than you might imagine." He paused, and smiled a little. "In fact, Dr. Scarpetta, you have not been as alone at some points as you might have thought."

"I sincerely hope you'll thank Jerod and Ki Soo," I said, assuming they were SEALs.

But it was Wesley who replied, "I will, or perhaps you can yourself next time you visit HRT."

"General Sessions," I moved on to what seemed a rather more mundane topic. "Would you happen to know if rats are a concern in decommissioned ships?"

"Rats are always a worry in any ship," he said.

"One of the uses of cyanide is to exterminate rodents in the hulls of ships," I said. "The Inactive Yard may keep a supply of it."

"As I've indicated, Captain Green is of great concern to us." He knew just what I meant.

"Vis-à-vis the New Zionists?" I asked.

"No," Wesley answered for him. "Not as opposed to but

as with. My speculation is that Green is the New Zionists' direct link to anything military, such as the shipyard, while Roche is simply his toady. Roche is the one who harasses, snoops and snitches."

"He didn't kill Danny," I said.

"Danny was killed by a psychopathic individual who blends well enough with normal society that he did not draw any attention to himself as he waited outside the Hill Cafe. I'd profile this individual as a white male, early thirties to early forties, experienced in hunting and in guns, in general."

"Sounds like the spitting image of the drones who took over Old Point," Marino remarked.

"Yes," Wesley said. "Killing Danny, whether he was the intended victim or not, was a hunting assignment, like shooting a groundhog. The individual who did this probably bought the Sig forty-five at the same gun show where he got the Black Talons."

"I thought you said the Sig once belonged to a cop," the general reminded him.

"Right. It ends up on the street and eventually gets sold secondhand," Wesley said.

"To one of Hand's followers," Marino said. "The same kind of guy that took out Shapiro in Maryland."

"The exact same kind of guy."

"My big question is what they think you know," the general asked me.

"I've thought about that a lot and can't come up with anything," I replied.

"You have to think like they do," Wesley said to me. "What is it they think you might know that others don't?"

"They might think I have the Book," I said for lack of anything else that came to mind. "And apparently that is as sacred as an Indian burial ground to them."

"What's in it that they wouldn't want anyone else to know?" Sessions asked.

"It would seem that the revelation most dangerous to them would be the plan they've already carried out," I replied.

"Of course. They couldn't carry it out if someone tipped their hand." Wesley looked at me, a thousand thoughts in his eyes. "What does Dr. Mant know?"

"I haven't had the chance to ask him. He doesn't answer my calls, and I've left messages numerous times."

"You don't think that's rather strange?"

"I absolutely think it's strange," I said to him. "But I don't think anything extreme has happened, or we would have heard. I think he's afraid."

Wesley explained to the general, "He's the medical examiner in charge of the Tidewater District."

"Well, then, perhaps you should go see him," the general suggested to me.

"In light of circumstances, this doesn't seem the ideal time," I said.

"On the contrary," the general said. "I think this is precisely the ideal time."

"You might be right," Wesley agreed. "Our only hope, really, is to get inside these people's heads. Maybe Mant has information that could help. Maybe that's why he's hiding."

General Sessions shifted in his chair. "Well, I vote for it," he said. "For one thing, we've got to worry about this same kind of thing happening over there, as you and I have already discussed, Benton. So that business already awaits anyway, doesn't it? It won't be any big deal for another person to go along, providing British Airways doesn't mind, short notice and all." He seemed amused in a wry way. "If they do, I expect I'll just have to call the Pentagon."

"Kay," Wesley explained this to me while Marino looked on with angry eyes, "we don't know that an Old Point isn't already happening in Europe because what's going on in Virginia didn't happen overnight. We're worried about major cities elsewhere."

"So, are you telling me these New Zionist fruit loops are in England, too?" It was Marino who asked, and he was about to boil over.

"Not that we are aware of, but unfortunately, there are plenty of others to take their place," Wesley said.

"Well, I got an opinion." Marino looked accusingly at me. "We got a possible nuclear disaster on our hands. Don't you think you ought to stick around?"

"That would be my preference."

The general made the salient remark, "If you help, hopefully it won't be necessary for you to stick around because there won't be anything for you to do."

"I understand that, too," I said. "No one believes in prevention more than I do."

"Can you manage it?" Wesley asked.

"My offices are already mobilizing to handle whatever

happens," I said. "The other doctors know what to do. You know I'll help in any way I possibly can."

But Marino was not to be soothed. "It ain't safe." He stared at Wesley now. "You can't just go sending the doc through airports and all the hell over the place when we don't know who's out there or what they want."

"You're right, Pete," Wesley thoughtfully said. "And we're not going to do that."

14

That night I went home because I needed clothes, and my passport was in the safe. I packed with nervous hands as I waited for my pager to beep. Fielding had been calling me on the hour to hear updates and air his concerns. The bodies at Old Point remained where the gunmen had left them, as best we knew, and we did not know how many of the plant's workers remained imprisoned inside.

I slept restlessly under the watch of a police car parked on my street, and I sat up when the alarm clock startled me awake at five A.M. An hour and a half later, a Learjet awaited me at the Millionaire Terminal in Henrico County, where the area's wealthiest businessmen parked their helicopters and corporate planes. Wesley and I were polite but guarded as we greeted each other, and I was having trouble believing we were about to fly overseas together. But it had been planned that he would visit the embassy before it was suggested that I should go to London, too, and General Sessions did not know about our history. Or at least this was how I chose to view a situation that was out of my hands.

"I'm not sure I trust your motives," I said to Wesley as the jet took off like a race car with wings. "And what about this?" I looked around. "Since when does the Bureau use Learjets, or did the Pentagon arrange this, too?"

"We use whatever we need," he said. "CP&L has made available any resource it has to help us resolve this crisis, and this Learjet belongs to them."

The white jet was sleek, with burlwood and teal green leather seats, but it was loud, so we could not speak softly.

"You don't have to worry about using something of theirs?" I said.

"They're just as unhappy about all this as we are. As far as we know, with the exception of one or two bad apples, CP&L is blameless. In fact, it and its employees are clearly the most profoundly victimized."

He stared ahead at the cockpit and its two well-built pilots dressed in suits. "Besides, the pilots are HRT," he added. "And we checked every nut and bolt of this thing before we took off. Don't worry. As for my going with you"—he looked at me—"I'll say it again. What happens now is operational. The ball has been passed to HRT. I will be needed when terrorists begin to communicate with us, when we can at least identify them. But I don't think that will be for several days."

"How can you possibly know that?" I poured coffee.

He took the cup from my hand and our fingers brushed. "I know because they're busy. They want those assemblies, and there are only so many they can get per day."

"Have the reactors been shut down?"

"According to the power company, the terrorists shut down the reactors immediately after storming the plant. So they know what they want, and they are down to business."

"And there are twenty of them."

"That's approximately how many went in for their alleged seminar in the mock control room. But we really can't be sure how many are there now."

"This tour," I said, "when was it scheduled?"

"The power company said it was originally scheduled in early December for the end of February."

"Then they moved it up." I wasn't surprised in light of what had happened lately.

"Yes," he said. "It was suddenly rescheduled a couple of days before Eddings was killed."

"It sounds like they're desperate, Benton."

"And probably more reckless and not as prepared," he said. "And that's better and worse for us."

"And what about hostages? Is it likely they will let all of them go, based on your experience?"

"I don't know about all of them," he said, staring out the window, his face grim in soft side lights.

"Lord," I said, "if they try to get the fuel out, we could have a national disaster on our hands. And I don't see how they think they can pull this off. Those assemblies probably weigh several tons each and are so radioactive they could cause instant death if you got close. And how will they get them away from Old Point?"

"The plant's surrounded by water for purposes of cooling the reactors. And nearby, on the James, we're watching a barge we believe belongs to them."

I remembered Marino telling me of barges delivering large crates to the New Zionist compound, and I said, "Can we take it?"

"No. We can't take barges, submarines, nothing right now. Not until we can get those hostages out." He sipped coffee, and the horizon was turning a pale gold.

"Then the best-case scenario is they will take what they want and leave without killing anybody else," I supposed, although I did not think this could happen.

"No. The best-case scenario is we stop them there." He looked at me. "We don't want a barge full of highly radioactive material on Virginia's rivers or out at sea. What are we going to do, threaten to sink it? Besides, my guess is they'll take hostages with them." He paused. "Eventually, they'll shoot them all."

I could not help but imagine those poor people now as fright shocked every nerve cell every moment they breathed. I knew about the physical and mental manifestations of fear, and the images were searing and I seethed inside. I felt a wave of hatred for these men who called themselves the New Zionists, and I clenched my fists.

Wesley looked down at my white knuckles on the armrests,

and thought I was afraid of flying. "It's only a few more minutes," he said. "We're starting our descent."

We landed at Kennedy, and a shuttle waited for us on the tarmac. It was driven by two more fit men in suits, and I did not ask Wesley about them because I already knew. One of them walked us inside the terminal to British Airways, which had been kind enough to cooperate with the Bureau, or maybe it was the Pentagon, by making two seats available on their next Concorde flight to London. At the counter, we discreetly showed our credentials and said we had not packed guns. The agent assigned to keep us safe walked with us to the lounge, and when I looked for him next, he was perusing stacks of foreign newspapers.

Wesley and I found seats before expansive windows looking out over the tarmac where the supersonic plane waited like a giant white heron being fed fuel through a thick hose attached to its side. The Concorde looked more like a rocket than any commercial craft I had seen, and it appeared that most of its passengers were no longer capable of being impressed by it or much of anything. They served themselves pastries and fruit, and some were already mixing Bloody Marys and mimosas.

Wesley and I talked little and constantly scanned the crowd as we held up newspapers like every other proverbial spy or fugitive on the run. I could tell that Middle Easterners, in particular, caught his eye, while I was more wary of people who looked like us, for I remembered Joel Hand that day I had faced him in court and had found him attractive and genteel. If he sat next to me right now and I did not know him, I would have thought he belonged in this lounge more than we.

"How are you doing?" Wesley lowered his paper.

"I don't know." I was agitated. "So tell me. Are we alone or is your friend still here?"

His eyes smiled.

"I don't see what's amusing about this."

"So you thought the Secret Service might be nearby. Or undercover agents."

"I see. I guess that man in the suit who walked us here is special services for British Airways."

"Let me answer your question this way. If we're not alone, Kay, I'm not going to tell you."

We looked at each other a moment longer—we had never traveled abroad together, and now did not seem like a good time to start. He was wearing a blue suit so dark it was almost black, and his usual white shirt and conservative tie. I had dressed with similar somber deliberation, and both of us had our glasses on. I thought we looked like partners in a law firm, and as I noticed other women in the room I was reminded that what I did not look like was anybody's wife.

Paper rustled as he folded the London *Times* and glanced at his watch. "I think that's us," he said, getting up as Flight 2 was called again.

The Concorde held a hundred people in two cabins with two seats on either side of the aisle. The decor was muted gray carpet and leather, with spaceship windows too small to gaze out. Flight attendants were British and typically polite, and if they knew we were the two passengers from the FBI, Navy, or God knows, the CIA, they did not indicate so in any way. Their only concern seemed to be what we wanted to drink, and I ordered whiskey.

"It's a little early, isn't it?" Wesley said.

"Not in London it's not," I told him. "It's five hours later there."

"Thank you. I'll set my watch," he dryly said as if he'd never been anywhere in his life. "I guess I'll have a beer," he told the attendant.

"There, now that we're on the proper time zone, it's easier to drink," I said, and I could not keep the bite out of my voice.

He turned to me and met my eyes. "You sound angry."

"That's why you're a profiler, because you can figure out things like that."

He subtly looked around us, but we were behind the bulkhead with no one across the aisle, and I almost did not care who was at our rear.

"Can we talk reasonably?" he quietly asked.

"It's hard to be reasonable, Benton, when you always want to talk after the fact."

"I'm not sure I understand what you mean. I think there's a transition missing somewhere."

I was about to give him one. "Everyone knew about your separation except me," I said. "Lucy told me because she heard about it from other agents. I would just like to be included in our relationship for once."

"Christ, I wish you wouldn't get so upset."

"Not half as much as I do."

"I didn't tell you because I didn't want to be influenced by you," he said.

We were talking in low voices, leaning forward and together so that our shoulders were touching. Despite the grim circumstances, I was aware of his every move and how it felt against me. I smelled his wool jacket and the cologne he liked to wear.

"Any decision about my marriage can't include you," he went on as our drinks arrived. "I know you must understand that."

My body wasn't used to whiskey at this hour, and the effect of it was quick and strong. I instantly began to relax, and shut my eyes during the roar of takeoff as the jet leaned back and throbbed, thundering up through the air. From then on, the world below became nothing but a vague horizon, if I could see anything out the window at all. The noise of engines remained loud, making it necessary for us to continue sitting very close to each other as we intensely talked on.

"I know how I feel about you," Wesley was saying. "I have known that for a long time."

"You have no right," I said. "You have never had a right."

"And what about you? Did you have a right to do what you did, Kay? Or was I the only one in the room."

"At least I'm not married or even with anyone," I said. "But no, I shouldn't have."

He was still drinking beer and neither of us was interested

in the canapes and caviar that I suspected would prove the first inning of a long gourmet game. For a while we fell silent, flipping through magazines and professional journals while almost everyone else inside our cabin did the same. I noticed that people on the Concorde did not talk to each other much, and I decided that being rich and famous or royal must be rather boring.

"So I guess we've resolved that issue then," Wesley started again, leaning closer as I picked at asparagus.

"What issue?" I set down my fork, because I was left-handed and he was in the way.

"You know. About what we should and shouldn't do." He brushed against my breast and then his arm stayed there as if all we had said earlier was voided at Mach two.

"Yes," I said.

"Yes?" His voice was curious. "What do you mean, yes?"

"Yes about what you just said." With each breath I took, my body moved against him. "About resolving things."

"Then that's what we'll do," he agreed.

"Of course we will," I said, not entirely certain what we had just agreed to. "One other thing," I added. "If you ever get divorced and we want to see each other, we start over."

"Absolutely. That makes perfect sense."

"In the meantime, we're colleagues and friends."

"That's exactly what I want, too," he said.

At half past six, we sped along Park Lane, both of us silent in the backseat of a Rover driven by an officer of the

Metropolitan Police. In darkness, I watched the lights of London go by, and I was disoriented and vividly alive. Hyde Park was a sea of spreading darkness, lamps smudges of light along winding paths.

The flat where we were staying was very close to the Dorchester Hotel, and Pakistanis pooled around that grand old hotel this night, protesting their visiting prime minister with fervor. Riot police and dogs were out in numbers, but our driver seemed unconcerned.

"There is a doorman," he said as he pulled in front of a tall building that looked relatively new. "Just go in and give him your identification. He will get you into your accommodations. Do you need help with your bags?"

Wesley opened his door. "Thanks. We can manage."

We got out and went inside a small reception area, where an alert older man smiled warmly at us from behind a polished desk.

"Oh right. I've been expecting you," he said.

He got up and took our bags. "If you'll just follow me to the lift here."

We got on and rose to the fifth floor, where he showed us a three-bedroom flat with wide windows, bright fabrics and African art. My room was comfortably appointed, with the typical English tub large enough to drown in and toilet that flushed with a chain. Furniture was Victorian with hardwood floors covered in worn Turkish rugs, and I went over to the window and turned the radiator up high. I switched off lamps and gazed out at cars rushing past and dark trees in the park moving in the wind.

Wesley's room was down the hall at the far end, and I did not hear him walk in until he spoke.

"Kay?" He waited near my doorway, and I heard ice softly rattle. "Whoever lives here keeps very fine Scotch. I've been told we are to help ourselves."

He walked in and set tumblers on the sill.

"Are you trying to get me drunk?" I asked.

"It's never been necessary in the past."

He stood next to me, and we drank and leaned against each other as we looked out together. For a long time we spoke in small, quiet sentences, and then he touched my hair, and kissed my ear and jaw. I touched him, too, and our love for each other got deeper as our kisses and caresses did.

"I've missed you so much," he whispered as clothing became loosened and undone.

We made love because we could not help ourselves. That was our only excuse and would hold up in no court I knew. Separation had been very hard, so we were hungry with each other all night. Then at dawn I drifted off to sleep long enough to awaken and find him gone, as if it all had been a dream. I lay beneath a down-filled duvet, and images were slow and lyrical in my mind. Lights danced beneath my lids and I felt as if I were being rocked, as if I were a little girl again and my father were not dying of a disease I did not understand back then.

I had never gotten over him. I supposed my attachments to all men had sadly relived my being left by him. It was a dance I moved to without trying, and then found myself in silence in the empty room of my most private life. I realized how much Lucy and I were alike. We both loved in secret and would not speak of pain.

Getting dressed, I went out into the hall and found Wesley in the living room drinking coffee as he looked out at a cloudy day. He was dressed in suit and tie, and did not seem tired.

"There's coffee on," he said. "Can I get you some?"

"Thanks, I'll get it." I stepped into the kitchen. "Have you been up long?"

"For a while."

He made coffee very strong, and it struck me that there were so many domestic details about him I did not know. We did not cook together or go on vacations or do sports when I knew we both enjoyed so many of the same things. I walked into the living room and set my cup and saucer on a windowsill because I wanted to look out at the park.

"How are you?" His eyes lingered on mine.

"I'm fine. What about you?"

"You don't look fine."

"You always know just the thing to say."

"You look like you didn't get much sleep. That's what I meant."

"I got virtually no sleep, and you're to blame."

He smiled. "That and jet lag."

"The lag you cause is worse, Special Agent Wesley."

Already traffic was loud rushing past, and punctuated periodically by the odd cacophony of British sirens. In the cold, early light, people were walking briskly along sidewalks, and some were jogging. Wesley got up from his chair.

"We should be going soon." He rubbed the back of my neck and kissed it. "We should get a little something to eat. It's going to be a long day."

"Benton, I don't like living this way," I said as he shut the door.

We followed Park Lane past the Dorchester Hotel, where some Pakistanis were still taking their stand. Then we took Mount Street to South Audley where we found a small restaurant open called Richoux. Inside were exotic French pastries and boxes of chocolates beautiful enough to display as art. People were dressed for business and reading newspapers at small tables. I drank fresh orange juice and got hungry. Our Filipino waitress was puzzled because Wesley had only toast while I ordered bacon and eggs with mushrooms and tomatoes.

"You wish to share?" she asked.

"No, thank you." I smiled.

At not quite ten A.M., we continued on South Audley to Grosvenor Square, where the American Embassy was an unfortunate granite block of 1950s architecture guarded by a bronze eagle rampant on the roof. Security was extremely tight, with somber guards everywhere. We produced passports and credentials, and our photographs were taken. Finally, we were escorted to the second floor where we were to meet with the FBI's senior legal attaché, or legate, for Great Britain. Chuck Olson's corner office afforded a perfect view of people waiting in long lines for visas and green cards. He was a stocky man in a dark suit, his neatly trimmed hair almost as silver as Wesley's.

"A pleasure," he said as he shook our hands. "Please have a seat. Would anybody like coffee?"

Wesley and I chose a couch across from a desk that was clear except for a notepad and file folders. On a cork board behind Olson's head were drawings that I assumed were done by his children, and above these hung a large Department of Justice seal. Other than shelves of books and various commendations, the office was the simple space of a busy person unimpressed with his job or self.

"Chuck," Wesley began, "I'm sure you already know that Dr. Scarpetta is our consulting forensic pathologist, and though she does have her own situation in Virginia to handle, she could be called back here later."

"God forbid," Olson said, for if there was a nuclear disaster in England or anywhere in Europe, chances were I would be brought in to help handle the dead.

"So I wonder if you could give her a clearer picture of our concerns," Wesley said.

"Well, there's the obvious," Olson said to me. "About a third of England's electricity is generated by nuclear power. We're worried about a similar terrorist strike, and don't know, in fact, if one hasn't already been planned by these same people."

"But the New Zionists are rooted in Virginia," I said. "Are you saying they have international connections?"

"They aren't the driving force in this," he said. "They aren't the ones who want plutonium."

"Who specifically, then?" I said.

"Libya."

"I think the world has known that for a while," I replied.

"Well, now it's happening," Wesley said. "It's happening at Old Point."

"As you no doubt know," Olson went on, "Qaddafi has wanted nuclear weapons for a very long time and has been thwarted in his every attempt. It appears he finally found a way. He found the New Zionists in Virginia, and certainly, there are extremist groups he could use over here. We also have many Arabs."

"How do you know it's Libya?" I asked.

It was Wesley who replied, "For one thing, we've been going through Joel Hand's telephone records and they include numerous calls—mainly to Tripoli and Benghãzi—made over the past two years."

"But you don't know that Qaddafi is trying anything here in London," I said.

"What we fear is how vulnerable we would be. London is the stepping-off point to Europe, the U.S. and the Middle East. It is a tremendous financial center. Just because Libya steals fire from the U.S. doesn't mean the U.S. is the ultimate target."

"Fire?" I asked.

"As in the myth about Prometheus. Fire is our code for plutonium."

"I understand," I said. "What you're saying makes chilling sense. Tell me what I can do."

"Well, we need to explore the mind-set of this thing, both for purposes of what's happening now and what might happen later," Olson said. "We need to get a better handle on how these terrorists think, and that, obviously, is Wesley's department. Yours is to get information. I understand you have a colleague here who might prove useful."

"We can only hope," I said. "But I intend to speak to him."

"What about security?" Wesley asked him. "Do we need to put someone with her?"

Olson looked at me oddly as if assessing my strength, as if I were not myself but an object or fighter about to step into the ring.

"No," he said. "I think she's absolutely safe here, unless you know otherwise."

"I'm not sure," Wesley said as he looked at me, too. "Maybe we should send someone with her."

"Absolutely not. No one knows I'm in London," I said. "And Dr. Mant already is reluctant, if not scared to death, so he's certainly not going to open up to me if someone else is along. Then the point of this trip is defeated."

"All right," Wesley reluctantly said. "Just so long as we know where you are, and we need to meet back here no later than four if we're going to catch that plane."

"I'll call you if I get hung up," I said. "You'll be here?"

"If we're not, my secretary will know where to find us," Olson said.

I went down to the lobby where water splashed loudly in a fountain and a bronze Lincoln was enthroned within walls lined with portraits of former U.S. representatives. Guards were severe as they studied passports and visitors. They let me pass with cool stares, and I felt their eyes follow me out the door. On the street in the cold, damp morning, I hailed a cab and gave the driver an address not very far away in Belgravia off Eaton Square.

The elderly Mrs. Mant had lived in Ebury Mews in a three-story town house that had been divided into flats. Her building was stucco with red chimney pots piled high on a variegated shingle roof, and window boxes were filled with daffodils, crocuses and ivy. I climbed stairs to the second floor and knocked on her door, but when it was answered, it was not by my deputy chief. The matronly woman peering out at me looked as confused as I did.

"Excuse me," I said to her. "I guess this has already been sold."

"No, I'm sorry. It's not for sale a'tall," she firmly said.

"I'm looking for Philip Mant," I went on. "Clearly I must have the wrong . . ."

"Oh," she said. "Philip's my brother." She smiled pleasantly. "He just left for work. You just missed him."

"Work?" I said.

"Oh yes, he always leaves right about this time. To avoid traffic, you know. Although I don't think that's really possible." She hesitated, suddenly aware of the stranger before her. "Might I tell him who dropped by?"

"Dr. Kay Scarpetta," I said. "And I really must find him."

"Why of course." She seemed as pleased as she was surprised. "I've heard him speak of you. He's enormously fond of you and will be absolutely delighted to hear you came by. What brings you to London?"

"I never miss an opportunity to visit here. Might you tell me where I could find him?" I asked again.

"Of course. The Westminster Public Mortuary on Horseferry Road." She hesitated, uncertain. "I should have thought he would have told you."

"Yes." I smiled. "And I'm very pleased for him."

I wasn't certain what I was talking about, but she seemed very pleased, too.

"Don't tell him I'm coming," I went on. "I intend to surprise him."

"Oh, that's brilliant. He will be absolutely thrilled."

I caught another taxi as I thought about what I believed she had just said. No matter Mant's reason for what he had done, I could not help but feel slightly furious.

"You going to the Coroner's Court, ma'am?" the driver asked me. "It's right there." He pointed out the open window at a handsome brick building.

"No, I'm going to the actual mortuary," I said.

"All right. Well that's right here. Better that you walk in," he said with a hoarse laugh.

I got out money as he parked in front of a building small by London standards. Brick with granite trim and a strange parapet along the roof, it was surrounded by an ornate wrought-iron fence painted the color of rust. According to the date on a plaque at the entrance, the mortuary was more than a hundred years old, and I thought about how grim it would have been to practice forensic medicine in those days. There would have been few witnesses to tell the story except for the human kind, and I wondered if people had lied less in earlier times.

The mortuary's reception area was small but pleasantly

furnished like a typical lobby for a normal business. Through an open door was a corridor, and since I did not see anyone, I headed that way just as a woman emerged from a room, her arms loaded with oversized books.

"Sorry," she said, startled. "But you can't come back here."

"I'm looking for Dr. Mant," I said.

She wore a loose-fitting long dress and sweater, and spoke with a Scottish accent. "And who may I tell him is here to see him?" she politely said.

I showed her my credentials.

"Oh very good. I see. And he must be expecting you."

"I shouldn't think so," I said.

"I see." She shifted the books to another arm, and she was very confused.

"He used to work with me in the States," I said. "I'd like to surprise him, so I prefer to find him if you'll just tell me where."

"Dear me, that would be the Foul Room just now. If you go through this door here." She nodded at it. "And you'll see locker rooms to the left of the main mortuary. Everything you need is there, then turn left again through another set of doors, and right beyond that. Is that clear?" She smiled.

"Thank you," I said.

In the locker room I put on booties, gloves and mask, and loosely tied a gown around me to keep the odor out of my clothes. I passed through a tiled room where six stainless-steel tables and a wall of white refrigerators gleamed. The doctors wore blue, and Westminster was keeping them busy this morning. They scarcely glanced at me as I walked past. Down the hall I found my deputy chief in tall rubber boots, standing on a footstool as he worked on a badly decomposing body that I suspected had been in water for a while. The stench was terrible, and I shut the door behind me.

"Dr. Mant," I said.

He turned around and for an instant did not seem to know who I was or where he was. Then he simply looked shocked.

"Dr. Scarpetta? My God, why I'll be bloody damned." He heavily stepped off the stool, for he was not a small man. "I'm so surprised. I'm rather speechless!" He was sputtering, and his eyes wavered with fear.

"I'm surprised, too," I somberly said.

"I quite imagine that you are. Come on. No need to talk in here with this rather ghastly floater. Found him in the Thames yesterday afternoon. Looks like a stabbing to me but we have no identity. We should go to the lounge," he nervously talked on.

Philip Mant was a charming old gentleman impossible not to like, with thick white hair and heavy brows over keen pale eyes. He showed me around the corner to showers, where we disinfected our feet, stripped off gloves and masks and stuffed scrubs into a bin. Then we went to the lounge, which opened onto the parking lot in back. Like everything else in London, the stale smoke in this room had a long history, too.

"May I offer you some refreshment?" he asked as he got

out a pack of Players. "I know you don't smoke anymore, so I won't offer."

"I don't need a thing except some answers from you," I said.

His hands trembled slightly as he struck a match.

"Dr. Mant, what in God's name are you doing here?" I started in. "You're supposed to be in London because you had a death in the family."

"I did. Coincidentally."

"Coincidentally?" I said. "And what does that mean?"

"Dr. Scarpetta, I fully intended to leave anyway and then my mother suddenly died and that made it easy to choose a time."

"Then you've had no intention of coming back," I said, stung.

"I'm quite sorry. But no, I have not." He delicately tapped an ash.

"You could at least have told me so I could have begun looking for your replacement. I've tried to call you several times."

"I didn't tell you and I didn't call because I didn't want them to know."

"Them?" The word seemed to hang in the air. "Exactly who do you mean, Dr. Mant?"

He was very matter-of-fact as he smoked, legs crossed and belly roundly swelling over his belt. "I have no idea who they are, but they certainly know who we are. That's what alarms me. I can tell you exactly when it all began. October thirteenth, and you may or may not remember the case."

I had no idea what he was talking about.

"Well, the Navy did the autopsy because the death was at their shipyard in Norfolk."

"The man who was accidentally crushed in a dry dock?" I vaguely recalled it.

"The very one."

"You're right. That was a Navy case, not ours," I said as I began to anticipate what he had to say. "Tell me what that has to do with us."

"You see, the rescue squad made a mistake," he continued. "Instead of transporting the body to Portsmouth Naval Hospital, where it belonged, they brought it to my office, and young Danny didn't know. He began drawing blood, doing paperwork, that sort of thing, and in the process found something very unusual amongst the decedent's personal effects."

I realized Mant did not know about Danny.

"The victim had a canvas satchel with him," he went on. "And the squad had simply placed it on top of the body and covered everything with a sheet. Poor form as it may be, I suppose had that not occurred we wouldn't have had a clue."

"A clue about what?"

"What this fellow had, apparently, was a copy of a rather sinister bible that I came to find out later is connected to a cult. The New Zionists. An absolutely terrible thing, that book was, describing in detail torture, murder, things like that. It was terribly unsettling, in my view."

"Was it called the *Book of Hand*?" I asked.

"Why yes." His eyes lit up. "It was, indeed."

"Was it in a black leather binder?"

"I believe it was. With a name stamped on it that oddly enough was not the name of the decedent. Shapiro, or something."

"Dwain Shapiro."

"Of course," he said. "Then you already know about this."

"I know about the Book but not why this individual had it in his possession, because certainly his name was not Dwain Shapiro."

He paused to rub his face. "I think his name was Catlett."

"But he could have been Dwain Shapiro's killer," I said. "That could be why he had the bible."

Mant did not know. "When I realized we had a naval case in our morgue," he said, "I had Danny transport the body to Portsmouth. Clearly, the poor man's effects should have gone with him."

"But Danny kept the book," I said.

"I'm afraid so." He leaned forward and crushed out the cigarette in an ashtray on the coffee table.

"Why would he do that?"

"I happened to walk into his office and spotted it, and I asked him why in the world he had it. His explanation was that since the book had another individual's name on it, he wondered if it hadn't been accidentally picked up at the scene. That perhaps the satchel belonged to someone else, as well." He paused. "You see, he was still rather new and I think he'd simply made an honest mistake."

"Tell me something," I said, "were any reporters calling the office or coming around at this time? For example, might anyone have inquired about the man crushed to death in the shipyard?"

"Oh yes, Mr. Eddings showed up. I remember that because he was rather keen on finding out every detail, which puzzled me a bit. To my knowledge, he never wrote anything about it."

"Might Danny have talked to Eddings?"

Mant stared off in thought. "It seems I did see the two of them talking some. But young Danny certainly knew better than to give him a quote."

"Might he have given Eddings the Book, assuming that Eddings was doing a story on the New Zionists?"

"Actually, I wouldn't know. I never saw the Book again and assumed Danny had returned it to the Navy. I miss the lad. How is he, by the way? How is his knee? I called him Hop-Along, you know." He laughed.

But I did not answer his question or even smile. "Tell me what happened after that. What made you afraid?"

"Strange things. Hang-ups. I felt I was being followed. My morgue supervisor, as you recall, abruptly quit with no good explanation. And one day when I went out to the parking lot, there was blood all over the windshield of my car. I actually had it tested in the lab, and it was type butcher shop. From a cow, in other words."

"I presume you have met Detective Roche," I said.

"Unfortunately. I don't fancy him a'tall."

"Did he ever try to get information from you?"

"He would drop by. Not for postmortems, of course. He doesn't have the stomach for them."

"What did he want to know?"

"Well, the Navy death we talked about. He had questions about that."

"Did he ask about his personal effects? The satchel that inadvertently came into the morgue along with the body?"

Mant was trying to remember. "Well, now that you're prodding this rather pathetic memory of mine, it seems I do recall him asking about the satchel. And I referred him to Danny, I believe."

"Well, Danny obviously never gave it to him," I said. "Or at least not the Book, because that has turned up since."

I did not tell him how because I did not want to upset him.

"That bloody Book must be terribly important to someone," he mused.

I paused as he smoked again. Then I said, "Why didn't you tell me? Why did you just run and never say a word?"

"Frankly, I didn't want you dragged into it, as well. And it all sounded rather fantastic." He paused, and I could tell by his face he sensed other bad events had occurred since he had left Virginia. "Dr. Scarpetta, I'm not a young man. I only want to peacefully do my job a little while longer before I retire."

I did not want to criticize him further because I understood what he had done. I frankly could not blame him and was glad he had fled, for he probably had saved his own life. Ironically, there had been nothing important he knew, and had he been murdered, it would have been for no cause, as Danny's murder was for no cause.

Then I told the truth as I pushed back images of a knee brace as bright red as blood spilled, and leaves and trash clinging to gory hair. I remembered Danny's brilliant smile and would never forget the small white bag he had carried out of the cafe on a hill, where a dog had barked half the night. In my mind, I would always see the sadness and fear in his eyes when he helped me with the murdered Ted Eddings, who I now realized he had known. Together, the two young men had inadvertently led each other a step closer to their eventual violent deaths.

"Dear Lord. The poor boy," was all Mant could say.

He covered his eyes with a handkerchief, and when I left him, he was still crying.

15

Wesley and I flew back to New York that night, and arrived early because tail winds were more than a hundred knots. We went through customs and got our bags, then the same shuttle met us at the curb and returned us to the private airport where the Learjet was still waiting.

The weather had suddenly warmed and was threatening rain, and we flew between colossal black thunderheads lighting up with violent thoughts. The storm loudly cracked and flashed as we sped through what seemed the middle of a feud. I had been briefed a little as to the current state of affairs, and it had come as no surprise that the Bureau had established an outpost along with others set up by police and rescue crews.

Lucy, I was relieved to hear, had been brought in from the field, and was working again in the Engineering Research Facility, or ERF, where she was safe. What Wesley did not tell me until we reached the Academy was that she had been deployed along with the rest of HRT and would not be at Quantico long.

"Out of the question," I said to him as if I were a mother refusing permission.

"I'm afraid you don't have a say in this," he replied.

He was helping me carry my bags through the Jefferson lobby, which was deserted this Saturday night. We waved to the young women at the registration desk as we continued arguing.

"For God's sake," I went on, "she's brand new. You can't just throw her into the middle of a nuclear crisis."

"We're not throwing her into anything." He pushed open glass doors. "All we need are her technical skills. She's not going to be doing any sniper-shooting or jumping out of planes."

"Where is she now?" I asked as we got on an elevator.

"Hopefully in bed."

"Oh." I looked at my watch. "I guess it is midnight. I thought it was tomorrow and I should be getting up."

"I know. I'm screwed up, too."

Our eyes met and I looked away. "I guess we're supposed to pretend nothing happened," I said with an edge to my voice, for there had been no discussion of what had happened between us.

We walked out into the hall and he pressed a code into a digitalized keypad. A lock released and he opened another glass door.

"What good would it do to pretend?" he said, entering another code and opening another door.

"Just tell me what you want to do," I said.

We were inside the security suite where I usually stayed when work or danger kept me here overnight. He carried my bags into the bedroom as I drew draperies across the large window in the living room. The decor was comfortable but plain, and when Wesley did not respond, I remembered it probably was not safe to talk intimately in this place where I knew at the very least phones were monitored. I followed him back out into the hall and repeated my question.

"Be patient," he said, and he looked sad, or maybe he was just weary. "Look, Kay, I've got to go home. First thing in the morning we've got to do a surveillance by air with Marcia Gradecki and Senator Lord."

Gradecki was the United States attorney general, and Frank Lord was the chairman of the Judiciary Committee and an old friend.

"I'd like you along since overall you seem to know more of what's been going on than anyone else. Maybe you can explain to them the importance of the bible these wackos believe. That they'll kill for it. They'll die for it."

He sighed and rubbed his eyes. "And we need to talk about how we're going to—God forbid—handle the contaminated dead should these goddamn assholes decide to blow up the reactors." He looked at me again. "All we can do is try," he said, and I knew he referred to more than the present crisis.

"That's what I'm doing, Benton," I said, and I walked back inside my suite.

I called the switchboard and asked them to ring Lucy's room, and when there was no answer, I knew what that meant.

She was at ERF, and I could not call there because I did not know where in that building the size of a football field she might be. So I put on my coat and walked out of Jefferson because I could not sleep until I saw my niece.

ERF had its own guard gate not far from the one at the entrance of the Academy, and most of the FBI police, by now, knew me pretty well. The guard on duty looked surprised when I appeared, and he walked outside to see what I wanted.

"I think my niece is working late," I began to explain.

"Yes, ma'am. I did see her go in earlier."

"Is there any way you can contact her?"

"Hmmm." He frowned. "Might you have any idea what area she'd likely be in?"

"Maybe the computer room."

He tried that to no avail, then looked at me. "This is important."

"Yes, it is," I said with gratitude.

He raised his radio to his mouth.

"Unit forty-two to base," he said.

"Forty-two, come in."

"You ten-twenty-five me at ERF gate?"

"Ten-four."

We waited for the guard to arrive, and he occupied the booth while his partner let me inside the building. For a while we roamed long empty hallways, trying locked doors that led into machine shops and laboratories where my niece might be. After about fifteen minutes of this, we got lucky. He tried a door and it opened onto an expansive room that was a Santa's workshop of scientific activity.

Central to this was Lucy, who was wearing a data glove and head-mounted display connected to long thick black cables snaking over the floor.

"Will you be okay?" the guard asked me.

"Yes," I said. "Thank you so much."

Co-workers in lab coats and coveralls were busy with computers, interface devices and large video screens, and they all saw me walk in. But Lucy was blind. She really was not in this room but the one in the small CRTs covering her eyes as she conducted a virtual-reality walk-through along a catwalk in what I suspected was the Old Point nuclear power plant.

"I'm going to zoom in now," she was saying as she pressed a button on top of the glove.

The area on the video screen suddenly got bigger as the figure that was Lucy stopped at steep grated stairs.

"Shit, I'm zooming out," she said impatiently. "No way this is going to work."

"I promise it can," said a young man monitoring a big black box. "But it's tricky."

She paused and made some other adjustment. "I don't know, Jim, is this really high-res data or is the problem me?"

"I think the problem's you."

"Maybe I'm getting cyber sick," my niece then said as she moved around inside what looked like conveyor belts and huge turbines that I could see on the video screen.

"I'll take a look at the algorithm."

"You know," she said, making her way down the virtual stairs, "maybe we should just put it in C code and go from a delay of three-four to three hundred and four microseconds, et cetera, instead of whatever's in the software we got."

"Yeah. The transfer sequences are off," said someone else. "We got to adjust the timing loops."

"What we don't have is the luxury of massaging this too much," another opinion sounded. "And, Lucy, your aunt's here."

She briefly paused, then went on as if she had not heard what the person just said. "Look, I'll do the C code before morning. We gotta be sharp or Toto's going to end up stuck or falling down stairs. And then we're totally screwed."

Toto, I could only conclude, was the odd bubble head with one video eye that was mounted on a boxy steel body no more than three feet high. Legs were cleated tracks, arms had grippers, and in general he reminded me of a small animated tank. Toto was parked to one side, not far from his master, who was taking off her helmet.

"We got to change the bio-controllers on this glove," she said as she began carefully pulling it off. "I'm used to one finger meaning forward and two meaning back. Not the other way around. I can't afford a mix-up like that when we're in the field."

"That's an easy one," said Jim, and he went to her and took the glove.

Lucy looked keyed up to the point of being crazed when she met me near the door.

"How'd you get in?" She wasn't the least bit friendly.

"One of the guards."

"Good thing they know you."

"Benton told me they'd brought you back, that HRT needs you," I said.

She watched her colleagues continue to work. "Most of the guys are already there."

"At Old Point," I said.

"We've got divers around the area, snipers set up nearby, choppers waiting. But nothing's going to do any good unless we can get at least one person in."

"And obviously, that's not you," I said, knowing that if she claimed otherwise I would kill the FBI, the entire Bureau, all of them at once.

"In a way it's me going in," my niece said. "I'll be the one working Toto. Hey, Jim," she called out. "While you're at it, let's add a fly command to the pad."

"So Toto's gonna have wings," someone cracked. "Good thing. We're gonna need a smart guardian angel."

"Lucy, do you have any idea how dangerous these people are?" I could not help but say.

She looked at me and sighed. "I mean, what do you think, Aunt Kay? Do you think I'm just a kid playing with Tinkertoys?"

"I think that I can't help but feel very worried."

"We should all be worried right now," she said, drained. "Look, I got to get back to work." She glanced at her watch and blew out a big breath. "You want a quick overview of my plan so you at least know what's going on?"

"Please."

"It starts with this." She sat on the floor and I got down beside her, our backs against the wall. "Normally, a robot like Toto would be controlled by radio, which would never work inside a facility with so much concrete and steel. So I've come up with what I think is a better way. Basically, he'll carry a spool of fiber optic cable that he'll leave behind like a snail's trail as he moves around."

"And where is he going to move around?" I asked. "Inside the power plant?"

"We're trying to determine that now," she said. "But a lot will depend on what happens. We could be covert, such as in information gathering. Or we could end up with an overt deployment on our hands, such as if the terrorists want a hostage phone, which we're banking on. Toto has to be ready to go anywhere instantly."

"Except stairs."

"He can do stairs. Some better than others."

"The fiber optics cable will be your eyes?" I said.

"It will hook right into my data gloves." She held up both hands. "And I will move as if it's me going in instead of Toto. Virtual reality will allow me to have a remote presence so I can react instantly to whatever his sensors pick up. And by the way, most of them are in that lovely shade of gray we made him." She pointed to her friend across the room. "His smart paint helps him not to bump into things," she added as if she might have feelings for him.

"Did Janet come back with you?" I then asked.

"She's finishing up in Charlottesville."

"Finishing up?"

"We know who's been breaking into CP&L's computer," she said. "A woman graduate assistant in nuclear physics. Surprise, surprise."

"What's her name?"

"Loren something." She rubbed her face with her hands. "God, I should never have sat down. You know cyberspace really can make you dizzy if you stay in it too long. Lately, it's almost been making me sick. Uh." She snapped her fingers several times. "McComb. Loren McComb."

"And she's how old?" I asked as I remembered Cleta saying that the name of Eddings's girlfriend was Loren.

"Late twenties."

"Where is she from?"

"England. But she's actually South African. She's black."

"Thus explaining her poor character, according to Mrs. Eddings."

"Huh?" Lucy looked bizarrely at me.

"What about a connection with the New Zionists?" I asked.

"Apparently she got associated with them over the net. She's very militant and antigovernment. My theory is she got brainwashed by them the longer they communicated."

"Lucy," I said, "I think she was Eddings's girlfriend and source, and in the end, she may have helped the New Zionists kill him, probably by way of Captain Green."

"Why would she help him and then do that?"

"She may have believed she had no choice. If she had assisted him with information that could have hurt Hand's cause, she may have been convinced to help them or they may have threatened her."

I thought of the Cristal Champagne in Eddings's refrigerator, and wondered if he had planned to spend New Year's Eve with his girlfriend.

"How would they have wanted her to help them?" Lucy was asking.

"She probably knew his burglar alarm code, maybe even the combination to his safe." My final thought was the worst. "She may have been with him in the boat the night he died. For that matter, we don't know that she wasn't the one who poisoned him. After all, she's a scientist."

"Damn."

"I'm assuming you've interviewed her," I said.

"Janet has. McComb claims she was on the Internet about eighteen months ago when she came across a note posted on a bulletin board. Allegedly, some producer was working on a movie that had to do with terrorists taking over a nuclear power plant so they could re-create a North Korea situation and get weapons-grade plutonium, et cetera, et cetera. This alleged producer needed technical help, for which he was willing to pay."

"Did she have a name for whoever this was?" I asked.

"He just always called himself 'Alias,' as if to imply he might be famous. She bit big time and the relationship began. She started sending him information from graduate papers she had access to because of her graduate assistantship. She gave this Alias asshole every recipe you might think of for essentially taking over Old Point and shipping fuel assemblies to the Arabs."

"What about making casks?"

"Right. Steal tons of the depleted uranium from Oak Ridge. Have it sent to Iraq, Algeria, wherever, to be made into the hundred-twenty-five-ton casks. Then ship them back here where they're stored until the big day. And she went into the whole bit about when uranium turns into plutonium inside a reactor." Lucy stopped and glanced over at me. "She claims it never occurred to her that what she was doing might be real."

"And was it real to her when she began breaking into CP&L's computer?"

"That's one she can't explain, nor will she supply a motive."

"I expect motive is easy," I said. "Eddings was interested in any phone calls to Arab nations that certain people might have been making. And he got his list via the gateway in Pittsburgh."

"You don't think she would have realized that the New Zionists wouldn't appreciate her helping her boyfriend, who happened to be a reporter?"

"I don't think she cared," I angrily said. "I suspect she enjoyed the drama of playing both sides. If nothing else, it had to make her feel very important when she probably had not felt that way before in her quiet academic world. I doubt reality hit until Eddings started poking around NAVSEA, Captain Green's office or who knows where, and then the New Zionists were tipped that their source, Ms. McComb, was threatening the entire mission."

"If Eddings had figured it out," Lucy said, "they never could have pulled it off."

"Exactly," I said. "If any of us had figured it out in time, this wouldn't be happening." I watched a woman in a lab coat maneuver Toto's arms to lift a box. "Tell me," I said, "what was Loren McComb's demeanor when Janet interviewed her?"

"Detached. Absolutely no emotion."

"Hand's people are very powerful."

"I guess so if you can help your boyfriend one minute and they can get you to murder him the next." Lucy was watching her robot, too, and didn't seem pleased by what she was seeing.

"Well, wherever the Bureau is detaining Ms. McComb, I hope it's where the New Zionists can't find her."

"She's secluded," Lucy said as Toto suddenly stopped in his tracks and the box thudded heavily to the floor. "What have you got the shoulder joint's rpm set at?" she called out.

"Eight."

"Let's lower it to five. Damn." She rubbed her face again. "That's all we need."

"Well, I'm going to leave you and go on back to Jefferson," I said as I got up.

She got a strange look in her eyes. "You staying on the security floor, as usual?" she asked.

"Yes."

"I guess it doesn't matter, but that's where Loren McComb is," she said.

In fact, my suite was next to hers, but, unlike me, she was confined. But as I sat up in bed for a while trying to read, I could hear her TV through the wall. I could hear channels switch, and then I recognized "Star Trek" sounds as she watched an old episode rerun.

For hours we were only several feet apart and she did not know it. I imagined her calmly mixing hydrochloric acid and cyanide in a bottle, and directing gas into the compressor's intake valve. Instantly, the long black hose would have violently jerked in the water, and then only the river's sluggish current would have moved it anymore.

"See that in your sleep," I said to her, though she could not hear me. "In your sleep for the rest of your life. Every single goddamn night." I angrily snapped off my lamp.

16

Early the next morning, fog was dense beyond my windows, and Quantico was quieter than usual. I did not hear a single gunshot on any range, and it seemed the Marines were sleeping in. As I walked out of double glass doors leading to the area where the elevators were, I heard a door shut and security locks click free next door to my room.

I punched the down button and glanced around as two female agents in conservative suits walked on either side of a light-skinned black woman who was staring straight at my face as if we had met before. Loren McComb had defiant dark eyes, and pride ran deep within her, as if it were the spring that fed her survival and made all that she did flourish.

"Good morning," I said with no feeling.

"Dr. Scarpetta," one of the agents somberly greeted me as the four of us boarded the elevator together.

Then we were silent to the first floor, and I could smell the sour staleness of this woman who had taught Joel Hand how to build a bomb. She was wearing tight faded jeans, sneakers, and a long, full white blouse that could not hide an impressive build that must have contributed to Eddings's fatal error. I stood behind her and her wardens and watched the sliver of her face that I could see. She licked her lips often, staring straight ahead at doors which did not open soon enough for me.

Silence was thick like the fog outdoors, and then we were released on the first floor. I took my time getting off, and I watched the two agents lead McComb away without laying a finger on her. They did not have to, because they could, were it needed, just like that. They escorted Loren McComb down a corridor, then turned into one of the myriads of enclosed walkways called gerbil tubes, and I was surprised when she paused to look back at me again. She met my unfriendly stare and moved on, one step closer to what I hoped would be a long pilgrimage in the penitentiary.

Climbing stairs, I walked into the cafeteria where flags for every state in the union were hung on the walls. I met Wesley in a corner beneath Rhode Island.

"I just saw Loren McComb," I said, setting down my tray.

He glanced at his watch. "She'll be interviewed most of today."

"Do you think she'll be able to tell us anything that might help?"

He slid salt and pepper closer. "No. It's too late," he simply said.

I ate scrambled egg whites and dry toast, and drank my coffee black as I watched new agents and cops in the National Academy fix omelets and waffles. Some made sandwiches with bacon and sausage, and I thought how boring it was to get old.

"We should go." I picked up my tray, because sometimes eating wasn't worth it.

"I'm still eating, Chief." He played with his spoon.

"You're eating granola and it's all gone."

"I might get more."

"No, you won't," I said.

"I'm thinking."

"Okay." I looked at him, interested to hear what he had to say.

"Just how important is this *Book of Hand?*"

"Very. Part of the problem started when Danny basically took one and probably gave it to Eddings."

"Why do you think it's so important?"

"You're a profiler. You should know. It tells us how they will behave. The Book makes them predictable."

"A terrifying thought," he said.

At nine A.M. we walked past firing ranges to a half acre of grass near the tire house HRT used in the very maneuvers they would need now. This morning, they were nowhere to be seen, all of them at Old Point except our pilot, Whit. He was typically silent and fit in a black flight suit, standing by a blue and white Bell 222, a corporate twin-engine helicopter also owned by CP&L.

"Whit." Wesley nodded at him.

"Good morning," I said as we boarded.

Inside were four seats in what looked like the cabin of a small plane and a co-pilot was busy studying a map. Senator Lord was completely engrossed in whatever he was reading, the attorney general across from him preoccupied with paperwork, too. They had been picked up first in Washington, and did not look like they had slept much, either, the last few nights.

"How are you, Kay?" The senator did not look up.

He was dressed in a dark suit and a white shirt with stiff collar. His tie was deep red, and he wore Senate cuff links. Marcia Gradecki, in contrast, wore a simple pale blue skirt and jacket, and pearls. She was a formidable woman with a face that was attractive in a strong, dynamic way. Although she had gotten her start in Virginia, before this moment we had never met.

Wesley made certain we knew each other as we lifted into a sky that was perfectly blue. We flew over bright yellow school buses that were empty this time of day, then buildings quickly gave way to swamps with duck blinds and vast acres of woods. Sunlight painted paths through the tops of trees, and as we began to follow the James, our reflection silently flew after us along the water.

"In a minute here, we're going to fly over Governor's Landing," said Wesley, and we did not need headphones to speak to one another, only to the pilots. "It's the real-estate arm of CP&L, and where Brett West lives. He's the vice president in charge of operations and lives in a nine-hundred-thousand-dollar house down there." He paused as everybody looked down. "You can just about see it. There. The big brick one with the pool and basketball court in back."

The development had many huge brick homes that had pools and painfully young vegetation. There was also a golf course and a yacht club where we were told West kept a boat that right now was not there.

"And where is this Mr. West?" the attorney general asked as our pilots turned north where the Chickahominy met the James.

"At the moment we don't know." Wesley continued looking out the window.

"I'm assuming you believe he's involved," the senator said.

"Without question. In fact, when CP&L decided to open a district office in Suffolk, they built it on land they bought from a farmer named Joshua Hayes."

"His records were also accessed in their computer," I interjected.

"By the hacker," Gradecki said.

"Right."

"And you have her in custody," she said.

"We do. Apparently, she was dating Ted Eddings, and that's how he got into this and ended up murdered." Wesley's face was hard. "What I am convinced of is that West has been an accomplice to Joel Hand from the start. You can see the district office now." He pointed. "And what do you know," he added ironically, "it's right next to Hand's compound."

The district office was basically a large parking lot of utility trucks and gas pumps, and modular buildings with CP&L

painted in red on the roofs. As we flew around it and over a stand of trees, the terrain beneath us suddenly turned into the fifty-acre point on the Nansemond River where Joel Hand lived within a high metal fence that according to legend was electrified.

His compound was a cluster of multiple smaller homes and barracks, his own mansion weathered and with tall, white pillars. But it was not those buildings that worried us. It was others we saw, large wood structures that looked like warehouses built in a row along railroad tracks leading to a massive private loading dock with huge cranes on the water.

"Those aren't normal barns," the attorney general observed. "What was being shipped off his farm?"

"Or on it," the senator said.

I reminded them of what Danny's killer had tracked into the carpet of my former Mercedes. "This might be where the casks were stored," I added. "The buildings are big enough, and you would need cranes and trains or trucks."

"Then that would certainly link Danny Webster's homicide to the New Zionists," the attorney general said to me as she nervously fingered her pearls.

"Or at least to someone who was going in and out of the warehouses where the casks were kept," I answered. "Microscopic particles of depleted uranium would be everywhere, saying that the casks are, in fact, lined with depleted uranium."

"So this person could have had uranium on the bottom of his shoes and not known it," Senator Lord said.

"Without a doubt."

"Well, we need to raid this place and see what we find," he then said.

"Yes, sir," Wesley agreed. "When we can."

"Frank, so far they haven't done anything that we can prove," Gradecki said to him. "We don't have probable cause. The New Zionists haven't claimed responsibility."

"Well, I know how it works, too, but it's ridiculous," Lord said, looking out. "There's no one down there but dogs, looks like to me. So you explain that, if the New Zionists are not involved. Where is everyone? Well, I think we damn well know."

Doberman pinschers in a pen were barking and lunging at the air we circled.

"Christ," Wesley said. "I never thought all of them might be inside Old Point."

Neither had I, and a very scary thought was forming.

"We've been assuming the New Zionists maintained their numbers over recent years," Wesley went on. "But maybe not. Maybe eventually the only people here were the ones in training for the attack."

"And that would include Joel Hand." I looked at Wesley.

"We know he's been living here," he said. "I think there's a very good chance he was on that bus. He's probably inside the power plant with the others. He's their leader."

"No," I said. "He's their god."

There was a long pause.

Then Gradecki said, "The problem with that is he's insane."

"No," I said. "The problem with that is he's not. Hand is evil, and that's infinitely worse."

"And his fanaticism will affect everything he does in there," Wesley added. "If he is in there"—he measured his words—"then the threat goes bizarrely beyond escaping with a barge of fuel assemblies. At any time, this could turn into a suicide mission."

"I'm not sure why you're saying that," said Gradecki, who did not want to hear it in the least. "The motive is very clear."

I thought of the *Book of Hand*, and of how hard it was for the uninitiated to understand just what a man like its author was capable of doing. I looked at the attorney general as we flew over rows of old gray tankers and transport ships, known as the Navy's Dead Fleet. They were parked in the James, and from a distance it looked like Virginia was under siege, which in a way, it was.

"I don't believe I've ever seen that," she muttered in amazement as she looked down.

"Well, you should have," Senator Lord retorted. "You Democrats are responsible for the decommissioning of half the Navy's fleet. In fact we don't have room to park them. They're scattered here and there, ghosts of their former selves and not worth a tinker's damn if we need seaworthy vessels fast. By the time you'd get one of those old tubs going, the Persian Gulf would be as long past as that other war they fought around here."

"Frank, you've made your point," she crisply said. "I believe we have other matters to attend to this morning."

Wesley had put on a set of headphones so he could talk to the pilots. He asked for an update and then listened for a long time as he stared out at Jamestown and its ferry. When he got off the radio his face was anxious.

"We'll be at Old Point in several minutes. The terrorists still have refused contact and we don't know how many casualties might be inside."

"I hear more helicopters," I said.

We were silent, and then the sound of thudding blades was unmistakable. Wesley got back on the air.

"Listen, dammit, the FAA was supposed to restrict this airspace." He paused as he listened. "Absolutely not. No one else has clearance within a mile—" Interrupted, he listened again. "Right, right." He got angrier. "Christ," he exclaimed as the noise got louder.

Two Hueys and two Black Hawks loudly rumbled past, and Wesley unfastened his seat belt as if he were going somewhere. Furious, he rose and moved to the other side of the cabin, looking out windows.

He had his back to the senator when he said with controlled fury, "Sir, you should not have called in the National Guard. We have a very delicate operation in place and cannot—let me repeat—cannot afford any sort of interference in either our planning or our airspace. And let me remind you the jurisdiction here is police, not military. This is the United States—"

Senator Lord cut in, "I did not call them, and we're in complete agreement."

"Then who did?" asked Gradecki, who was Wesley's ultimate boss.

"Probably your governor," Senator Lord said, looking at me,

and I knew by his manner that he was enraged, too. "He would do something stupid like that because all he thinks about is the next election. Patch me into his office, and I mean now."

The senator slipped the headset on and did not care who overheard when he launched in several minutes later.

"For God's sake, Dick, have you lost your mind?" he said to the man who held the Commonwealth's highest office. "No, no, don't even bother telling me any of that," he snapped. "You are interfering with what we're doing out here, and if it costs lives you can be assured I'm going to announce who's to blame . . ."

He fell silent for a moment, and the expression on his face as he listened was scary. Then he made several other salient points as the governor ordered the National Guard back in. In fact, their huge helicopters never landed, but suddenly changed formation as they gained altitude. They flew right past Old Point, which just now we could see, its concrete containments rising in the clean blue air.

"I'm very sorry," the senator apologized to us, because he was, above all, a gentleman.

We stared out at scores of police and law enforcement vehicles, ambulances and fire trucks, and flowering satellite dishes and news vans. Dozens of people were outside as if enjoying a lovely, brisk day, and Wesley informed us that where they were congregating was the visitors' center, which was the command post for the outer perimeter.

"As you can see," he explained, "it's no closer than half a mile away from the plant and the main building, which is there." He pointed.

"The main building is where the control room is?" I asked.

"Right. That three-story beige brick building. That's where they are, at least most of them, we think, including the hostages."

"Well, it's where they'd have to be if they planned on doing anything with the reactors, like shutting them down, which we know they've already done," Senator Lord remarked.

"And then what?" the attorney general asked.

"There are backup generators, so no one's going to lose electricity. And the plant itself has an emergency power supply," Lord said, and he was known for being an ardent advocate of nuclear energy.

Wide waterways ran on the plant's two sides, one leading from the nearby James, the other to a man-made lake nearby. Then there were acres of transformers and power lines, and parking lots with many cars, belonging to hostages and the people who had arrived to help. There did not seem an easy way to access the main building without being seen, for any nuclear power plant is designed with the most stringent security in mind. The point was to keep out everyone not authorized, and, unfortunately, that included us. A roof entry, for example, would require cutting holes in metal and concrete, and could not be done without risk of being seen.

I suspected Wesley was thinking about a possible amphibious plan, for HRT divers could enter undetected either the river or the lake, and follow a waterway very close to one side of the main building. It looked to me that they could swim within twenty yards of the very door the terrorists had stormed, but how the agents would escape detection once ashore, I could not imagine.

Wesley did not spell out any plan, for the senator and the attorney general were allies, even friends, but they were also politicians. Neither the FBI nor the police needed Washington inserting itself into this mission. What the governor had just done was bad enough.

"Now if you'll notice the large white RV that's close to the main building," Wesley said, "that's our inner perimeter command post."

"I thought that belonged to a news crew," the attorney general commented.

"That's where we try to establish a relationship with Mr. Hand and his Merry Band."

"How?"

"For starters, I want to talk with them," Wesley said.

"No one's talked to them yet?" the senator asked.

"So far," he said, "they don't seem interested in talk."

The Bell 222 slowly made its loud descent as news crews assembled near a helipad across the road from the visitors' center. We grabbed briefcases and bags, and disembarked in the strong wind of flying blades. Wesley and I walked swiftly and in silence. I glanced back only once and saw Senator Lord surrounded by microphones while our nation's most powerful lawyer delivered a string of emotional quotes.

We walked inside the visitors' center with its many displays intended for school children and the curious. But now the entire area was divided by local and state police. They were drinking sodas, eating fast food and snacks near plats and maps on easels, and I could not help but wonder how much of a difference any of us could make.

"Where's your outpost?" Wesley asked me.

"It should be out with the squads. I think I spotted our refrigerator truck from the air."

His eyes were roaming around. They stopped on the men's room door opening and swinging shut. Marino walked out, hitching up his pants again. I had not expected to see him here. If for no other reason, I would have thought his fear of radiation would have kept him home.

"I'm getting coffee," Wesley said. "Anybody?"

"Yo. Make it a double."

"Thanks," I said, then to Marino I added, "This is the last place I would have expected to see you."

"See all these guys walking around in here?" he said. "We're part of a task force so all the local jurisdictions got somebody here that can call home and say what the hell's going on. Bottom line is, the chief sent my ass out here, and no, I'm not thrilled about it. And by the way, I saw your buddy Chief Steels out here, and you'll be happy to know Roche has been suspended without pay."

I did not reply, for Roche was not important right now.

"So that ought to make you feel a little better," Marino went on.

I looked at him. His stiff white collar was rimmed in sweat, and his belt with all its gear creaked as he moved.

"While I'm here, I'll do my best to keep an eye on you.

But I'd appreciate it if you didn't go wandering into the crosshairs of some drone's high-powered rifle," he added, smoothing back strands of hair with a big, thick hand.

"I'd appreciate it if I didn't do that either. I need to check on my folks," I said. "Have you seen them?"

"Yeah, I saw Fielding in that big trailer the funeral home people bought for you. He was cooking eggs in the kitchen like he's camping out or something. There's a refrigerator truck, too."

"Okay. I know exactly where it is."

"I'll take you over there, if you want," he nonchalantly said, as if he didn't care.

"I'm glad you're here," I said, because I knew I was part of the reason, no matter what he claimed.

Wesley was back, and he had balanced a paper plate of doughnuts on top of cups of coffee. Marino helped himself while I looked out windows at the bright, cold day.

"Benton," I said, "where is Lucy?"

He did not reply, so I knew. My worst fears were confirmed right then.

"Kay, all of us have a job to do." His eyes were kind, but he was unequivocal.

"Of course we do." I set down my coffee because my nerves were bad enough. "I'm going out to check on things."

"Hold on," Marino said as he started his second doughnut.

"I'll be fine."

"Yeah, you will," he said. "I'm going to make sure of that."

"You do need to be careful out there," Wesley said to me. "We know there's someone in every window, and they could start shooting whenever they want."

I looked at the main building in the distance, and I pushed open the glass door that led outside. Marino was right behind me.

"Where's HRT?" I asked him.

"Where you can't see them."

"Don't talk to me in riddles. I'm not in the mood."

I walked with purpose, and because I could not see any sign of terrorism or its victims, this ordeal seemed a drill. Fire and refrigerator trucks and ambulances seemed part of a mock emergency, and even Fielding arranging disaster kits inside the large white trailer that was my outpost did not strike me as reality. He was opening one of the blue Army footlockers stamped with OCME, and inside was everything from eighteen-gauge needles to yellow pouches designed to hold the personal effects of the dead.

He looked up at me as if I had been here all along. "You got any idea where the stakes are?" he asked.

"Those should be in separate boxes with hatchets, pliers, metal ties," I replied.

"Well, I don't know where they are."

"What about the yellow body pouches?" I scanned lockers and boxes stacked inside the trailer.

"I guess I'm just going to have to get all that from FEMA," he said, referring to the Federal Emergency Management Agency.

"Where are they?" I asked, because hundreds of people from many agencies and departments were here.

"You go out and you'll see their trailer directly to the left, next to the guys from Fort Lee. Graves Registration. And FEMA's got the lead-lined suits."

"And we'll pray we don't need them," I said.

Fielding said to Marino, "What's the latest on hostages? Do we know how many they've got in there?"

"We're not really sure because we don't know exactly how many employees were in the building," he said. "But the shift was small when they hit, which I'm sure was part of the plan. They've released thirty-two people. We're thinking there's maybe about a dozen left. We don't know how many of them are still alive."

"Christ." Fielding's eyes were angry as he shook his head. "You ask me, every one of the assholes ought to be shot on the spot."

"Yeah, well, you won't get an argument out of me," Marino said.

"At this moment," Fielding said to me, "we can handle fifty. That's the max between the truck we got here and our morgue back in Richmond, which is already pretty crowded. Beyond that, MCV's mobilized if we need them for storage."

"The dentists and radiologists are also mobilized," I assumed.

"Right. Jenkins, Verner, Silverberg, Rollins. They're all on standby."

I could smell eggs and bacon and didn't know if I felt hungry or sick. "I'm on the radio, if you need me," I said, opening the trailer's door.

"Don't walk so fast," Marino complained when we were back outside.

"Have you checked out the mobile command post?" I asked. "The big blue and white RV? I saw it when we were flying in."

"I don't think we want to go over there."

"Well, I do."

"Doc, that's the inner perimeter."

"That's where HRT is," I said.

"Let's just check it out with Benton first. I know you're looking for Lucy, but for God's sake, use your head."

"I am using my head and I am looking for Lucy." I was getting angrier with Wesley by the moment.

Marino put his hand on my arm and stopped me, and we squinted at each other in the sun. "Doc," he said, "listen to me. What's going down ain't personal. No one gives a shit that Lucy's your niece. She's a friggin" FBI agent, and it ain't Wesley's duty to give you a report on everything she's doing for them."

I did not say anything, and he did not need to, either, for me to know the truth.

"So don't be pissed at him." Marino was still gently holding my arm. "You want to know? I don't like it, either. I couldn't stand it if something happened to her. I don't know what I'd do if anything happened to either of you. And right now I'm about as scared as I've ever been in my goddamn fucking life. But I got a job to do and so do you."

"She's at the inner perimeter," I said.

He paused. "Come on, Doc. Let's go talk to Wesley."

But we did not get a chance to do that, because when we walked into the visitors' center, we found him on the phone. His tone was iron-calm and he was standing tensely.

"Don't do anything until I get there, and it is very important that they know I'm on my way," he was saying, slowly.

"No, no, no. Don't do that. Use a bullhorn so no one gets close." He glanced at Marino and me. "Just hold tight. Tell them you've got someone coming who will get a hostage phone to them immediately. Right."

He hung up and headed straight for the door, and we were right behind him.

"What the hell's going on?" Marino asked.

"They want to communicate."

"What'd they do? Send a letter?"

"One of them yelled out a window," Wesley replied. "They're very agitated."

We walked fast past the helipad, and I noted it was empty, the senator and attorney general long gone.

"So they don't already have a phone?" I was very surprised.

"We shut down the phones in that building," Wesley said. "They have to get a phone from us, and before this minute they haven't wanted one. Now, suddenly they do."

"So there's a problem," I said.

"That's the way I'm reading it." Marino was out of breath.

Wesley did not reply, but I could tell he was unnerved, and it was rare that anything made him this way. The narrow road led us through the sea of people and vehicles waiting to help, and the tan building loomed larger. The mobile command post gleamed in the sun and was parked on the grass, the conical containments and the waterway they needed for cooling so close I could have hit them with a stone.

I had no doubt that New Zionists had us in their rifle sights and could pull the trigger, if they chose, to pick us off one at a time. The windows where we believed they watched were open, but I could not see anything behind their screens.

We walked around to the front of the RV where half a dozen police and agents were in plain clothes surrounding Lucy, and the sight of her almost stopped my heart. She was in black fatigues and boots, and was attached to cables again, as she had been at ERF. Only this time she wore two gloves, and Toto was awake on the ground, his thick neck connected to a spool of fiber optics line that looked long enough to walk him to North Carolina.

"It's better if we tape down the receiver," my niece was saying to men she could not see because of the CRTs over her eyes.

"Who's got tape?"

"Hold on."

A man in a black jumpsuit reached inside a large toolbox and tossed a roll of tape to someone else. This person tore off several strips of it and secured the receiver to the cradle of a plain black phone in a box firmly held in the robot's grippers.

"Lucy," Wesley spoke. "This is Benton Wesley. I'm here."

"Hi," she said, and I could feel her nervousness.

"As soon as you get the phone to them, I'm going to start talking. I just want you to know what I'm doing."

"Are we ready?" she asked, and she had no idea I was there.

"Let's do it," Wesley tensely said.

She touched a button on her glove and Toto came to life in a quiet whir, and the one eye beneath his domed brain turned, as if focusing like a camera lens. His head swiveled as Lucy touched another button on a glove, and everyone watched in hushed anticipation as my niece's creation suddenly moved. It plowed forward on rubber tracks, telephone tight in its grippers, the fiber optics and telephone cable unrolling from spools.

Lucy silently conducted Toto's journey like an orchestra, her arms out and gently moving. Steadily, the robot rolled down the road, over gravel and through grass, until he was far enough away that one of the agents passed out field glasses. Following a sidewalk, Toto reached four cement steps leading up to the glass front entrance of the main building, and he stopped. Lucy took a deep breath as she continued to make her telepresence known to her metal and plastic friend. She touched another button, and the grippers extended with arms. They slowly lowered and set the telephone on the second step. Toto backed up and swiveled around, and Lucy began to bring him home.

The robot had not gotten far when all of us could see that glass door open, and a bearded man in khakis and a sweater swiftly emerged. He grabbed the telephone off the step and vanished inside.

"Good work, Lucy," Wesley said, and he sounded very relieved. "Okay, goddamn it, now call," he added, and he was not talking to us, but them. "Lucy," he added, "when you're ready, come on in."

"Yes, sir," she said as her arms coaxed Toto over every dip and bump.

Then Marino, Wesley and I climbed steps leading into the

mobile command post, which was upholstered in gray and blue, with tables between seats. There was a small kitchen and bath, and windows were tinted so one could see out, but not in. Radio and computer equipment had been set up near the back, and overhead five televisions were turned to the major networks and CNN, the volume set low. A red phone on a table started ringing as we were walking down the aisle. It sounded urgent and demanding, and Wesley ran to pick it up.

"Wesley," he said, staring out a window, and he pushed two buttons that both taped the caller and put him on speakerphone.

"We need a doctor." The male voice sounded white and southern, and he was breathing hard.

"Okay, but you're going to need to tell me more."

"Don't bullshit with me!" he screamed.

"Listen." Wesley got very calm. "We're not bullshitting, all right? We want to help, but I need more information."

"He fell in the pool and went into like a coma."

"Who did?"

"Why the fuck does it matter who?"

Wesley hesitated.

"He dies, we've got this place wired. You understand? We're going to blow you fucking up if you don't do something now!"

We knew who he meant, so Wesley did not ask again. Something had happened to Joel Hand, and I did not want to imagine what his followers might do if he died.

"Talk to me," Wesley said.

"He can't swim."

"Let me make certain I understand. Someone almost drowned?"

"Look. The water's radioactive. It had the fucking fuel assemblies in it, you understand?"

"He was inside one of the reactors."

The man screamed again, "Just shut the fuck up with your questions and get someone to help. He dies, everybody dies. You understand that?" he said as a gun loudly went off over the phone and cracked from the building at the same time.

Everyone froze, and then we could hear crying in the background. I thought my heart would beat out of my ribs.

"You make me wait another minute," the man's excited voice was back on the line, "and another one gets killed."

I moved closer to the phone and before anyone could stop me, I said, "I'm a doctor. I need to know exactly what happened when he fell into the reactor pool."

Silence. Then the man said, "He almost drowned, that's all I know. We tried to pump water out of him but he was already unconscious."

"Did he swallow water?"

"I don't know. Maybe he did. Some was coming out of his mouth." He was becoming more agitated. "But if you don't do something, lady, I'm going to turn Virginia into a goddamn desert."

"I'm going to help you," I said. "But I need to ask you several more questions. Tell me his condition now?"

"Like I said. He's out. It's like he's in a coma."

"Where do you have him?"

"In the room here with us." He sounded terrified. "He don't react to anything, no matter what we try to do."

"I'm going to have to bring in a lot of ice and medical supplies," I said. "It's going to take several trips unless I have some help."

"You'd better not be FBI," he raised his voice again.

"I'm a doctor out here with a lot of other medical personnel," I said. "Now, I'm going to come and help, but not if you're going to give me a hard time."

He was silent. Then he said, "Okay. But you come alone."

"The robot will help me carry things. The same one that brought you your phone."

He hung up, and when I did, Wesley and Marino were staring at me as if I had just committed murder.

"Absolutely not," Wesley said. "Jesus Christ, Kay. Have you lost your mind?"

"You ain't going if I have to put you in a goddamn police hold," Marino chimed in.

"I have to," I said simply. "He's going to die," I added.

"And that's the very reason why you can't go in there," Wesley exclaimed.

"He has acute radiation sickness from swallowing water in the pool," I said. "He can't be saved. Soon he will die, and then I think we know what the consequences might be. His followers will probably set off the explosives." I was looking at Wesley and Marino, and the commander of HRT. "Don't you understand? I've read their Book. He is their messiah, and they won't just walk away when he dies. This whole thing will turn into a suicide mission, as you predicted." I looked at Wesley again.

"We don't know that they'll do that," he said to me.

"And you'll take the chance they won't?"

"And what if he comes to," Marino said. "Hand's going to recognize you and tell all his assholes who you are. Then what?"

"He's not going to come to."

Wesley stared out a window, and it wasn't very hot in the RV, but he looked like it was summer. His shirt was limp from dampness, and he kept wiping his brow. He did not know what to do. I had one idea, and I did not think there could be another one.

"Listen to me," I said. "I can't save Joel Hand, but I can make them think he's not dead."

Everyone just stared at me.

Then Marino said, "What?"

I was getting frantic. "He could die any minute," I said. "I've got to get in there now and buy you enough time to get in, too."

"We can't get in," Wesley said.

"Once I'm in there, maybe you can," I said. "We can use the robot to find a way. We'll get him in, and then he can stun and blind them long enough for your guys to get in. I know you have the equipment to do that."

Wesley was grim and Marino looked miserable. I understood the way they felt, but I knew what must be done. I went out to the nearest ambulance and got what I needed from paramedics while other people found ice. Then Toto and

I made our approach with Lucy at the controls. The robot carried fifty pounds of ice while I was in charge of a large medical chest. We walked toward the front door of Old Point's main building as if this were any other day and our visit was normal. I did not think of the men who had me in their scopes. I refused to imagine explosives or the barge loading up material that could help Libya build an atom bomb.

When we reached the door, it was immediately opened by what looked like the same bearded man who had appeared to get the hostage phone not long ago.

"Get in," he gruffly said, and he was carrying an assault rifle on a strap.

"Help me with the ice," I said.

He stared at the robot with its five bags held fast in grippers. He was reticent, as if Toto were a pit bull that might suddenly hurt him in some way. Then he reached for the ice and Lucy programmed her friend through fiber optics to release it. Next, this man and I were inside the building with the door shut, and I saw that the security area had been destroyed, X-ray and other scanning devices ripped out of place and riddled with bullets. There were blood drips and drag marks, and when I followed him around a corner, I smelled the bodies before I saw the slain guards who had been gathered into a ghastly, gory pile down the hall.

Fear rose in my throat like bile as we passed through a red door, and the rumble of combines shook my bones and made it impossible to hear anything said by this man who was a New Zionist. As I noticed the large black pistol on his belt, I thought about Danny and the .45 that had so coldly killed him. We climbed grated stairs painted red, and I did not look down because I would get dizzy. He led me along a catwalk to a door that was very heavy and painted with warnings, and he punched in a code as ice began to drip on the floor.

"Just do as you're told," I vaguely heard him say as we walked into the control room. "You understand me?" He nudged my back with his rifle.

"Yes," I said.

There were maybe a dozen men inside, all dressed in slacks and sweaters or jackets, and carrying semiautomatic rifles and machine guns. They were very excited and angry, and seemed indifferent to the ten hostages sitting on the floor against a wall. Hands were tied in front of hostages, and pillow cases had been pulled over their heads. Through holes cut out for eyes, I could see their terror. The openings for their mouths were stained with saliva and they sucked in and out with rapid, shallow breaths. I noted bloody drag marks on the floor here, too, only these were fresh and led behind a console where the latest victim had been dumped. I wondered how many bodies I would later find should mine not be among them.

"Over there," my escort ordered.

Joel Hand was on his back on the floor, covered by a curtain someone had ripped from a window. He was very pale and still wet from the pool where he had swallowed water that would kill him, no matter what I tried to do. I recognized his fair, full-lipped face from when I had seen him in court, only he looked puffier and older.

"How long has he been like this?" I spoke to the man who had brought me in.

"Maybe an hour and a half."

He was smoking and pacing. He would not meet my eyes, one hand nervously resting on the barrel of his gun, which was aimed at my head as I set down the medical chest. I turned around and stared at him.

"Don't point that at me," I said.

"You shut up." He stopped pacing and looked as if he would crack my skull.

"I'm here because you invited me, and I'm trying to help." I met his glassy gaze and my voice meant business, too. "If you don't want me to help, then go ahead and shoot me or let me leave. Neither one is going to help him. I'm trying to save his life and don't need to be distracted by your goddamn gun."

He did not know what to say as he leaned against a console with enough controls to fly a spaceship. Video displays on walls showed that both reactors were shut down, and areas in a grid lighted up red warned of problems I could not comprehend.

"Hey, Wooten, take it easy." One of his peers lit a cigarette.

"Let's open the bags of ice now," I said. "I wish we had a tub, but we don't. I see some books on those countertops, and it looks like there's a lot of stacks of paper over there by that fax machine. Bring anything like that you can for a border."

Men brought to me all sorts of thick manuals, reams of

papers and briefcases that I assumed belonged to the employees they had captured. I formed a rectangular border around Hand as if I were in my backyard making a flower bed. Then I covered him with fifty pounds of ice, leaving only his face and an arm exposed.

"What will that do?" The man called Wooten had moved closer, and he sounded as if he were from out west somewhere.

"He's been acutely exposed to radiation," I said. "His system is being destroyed and the only way to put a stop to it is to slow everything down."

I opened the medical chest and got out a needle, which I inserted into their dying leader's arm and secured with tape. I connected an IV line leading to a bag on a stand that contained nothing but saline, a harmless salty solution that would do nothing one way or another. It dripped as he got cooler beneath inches of ice.

Hand was barely alive, and my heart was thudding as I looked around at these sweating men who believed that this man I pretended to save was God. One had taken his sweater off, and his undershirt was almost gray, the sleeves drawn up from years of washing. Several of them had beards, while others had not shaved in days. I wondered where their women and children were, and I thought of the barge in the river and what must be going on in other parts of the plant.

"Excuse me," a quavering voice barely said, identifying at least one of the hostages as a woman. "I need to go to the bathroom."

"Mullen, you take her. We don't want nobody shitting in here."

"Excuse me, but I have to go, too," said another hostage, who was a man.

"So do I."

"All right, one at a time," said Mullen, who was young and huge.

I knew at least one thing the FBI did not. The New Zionists had never intended to let anyone else go. Terrorists place hoods over their hostages because it is easier to kill people who have no faces. I got out a vial of saline and injected fifty milliliters into Hand's IV line, as if I were giving him some other magic dose.

"How's he doing?" one of the men loudly asked as another hostage was led off to the bathroom.

"I've got him stabilized at the moment," I lied.

"When's he going to come around?" asked another.

I took their leader's pulse again, and it was so faint I almost could not find it. Suddenly, the man dropped down beside me and felt Hand's neck. Digging his fingers in the ice, he pressed them over the heart, and when he looked up on me, he was frightened and furious.

"I don't feel nothing!" he yelled, his face red.

"You're not supposed to feel anything. It's critical to keep him in a hypothermic state so we can arrest the rate of irradiation damage to blood vessels and organs," I told him. "He's on massive doses of diethylene triamine penta-acetic acid, and he is quite alive."

He stood, his eyes wild as he stepped closer to me, finger

on the trigger of his Tec-9. "How do we know you aren't just bullshitting or making him worse."

"You don't know." I showed no emotion because I had accepted this was the day I would die, and I was not afraid of it. "You have no choice but to trust that I know what I'm doing. I've profoundly slowed down his metabolism. And he's not going to come to any time soon. I'm simply trying to keep him alive."

He averted his gaze.

"Hey, Bear, take it easy."

"Leave the lady alone."

I continued kneeling by Hand as his IV dripped and melting ice began to seep through the barricade, spreading over the floor. I took his vital signs many times and made notes, so it seemed that I was very busy in my attendance of him. I could not help but glance out windows whenever I could, and wonder about my comrades. At not quite three P.M., his organs failed him like followers that suddenly aren't interested anymore. Joel Hand died without a gesture or sound as cold water ran in small rivers across the floor.

"I need ice and I need more drugs," I looked up and said.

"Then what?" Bear came closer.

"Then at some point you need to get him to a hospital."

No one responded.

"If you don't give me these things I've requested, I can do nothing more for him," I flatly said.

Bear went over to a desk and got on the hostage phone. He said we needed ice and more drugs. I knew Lucy and her team had better act now or I probably would be shot. I moved away from Hand's spreading puddle, and as I looked at his face it was hard for me to believe that he had so much power over others. But every man in this room and those in the reactor and on the barge would kill for him. In fact, they already had.

"The robot's bringing the shit. I'm going out to get it," said Bear as he looked out the window. "It's on its way now."

"You go out there you're probably going to get your ass shot off."

"Not with her in here." Bear's eyes were hostile and crazed.

"The robot can bring it to you," I surprised them by saying.

Bear laughed. "You remember all those stairs? You think that tin-ass piece of shit's going to get up those?"

"It's perfectly capable," I said, and I hoped this was true.

"Hey, make it bring the stuff in so no one has to go out," another man said.

Bear got Wesley on the hostage phone again. "Make the robot bring the supplies to the control room. We're not coming out." He slammed the receiver down, not realizing what he had just done.

I thought of my niece and said a prayer for her because I knew this would be the hardest thing she had ever done, and I jumped as I suddenly felt the barrel of a gun against the back of my neck.

"You let him die, you're dead, too. You got that, bitch?"

I did not move.

"Pretty soon, we got to sail out of here, and he'd better be going with us."

"As long as you keep me in supplies, I will keep him alive," I quietly said.

He removed the gun from my neck and I injected the last vial of saline into their dead leader's IV line. Beads of sweat were rolling down my back, and the skirt of the gown I had put over my clothes was soaked. I imagined Lucy this minute outside the mobile outpost in her virtual reality gear. I imagined her moving her fingers and arms and stepping here and there as fiber optics made it possible for her to read every inch of the terrain on her CRTs. Her telepresence was the only hope that Toto would not get stuck in a corner or fall somewhere.

The men were looking out the window and commented when the robot's tracks carried him up the handicap ramp and he went inside.

"I wouldn't mind having one of those," one of them said.

"You're too stupid to figure out how to use it."

"No way. That baby ain't radio-controlled. Nothing radio-controlled would work in here. You got any idea how thick the walls are?"

"It'd be great for carrying in firewood when the weather sucks."

"Excuse me, I need to use the bathroom," one of the hostages timidly said.

"Shit. Not again."

My tension got unbearable as I feared what would happen if they went out and were not back when Toto appeared.

"Hey, just make him wait. Damn, I wish we could close these windows. It's cold as shit in here."

"Well, you won't get none of that clean, cold air in Tripoli. Better enjoy it while you can."

Several of them laughed at the same time the door opened and another man walked in who I had not seen before. He was dark-skinned and bearded, wearing a heavy jacket and fatigues, and he was angry.

"We have only fifteen assemblies out and in casks on the barge," he spoke with authority and a heavy accent. "You must give us more time. Then we can get more."

"Fifteen's a hell of a lot," Bear said; and he did not seem to care for this man.

"We need twenty-five assemblies at the very least! That was the arrangement."

"No one's told me that."

"He knows that." The man with the accent looked at Hand's body on the floor.

"Well, he ain't available to discuss it with you." Bear crushed out a cigarette with the toe of his boot.

"Do you understand?" The foreign man was furious now. "Each assembly weighs a ton, and the crane has to pull it from the flooded reactor to the pool, then get it into a cask. It is very slow and very difficult. It is very dangerous. You promised we would have at least twenty-five. Now you are rushing and sloppy because of him." The man angrily pointed at Hand. "We have an agreement!"

"My only agreement is to take care of him. We gotta get him on the barge and take the doctor with us. Then we get him to a hospital."

"This is nonsense! He looks already dead to me! You are lunatics!"

"He's not dead."

"Look at him. He is white as snow and does not breathe. He is dead!"

They were screaming at each other, and Bear's boots were loud as he strode over to me and demanded, "He's not dead, is he?"

"No," I said.

Sweat rolled down his face as he drew the pistol from his belt and pointed it first at me. Then he pointed it at the hostages, and all of them cowered and one began to cry.

"No, please. Oh please," a man begged.

"Who is it who needs to use the john so bad?" Bear roared.

They were silent, shaking as hoods sucked in and out and wide eyes stared.

"Was it you?" The gun pointed at someone else.

The control-room door had been left open, and I could hear the whirring of Toto down the hall. He had made it up the stairs and along a catwalk, and he would be here in seconds. I retrieved a long metal flashlight that had been designed by ERF and tucked into the medical chest by my niece.

"Shit, I want to know if he's dead," one of the men said, and I knew my charade was over.

"I'll show you," I said as the whirring got louder.

I pointed the flashlight at Bear as I pushed a button, and he shrieked at the dazzling pop as he grabbed his eyes and I swung the heavy flashlight like a baseball bat. Bones shattered in his wrist, the pistol clattering to the floor, and the robot rolled in empty-handed. I flung myself down flat on my face, covering my eyes and ears as best I could, and the room exploded in blazing white light as a concussion bomb blew off the top of Toto's head. There was screaming and cursing as terrorists blindly fell against consoles and each other, and they could not hear or see when dozens of HRT agents stormed in.

"Freeze, motherfuckers!"

"Freeze or I'm gonna blow your motherfucking brains out!"

"Don't anybody move!"

I did not budge in Joel Hand's icy grave as helicopters shook windows and feet of fast-roping agents kicked in screens. Handcuffs snapped, and weapons clattered across the floor as they were kicked out of the way. I heard people crying and realized they were the hostages being taken away.

"It's all right. You're safe now."

"Oh my God. Oh thank you, God."

"Come on. We need to get you on out of here."

When I finally felt a cool hand on the side of my neck, I realized the person was checking for vital signs because I looked dead.

"Aunt Kay?" It was Lucy's strained voice.

I turned over and slowly sat up. My hands and the side of my face that had been in water were numb, and I looked around, dazed. I was shaking so badly my teeth were chattering as she squatted beside me, gun in hand. Her eyes roamed the room as other agents in black fatigues were taking the last prisoners out.

"Come on, let me help you up," she said.

She gave me her hand, and my muscles trembled as if I were about to have a seizure. I could not get warm, and my ears would not stop ringing. When I was standing, I could see Toto near the door. His eye had been scorched, his head blackened, the domed top of it gone. He stood silent in his cold trail of fiber optic cable, and no one paid him any mind as one by one all of the New Zionists were taken away.

Lucy looked down at the cold body on the floor, at the water and IV, the syringes and empty bags of saline.

"God," she said.

"Is it safe to go out?" I had tears in my eyes.

"We've just now taken control of the containment area, and we took the barge the same time we took the control room. Several of them had to be shot because they wouldn't drop their weapons. Marino got one in the parking lot."

"He shot one of them?"

"He had to," she said. "We think we got everyone—I guess about thirty—but we're still being careful. This place is wired with explosives, come on. Are you able to walk?"

"Of course I am."

I untied my soaked gown and yanked it off because I could not stand it anymore. Tossing it on the floor, I pulled off my gloves and we walked quickly out of the control room. She snatched her radio off her belt and her boots were loud on the catwalk and the stairs Toto had maneuvered so well.

"Unit one-twenty to mobile unit one," she said.

"One."

"We're clearing out now. Everything secure?"

"You got the package?" I recognized Benton Wesley's voice.

"Ten-four. Package is a-okay."

"Thank God," came a reply unusually emotional for the radio. "Tell the package we're waiting."

"Ten-four, sir," Lucy said. "I believe the package knows."

We walked fast beyond bodies and old blood, and turned in to a lobby that could not keep anyone in or out anymore. She pulled open a glass door, and the afternoon was so bright I had to shield my eyes. I did not know where to go and felt very unsteady on my feet.

"Watch the steps." Lucy put an arm around my waist. "Aunt Kay," she said, "just hold on to me."

FROM POTTER'S FIELD

Patricia Cornwell

It's Christmas and a naked body is discovered in Central Park . . .

Although a holiday for most, the festivities always seem to heighten the alienation felt by society's criminals; and that usually means more work for Dr Kay Scarpetta, Virginia's Chief Medical Examiner and consulting forensic pathologist for the FBI.

The body is found propped against a fountain in a bleak area of New York's Central Park. The unknown female's apparent manner of death points to a modus operandi that is chillingly familiar: the gunshot wound to the head, the sections of skin excised from the body, the displayed corpse – all suggest that Temple Brooks Gault, Scarpetta's nemesis, is back at work.

Calling on all her reserves of courage and skill, and the able assistance of colleagues Marino and Wesley, Scarpetta must track this most dangerous of killers, in pursuit of survival as well as justice – heading inexorably to an electrifying climax amid the dark, menacing labyrinths of the New York subway.

'Cornwell is on magnificent form' *Evening Standard*

978-0-7515-4463-3

UNNATURAL EXPOSURE

Patricia Cornwell

A sadistic serial killer, a deadly virus

Dublin, Ireland and Richmond, Virginia: separated by thousands of miles – linked by murder. For Dr Kay Scarpetta a lecture stint in Ireland provides the perfect opportunity to find out if the murders on both sides of the Atlantic are indeed connected. Five dismembered, beheaded bodies were found in Ireland years ago – now four have been discovered in the States.

The tenth corpse, found in Virginia, is different. There are vital discrepancies, and an indication that the elderly victim was already seriously ill. A copy-cat killing. Ghoulish, perhaps, but not unusual.

And then abject terror grips Scarpetta and her colleagues when the next body is found. The circumstances of death broadcast a clear and horrifying message: the killer is armed with the most lethal weapon on earth – smallpox.

'Nobody does it like Cornwell' *Literary Review*

978-0-7515-4473-2